Polrudden

E. V. Thompson was born in London. He spent nine years in the Navy before joining the Bristol police force where he was a founder member of the 'Vice Squad'. Since then he has been an investigator with BOAC, worked with the Hong Kong Police Narcotics Bureau and was Chief Security Officer of Rhodesia's Department of Civil Aviation. On his return to England he set out to be a full-time writer. A year later, broke but still writing, he swept factory floors, was a hotel detective in London and a civil servant in Plymouth Dockyard. Then in 1977 his first book, *Chase the Wind*, won the 'Best Historical Novel Competition' and became a bestseller, followed a year later by the equally successful *Harvest of the Sun. Polrudden*, the sequel to *The Restless Sea*, is his ninth book.

Also by E. V. Thompson
in Pan Books

E.V. Thompson

Polrudden

PAN BOOKS
in association with
Macmillan London

First published 1985 by Macmillan London Limited
This edition published 1987 by Pan Books Ltd
Cavaye Place, London SW10 9PG
in association with Macmillan London Limited
9 8 7 6 5 4 3 2
© E.V. Thompson 1985
ISBN 0 330 29694 9

Reproduced, printed and bound in Great Britain by
Hazell Watson & Viney Limited,
Member of the BPCC Group,
Aylesbury, Bucks

CHAPTER ONE

Latecomers to the cliff-top manor-house of Polrudden shrugged coat collars higher and bowed their heads in homage to wind and rain. Blowing from off the sea, the wind increased in strength to a severe gale as it rose to clear the barrier of cliffs guarding Pentuan village. At Polrudden the sound of waves booming against the base of the cliffs could be clearly heard above the noise of the storm.

Once inside the great high-roofed barn, the villagers peeled off waterproof coats and agreed this was the roughest September weather anyone there could remember.

However, it was not long before the wind and rain rattling the tiles high above their heads were quickly forgotten as the newcomers accepted tankards of ale and took in the scene about them.

They collected in small, excited groups in the centre of the ancient barn, surrounded by long, rough-planked trestle-tables that sagged beneath the weight of more food than the noisy, wide-eyed Pentuan children had ever seen.

There were many fish dishes, of course, for this was a fishing community: marinated pilchards; 'fumadoes', the smoked fish so loved by the Spanish and Portuguese peasants; fat mackerel baked in bay leaves; and 'starry-gazy pie' containing whole cooked pilchards, their heads protruding through the centre of the pastry, eyes gazing balefully and sightlessly at the high rafters above.

But there was more than fish on offer today. Each table bore at least one fat cooked goose, its plump legs angled indecently in the air. There were rabbits, pasties, hams, pigs' heads, and loaves of barley bread stacked like quarry waste in great baskets. For the children there was hobbin pudding, jam tarts, cakes and gingerbread.

Nathan Jago stood at one end of the great barn, where a pit had been dug in the floor and filled with a charcoal fire, the smoke disappearing through a hole in the cob-and-stone wall. Over the fire a whole bullock rotated on an iron spit, turned by a team of red-faced, perspiring men. Their colour owed as much to the vast quantity of ale they were consuming as to heat from the fire.

'You've done the villagers proud today, Nathan. It does my heart good to see so many happy faces.'

Nathan turned to where his father was running a spotted Kerchief about the damp neckband of his frayed collar. In his other hand, Josiah Jago held a preacher's hat, Its wide felt brim limp and wet. Beside him, ill at ease in the manner of a young man in unfamiliar surroundings, stood the Reverend Damian Roach. Sent to Josiah Jago by the Methodist Society to gain experience 'in the field', the close-knit Cornish community in which he found himself.

Nodding to the younger man, Nathan replied to his father: 'They've had little cause for merry-making these past few years. The pilchards haven't run in any numbers for nigh on two years – and when they have we've been unable to get good French salt to cure them, thanks to this damned war. Add to this the crippling cost of corn . . . ! It's a wonder half of Cornwall hasn't starved to death.'

'More than half *are* starving,' replied Josiah Jago unhappily. 'All tithe-holders aren't as generous as you. They demand their dues, even though it means taking food from the mouths of children. They'll have a hard time explaining their actions to the Lord when the Day of Judgement comes. In Matthew eighteen, verse six, it's written: "But whoso shall offend one of these little ones – " '

'I don't doubt you're right,' Nathan interrupted hurriedly. He knew from experience that his father would launch into a lengthy sermon given the slightest provocation. 'But everyone is waiting for you to say a prayer, so we can begin the celebrations. I'll call for quiet.'

As Nathan made himself heard above the babble of voices, the conversations faltered and died, erupting again in a sibilant 'Sh!' when some of the children continued to play a noisy game of tag at the end of the barn farthest from the spitted steer.

'Friends' – Preacher Jago's voice was quite capable of carrying above such minor interruptions – 'I have been asked to call on Our Lord to bless this feast today. Before I do, I know you'll want to join with me in giving thanks for the joyful events that have occasioned such a splendid repast. It also gives me the opportunity of introducing the Reverend Damian Roach to those of you who have not yet met him. Recently ordained in the Established Church, he has decided to devote his future to the Methodist movement and has come here to learn the ways of a Cornish circuit.'

After a brief outburst of polite applause had subsided, Josiah Jago continued: 'But the main reason for our celebration is, of course, the return to us of our brethren – Matthew Clarke, Jonathan Hunkin, Hannibal Truscott, Lewis Dart and Samson Harry. Taken by the enemy whilst peaceably reaping the harvest of the sea within sight of their own homes, they remained in French hands for five years until they and seven Mevagissey fishermen were released by the victorious army of our noble Lord Wellington in far-off Spain.'

As Preacher Jago paused to cast a glance over the villagers gathered about him, a gust of wind rattled the slates on the high roof of the barn and one or two faces looked up anxiously.

Preacher Jago was unaware of the momentary diversion as he picked out the faces of the five rescued men among the celebrating villagers. 'We thank Thee for the deliverance of our brethren, O Lord, and pray this war may soon come to an end and all those who fight for king and country return safely to us once again.'

The murmured 'Amen' from the assembled villagers was

followed quickly by Nathan.

'Thank you, Father. Now, everyone, get something to eat. Don't stint yourselves. There's plenty of food and drink. I want nothing left behind to feed the mice and rats.'

Preacher Jago had intended saying much more, as the villagers knew, and they were smiling as they surged forward, heading for the heavily laden tables.

After only a moment's hesitation, Preacher Jago followed in the wake of the villagers. A dedicated, hardworking preacher, he lived as frugally as the poorest fisherman there. Any money that came into his hands went immediately into the ever-empty coffers of the Methodist Church.

As Nathan watched the Pentuan villagers heaping food upon their plates, a small, slight girl moved to his side, her fingers finding his hand. It was Amy, his wife. Her gaze upon the busy scene about the tables, she said: 'I didn't realise there were so many villagers. Do you think there will be enough food to go round?'

Nathan squeezed her fingers affectionately. 'There *has* to be. I've already spent enough money to keep the St Austell poorhouse going for a full year.'

St Austell was the market-town, four miles away. There had been a recent slump in the ore from the many tin mines to the north of the town. The poorhouse, already overfull with the widows and orphans of Wellington's soldiers, was placing a severe strain on the parish.

'I'm sorry, Nathan. I know this celebration was *my* idea, but I didn't realise how many people would come. Has it cost *too* much?'

'We'll survive – if the pilchards appear off the coast soon. We've got three boats operating out of Portgiskey, yet they haven't caught enough to pay *one* crew's wages this year.' Nathan squeezed Amy's hand again. 'One thing is certain, we're giving everyone a meal they'll talk about for years to come.'

Further conversation became impossible as villagers returned from the tables with laden plates and drew Nathan and Amy into conversation.

Nathan had moved on to supervise the distribution of meat from the spit-roasted bullock when one of the maids from the house entered the barn. A coat was raised above her head to protect her from the rain. Pausing in the doorway, her eyes searched the crowd. When she saw Nathan, she hurried to him.

'Begging your pardon, Master. I just went up to my room over in the house – it's in the attic. While I was there I . . . I saw something. When I told Cook, she said I must hurry across here and tell you straightaway.'

Nathan nodded, slightly impatient. 'What was it? Has the storm damaged the roof? Is rain coming in? If it is, you'd best go and find – '

''Twasn't the roof, Master. It were a ship.'

Nathan looked from the girl to the stormy-grey sky, visible through the high window-slits of the barn.

'You saw a ship, in this weather? You can hardly see the cliff-edge from the house.'

'No, Master, but it's squally, see. Belts of rain coming in across the bay. In between it's a bit clearer. That's when I saw this ship. It was a big one, with three masts. It were leaning right over in the water, heading north towards Black Head.'

Nathan's scepticism left him. The girl's description had been too detailed for the vessel to be a figment of her imagination. He would need to take some action. Any ship heading northwards and close enough to shore to be seen in this light would be unable to avoid Black Head, the high promontory jutting out into the sea, half a mile away.

'How long ago was this?'

'Not more than five minutes, Master – ten at the most.'

Nathan looked at the men standing about him. All were dressed in their Sunday clothes. They would not relish tramping through the mud of a cliff-top path in search of a ship that might or might not be about to go aground on Black Head.

Amy was at the far end of the large tithe-barn. Nathan decided there was no need to tell her what he was about to do. To the housemaid he said: 'Tell Will Hodge to saddle two horses and bundle up a few pitch torches in an oilskin while I change. We'll try heading the boat off – if it's still afloat.' Will Hodge was the Polrudden groom.

Preacher Jago had heard the exchange and he said: 'I'll come with you . . .'

'No. You stay and keep everyone happy. Tell Amy where I've gone only if she asks. There's no need for her to worry unnecessarily. If I'm not back in the hour, send someone out to find me.'

Ten minutes later Nathan and Will Hodge were riding in single file along the cliff-top. The weather was just as the maid had described it. Most of the time driving rain and mist reduced visibility to no more than forty or fifty yards. Then the rain would ease off, and for a few minutes it was possible to see out across the white-crested waves for a few hundred yards.

During one such lull, Nathan pulled his horse to a startled halt. Behind him Will Hodge was forced to do the same.

Pointing out to sea, Nathan cried: 'There's something out there, Will. Can you see what it is?'

The groom peered out across the bay, but the rain had closed in again and approaching dusk restricted visibility still further.

Will Hodge ran a hand across his wet face. 'I can't see anything.'

'There. Now!'

This time Will Hodge saw what Nathan had seen before. 'It's a ship, right enough, but it's heading *south*.'

'And far too close to shore. They'll never clear Chapel Point in this sea.'

Mevagissey Bay curved in a shallow crescent, with Black Head to the north and Chapel Point to the south. A safe anchorage, favoured by ships when the prevailing westerly winds were blowing, it was an inescapable trap for a sailing vessel caught in an easterly storm.

Nathan also observed something that had escaped the attention of the groom, but he said nothing. Flying from the masthead of the doomed ship was a tricolour flag of red, white and blue. The ship battling against the storm was a French vessel.

'Their only hope is to put in to Pentuan,' shouted Nathan above the noise of the wind. Pointing to the wrapped torches, he added: 'If we can light these, we might be able to guide the ship in.'

Will Hodge shook his head doubtfully, but he, too, realised this was probably the only chance the ship had of reaching safety.

The two men were halfway to Pentuan across the clifftop when Nathan heard Will Hodge's shout above the noise of the storm.

The groom was pointing out to sea, his face registering disbelief. Following the direction of Will Hodge's startled gaze, Nathan saw the ship again – but now she was heading straight towards them. Steering towards the cliffs!

Nathan realised immediately the reason for the vessel's extraordinary new course. There was a quarry dug deep into the cliff below Polrudden, with a small quay from which stone was loaded directly into ships. Over the centuries the quarry workings had eaten farther and farther into the cliffs. It would be easy for a stranger to the coast to mistake the quarry for a small harbour. By the time the ship's captain realised his mistake it would be too late. The channel to the quarry quay was narrow and angled. It required a coxswain with detailed knowledge of the coast to bring a ship in, even in the most favourable conditions. In weather like this such an attempt would be suicidal for a stranger.

At that moment the ship made an alteration in course, and Nathan noticed the sluggish manner in which the vessel responded. The French ship was so low in the water that the deck was almost awash. Nathan realised the ship was taking water. The captain *had* to take a desperate chance. He was in charge of a sinking vessel.

'Give me the torches and ride to Polrudden. Get all the men you can – and ropes.'

Will Hodge handed over the oilskin-wrapped bundle. 'What are you going to do?' He shouted the words, but a fresh gust of wind off the sea snatched them away and he had to repeat them.

'I'm going down to the quarry to do whatever I can. Hurry!'

Nathan left his horse at the top of the steep path that led down the cliff to the quarry. In this weather it would be safer going down on foot. He could not see the ship now, but knew it must be close to the narrow quarry channel.

On the quay was a small disused checking-house. Although derelict, it provided shelter from the wind, and Nathan crouched here and set about lighting the pitch-impregnated torches. It was difficult. Water from Nathan's saturated coat constantly threatened to soak the tinder in the box containing flint and steel. Not until Nathan peeled off his dripping coat was he able to raise a flame from the tinder. Cursing impatiently, he eventually managed to transfer the flame to the damp torch. When he felt the torch was burning sufficiently strongly to compete with rain and wind, Nathan ran to the seaward end of the small quay.

The French vessel was well off course for the channel. Hoping desperately that someone on board had a glass trained on the shore, Nathan began signalling with the torch, trying to convey the message that the ship needed to steer to the right of its present course.

Much to his relief, the ship heeled over slowly. Wallowing heavily in the rough water, she pursued a sluggish course towards the hazardous channel.

It was the beginning of the longest twenty minutes of Nathan's life. Half-filled with water, the French ship answered reluctantly to the hard-working helmsman. On one occasion it failed to respond at all, but the French captain was a skilful and resourceful sailor. Just when it seemed the ship would be dashed upon the smooth black rocks, an anchor was thrown overboard from the stern. It held for long enough to enable the ship to be swung away from disaster in the manner of a giant pendulum. Its purpose served, the anchor was cut free and the ship surged forward, caught in the grip of wind and tide.

Twice more the same device was used to bring the ship round the worse angles in the narrow channel, and Nathan began to believe the impossible might be achieved.

By now the first breathless villagers had reached the cliffside quarry from Polrudden. They watched with mixed feelings as Nathan worked to guide the ship to safety. Not all the fishermen joined Preacher Jago in his prayers for the safety of their fellow-men. For many, a shipwreck on this stretch of coastline meant the chance of plunder. It was 'the Lord's bounty', enjoyed by the fishing communities of Cornwall through the centuries.

Yet even those who disagreed with Nathan's attempt to save the ship kept their thoughts to themselves – until Samson Harry spotted the tricolour flying at the ship's masthead.

'Dammit! That's a *French* ship out there! Why are you trying to save her? She belongs to the King's enemies.'

'Do you see any gun-ports, Samson? It's a merchantman, manned by ordinary seamen – men like most of us here.'

'I suffered in French hands for five long years. I'll not lift a finger to save any one of 'em. Let 'em all die.'

Samson Harry's face was suffused with an anger fuelled by the drinks he had consumed at Polrudden. Five years as a French prisoner-of-war had left him unused to strong English ale. He took a step forward, as though to snatch the spluttering torch from Nathan's grasp, but one look at Nathan's face quickly brought him to his senses. Nathan Jago was not a man with whom to tangle.

'Damn you, Jago! It's well known you've made a fortune from trading with the French while we've been fighting a war with them.'

This time the expression on Nathan's face caused Samson Harry to take an involuntary pace backwards, but Nathan had more important things to do than quarrel with a returned prisoner-of-war. His attention returned to the ship and he signalled for the helmsman to keep the ship farther to the north of the narrow quarry opening. When he spoke again to Samson Harry it was done without shifting his gaze from the storm-bound vessel.

'I've done my share of fighting the French, as well you know, Samson. If you're not satisfied with what I'm doing, you can take it up with me when you're sober, if you've a mind. But speak to your wife first. If it hadn't been for French salt, shipped in during the night hours, there would have been no work for her in my fish-cellar. You'd have come home to find your wife in the poorhouse and your boys packed off in a man-o'-war by the poorhouse master.'

A moment later, Samson Harry was forgotten as the French vessel began to drift dangerously off course, all steering gone as the high cliffs played tricks with the wind. The ship swung diagonally across the channel, and now the waves had the vessel in their grip.

The most mercenary of the watchers on shore gasped in horror as the French ship was flung upon rocks as unyielding as a bulldog's teeth. The rocks held fast as successive waves pounded the stricken vessel. Their grip was broken only when a huge wave combined with the frenzied wind to lift the vessel and turn her upon her side.

As the rocks dug deep into the ship's flanks, timbers screeched in anguish. At that moment the villagers of Pentuan knew they were not to be cheated of their storm-driven bounty.

Only minutes after the ship had been thrown on her beam, half a dozen villagers were spoiling their Sunday clothes in the water at the edge of the quarry. Wading knee-deep, they jostled one another in a bid to be the first to reach a small wooden chest, washed from the clutches of one of the unfortunates who had been standing on deck when disaster struck the French ship *L'Emir*.

Rising above the din of the storm and the eager shouts of the Pentuan villagers, Nathan now heard a new sound. It was the terror-stricken cries of men brought face to face with death. Yet it was not only sailors who had been shipwrecked on board *L'Emir*. She was a passenger-carrying vessel, and soon Nathan could hear the shrill screams of women and children.

In the failing light, Nathan watched as passengers who had managed to fight their way to a hatchway began spilling out into the sea. He looked on helplessly as a loudly screaming woman rose high on a wave, midway between ship and sea, her skirts floating in a wide circle about her. At the mercy of the storm, she was given a cruel glimpse of the shore and safety, before being drawn out to sea, to vanish beneath the angry grey waters.

More and more figures began to appear at the hatchways. Confronted by glistening black rocks and frothing, bubbling water, they tried to draw back, only to be pushed headlong by those who came behind.

Will Hodge and two young village men hurried down the path to the quarry, long ropes slung over their shoulders.

'Quick, over here.'

Nathan took the rope from Will Hodge and hurled one end to a floating woman. Caught in the waters inside the quarry workings, she was being swept to and fro by the movement of the sea. She succeeded in catching the rope at Nathan's second throw, and he dragged her to the quay. From here she was hauled to safety by Will Hodge, helped by Preacher Josiah Jago.

'We'll need to get a rope to the ship,' Nathan shouted.

It was raining hard again now, stinging Nathan's face as he stared out to sea. Only Will Hodge heard him as the Polrudden groom struggled up the quay steps, supporting the rescued woman.

The majority of the Pentuan villagers were at the water's edge, some of them wading waist-deep to reach the flotsam drifting from the ship. One of the large hatch-covers had split open, and cargo of every description was drifting ashore.

Survivors from the doomed vessel were also struggling to the shore now. Nathan saw one, bleeding profusely from a gash on his forehead, actually knocked back into the sea by a fisherman eager to reach a leather sea-chest floating low in the water.

'You'll get no help from anyone tonight,' commented Will Hodge grimly. 'The pickings are too rich.'

Women from the village had reached the sea-edge quarry now and were behaving with even less restraint than their menfolk. A roll of silk had floated ashore, and four women fought over ownership. As fists flew and voices were raised in anger, they used language as foul as any uttered by their fisherman husbands.

Nathan looked to where the ship was now little more than a wildly pitching outline against the storm-darkened sky. For every passenger and crewman who had taken to the water, there were two clinging to the hull and tangled rigging, crying pitifully for help.

Nathan arrived at a sudden decision. Stripping off his coat and boots, he knotted one end of a rope about his waist, ignoring the alarmed protests of his father.

'Fasten the other end of the rope to something strong – one of the berthing-rings will do – then help Will to pay out the rope slowly behind me as I swim out to the ship.'

Nathan plunged into the water, his dive taking him well beneath the surface. The sudden silence as the water closed over him came as more of a shock than did the icy cold. He rose to the surface – only to be dragged down again by a desperately struggling woman. Gasping and choking, she clung to him in a frantic bid to save herself from drowning.

It needed considerable strength to break free from her grip and push her towards the quay. When hands reached out to pull the woman to safety, Nathan struck out once more for the wrecked vessel.

He was a strong man and a powerful swimmer, but he needed every ounce of his strength to battle his way clear of the quarry. More than once he narrowly avoided being dashed against the rocks by the waves that swept in from the bay. Then, when he was still ten yards from the ship, the swell lifted him and flung him into a tangle of rigging.

Scrambling upwards, Nathan finally sat on the side of the

heaving vessel. The noise out here was fearsome as the ship rose and fell on the rocks, her timbers screeching a protest to the wind.

Nathan worked his way aft, passing many survivors who clung helplessly to the wreck, shrieking for help.

The mainmast had been snapped off about ten feet above the deck, but enough of the boom remained to enable him to secure the rope. Providing those on shore took up the slack without allowing the rope to tauten to breaking-point, many lives could now be saved. All that remained was to let the panic-stricken survivors know there was now a life-saving link with the shore.

Communicating his message proved far more difficult than Nathan had anticipated. Most of the passengers approached by Nathan continued to wail hysterically. Only one woman seemed to understand what he was saying, but she refused point-blank to leave her uncertain sanctuary amidst a tangle of sodden rigging and canvas.

Then Nathan found a Frenchman wedged in the after passenger hatchway, braced against the constant rise and fall of the trapped ship. The Frenchman was helping passengers to make their way to places where they might cling on, in hopeful anticipation of eventual rescue.

Nathan repeated his message twice before the man showed signs of understanding. Gripping Nathan's arm in sudden hope, the Frenchman called inside the hatch before easing himself from his uncomfortable position and motioning for Nathan to take his place.

Putting his mouth close to Nathan's ear, he shouted in excellent English: 'Direct them to the rope. I will be there to help them.' Gripping Nathan's arm once more, he added: 'God Bless you, Englishman.'

The Frenchman disappeared into the near-darkness, collecting survivors along the way, confidently calling on his compatriots to follow him to safety.

Nathan remained at the hatchway, helping more than a dozen men and women through the hatch, until he was told there were no more passengers left inside.

Gratefully, Nathan eased his aching limbs from the uncomfortable position he had been forced to adopt. He was about to follow the others, when he thought he heard a cry from inside the ship.

He could not be certain; there was too much noise about him. He had almost convinced himself he had been mistaken when he heard the sound once again. This time there could be no doubt. It was the cry of a small child.

The ship was trapped firmly on the rocks now, with the tide still rising and the storm showing no sign of abating. There was a very real danger that the ship would roll over. If it did, it would either drop back and sink in the deeper waters of the bay, or be smashed to pieces at the foot of the cliffs.

Clinging to the edge of the hatchway, Nathan climbed inside the solid darkness of the ship. In here he was away from the howling of the wind and the sound of the sea crashing against miles of cliff-face. There *was* noise, of course – a constant battering of the sea against the hulk, and the screeching of tortured timbers – but he could hear the crying more clearly now. It was coming from farther along the side-tilted passageway.

Nathan made his way towards the sound. Crouching low in the narrow corridor, his greatest danger lay in falling inside one of the cabins where heavy furniture was being flung from side to side in the swirling water.

He was halfway along the passageway when the ship unexpectedly shifted position. Rising on a great wave, she crashed back on the rocks, sliding between two of the largest. The movement brought the ship almost upright once more. It also caused a surge of water along the passageway, strong enough to bowl Nathan over. He regained his feet quickly, but the water now lapped about his waist. He knew there must be a great hole torn in the ship's bottom. It was necessary to find the child quickly and leave the ship.

The cries had stopped, but Nathan splashed on. If the

child had fallen in the water, it might be drowning at this very moment.

Suddenly, he heard the whimpering of a terrified child. There was another sound, too: the comforting murmur of a woman's voice. They came from inside a cabin close to Nathan. At that moment the ship crunched against the rocks and Nathan fell against the edge of a door-frame, cursing involuntarily.

There was an immediate response from inside the cabin. A woman's voice spoke in rapid French, unintelligible to Nathan, and he cut the tirade short.

'Do you understand English?'

After the briefest hesitation, a soft, heavily accented voice answered.

'Yes . . . A little.'

There was no time to ask the woman why she had not made her way to the hatchway with the other passengers. 'You've got to get out of here quickly. The ship is likely to go down at any moment.'

'Then, take my son. Go.'

A child was thrust into Nathan's arms. It clung to him, at the same time setting up a frightened howl at being parted from its mother so abruptly.

Nathan settled the child in one arm and reached out in the darkness for the woman. 'We'll all go together. There's nothing to be frightened of.'

'I am not frightened. I . . . My leg. It is broken. Take my son and leave, I beg you.'

The ship shuddered beneath the weight of yet another wave, and Nathan felt the bow of the ship drop.

'You'll come, too.' Reaching out, he found the woman slumped in a corner of the cabin, wedged between the bulkhead and a wooden deck-support. 'Hold me, I'll float you to the hatchway.'

It was doubtful whether the woman fully understood, but there was no time to explain. When she made no move, Nathan took her arm and pulled her towards him.

She cried out in pain, but instinctively clutched at him for support.

'Good. Now, float . . . *Float*!'

As he shouted the last word, he dragged her to the doorway, ignoring her cries. The child began to wail with renewed terror, but once in the passageway the woman seemed to understand what was required of her and she stopped struggling. Clinging tightly to Nathan's shirt, occasionally twisting painfully in the water as the seas buffeted the ship, she stayed with him.

The water had risen to chest height now. Once, when Nathan was thrown off balance by a more violent movement than usual, the woman lost her grip on his shirt. She flailed helplessly about in the water until he was able to pull her back to him.

At the hatchway steps he pulled the woman up behind him, gritting his teeth against her cries of pain. Not until her head and upper body were clear of the hatchway did he allow her a brief respite.

'Please . . . leave me and take my son to safety.' Her voice gave a clear indication of the great pain she felt.

'It's not much farther now. The worst is over.'

'Then, take him first. Come back for me.'

Nathan hesitated for only a few moments. She was right. There was no way he could carry both the boy and his mother to shore together. But leaving her might be condemning her to certain death.

'All right – but you hold on here. I *will* be back for you. Do you understand?'

'I understand. May God go with you. Please . . . What is your name?'

'Jago. Nathan Jago.'

'My son is Jean-Paul Duvernet. You will remember?'

'I will – but I want you around to remind me. Stay exactly where you are until I return.'

'Take care of my son, Nathan Jago. Take very good care of him, I beg you . . .'

At the splintered mainmast Nathan found the Frenchman whose place he had taken at the hatchway. Putting his mouth to Nathan's ear, the Frenchman shouted: 'I have made a sling. It is only a loop about the rope you brought to the ship, but it is successful. People are reaching shore alive . . .'

The ship gave a sudden lurch and heeled over at least forty-five degrees. Thrusting the boy into the Frenchman's arms, Nathan shouted above the wind: 'Take him ashore. I'm going back for his mother. She's broken a leg.'

As Nathan made his way back to the hatchway, the ship shifted yet again. This time he thought the vessel was going right over, but at the last moment she grounded on the rocks and held. However, she now lay completely on her side again, and the last few yards to the hatchway required the agility of a monkey.

The woman was nowhere to be found. Nathan searched the surrounding rigging and called into the darkness again and again, but there was no reply. After a moment's hesitation, he climbed through the hatchway. Water completely filled the cabins on one side of the ship now, leaving only a couple of feet of space in the passageway. There was no sign of the woman, and Nathan's voice was lost in the sound of protesting timbers.

Another movement of the ship reminded Nathan of his own danger. He clambered out through the hatchway once more.

Carried on the wind, he imagined he heard the soft voice calling to him once more.

'Take care of my son, Nathan Jago. Take very good care of him, I beg you . . .'

CHAPTER TWO

The following morning it was as though the storm and the wrecking of the French ship *L'Emir* had never happened. The sky was the colour of soft washed canvas and the sea lay low, ashamed of its recent anger. In Pentuan village the wind picked desultorily at leaves and broken twigs strewn in profusion about the cottages flanking the square.

The flotsam choking the waters of the tiny quarry harbour had long been gathered in, but boats from Pentuan were trawling the waters about the sunken ship in search of gleanings.

On land, boys and men scoured the shoreline. Their harvest was a grim one. Seventeen bodies were carried to the small Methodist chapel in Pentuan to await burial. Seven more would be found before the day ended. Others would be discovered on the beaches of nearby Cornish parishes and buried without record below high-water mark. Times were hard for the *living* in Cornwall. No one wasted effort on unknown dead – especially *French* dead.

Grieving friends and relatives who had survived the wreck sat about the chapel burial-ground. Their earlier noisy grief had given way to a sense of loss, accentuated by the knowledge they were in a country with which France was at war.

One of the bodies lying in the chapel in Pentuan was that of Marie-Louise Duvernet. She had been identified by the Frenchman who had been responsible, with Nathan, for saving many lives the previous night.

Dark-skinned, Marie-Louise Duvernet possessed a beauty that death had not yet been able to steal from her.

When Nathan commented on this, the Frenchman smiled wryly.

'In Martinique men fought duels for a smile from Marie-Louise. Yet many eyebrows were raised when Captain Charles Duvernet married her. One takes a – a "lady of colour"? – for a mistress, not as a wife. But how is her son? He is still at your house?'

'Yes. This morning he seems far more interested in my own son's rocking-horse than in what's happened.'

'Good. He will have a lifetime to feel sad at the loss of his mother.'

The Frenchman looked thoughtful. 'My compatriots and I will become prisoners-of-war. What will you do with the boy?'

Nathan frowned. 'He'll be nobody's prisoner; my wife will see to *that*. Unless there are objections from your people we'll keep him until this war is over.'

'There will be no objections. Each of us will need to be selfish in order to survive captivity. No one will want the added responsibility of one who may be an orphan. His mother was on her way to France from Martinique to seek news of the boy's father. He accompanied Napoleon Bonaparte on the Russian campaign. Half a million soldiers set off with banners flying and drums beating to conquer Russia. Only one in ten survived. It is not known whether Captain Duvernet is among their number. If he is, then he has reason to be grateful to you, M'sieur Jago. You saved the life of his son – and the lives of many others, too.'

The Frenchman nodded towards the line of bodies laid out in the aisle between the high enclosed pews. 'But for your bravery there would be many more of us lying here.'

'I still don't know why your ship was so close to the English coast if you were on passage from Martinique to France.'

The Frenchman spread his arms wide in a gesture of despair. 'This is the year 1813. Martinique is occupied by your soldiers. *L'Emir* managed to escape from the island, but we were pursued all the way from the Indies – only to meet up with a British fleet when we reached the Channel. We hoped to lose our pursuers in the storm. The remainder of the story is known to you.'

At that moment there was the sound of shouting from outside the chapel. Walking to the door, Nathan saw a detachment of the South Cornwall Militia drawn up in the burial-ground. All were perspiring freely as a result of a forced march from St Austell, led by a sergeant who was himself mounted on a horse.

Denying his protesting men the opportunity to relax, the sergeant ordered them to round up the bewildered French survivors who were resting in the chapel burial-ground.

'There's no need for this,' Nathan called angrily. 'These people have dead relatives inside the chapel. They'll not run away.'

The militia sergeant looked down at Nathan, seeing a tall, powerfully built man with an air of authority that belied the simple clothes he wore. 'And who might you be?'

'Nathan Jago, from Polrudden Manor. The remainder of the survivors are in my barn. When they're ready to move off I'll supply wagons for them.'

'My orders were to come here as quickly as possible and take the French men prisoner, to Bodmin Gaol.'

'There are French women and children, too – and some are hurt. There's to be a burial here today. When it's over these people will be ready to go with you. In the meantime, take your men to the barn up at the manor. There's food and ale there.'

The mention of ale put new life into the flagging militiamen, and the sergeant knew better than to risk an outright flouting of his tenuous authority.

'All right, sir. We'll go on to the manor – and thank you kindly.' Suddenly remembering that when he was on duty he was not merely a tenant farmer, but a sergeant of militia, he added: 'But these people are prisoners-of-war. I'm making you personally responsible for them.'

Honour satisfied, the militia sergeant rode off after his thirsty men.

There was a smile on the face of the Frenchman when he said: 'It would appear authority weighs as heavily upon an Englishman as it does on a Frenchman, M'sieur Jago. I fear the sergeant intends treating us as though we have been captured by him in battle.'

'He'll maybe shout at you when you go through a town or village, but no one will be harmed. However, it does mean you must now consider yourself a prisoner. Tonight you will be locked inside an English gaol.'

The Frenchman shrugged. 'It is all part of the foolishness of war, M'sieur Jago.'

Nathan suddenly realised he did not know the other man's name. When he asked, the Frenchman replied: 'Argon. Louis d'Argon. When a French king returns to the throne of France I will once more be Louis, comte d'Argon. Until then it is more convenient in present-day France to be *Citizen* d'Argon.'

Nathan was impressed by Louis d'Argon as a man, and intrigued by his title. However, when he began to question him about it, the Frenchman brushed the questions aside. 'When the time is right the past will be remembered. Until then it is wiser to allow it to sleep undisturbed.'

His words made little sense to Nathan, but he did not pursue the matter. Instead he said: 'You'll no doubt be transferred from Bodmin to the hulks at Plymouth. French prisoners-of-war have been sent there since they began lodging Americans in Dartmoor. A prison hulk is no place for a gentleman. Should the opportunity of parole present itself, you may use my name on your behalf. I'll be happy to have you here, at Polrudden. In the meantime, if you have any message for your family in France, I can arrange for it to be delivered.'

Louis d'Argon smiled delightedly. 'I am flattered. I feel sure you have said more to me than you would to a stranger of your own people. Only an Englishman who trades in undutied goods can be confident of having a letter delivered in France. Perhaps I should have guessed. I have already learned you are a man who goes where others fear to go. Do not worry, my friend. Your secret is safe with me – just as the lives of my compatriots were with you. We owe you much. I do not think I will need to burden you further with the matter of my parole. Letters . . . Ah! This could be another matter – but you need have no misgivings that you might be betraying your country. *All* Frenchmen do not believe that Napoleon Bonaparte rules by divine providence. Realisation is dawning that France will one day soon have to pay a great price for this Bonaparte's ambitions. For now, I can only give you my deepest thanks for all you have done for me and my fellow-passengers in *L'Emir*.'

The bodies of the shipwreck victims were buried in a simple ceremony at noon that day. The service was kept brief because even the garrulous Preacher Jago realised that few of his listeners could understand a word that was being said. Another factor was the reappearance of the sergeant of militia. Red-faced, and fortified by a large quantity of ale, he was now insisting that the French prisoners move off, in order to arrive at Bodmin Gaol by nightfall.

The service over, the militiamen began grumbling about wagons being supplied to convey French prisoners to gaol, while they were obliged to walk alongside them. This matter was solved to the satisfaction of everyone except the sergeant when Nathan supplied an additional wagon to carry the part-time soldiers.

Leaving his father kneeling at the side of the mass grave containing the bodies of the seventeen shipwreck victims, Nathan made his way home to Polrudden Manor. Amy met him at the door and led him upstairs, a finger to her lips. Quietly opening the door to the nursery, she beckoned him to look inside.

Two children lay on the floor. The first was Beville, Nathan's son by his first wife, Elinor. Polrudden had been her family home and she had died here, giving birth to

Beville. The second child was the French boy, Jean-Paul Duvernet. Fast asleep now, they had been playing together, and Beville's toys were strewn all about them. There were wooden animals and figures, and a wooden Noah's ark, complete with animals, real and imagined, assembled in pairs about the wooden Noah, his wife and their sons.

'It's as though Jean-Paul has *always* lived here,' whispered Amy happily. 'Isn't he a lovely little boy? He asked after "Mamma" only once – and I think that's the only word he can say. The rest of the time he and Beville have played together.'

'Does the militia sergeant know he's here?'

'Yes.' The tenderness left Amy's face. 'Someone must have told him. I suspect it was Samson Harry. I saw the two of them talking together at the end of the driveway. The sergeant wanted to take Jean-Paul away, but I told him no motherless boy was going to Bodmin Gaol from my house. If you agree, I think Jean-Paul should remain here until the war is over, or until he's claimed by his father.'

'He could be here for a very long time!' Nathan reported what Louis d'Argon had told him.

'Poor little soul!' Sympathy was suddenly replaced by ferocity as Amy added: 'It's all the more reason for us to keep him here. You don't mind, do you, Nathan?'

'You don't need to ask such a question. I took him from the arms of his mother and I have just seen her laid in the ground. This will be his home for as long as he needs us.'

'I'm glad you feel that way about him. *Very* glad. He'll be a wonderful playmate for Beville – and I think *I* love him already!' Amy kissed Nathan, and as they walked down the stairs together Nathan felt a happiness that caused him temporarily to forget the anxiety he felt about his fishing venture and the future of Polrudden, the house that would one day belong to his son.

Beville would one day inherit a baronetcy from his grandfather, Sir Lewis Hearle, father of Nathan's first wife, Elinor. She and Nathan had met and married soon after he returned to his childhood home to begin drift-fishing. His boat had been bought with money won in the prize-fighting rings of England. After Elinor died, Sir Lewis Hearle had put Polrudden up for sale. Amy had staked the fortune left to her by her father on Nathan's last prize-fight. He won, and with her money she bought Polrudden, bringing it with her as a dowry when she married Nathan. The house was to be Beville's inheritance when he came of age. Amy had known Beville from babyhood and she loved him as though he were her own, but she had love to spare for the small French castaway who now slept on the nursery floor at Polrudden.

Nathan looked at Amy as they walked together down the stairs and suddenly put out an arm to bring her to a halt. Drawing her close, he kissed her hard and long, and she responded with a passion that matched his own.

As he held her to him his gaze strayed to the window and the sea that stretched, calm and blue, to the far horizon. He was happy now, but the sea held the key to their future. The fish had to arrive soon if Polrudden was to remain their home and one day pass to Beville.

The pilchards returned to Mevagissey Bay exactly one week after the loss of the French merchantman. So vital was the event to the fishing community of Pentuan that look-outs had been posted on the cliffs either side of the wide sandy beach for days. The men went to their posts at dawn and remained there, constantly scanning the bay, until dusk made further observation impossible.

On this particular morning the look-out had not even reached his post when he was alerted by gulls wheeling and screaming, no more than half a mile from shore. Beneath the birds the sea was ruffled as though by a localised wind, the surface momentarily turned to silver as millions of small fish changed direction in unison.

The look-out's excited cry of 'Hevva! Hevva!' was a sound that had prompted a flurry of activity in Cornish fishing settlements for many centuries. Today was no exception. Men, women and children spilled from their houses, taking up the cry as the men ran for their boats. Some, called from their beds, were pulling on jerseys and tucking shirts inside trousers as they went. As the smaller children scrambled to the cliff-top to view the great shoal for themselves, women and older boys ran for the beach to help launch the heavy, net-laden seine-boats, each rowed by six hefty men.

At Polrudden the news was brought to the house by Will Hodge, the groom. He had heard the shout go up while exercising the horses along the cliff-edge.

By the time Nathan ran from the house, the groom had a horse waiting at the door. On the way down the hill Nathan could see a line of drifters far out on the horizon, well to the east of Gribbin Head. His own boat, *The Brave Amy H,* would be one of them. Nathan cursed his bad luck. The pilchards were running now, but Nathan knew from experience they would be coming from the opposite direction, from the west. The drift-fishermen were frequently accused of taking pilchards before they came close enough inshore to benefit the seine-fishermen. Indeed, many seine-fishermen believed that the larger boats with their long nets broke up the shoals, preventing them from coming close inshore, but the accusation could not be levelled at drift-fishermen today. The arrival of the pilchards had taken the drift-fishermen unawares. They would not know of their presence until they saw the activity ashore.

At the foot of Pentuan hill Nathan turned his horse across the narrow bridge before shaking out the reins. He allowed the horse to gallop along the firm sands of the beach that stretched almost to Portgiskey Cove. It was here, beside his fish-cellar, that Nathan berthed his boats.

By now the Pentuan boats were at sea, heading for the great shoal, guided by the stentorian shouts of the look-out, the 'huer', who used his arms to add emphasis to his words. When the boats reached the shoal they would cast their nets to encircle as many fish as possible and then carry the long ropes attached to the nets back to the shore. Every available member of the community, young and old, would find a place on the ropes and help haul the trapped fish close inshore, where the fishermen would reap the harvest of the sea.

Galloping along the sand, Nathan passed some of the crewmen of his own boats, running to Portgiskey Cove. The remainder were already here, dragging the large drift-boats into deep water, ready to put to sea. The nets had been placed on board many days before.

Waving to Ahab Arthur, skipper of *Peggy Hoblyn*, which was already hoisting sail and forging out of the cove, Nathan called: 'Take a line on Chapel Point from The Gwineas. Lay your nets as close in as you dare.'

Ahab Arthur waved an acknowledgement, and Nathan knew the experienced fisherman would probably have fished off The Gwineas, even had Nathan said nothing. He had been drift-fishing before Nathan was born, owning two drifters of his own until he was put out of business by the prejudice of the neighbouring Mevagissey seiners.

Nathan handed his horse into the care of the young son of one of the fishermen. The boy would ride it back to the stables at Polrudden. Splashing through the shallows, Nathan swung himself on board his third fishing-boat, *Sir Beville*. Named in anticipation of the title that would one day be his son's, *Sir Beville* was Nathan's largest and newest fishing-boat. Bought at auction in Falmouth, she had been a naval 'prize', captured off the Brittany coast by a patrolling frigate. Larger than any other drifter on the south Cornish coast, *Sir Beville* was capable of deep-sea work. Her purchase had been a gamble for Nathan. He had hoped a good season would see her bringing home catches twice the size of his other boats. So far, the gamble had not paid off.

The last of the fishermen was dragged on board, grinning his relief, as *Sir Beville*'s foresail bellied out in the breeze and drove her on, into deep water. Each of the five fishermen on board received one twenty-fifth of the value of the catch, by way of salary. For too long now that share had been one twenty-fifth of nothing. Today the men hoped for a change of luck.

Sir Beville was a fast-sailing boat and overhauled *Peggy Hoblyn* halfway to the rocky island known as The Gwineas. Nathan knew that when shoals of pilchards were on the move they frequently took a route to the south of here. Sometimes, if the water temperature was not right, they would swim too deep to be caught, but today they behaved exactly as Nathan had predicted.

By the time the two drifters had their nets paid out in a long line stretching out to sea, they had been joined by Nathan's third fishing-boat, *The Brave Amy H,* and two drifters from Mevagissey.

The boats remained at sea all day. By the time they returned to Portgiskey Cove they had made a record catch, being loaded with enough pilchards to busy the wives of the fishermen, at the Portgiskey fish-cellar, for many days to come.

Nathan walked up the hill to Polrudden a tired but happy man. He would need a good many such catches before all his troubles were over, but the pilchards had come at the right time. The fishermen needed a fillip; now they had one – drift fishermen and seiners alike.

Nathan found Amy playing with Beville and Jean-Paul in the garden at Polrudden. She saw how tired he was and, after he had been the object of the small boys' attention for some minutes, she called Rose, the servant-girl whose task it was to take care of the children, and led Nathan away.

As they walked to the house, Amy slipped her arm through his. Looking up at him, she smiled. 'Are we rich again?'

Nathan grimaced good-humouredly. 'We're not rich, but we *can* afford to pay the servants and keep the house going for another month or two. What sort of a day have you had?'

Amy tightened her grip on his arm. 'Jean-Paul cried for his "Mamma" when he sat down for lunch. It's the first time. It was very upsetting, but it didn't last too long. He's a lovely little boy, but not being able to understand English is a problem for him.'

'He'll learn – if he's with us long enough. Ahab Arthur gave some of his catch to a British frigate passing up-Channel with despatches. Wellington has given a drubbing to Napoleon's army in Spain. The French are retreating everywhere. It's said the war can't last for many more months.'

'That will please many wives and mothers, but it's come too late for Jean-Paul. He may never know any family but us.'

When Nathan saw Amy's expression, he stopped and turned her towards him.

'Amy, don't get *too* fond of the boy. His relatives will want him back.'

'Yes,' agreed Amy unhappily, 'but there's nothing to prevent me giving him lots of love while he's here.'

Nathan kissed her then. 'I can't stop you loving Jean-Paul, even if I wanted to. It would have made his mother very happy to know how much you care for him. Just don't love him *too* much, that's all.'

CHAPTER THREE

The seasonal bustle in the Portgiskey fish-cellar died with September. It returned briefly, when a ship put in to the tiny harbour of Pentuan to load salted pilchards, now tightly packed in large wooden hogsheads, but the fishermen would see no large shoals of pilchards again this season.

By early December the smell of fish, strong enough to guide fishermen to port from five miles out on a dark night, had been dispersed by early winter storms. Nathan was catching a few fish with his three drifters, but they were hardly enough to cover the cost of repairing torn nets and sails, or to pay the women who worked in the fish-cellar.

Yet Nathan was luckier than most. The Pentuan seine-fishermen had pulled their boats ashore in preparation for the long winter ahead. Larger vessels lay upside down, well above the high-water mark. Smaller boats would spend the winter leaning against cottage walls in the village.

Enterprising village men went inland, carrying seaweed and sea sand to surrounding farms. For this they might receive a bushel of wheat, a side of bacon, or a few eggs and butter. But such resourcefulness was resented by the farm-workers, themselves suffering hard times. Fights became frequent between those who worked the land and those who harvested the sea.

One day Nathan returned to Portgiskey in *The Brave Amy H* with a catch of mackerel and found Samson Harry, the returned prisoner-of-war, waiting on the Portgiskey quay.

'You'll not make a fortune fishing mackerel.' Samson Harry's dour observation was directed at Nathan.

'You're telling me nothing I don't already know.'

The catch looked impressive as it was landed, but no satisfactory method of curing the oily fish had yet been found. It would need to be sold locally – and quickly, at prices local people could afford.

Nathan did not like the stocky, unsmiling fisherman. Samson Harry felt the world owed him a debt because of the five years he had spent inside French prisons. 'If you want some fish for your family, you're welcome to help yourself.'

'I've not come to beg,' Samson Harry's reply was sharp. 'I'm here to ask for work.'

Nathan's immediate reaction was to tell the man standing before him that he had no work. Samson Harry would not fit in with the other crewmen. His constant grumbling would create dissatisfaction. On the other hand, Harry had a large, dependent family, the youngest born three months after he was taken prisoner. They had suffered great hardship during his five years' absence, kept from the poorhouse only by the genorisity of Pentuan villagers.

Nathan hesitated. 'I've got nothing for you immediately, but you're welcome to be one of my reserve fishermen. Winter's here and there'll be the usual sickness. You'll get a fair share of work.'

'I'm no *reserve* fisherman! I was out fishing with my father on the day you were born. By the time you ran away from home, at fifteen, I was skippering a deep-sea lugger. When I watched Nelson's ships limping back from Trafalgar – yours among them – I *owned* the boat I sailed. If it hadn't been for the French, I'd have a fleet of deep-sea fishing-boats now. What I have to offer is my *skill* – as a skipper. The know-how to find fish when no one else can. The guts to put to sea when other men are peeping around a curtain at the weather. By the look of your empty cellar you could do with a good skipper. I'm offering to do you a favour, Nathan Jago, not begging one.'

Nathan remembered that Samson Harry had been known as a hard man for whom to work. He stayed out longer and sailed further than any other fishing-boat in search for fish. Some said, unkindly, this was the reason he had been captured by the French man-of-war while other fishing-boats reached the safety of Mevagissey harbour. Even so, Nathan did not recall that Samson Harry had won fame for returning with exceptionally heavy catches.

'I've no vacancy for a skipper. My advice to you is to take out a loan and buy your own boat. You'll never be happy working for another man.'

'If it was advice I wanted, I'd hardly have come to a man who's spent much of his life prize-fighting. I'd have gone where I'd be sure of getting *sound* advice. There's no bank will loan money to a man who's spent the last five years in French gaols. Years ago I could have gone cap in hand to the lord of the manor and asked for help, but *you're* living in the manor now. You'd hardly loan money to a man who's likely to put you out of business.'

'I haven't money to loan anyone,' said Nathan honestly. 'If I had, I doubt if I'd give it to you. It's not that I'm worried about being put out of business. In a good year there's fish for everyone, but the fish haven't been running lately. Fishermen are going out of business all along the coast. No sane man would risk money financing a fishing business.'

'If I had a boat, it *would* make money. I'd see to that – and I wouldn't need to deal with the King's enemies to see a profit, either.'

'The war's almost over, Samson. Soon we'll all be doing business with the French again – by day as well as by night.'

Nathan was showing exceptional patience with Samson Harry. Any man who lost his boat, for whatever reason, had every right to feel embittered.

'No doubt you'll be well ahead of everyone else, Jago. With your experience of night-trading and a French brat living under your roof, *you'll* be the one the French come to. Then perhaps you'll *really* be the squire of Pentuan.'

Nathan glanced to where the crew of his fishing-boat were listening to the exchange. Not one of them met his eyes. Out on the water, pulling in nets, elbow-deep in mackerel, they sweated and swore together, sharing the same jokes. Samson Harry had reminded them Nathan was no longer one of their number. Nathan's home was in the manor-house where his first wife had been born. His son, Beville, would one day inherit his grandfather's baronetcy. Nathan owned the boats in which the fishermen worked. He set the tithe payments which every Pentuan boat-owner was obliged to pay to the manor in respect of the fish he caught.

'You've said enough, Samson. The French child was saved from the sea and has no family to care for him. As for night-trading, it's kept *your* family together, as I've told you before, and the less said about it the better. Loose tongues have resulted in more than one Pentuan fishermen being taken by Revenue men. Your homecoming will turn sour if it happens again because of you.'

'My homecoming's turned sour already. Too much has changed while I've been away – and nothing for the better. I've offered you my skills as a fisherman and you've turned me down. You'll regret it one day, Nathan Jago. A man has to look after his own – and the Devil can take all others.' Still angry, Samson Harry broke off the exchange and strode stiffly away from Portgiskey.

There was a movement behind Nathan, and Ahab Arthur came to stand beside him, his gaze on the departing man.

'Be careful of him, Nathan. Samson Harry believes he's owed recompense for his misfortunes. He'll seek it from those who have what he's lost.'

Ahab Arthur's words were disturbingly prophetic. The following week Samson Harry moved his family to Fowey Town, six miles across the bay. He had been made coxswain of the Fowey Revenue cutter. In the future, neither Samson Harry nor his family would be welcome among a fishing community to whom smuggling was as traditional as fishing itself.

Nathan had a long-standing arrangement with a French smuggling vessel. Once a month he took out *The Brave Amy H* with a trusted crew, to make a rendezvous with the French ship. Golden sovereigns and sometimes tin ingots were passed to the Frenchman. In return, brandy, tea and salt were loaded in *The Brave Amy H*.

After Samson Harry's appointment to the Preventive Service, Nathan made hurried contact with the French vessel and set a new date and place for the rendezvous. Justification for his caution came on the night when he would otherwise have made his smuggling trip. All night unknown boats followed the Portgiskey vessels as they went about their fishing. In the morning, on their way back to Portgiskey, they were intercepted by Revenue cutters drawn from the ports of Fowey, Looe and Falmouth. The fishing-boats and, later, the fish-cellar at Portgiskey were thoroughly searched before the cutters returned to their respective stations to report a wasted night's work.

The increased activities of the Preventive men caused Nathan some concern, as well as reducing his profits – as Samson Harry knew they would. Henceforth, Nathan would only bring ashore unexcised goods for immediate delivery to his customers. He could no longer run the risk of storing them in the fish-cellar or at Polrudden.

Amy urged Nathan to cease his smuggling activities altogether, but he could not afford to do this. Certainly not at this time of the year, after experiencing a poor fishing season.

Then, in January 1814, something occurred to change everything.

Late one evening, Nathan was seated with Amy in the smallest of the manor's lounges, a cosy fire burning in the hearth, when there was a heavy knocking at the main door of the house. The urgency of the sound brought Nathan from his chair, and Amy looked at him in consternation. Good news seldom came to the house at this time of the night.

The noise of the heavy bolt being drawn back echoed along the corridor outside, and it was followed by the sound of raised voices. Nathan reached the door and flung it open in time to allow a tall, loose-limbed man dressed for riding to stride into the room. It was Louis d'Argon!

Behind him a young housemaid wrung her hands anxiously. 'I'm sorry, Master. I tried to stop him. He walked right in.'

'It's all right, Winnie. Find Will Hodge and tell him to take care of the gentleman's horse. Then you can lock up again.'

As the door closed behind the servant-girl, Nathan turned to find the Frenchman bowing low over Amy's hand.

'Louis! What are you doing here? Have you escaped from the hulks? Is there a pursuit?'

Releasing Amy's hand with exaggerated reluctance,

Louis d'Argon smiled at Nathan. 'Were I to admit to being a fugitive, would you offer me sanctuary?' Clasping Nathan in an embrace, the Frenchman looked searchingly into Nathan's eyes. 'Why, yes, I think you would! Thank you, my friend, I am deeply moved. But you need have no fear. I am *not* being hunted. However, I *am* here to solicit your aid.'

Amy rose from her seat. 'I'll find a servant and have a meal prepared while you talk business.'

'No . . . please! I am about to ask your husband to do something that may prove to be dangerous. I would like you to hear what I have to say. If you do not approve . . .' Louis d'Argon shrugged expressively. 'He has already risked his life once for me and my fellow-passengers in *L'Emir.* I will understand.'

Louis, comte d'Argon took few things in life seriously, but the expression on his face now caused Nathan to cross to a small table and fill three pot-bellied glasses from a decanter filled with best Armagnac. The drink had been a Christmas gift from the master of the French vessel with whom Nathan had nocturnal meetings.

'Perhaps we should drink this while you tell us why you're here – and how it is you're riding the roads of England a free man, and not rotting in a Plymouth prison hulk.'

The smile returned to Louis d'Argon's face, and a movement of his hand drew attention to his clothes. From the heavy blue cutaway coat buttoned around his throat to tight buff-coloured pantaloons, encased below the knee in polished black riding boots, the Frenchman was fashionably elegant.

'The necessities of *my* life are not to be found in a prison hulk, my dear friend. As for the company I was expected to keep there . . .!' Louis d'Argon wrinkled his nose in distaste. 'Four days and nights in such a dreadful place were all I could endure.'

'How did you obtain your release? We *are* at war with France.'

'True – but every Frenchman is not a slave to the Revolution. My father was a courtier to King Louis XVI. He shared the King's confidence. He also shared his fate. He was guillotined while the blood of the King was still wet upon the blade that had taken his life. My mother would have died, too, had she not fled to the country, where mobs were not clamouring for aristocratic blood. Now the war has turned against Napoleon Bonaparte. When he is toppled the crown will be returned to the Bourbons. There is more than one claimant to the throne of France, but your government favours the comte de Provence. I am to go to France to speak to Bonaparte's marshals. They are the men who can force their leader to step down, and so ease the comte de Provence's path to the throne.'

Nathan looked with renewed respect at the man whose life he had helped to save on a stormy night. The responsibility of the task entrusted to Louis was enormous. He had to be a man of considerable stature and influence to be entrusted by the British government with such a mission. But why had he come here, to Polrudden?

When Nathan asked the question it was the turn of the Frenchman to appear surprised. 'How else am I to return to France? As you have said, our two countries are at war. But you are a resourceful man, Nathan. Before I was taken away by your militia you offered to have a letter taken to France for me. If you can send a letter, why not a man also?'

Nathan frowned. The French smuggler with whom Nathan had traded illegally for more than two years would take a letter without comment. A *man* – and a French aristocrat at that – was a very different matter.

Louis d'Argon shrugged off Nathan's doubts. 'I am a prisoner returning to France. I carry with me proposals to end a war that has dragged on for twenty years. Proposals to save thousands of French lives. My countrymen are sick of war and bloodshed, Nathan. The Revolution spawned a whole generation born to bloodshed. Young men have lived and died without knowing the meaning of peace. If this man with whom you trade is a true Frenchman, he will take me as a passenger – for the good of France. If he is also a father, he will be *eager* to take me, for the sake of his children.'

His impassioned declaration over, Louis d'Argon's face relaxed in a sudden smile once more. 'I realise this man is also a smuggler, so I have brought gold with me. He will be paid well for taking me quickly to France and putting me ashore on a quiet beach.'

Nathan thought of one-legged Captain Pierre. A skilful sailor and experienced smuggler, he had lost a leg at the great sea-battle of Trafalgar. He had been fighting for France – but not, as he frequently reminded Nathan, for the greater glory of Napoleon Bonaparte.

'You won't need your gold. Be honest with Cap'n Pierre and he'll take you wherever you wish to go – for the sake of France.'

Three nights later Nathan's boat, *Sir Beville,* slipped quietly out of Portgiskey, the fishing-boat's sails swelled by a fresh south-westerly wind. On board with Nathan was a full fishing crew – and Louis, comte d'Argon.

The three days of Louis d'Argon's clandestine visit had totally disrupted the routine of Polrudden Manor. A man of tremendous energy, the Frenchman had been frustrated by Nathan's warning not to leave the grounds of the ancient manor-house. News of the Frenchman's arrival would reach Pentuan within hours of his arrival. The villagers would be incensed by the presence of an 'enemy' at Polrudden, but the gossips would assume that Louis d'Argon had been paroled and do no more than grumble at the 'soft' attitude of the prison authorities. However, if Louis showed his face in the village, tempers would flare and perhaps place his mission in jeopardy.

To pass away time at Polrudden, Louis d'Argon taught everyone to play 'royal tennis', an ancient French ball game that was currently gaining popularity in London. He also broke a newly acquired pony to the saddle, redesigned a formal garden at the side of the house, played with the children and flirted outrageously with Amy and Nell Quicke, Nathan's happily married sister. Nathan also suspected that Louis bedded at least two of the servant-girls, but he made no attempt to confirm his suspicions.

Nathan set a course for Looe, a port sixteen miles to the east. Captain Pierre had a regular rendezvous five miles off Looe Island with smugglers from nearby Talland Bay.

Sir Beville was off Fowey when Nathan saw the outline of a much larger vessel slicing through the water on an identical course not five hundred yards distant. In a low voice, Nathan ordered the mainsail lowered, allowing the other vessel to forge ahead.

'What is it?' Louis d'Argon's question was barely audible above the combined voices of wind and sea.

'A man-of-war.' Nathan's equally quiet reply was terse. 'The Navy has taken to stationing a ship at Fowey – on Preventive duty.'

'Will it present problems for us?' Louis d'Argon's anxious question was in marked contrast to his usual care-free manner. 'It is important that I reach France as soon as possible.'

Nathan watched the shadowy form of the man-of-war drawing steadily ahead of them. 'She may be setting off on a patrol. If so, she'll probably be working the area where Cap'n Pierre is due to make his rendezvous and we'll need to forget it for tonight.'

'When is the next time we can meet with him?'

'A fortnight's time, off Mevagissey.'

'I cannot wait that long.' Louis d'Argon was deadly serious now. 'The marshals are meeting in Paris in a week's time. I must speak with them then. Should I fail, and Bonaparte return to Paris before they reach a decision, this war will continue until France is reduced to a wasteland by the armies of Europe. Are there no more smugglers trading with your people?'

'Probably but I don't know them – and not all men who sell unexcised goods are to be trusted. We'll go on; the man-of-war might merely be on passage to Plymouth.'

Nathan's hope proved unduly optimistic. Shortly before reaching the smuggler's rendezvous, *Sir Beville* was almost run down by the warship as it tacked slowly across the wind. Only Nathan's quick action in changing course saved his vessel from certain destruction.

Cursing the naval look-out who had failed to see him in the moonlit darkness, Nathan took *Sir Beville* farther out to sea.

'With look-outs like that there's little fear of Cap'n Pierre and his boat being taken,' he said. 'But they'll frighten him away, for certain. There's no sense in looking for him tonight.'

'Can you intercept him before he reaches the rendezvous? Perhaps farther along the coast?' There was desperation in Louis d'Argon's voice.

'We'd never find him. Cap'n Pierre has survived for so long because he's an elusive man. He approaches a rendezvous from a different direction each trip.' Nathan studied Louis d'Argon's face and saw his anxiety, discernible even in the pale moonlight. 'Do you *honestly* think you can help bring this war to a close?'

'If I believed otherwise, I would not be returning to France on a mission that will put my life at risk. Exiled Frenchmen of rank can find a welcome in any court in Europe – and nothing is expected of them. I am *convinced* I can persuade the marshals of France to depose Napoleon Bonaparte and seek an honourable peace.'

Nathan thought of his many friends who had been killed in the bloody war that had dragged on in Europe for so many years. Each day that passed saw more men killed on the high seas and the battlefields of Europe. There *was* a way to deliver Louis d'Argon to France, but it was an alternative Nathan had been trying to ignore. It could be ignored no longer.

'How well do you know the Brittany coastline?' Brittany was the French province closest to Cornwall, no more than 120 miles across the English Channel.

'As well as you know Cornwall. My family's estates are there.' Suddenly the reason for Nathan's question sank home. '*You* are taking me to France?'

'There's no other way to get you there quickly.'

'It will be dangerous for you.'

'Possibly, but *Sir Beville* is a French-built boat and we have the nets on board. With this wind we'll reach the Brittany coast before noon tomorrow, find a place you know, and put out our nets. We can fish while you choose a good spot to land after dark. But you'll need to change your clothes if you're to be taken for a fisherman. You'll find some spare fishing clothes in the locker, down below.'

When Nathan told the crew of his plans they were apprehensive about crossing the Channel. Their fears were assuaged somewhat when Louis d'Argon produced five guineas for each man, but throughout most of the night they formed a low-talking group huddled in the forecastle. Nathan knew they were discussing the dangers they would face across the English Channel. He could not blame them. He was thinking about them himself.

They sighted land soon after ten o'clock the next morning. As the fishing-boat drew nearer, Louis d'Argon identified it as the Ile de Batz. It lay a few miles from the French coast, close to the port of Roscoff.

'It is excellent!' Louis d'Argon was jubilant. 'The estates of my family are only a few miles inland. I will be able to obtain a horse and be on my way to Paris within hours of landing.'

'All we have to do now is look busy until nightfall.'

As the day wore on, Nathan became uneasy at the absence of other fishing-boats in the area. From the grey, overcast horizon to the indistinct shoreline there was not a sail to be seen. On such a day as this off the Cornish coast the fishing fleets would be out in strength. When he voiced his unease to Louis d'Argon, the Frenchman shrugged.

'Your British warships regularly patrol our coasts. French fishermen have learned it is not safe to fish during the day. Now they come out only at night.'

'Then, we must hope we don't meet up with a British man-of-war. We'd need to come up with a good explanation for fishing so close to the French coast – and in a French-built vessel. But, talking of fishing, this looks as good a spot as any to shoot the nets.'

An hour later, *Sir Beville* was drifting off the French coast, a long line of nets marked by bobbing corks reaching out from the boat.

Only once during the day did they see any sign of another vessel, and then it was no more than the topsail of a British frigate passing along the horizon from west to east.

As the fishing-boat drifted closer to the shore, Nathan could see a number of small villages that appeared little different from those in Cornwall. Only the strangely shaped spires informed the close observer that this was France, and not England.

There was more activity on shore than Louis d'Argon would have liked, but this was hardly surprising. The British armies of Lord Wellington were fighting their way into France from Spain. Napoleon himself was directing a desperate bid to contain the combined forces of Russia and the Prussian states in the east. The people's militia was mobilising in every corner of France, preparing to die in support of Emperor Napoleon Bonaparte and the motherland. The degree of mobilisation gave an added importance to Louis d'Argon's mission. If it failed, blood would be shed in every lane and every village in France.

Shortly before nightfall, Nathan and his crew began hauling in their nets. They discovered they had caught a surprising number of fish – enough to make the unplanned fishing expedition profitable.

Nathan and Louis d'Argon had jointly decided where the landing would take place. Once the nets were stowed inboard they set sail for the lights of a village which had a small walled harbour.

Louis d'Argon said the village was named Raulet. An inkeeper here was known to Louis. He would supply a horse without asking any awkward questions.

Sir Beville edged slowly in towards the harbour wall under a reduced foresail. The moon had not yet risen, and it was very dark. Only the lights of the village houses gave Nathan any idea of his position.

They heard voices long before they sighted the harbour wall, and Louis d'Argon listened intently before whispering to Nathan: 'They are militiamen, guarding the harbour. They have both agreed their duties are a waste of time and are leaving to drink with their friends.'

A few minutes later *Sir Beville* bumped gently against the harbour wall. The tide was falling and the harbour wall was high, having been built to withstand the great waves that swept in from the Atlantic. Nathan found it necessary to work the fishing-boat along the seaweed-hung wall until the boat reached steps cut into the stonework. Louis d'Argon bade Nathan a hurried farewell, then after a swift clasp of hands the Frenchman scrambled over the side of the fishing-boat – and was gone.

'Right! Let's get away from here and go home.'

It was not to be as simple as Nathan made it sound. The high harbour wall effectively robbed the sails of any wind. This, together with the long Atlantic rollers, kept them trapped against the wall.

'Hold the boat off and work it along the wall until we reach the harbour entrance,' Nathan hissed. 'There should be enough wind there for us to tack clear.'

Sir Beville was a large boat. It took the combined efforts of all the men on board to get her moving in the right direction as she rose and fell against the harbour wall. They succeeded with great difficulty, and the boat edged agonisingly slowly towards the harbour entrance.

Then, quite suddenly, the single foresail gathered the wind and *Sir Beville* surged through the water, leaving the French harbour astern.

'That was an anxious few minutes . . .' Nathan was at the helm and he grinned his relief at the nearest crew member.

The smile was lost in the darkness – and Nathan's relief was short-lived. Their course to clear the harbour was taking them towards the land. When Nathan estimated they had come as close as they dared, he put them about and, with increased sail, tacked close-hauled into the wind.

It should have been a perfectly safe manoeuvre to carry them into the open sea, but as they gathered speed the boat went aground. It happened with a suddenness that threw everyone on board to the deck. There was a brief moment of hope when *Sir Beville* lifted to the swell, only to be dashed when the boat grounded even more solidly than before, leaning over at an uncomfortable angle.

Scrambling to his feet, Nathan shouted: 'Throw out an anchor – as far forward as you can. We'll try to pull ourselves off.'

He knew where they were. While they were fishing he had seen a long sandbar – silt brought down by a small river to the east of Raulet. The sea and wind had combined to carry *Sir Beville* much closer to land than Nathan had realised.

One of the fishermen swung the anchor two or three times before sending it arcing into the darkness on the end of a stout rope. It was a grapnel-type anchor, and Nathan hoped it might catch on unseen rocks at the edge of the sandbar.

Three times the fisherman cast out the anchor while Nathan grew more concerned. The third time the anchor held, and he called all the crewmen to the rope. As *Sir Beville* rose on the swell, Nathan called: 'Heave . . . *now*!'

Their efforts succeeded in bringing the boat to a more upright position, but she was still securely lodged on the sandbar.

After half a dozen more attempts had failed, Nathan tried another tactic.

'Lighten the boat. Throw everything overboard that isn't absolutely essential. Hurry now; it's a falling tide, and we'll need to work fast if we're to get off.'

Everything that was not secured was carried to the side of the boat and committed to the sea. Heavy deep-water anchor, buckets, ballast – even the wet nets and their recent catch of fish. Meanwhile, Nathan set one of the crew to bailing all water from the bilges.

When the boat had been stripped of all but the most essential fittings, the desperate men tried once more to pull *Sir Beville* free. They succeeded in moving the vessel no more than eighteen inches before she settled once more, securely gripped by the sand and shingle of the bar.

'What do we do now?'

It was a cold January night, but Nathan could smell fear in the perspiration oozing from the young fisherman who asked the question.

'We sit here while the tide goes out and comes back again – and we pray as hard as we know how.'

CHAPTER FOUR

Within an hour of dawn, two boats manned by French militiamen put out from the village of Raulet and took Nathan and his five crewmen prisoner.

The Portgiskey fishermen had almost succeeded in freeing *Sir Beville* from the sandbar. The tide was at its lowest between three and four o'clock in the morning, and for two hours before this Nathan and his crew had been out on the now dry sanbar frantically digging a channel ahead of the boat. For spades they had used boards ripped from the gunwales. When the French boats reached them, water was beginning to lap against the sides of *Sir Beville*.

Even now they might have brought off a daring bluff. When the French boats drew close and one of the militiamen called out to them, Nathan spread his hands wide, looked sheepish, and made an unintelligible sound of despair. Then he threw a rope to the speaker, with signals to indicate that he expected a tow off the sandbar.

The Frenchman accepted the rope and had actually secured it to the stern of his boat when one of his colleagues in the other vessel called sharply to him. Nathan knew very little French, but he realised the Frenchman was commenting on the clothing worn by Nathan and his men.

The fishermen's clothing was distinctly Cornish, and Nathan realised the game was almost up. He tried to maintain the bluff by motioning once more for the men in the first boat to begin pulling *Sir Beville* free. The man responded with a question in French.

When Nathan made no reply, the man stooped down in the boat and rose with a musket in his hands. He repeated the question, this time with the gun pointing at Nathan.

The game was up.

'We're English.' Nathan repeated the statement twice, and when it was translated by one of the Frenchmen a murmur of anger rose from the two Raulet boats.

Many more guns appeared in view over the sides of the two French boats, and one of them began edging forward cautiously.

When the French boat bumped alongside, half a dozen Frenchmen clambered on board *Sir Beville*, covered determinedly by their companions.

Mustering the Pentuan fishermen in an apprehensive group at the stern of *Sir Beville*, two of the armed boarding-party stood guard over them while the remainder searched the grounded boat. When their task was completed, the Frenchmen relaxed a little and tried to converse with their prisoners, but neither party spoke the other's language.

Eventually, the Pentuan fishermen were divided into two groups and ordered to get in the French boats. Nathan's protest that he and his crew should stay together, accompanied by gestures, was ignored. He was pushed roughly over the side of his boat with two of his crew.

Nathan was furious with himself for allowing his boat and crew to fall into French hands. His chagrin increased when a rope was attached to *Sir Beville* and the fishing-boat pulled off the sandbar with little difficulty. Given another half-hour *Sir Beville* would have drifted clear by herself and the Pentuan fishermen might have sailed their boat home to Portgiskey.

Sir Beville was towed into harbour and berthed alongside the wall, the operation watched by a growing crowd of spectators. Then the six Cornishmen were taken ashore, surrounded by their captors and herded through the village to the lock-up.

On this walk the Pentuan fishermen encountered open hostility for the first time. Some of the young French boys began to jeer. The sound was quickly taken up by some of their elders. As the prisoners passed along the narrow streets leading from the harbour, the sound became more menacing. The mood of their captors also underwent a change. The Pentuan fishermen were prodded with muskets, and once a woman ran from a doorway and spat in the face of Saul Piper, the most quick-tempered member of Nathan's crew.

Reacting angrily, Saul Piper cursed the woman soundly until Nathan took his hand in a powerful grip.

'Hold on to your temper, Saul. If we start anything here in the street, we'll be beaten to death. These people have lost sons and husbands in the war and we're probably the first Englishmen they've ever seen.'

Scowling at the woman, who ran beside them, screaming angry abuse, Saul Piper wiped his bearded face and heeded Nathan's words, ignoring the captor who prodded him provocatively with a musket.

Nathan was relieved when the procession arrived at the village 'lock-up', a small building with a stout wooden door, heavily studded with square-headed iron nails. The six men were bundled roughly inside and the door slammed shut, leaving the men in cold, windowless gloom.

'What will they do to us now?' The tremulous question came from Cornelius Lanyon, the youngest member of Nathan's crew. Seventeen years of age, he had been taken on at the urgent request of his older brother, Pascoe. Orphaned when Cornelius was still a boy, Pascoe had worked hard to keep his young brother out of the poorhouse and bring him up as his mother would have wished. Both were in the crew captured by the French.

'They'll no doubt hand us over to the authorities in the nearest town and we'll be kept as prisoners until the war is over, in another month or two.'

Nathan spoke with more confidence than he felt. Louis d'Argon had predicted the war would soon be over, but that forecast depended upon the success of the Frenchman's own mission.

'A month or two? What'll my wife do in that time with no money coming in and a family to look after?'

The plaintive questions came from Matthew Mitchell. The eldest of a large family himself, Mitchell's own father had been lost at sea in a storm when Matthew was a boy. No one knew better than he how hard the next few months would be for a fatherless family.

'If the other boats are bringing in fish, Amy will see that no one goes hungry.' Nathan was determined to keep up the spirits of his crew. 'In the meantime we'd better all stick to the same story if we're questioned. We came across to this side of the Channel to fish well offshore. The wind and tide brought us closer to land than we realised and we ran aground. That's all you've got to remember. Don't try to add anything. We were fishing, that's all.'

'If they believe that, they'll believe anything!' The voice in the gloom came from the oldest member of the crew. Obadiah Hockin was a small, gnarled man of indeterminate age. He would admit only that he had been fishing for fifty years of his life.

'It's the best we can do – and the only story that's likely to ensure we suffer no more than imprisonment. Remember that, all of you.'

Nathan was well aware of the weakness of their story, but he was worried about a great deal more than the predicament in which he and his crew now found themselves. No one at Polrudden had any knowledge that *Sir Beville* had crossed the Channel to France. Amy believed they had gone along the coast to meet up with Captain Pierre. She would have been concerned when *Sir Beville* failed to return the previous morning. By now she would be frantic with worry, yet there was nothing Nathan could do to inform her of the plight of himself and his crew. Communications between France and England were non-existent, except through men like Captain Pierre.

Nathan was particularly concerned about what might happen to Polrudden in his absence. Ever since Beville's birth Nathan's life had been governed by a determination to keep Polrudden for him. When Beville inherited his grandfather's baronetcy it was doubtful whether it would be accompanied by any money. Polrudden was all he would have to go with the title. Nathan knew Amy was equally determined that Polrudden would one day be Beville's, but how long could she keep going on her own, believing Nathan to be dead?

It was a question that would keep sleep from Nathan on many tortured nights to come.

It was afternoon when the six Pentuan fishermen heard the sound of marching feet on the cobblestones outside their cramped prison. A few minutes later the door was swung open and the prisoners led outside.

Momentarily blinded by the winter sunlight after hours inside the darkened lock-up, they stumbled on the uneven roadway and a great howl went up from the assembled crowd. News of the capture of six Englishmen had spread quickly about the French countryside. Many workers had downed tools and hurried to Raulet for a glimpse of the arch-enemies of post-Revolutionary France.

Fortunately for Nathan and his crew, the men sent to escort them to the nearby town of St Pol-de-Léon were regular soldiers, well-disciplined veterans of Napoleon's Grand Army. No angry mob of unruly citizens would rob them of their charges.

The officer in charge of the escort was well aware of the mood of the citizens. Wisely, he commandeered an enclosed van to convey the six Englishmen. Removing the prisoners from the view of his countrymen would take the sting from their anger.

It proved to be a bumpy and uncomfortable ride, and for the first half-mile the rattle and thump of stones against the side of the van accompanied them on their way.

The Pentuan fishermen and their escort reached St Pol-de-Léon just as darkness fell. Here, too, they were given a noisy and angry reception while they were being ushered inside a large and imposing building which Nathan correctly identified as the town hall.

Inside the building the fishermen were formed into single file and marched along a number of corridors to a large chamber. The high-ceilinged room had a patterned marble floor and walls draped with the tricolour, symbol of the late Revolution.

At the end of the room three men sat behind a huge table which might comfortably have accommodated thirty persons at a banquet. Standing behind the men were a number of armed peasants dressed in the half-uniform of citizens' militia. Nearby, a small, grey-faced man fluttered his hands nervously as the central figure at the table spoke to him.

Turning to the six prisoners, the nervous man addressed himself to Nathan in halting but scholarly English. 'I am commanded to tell you this is a court of enquiry, convened to establish the reason why you were in French waters.'

Nathan shrugged. 'You don't need to hold a court of enquiry for that. We were fishing – drift-fishing, overnight. We drifted too far and ran aground. That's all there is to it.'

The principal judge snapped at the nervous interpreter, who hurriedly translated what Nathan had said. Before the interpreter came to an end, a large man at the end of the table waved him to silence and snapped at him angrily, his gaze upon Nathan.

'The mayor says you will speak only when you are asked a question by himself or either of the magistrates.'

So now Nathan knew the composition of the 'court of

enquiry'. He was about to question the interpreter when he saw the mayor glaring at him. Wisely, Nathan decided to keep quiet. It was foolish to antagonise the members of the court unnecessarily.

Shifting his attention from the prisoners, the mayor began questioning the Raulet militiamen. The interpreter made no attempt to keep the prisoners informed of what was being said, but Nathan realised the French militiamen were telling the court of enquiry how the capture had been made.

The mayor of St Pol-de-Léon nodded his satisfaction with the story told to him by the Frenchmen. He spoke to the nervous interpreter, who passed the gist of his questions on to the prisoners.

'The mayor wishes to know your name, and which of you is the captain of the vessel?'

Giving the names of his crew, Nathan declared he was both captain and owner of *Sir Beville*.

All three men comprising the court of enquiry were making notes, the mayor writing slowly and laboriously. When he finished, he looked at Nathan belligerently as he spoke to the interpreter.

'*Now* you may explain how you came to be aground on the sandbar outside Raulet.'

Nathan shrugged. 'What is there to explain? We were fishing off your coast and drifted too close inshore during the night. That's all.'

Nathan's words provoked another exchange between the Raulet men and the mayor. So far, neither of the magistrates had asked a question of the prisoners.

'The mayor says you lie. No nets were found on your boat.'

'We threw the nets and our catch overboard in a bid to get off the sandbar.'

'Why did you come so far for fish?'

'Because there has been none around the Cornish coast for many weeks. Cornish fishermen are becoming desperate. We'll go *anywhere* to find fish . . .'

The questioning continued for more than half an hour, covering the same ground time and time again. Finally, Nathan said: 'We *are* fishermen and, as such, present no threat to France. I demand we be released and allowed to sail back to England.'

When Nathan's words were interpreted, the mayor stood up and roared angrily at Nathan.

Trembling, the interpreter said: 'The mayor says you lie. You came here to spy on France – or perhaps to land a spy. You will be treated as agents of the enemy. As for your boat, it has already been given to the citizen who took you into custody.'

When Nathan began to protest, the mayor snapped an order to the citizen guards standing behind the prisoners. They rushed upon Nathan, and one of them was foolish enough to throw a punch at him. Nathan ducked instinctively and retaliated with a blow from the fist that had defeated every champion prize-fighter in England.

The Frenchman was unconscious before he hit the floor, and two of his fellow-citizens quickly joined him. Aware that his crew members were fighting alongside him, Nathan felt a mounting exhilaration as Frenchmen fell to the ground – but the outcome was inevitable.

A brass-bound musket-butt, wielded by one of the regular soldiers, struck Nathan behind the ear and he fell to the ground among the prone figures of the mayor's men.

CHAPTER FIVE

Amy was not concerned when Nathan failed to return immediately after his proposed rendezvous with Captain Pierre. She assumed he had taken the opportunity to fish new grounds on the way back to Portgiskey. By nightfall she was rather more anxious, but she was kept busy re-assuring the wives of Nathan's crewmen that *Sir Beville* would probably return with enough fish to keep them all busy in the cellar. Nathan and those with him were experienced sailors and the weather was fair.

In spite of her stated confidence, Amy woke more than once during the night, reaching out her hand in the hope that she would find Nathan lying beside her. Then she would lie awake, hoping to hear his footsteps crunching along the gravel path in front of the house.

When daylight filled the bedroom window with soft grey light, Amy rose from her bed and looked out from the house. From Polrudden the fields dropped away towards Pentuan. Through leafless branches of the trees surrounding the house she could see the long curve of Pentuan beach and the rocks marking the entrance to Portgiskey Cove.

Apart from a couple of small seine-boats drawn high up the sloping sand of the beach, there was not a boat to be seen. This was the moment when Amy faced the fact that she could find no more excuses for *Sir Beville*'s failure to return. Something had happened to the boat and her crew.

There was still a hope that *Sir Beville*'s failure to return had something to do with Louis d'Argon's mission. If the men had been taken by the Navy, or by the Preventive Service, the 'misunderstanding' would eventually be resolved. But Amy had waited long enough for information to come to her. It was time to seek some answers.

Downstairs, one of the early-rising maids was cleaning out grates and relighting the fires. Amy told the girl to leave all her chores and hurry to Venn Farm to fetch Nell Quicke, Nathan's married sister. Nell would take charge of the children while Amy did whatever proved necessary.

Slipping a warm cape over her shoulders, Amy let herself out of the house and made her way down the hill, heading for Portgiskey Cove.

The village of Pentuan was quiet. The only persons she saw in the street were two fishermen-turned-miners, returning from the night shift at one of the small mines farther along the valley. It was a cold morning with a strong onshore wind blowing, and the village fishermen would not be in a hurry to get out of bed. The two miners looked at Amy curiously and touched their hats to her before turning in at their cottages. Over breakfast the men would tell their wives they had seen Amy hurrying from the manor to Portgiskey. Together they would arrive at the reason for her early-morning haste. Within an hour the whole village would know that Nathan was missing, together with his boat and crew.

At Portgiskey, Amy was surprised to find Ahab Arthur, the oldest of Nathan's fishing captains, busying himself on board *The Brave Amy H*.

When she asked the old fisherman why he was at Portgiskey so early, he replied: 'Same reason as you, I reckon. I came down here hoping Nathan might have returned. When I found he hadn't, I thought I'd stay a while, just in case.'

'What do *you* think might have happened? Could they have made a good catch and taken it to Looe – or even to Plymouth?' Suddenly, Amy felt in great need of re-assurance.

Ahab Arthur shook his head. 'One of the Mevagissey boats came from Plymouth late last night. They saw nothing of *Sir Beville* there – nor along the way back.'

Amy's chin came up in sudden determination. 'They saw nothing of Nathan because they weren't looking for him. We *are*. I want you to get the crews together. Go to Plymouth yourself and send Dick Motam to Looe with *Peggy Hoblyn*. Speak to anyone who might have seen *Sir Beville*: fishermen, Preventive men – even the Navy. Tell them Nathan went fishing off Looe and hasn't returned.'

Amy remained at Portgiskey until all the crewmen had been called from their homes and each man knew what was expected of him. Not one of the fishermen complained about putting to sea in bad weather. A boat and six men were missing. Everything possible had to be done to find them. A mishap at sea could happen to any man who earned his living from fishing. It might be next year, next month, or that very night. A fishermean needed to know that his friends were ready to put to sea to search for him.

On her way back to Polrudden, Amy met Nathan's father, hurrying towards Portgiskey. The Pentuan preacher looked as though he had dressed in a hurry, and his first words provided confirmation of his appearance.

'I was roused from bed and told that Nathan and his boat are missing. It's not true, is it, Amy? When? We've had no bad weather . . .'

Amy took the preacher's arm. 'He set sail the night before last, heading for the Looe area. We expected him back yesterday morning. There's been no sighting of him.'

'What was he doing so far down as Looe?' Preacher Jago's face registered stern disapproval. 'He went to meet a smuggler? Then I don't doubt the Revenue men have him. I've warned him, Amy. I've warned *both* of you. John Wesley himself spoke on the evils of night-trading – right here in Cornwall. It's a calling that brings out the worst in a man.'

'Had Nathan been taken by Revenue men we'd have heard. They would have been here searching every inch of the fish-cellar. Besides, Nathan *wasn't* night-trading . . .' Amy's voice broke suddenly. 'I'm worried about him, Papa Jago. He's a good sailor . . . the *best,* but . . .'

'I'm sorry, my dear.' Preacher Jago's arm went about the shoulders of his distressed daughter-in-law. 'Nathan's missing, and a sermon from me is scant comfort. Forgive me.'

Amy squeezed the preacher's hand, but she said nothing. 'Where are you going now? Is there something I can do?'

'You can pray – but later. First, I must speak to the wives and relatives of Nathan's crewmen. I'd like you to come with me.'

It was not a pleasant morning for Amy. Two of the fishermen had large families. Saul Piper had a wife and four daughters, their ages ranging from ten to fifteen. Matthew Mitchell, a big, quiet man, also had four children: three boys aged five, nine and eleven, and two-year-old Kitty.

Mary Mitchell, a small, drab woman, lived in an untidy, none-too-clean cottage, tucked away behind the village square. She accepted the news with a quiet grief, more concerned with the effect the loss of their father would have on the children than with her own plight. Amy promised Mary Mitchell there would be work for her at the Portgiskey fish-cellar, but the mother of four declared she would move to St Austell to be near her own family. Hopefully, they would help to support her and the children.

Sophie Piper possessed none of Mary Mitchell's self-control. She greeted the news of the missing boat with a wail that startled half the village and set three of her four daughters to crying.

Amy tried to comfort the noisily weeping family by reminding Sophie Piper that the boat was merely overdue. No wreckage had been found, and there might be a perfectly good reason why *Sir Beville* was late returning to Portgiskey.

'You don't believe that, no more than I do,' wailed Sophie Piper. 'If you did, you wouldn't be here now with Preacher Jago, telling me about it. My man's gone. You knows it, and so do I.'

Josiah Jago also tried to reason with Sophie Piper, declaring it was far too early to abandon hope, but she had convinced herself that her husband was dead. Eventually, Amy walked from the house, leaving the Methodist preacher to give the weeping woman what comfort he could. Sophie Piper was simple-minded, as were two of her daughters: ten-year-old Lily and the plump thirteen-year-old, Tess. Another, eleven-year-old Harriet, had been crippled from birth, and the brunt of caring for the family fell upon fifteen-year-old Maud. It was Maud who followed Amy from the house.

'What are the chances of Dad coming home to us again, Mrs Jago?'

'I don't know,' replied Amy honestly. She knew how much responsibility rested upon this quiet young girl's thin shoulders. 'But Nathan is with your dad and *I'm* not giving up hope.'

'Thank you. I'll try to remember that.'

Amy's last two calls were easier than the others had been. Pascoe and Cornelius Lanyon had been orphaned when young, Cornelius being brought up by his older brother. When Pascoe married he brought his young bride to Pentuan, to share a house with Cornelius.

Rebecca Lanyon had been forced to give up her Quaker religion when she married Pascoe, but she still had firm religious beliefs and she leaned heavily on them now, when Amy broke the news of *Sir Beville*'s disappearance. Carefully controlling her emotions, Rebecca Lanyon declared she would leave the matter entirely in the Lord's hands.

'He hasn't failed me yet,' she said, the tremor in her voice belying the brave words. 'He'll not desert me now.'

As she left the tiny, neat cottage, Amy wished she had the young Quaker girl's faith. She was going to need all the strength she could find in the days ahead.

The final member of Nathan's crew was Obadiah Hockin. The aged fisherman lived alone in a tiny terraced cottage, his only relative a sister who lived in a rented home on the edge of Pentuan village. When Amy informed the woman that her brother was missing, the woman's pinched face became strangely animated, but her expression was not one of distress.

'Does this mean I can move into Obadiah's cottage right away?'

Amy bit back the words that would have expressed her disgust. 'Not unless you think Obadiah will be pleased to find you there, if he returns.'

Climbing the hill away from the village towards Polrudden, Amy thought of what she had said to Obadiah's avaricious sister '. . . *if* he returns.' For the first time she had admitted that Nathan and the men of *Sir Beville* might *not* be coming back.

The thought threatened to tear her apart. Amy stopped to look out to sea, her eyes blinded by tears. Then, clenching her hands tightly at her sides, Amy told herself fiercely she would *never* again allow herself, or anyone else, to suggest that Nathan might not return. He *would* come back to Polrudden. This would be her strength.

Nevertheless, there were many other unpalatable facts that had to be faced. Polrudden Manor and its grounds cost a great deal of money to staff and maintain. With only two fishing-boats to bring in the bulk of the manor's income they would need to be used to full advantage. Then there was Nathan's other profitable enterprise. Night-trading – smuggling. It assumed greater importance now. There was also the possibility that Captain Pierre might be able to throw some light on the fate of Nathan and the crew of *Sir Beville*. The difficulty was that the crew lost with Nathan had been the only one with experience of the illegal trade. Nathan was very cautious about involving others in his dealings with the Frenchman. No one, unless it were Amy herself, knew where and when Captain Pierre might be found.

In fact, Amy knew more about smuggling than most Cornishmen. Her father, Ned Hoblyn, had been one of Cornwall's most notorious smugglers during his lifetime, and Amy had helped him during the last years of his life. But that was before she had Beville to care for, and the responsibility for running Polrudden.

The boat sent to Looe tied up at Portgiskey that evening and Ahab Arthur brought *The Brave Amy H* back from Plymouth early the next morning. Both had the same tale to tell. Nothing had been learned about the fate of *Sir Beville*. What was more, an unusually forthcoming Port Officer had told Ahab Arthur there had been a Royal Navy frigate on anti-smuggling patrol off Looe that night. The man-of-war had met up with neither smugglers nor fishing-boats.

The crews of both boats were on the small quay at Portgiskey when Ahab Arthur gave his news to Amy. Not one of the fishermen would look directly at her. Each seemed to find the ground at his feet of more interest. It was left to Ahab Arthur to voice the question the fishermen were afraid to ask.

'What will you be doing now, Amy – now there's no hope? Will you sell off this place . . . and the boats?'

Once again Amy needed to remind herself that *she* had not given up hope. She felt like screaming the words at the fishermen – to know what right they had even to *say* there was no hope. Instead, she maintained a tight control on herself. It was not only *her* life that was affected by the disappearance of *Sir Beville*. These men were facing the loss of their livelihood and all it entailed. Times were hard and becoming worse. After a disastrous fishing season, many fishermen were being forced to turn to parish poor-houses, already overfull with farmworkers. In a poorhouse a man quickly learned that the first victim of his new way of life was pride. In return for two barely edible meals a day, a man sacrificed all control over his life, and over the lives of his wife and children. The wife would be found work apart from the husband and, wherever possible, the children would be placed in employment with someone else to provide their food, at no cost to their home parish.

'Nathan's two boats will continue to fish, and there will be more work than ever before. We've got to make two boats do the work of three. If there are no fish around here, you'll need to go farther out to find them. You'll work *harder*, but you *will* be working. If anyone's unhappy about this, now is the time to say so.' The men's heads were raised to look at her now, with new hope on their faces.

'You'll have no complaints about the way the men work, Amy. We'll see the clock round if need be.'

'That's exactly what we *will* be doing, Ahab. The only time I want to see the boats at Portgiskey is when they're unloading fish. For the rest of the time they'll be at sea, looking for fish. I've promised work in the cellar to Mary Mitchell, Rebecca Lanyon and Sophie Piper and her girls. It's up to you to see that promise is kept.'

When Amy left Portgiskey the fishermen were already preparing the boats for sea again, fired with a new determination; but Amy knew that inspiring words alone would not provide an answer to all the problems facing Polrudden.

Neither would words ease the vast, aching emptiness inside Amy. Her whole being cried out for Nathan, and this was a feeling she could share with no one. To do so would invite sympathy – and accepting sympathy was just another way of admitting that Nathan was lost to her.

Amy was glad she would have the two boys to keep her occupied, especially in the evenings, but her protective shell was cracked wide open that night as she put both boys to bed. Tucked in warmly, almost asleep, Beville suddenly asked: 'When is Daddy coming home?'

'Soon, darling. Soon now.'

Amy maintained normality until she put the door between herself and Beville. Then she fled to the privacy of her room. For the first time since Nathan's disappearance she broke down and wept with a raw emotion she had managed to hide from those who knew her.

CHAPTER SIX

The two Portgiskey fishing-boats were at sea day and night in a bid to keep the Jago fish-cellar working. Occasionally they would return with a reasonable catch; most days they had nothing at all to show for an exhausting trip.

Each day when the boats came in, Amy was on the small quay to meet them and check on their success, or the lack of it. She began to look gaunt and tired. The continuing uncertainty about Nathan's future, together with the responsibility of running both Polrudden and the fishing venture, were beginning to take their toll. She had promised work at the fish-cellar for the dependants of the missing crewmen. So far there had been only three full days' work for them. The catches were usually so small it was more profitable to sell the fish to local markets.

Early one morning when the two boats were tacking in towards Portgiskey in the face of a blustery westerly wind, Amy made her way to Portgiskey to meet them as usual. When the tide was low she could walk along the sands from Pentuan, but this morning the tide was lapping the base of the cliffs and she needed to approach along the path behind the cellar.

Toiling over the brow of the hill, Amy was startled to see an unfamiliar boat moored alongside the quay. She frowned. Portgiskey was a private cove; only Nathan's boats had a right to be here. Sudden excitement rocked her. Perhaps it *was* Nathan! Why else would a strange boat be here?

Amy began to run down the steep valley slope in her eagerness to reach the quay. She was almost at the fish-cellar before she saw the squat figure standing at the edge of the quay, his back towards her. She stopped her head-long flight immediately. It was not Nathan.

Hearing Amy's approach, the man turned. It was Samson Harry, coxswain of the Fowey Preventive Service cutter.

Observing her heaving chest and flushed face, Samson Harry gibed: 'You're in an almighty hurry. Are you afraid I might find something that shouldn't be here?'

'There's nothing at Portgiskey that shouldn't be here – except you and your boat. I thought –' Amy checked herself quickly. She owed no explanation to this man. 'It doesn't matter what I thought. Why *are* you here?'

'You needn't worry. It's not business – at least, not *Revenue* business. I came across the bay to look at the Portgiskey set-up, and at the boats. I'm pleased to see you're keeping them working right up to the last moment. That's sensible of you. Very sensible.'

'Sensible? Last moment? Stop talking in riddles and tell me what you're doing here at Portgiskey.'

'I've come to see what the cellar is worth. No doubt you'll be putting it up for sale soon. I'd like to make you an offer – as a going concern, of course. If you stop fishing and start selling things off piecemeal, my offer will be considerably reduced. You look surprised! Oh, yes, I know what you're thinking. Here's Samson Harry not long back from five years in a French gaol, and with hardly a penny piece to his name. Well, let me tell you. Before I went away I was a good fisherman. I had a sound business of my own. The bank over in Fowey knows this well. They'll be happy to loan me money to get started again, just so long as I have my job with the Preventive Service to back me up.'

'Samson Harry!' Amy had heard enough. 'Portgiskey belongs to Nathan. It's not for sale. No, not now or in the near future. What's more, if ever it *is* sold, I doubt whether *you'll* be considered as a buyer.'

'Think very carefully before making such a foolish statement, Mrs Jago. Other buyers are likely to be put off pretty quickly if they find Revenue men at Portgiskey rummaging the property every time they come looking around – especially the type of buyer you're most likely to attract!'

'Your threats impress me no more than your promises, Samson Harry. Now, move your boat from Portgiskey. I've got two working boats coming alongside to unload fish and there are people with work to do.'

The two fishing-boats were entering the cove now, one behind the other. Scowling, Samson Harry descended the stone steps and boarded his cutter. As he ordered his men to cast off, Amy walked to the fish-cellar and opened the doors in readiness for the fish she hoped the boats would be carrying.

Ahab Arthur's boat was first alongside the wall, and Amy was surprised to see the Reverend Damian Roach step ashore.

In answer to her question, Damian Roach replied: 'I am living and working in a fishing community. I should know something of their activities if I am to understand their problems. I'm sorry, I should have asked your permission.'

'That isn't necessary. You're welcome to go out with the men any time you wish.' Amy dismissed the matter; she had too many other things on her mind.

'The man who just left here . . . Ahab said he's the local Preventive Officer. Did he bring trouble for you?'

'He wants to buy the cellar and the boats. I've told him they aren't for sale.'

'The Preventive Service must be paying well,' commented Ahab Arthur, who had been listening to what was being said. 'When Samson moved his family to Fowey he needed to borrow money to pay the boatman who carried them across the bay.'

Amy felt disinclined to explain how Samson Harry proposed raising the money for Portgiskey, but Ahab Arthur needed no reply.

'All the same, you might do worse than to accept a good price right now. We've caught no more fish than we can sell from the quay. If we have to send it to St Austell, we'll be out of pocket.'

'If we can't make money fishing, we'll need to use the boat in other ways. Ahab, can you find a crew I can trust, for tomorrow night?'

'For night-trading?' Ahab Arthur shook his head in disapproval. 'All the men who knew about smuggling were with Nathan. None of us who are left ever went out with him. We know nothing of the rendezvous, or any of the signals –'

'You don't need to know anything,' Amy interrupted him. '*I'll* take care of all the details. All I want is a crew of men I can trust.'

'You're not considering going out smuggling . . . with your men?' The Reverend Damian Roach put the shocked question to Amy.

'It won't be the first time. I helped my father until he died and then I carried on alone for a while. I know where to find the French ship involved, and I know its captain. You tell me who's better to do what needs to be done.'

Ahab Arthur did not share her view. 'Preventive men

weren't so busy then. Now they're everywhere – and they're employing men like Samson Harry. Think what would happen if you were caught. Think of young Beville.'

'I *am* thinking of Beville. If things go on as they are, he'll grow up without a fishing business – and with no Polrudden.'

'Better than growing up an orphan. That's what he'll be if you're caught. You'll be transported for sure, and I've never heard of any woman returning to her home after transportation. Don't do it, Amy.'

The concern of the Reverend Damian Roach moved Amy far more than talk of the consequences of arrest and transportation. Temporarily blinded by tears that refused to be blinked away, she turned from him. 'I *must* go out tomorrow night. Captain Pierre might know something of Nathan.'

'*Sir Beville* was on a smuggling run when she went missing?'

'No, but Nathan had something to deliver to Captain Pierre. Something of great importance.'

'I see.' The Reverend Damian Roach was no more enlightened than before, but her words had helped him arrive at a decision. 'I'm no sailor, but if it will help *I'll* come along with you as a crewman.'

'You? As a Wesleyan preacher you must know that John Wesley was strongly opposed to smuggling. If you *don't* know, Preacher Jago will be quick to tell you.'

Damian Roach's smile made him appear even younger than he was. 'I have spent many years studying the details of John Wesley's life. Yes, he was opposed to smuggling, but it's also true to say that no lady in distress ever appealed to him in vain. Given such circumstances as this, I do not doubt he would have overlooked his views on smuggling, as he did on many occasions right here in Cornwall. My offer stands.'

'It won't be necessary, Preacher.' Ahab Arthur knocked out his pipe on the edge of the quay and spoke gruffly to Amy. 'I don't hold with night-trading any more than

Wesley did, but you'll have your crew and I'll skipper the boat wherever it needs to be taken. It'll be in everyone's best interest for you to forget this conversation, Preacher. Samson Harry would pay handsomely to know of our intentions.'

'I'll do better than forget it. I'll come with you. This is just one more aspect of Cornish life with which I should be familiar. Please let me know what time you intend sailing.'

As Amy watched the slight, boyish figure walking away, she realised it would be a mistake to dismiss Damian Roach as being no more than a young and inexperienced Methodist preacher.

The Brave Amy H cleared Portgiskey Cove and turned to tack into the teeth of a strong westerly wind. For a while the Reverend Damian Roach was able to treat this new experience with good humour, but gradually his light-hearted remarks grew fewer, the spaces between them longer.

When the fishing-boat cleared Deadman Point and met the swell rolling up-Channel from the Atlantic Ocean, the young preacher gave up all pretence of enjoying the voyage. Finding himself a space in the stern, he sat huddled in a heavy coat, the collar pulled high against the biting wind. His face emerged only occasionally as he sucked in great lungfuls of cold air.

Amy smiled to herself, safe in the knowledge that Damian Roach could not see her in the darkness. She was grateful to the young preacher for the kindness he had shown towards her since Nathan's disappearance. Uncritical, he had supported her when others hinted it would be impossible for her to run both Polrudden and Portgiskey without Nathan.

The rendezvous area was not reached until some three hours after setting out from Portgiskey. *The Brave Amy H* tacked backwards and forwards as Amy anxiously lit the prepared signals.

It was time for the rendezvous, but there was no sign of the French boat and the weather was deteriorating. Ahab

Arthur commented: 'I think we're out of luck, Amy. The French ship won't arrive tonight; the weather's too bad. We'll need to try another night.'

'No!' Amy's cry was one of sheer desperation. 'It's *got* to be tonight. I . . . I don't know anything about the alternative plans. They've all changed since I last took a boat out at night. I only know the time and place for the monthly rendezvous.'

'But it's useless staying out on a night like this, Amy. Some of these waves are so high we could be no more than a hundred feet from the Frenchman without our signal being seen.'

'We'll stay out for another thirty minutes.'

Her compromise brought a loud groan from the stern. The Reverend Damian Roach doubted whether he could survive another thirty minutes of the fishing-boat's violent movements. But Amy was already lighting another signal and peering out into the stormy night.

Half an hour later Amy, too, was ready to concede that there would be no meeting with the French smuggler tonight. It was more in desperation than in hope that she lit the last prepared signal. It flared into life inside the tin-lined box. Open only on one side, the box was held high, the light directed out to sea, faintly illuminating the white-capped, dark green waves surging about *The Brave Amy H*.

As the signal flickered and died, bitter disappointment swept over Amy. Suddenly, Damian Roach made a sound as though he were choking.

'Are you all right?'

Amy's anxiety was genuine, despite her own unhappiness.

'Out . . . there!' The Wesleyan preacher mumbled the words with difficulty. He was cold and trying desperately hard not to be sick. 'I saw . . . a light.' His hand pointed uncertainly out across the heaving water.

'Where?'

At that moment *The Brave Amy H* rose high on a wave and every man on board saw the signal light. It was not more than two hundred feet away.

Ten minutes later the two vessels were grinding against each other, kept from causing permanent damage by heavy plaited-rope fenders hung over the side of the French ship.

Helped to the swaying deck of the smuggling vessel by a push from Ahab Arthur, Amy rose to her feet and was caught up in an enthusiastic embrace by the exuberant Captain Pierre.

'Amy! It is good to see you after so much time. Please, come to my cabin. But what is your husband thinking of, allowing you at sea on a night like this? Why is he not with you? Is he ill?'

All Amy's hopes disappeared in that moment as she followed the French captain below decks. 'I had hoped you would have news of him. He hasn't been seen since he put to sea to meet you at your Looe rendezvous, more than two weeks ago.'

'Our Looe rendezvous . . .?' Captain Pierre opened the door to his cabin for her. 'Ah, yes! I remember now. We were unable to remain in the area. One of your English warships was on patrol there. Someone had given away our secret, I think.'

'So you didn't even see him.' Amy was thoroughly dejected. She had pinned too many hopes on this meeting, convinced Captain Pierre would have some news. She was no further forward than she had been two weeks ago.

A sudden thought came to her. Louis d'Argon had said his mission was of the utmost importance. If they had not met up with Captain Pierre, Nathan might have been foolhardy enough to risk a voyage across the English Channel, to France.

When she put the suggestion to Captain Pierre, he was startled. 'You think he might have gone to *France*? But why?' The French captain looked at her shrewdly. 'I suspect he did not come seeking me to buy goods. I am right, no?'

'He had something to be delivered in France. He believed it was of the utmost importance.'

'Ah! Well, these are unusual times. The war is moving closer to Paris. Suddenly many important letters are being carried between our two countries . . .'

Amy did not correct Captain Pierre's assumption that Nathan's mission had been to deliver a letter, and the Frenchman added: 'Soon there will be peace between us. Traders of each country will once more be welcomed by the other – unless they are *free*-traders, coming by night, eh?'

'You'll always be welcomed by all except Revenue men, Captain Pierre. Times would have been hard for Cornish fishermen had it not been for the salt you brought for our cellars. But you are right; there will be many changes. I suppose I must brave myself for a parting with Jean-Paul.'

'Jean-Paul? Who is he?'

'A small boy saved by Nathan from a French ship that was wrecked beneath the Polrudden cliffs in September last year. Jean-Paul Duvernet. He's one of the family now and will soon be speaking English as well as Beville. I'll . . Why, what's the matter?'

In the dim light from a swinging lamp, Amy could see a number of expressions battling for supremacy on the Frenchman's face. When he spoke his voice held excitement and incredulity. 'Jean-Paul *Devernet*? You are not talking of the son of the duc de Duvernet, one of the few remaining Bourbons?'

Now it was the turn of Amy to register astonishment. 'No, he can't be. His mother came from the Indies. From Martinique, I believe. She died in the wreck . . .' Amy suddenly remembered what Louis d'Argon had said about the boy. 'We were told he comes from a good family, but no one has mentioned anything about his father being a *duke*.'

Captain Pierre shrugged. 'Such titles have not been popular since the Revolution. Charles Duvernet scorned to use his, preferring the army rank given to him by Napoleon Bonaparte. The two men were good friends. However, if Duvernet is dead, as is rumoured, the title now belongs to his son – the boy you call Jean-Paul.'

The French smuggler became serious. 'Take care of the boy if you are really fond of him, Amy. Do not boast of his background. With his father dead he will be sought by the aristocracy and the people. The comte de Provence expects to claim the throne of France when Bonaparte is defeated. So many heads rolled in the days of "the Terror" there are few left to dispute his claim. A man, or a boy, bearing the title of the duc de Duvernet is one who might. The comte de Provence would be happy to have such a boy out of the way. Some citizens of the French Republic would agree with him. The intention is to cleanse France of the Bourbons once and for all. Guard the boy well, Amy. Let him enjoy being an ordinary little boy – while he may.'

The Brave Amy H nosed into Portgiskey Cove at three o'clock the next morning. As the boat bumped against the quay wall a dozen torches flickered into life.

'Everyone in the boat stay exactly where you are. If you attempt to escape, you'll be shot.'

It was Samson Harry. As he came down the stone steps to the fishing-boat the uncertain light of the torches reflected from the dull metal of muskets held in the hands of pale-faced, excited men.

'What are you doing here, Samson Harry? I thought Revenue men stayed in bed on such nights.'

'Many a smuggler's been captured because of such thoughts, Mrs Jago. No, don't try to step ashore. My men will search your boat first.'

'Search and be damned, but my fishermen aren't standing about in this wind while you take all night looking for something that isn't here. We'll be unloading the nets.'

Samson Harry hesitated. He was certain Amy and the crew of *The Brave Amy H* had been night-trading, but she was far too confident. He had an uneasy suspicion that he and his men would find nothing. If this were so, and innocent fishermen were shot, the subsequent outcry would probably cost him his very lucrative post.

He made no move to stop Amy as she pushed past him and made her way to the open doorway of the store where the nets would be stowed. Carrying the heavy drift-nets between them, the silent fishermen followed her example.

Last of all came the Reverend Damian Roach. Stepping unsteadily from the boat, he clutched at the wall of the quay for support.

'What's *he* doing here?' asked Samson Harry suspiciously, as his men filed on board *The Brave Amy H* to begin their search.

Damian Roach made no answer as he groped his way up the stone steps. It was left to Amy to answer for him.

'Preacher Roach felt he should sample life at sea if he were to understand the problems of fisherfolk. Unfortunately, it's been too rough to shoot the nets. After sheltering for a while in the lee of Deadman Point we decided we were wasting our time staying out. So we came back.'

Samson Harry looked at Amy for a long time as he fought to retain control of his temper. 'You've not been out fishing, Amy Jago,' he declared finally. 'And you had no intention of doing any fishing when you went out last night.'

'If you're out to prove me a liar, you'll need to put to sea yourself, Samson Harry. In the meantime I'll thank you not to come here with your men, making a nuisance of yourself. I've already told you I have no intention of selling you the fish-cellar and you'll not get it from me this way.'

Amy had laid the foundation stone of a complaint should she decide to level one against Samson Harry for any future harassment. Every man present at Portgiskey had heard Amy, and the Preventive Officer knew he had lost this particular battle.

Walking home to Polrudden in the darkness, Amy had reason to be well satisfied with her night's work. Not a quarter of a mile offshore, in the lee of the Polrudden cliffs, a long line of full brandy-kegs lay at the bottom of the bay, their position marked by a small lobster-pot float that differed only marginally from a half-hundred others dotted nearby.

As Amy made her way wearily up the staircase to her bedroom she wished she might have shared this moment with Nathan. He would have been proud of her.

CHAPTER SEVEN

A month to the day after *Sir Beville* failed to return to Portgiskey, Lavinia Hockin, spinster sister of Obadiah Hockin, Nathan's oldest fisherman, moved into her brother's cottage. She shifted her furniture and belongings with the help of a carrier from nearby Mevagissey, thus ensuring that the move came as a complete surprise to the Pentuan villagers.

The carrier was not allowed inside Obadiah's cottage. Instead, he was instructed to heap Lavinia's goods in the hard-packed earth yard, close to the back door. As he worked, she bustled back and forth from the house, taking in clothes and knick-knacks, leaving the furniture where it stood.

For two days curious neighbours heard the sound of an axe being wielded inside the cottage. As each piece of Lavinia's furniture was dragged inside the house, the space it had occupied was filled with splintered wood that had once been Obadiah's much-loved furniture.

In reply to a villager, more inquisitive than his fellows, Lavinia Hocking explained tearfully that she could not live with furniture that constantly reminded her of her dear lost brother. The villagers to whom her words were repeated believed neither the explanation nor her outward signs of grief.

Word quickly spread around Pentuan that Lavinia Hockin was wrecking her brother's home in a search for his life's savings. A small crowd gathered to watch the proceedings over the low garden wall. When Lavinia Hockin came from the house with an armful of splintered furniture, she was greeted by an increasing murmur of reproach from the watching villagers. Startled, Lavinia Hockin dropped the wood she was carrying and fled inside the house, slamming the door behind her.

Shut off from the view of the indignant villagers, the sounds of her activity continued, but for the next few days Lavinia Hockin transferred her furniture to the house only during the hours of darkness.

Lavinia Hockin was not the only one in Pentuan to have her lifestyle changed by the mysterious disappearance of *Sir Beville*; but, unlike Obadiah Hockin's sister, the change brought little hope for the future to the others.

Sophie Piper was used to having her big, domineering husband organise her life for her. He would discipline the children, tell her when to go to the fish-cellar for work, and even order her to clean the house when it became impossibly untidy. Now there was no one. Maud, her eldest daughter, took much of the burden of running the house upon her own, young shoulders, but it was not the same. Sophie could not turn to her daughter for comfort or advice.

Sophie was acutely lonely without Saul. It was especially bad during the long winter evenings when the girls had been put to bed to save fuel and candles.

Late one evening when the fire was no more than a faintly smoking memory in the hearth, Sophie Piper was laboriously taking up the hem of one of Maud's dresses. Maud had outgrown the old and well-patched garment, but it would serve the Piper family for a while yet.

Suddenly the candle began spluttering. Sophie Piper looked up to see the last half-inch of the wick swimming in a small pool of tallow. Too late she remembered there were no more candles in the house. She had meant to buy some from the store. Instead, she had spent the money on a large quantity of bacon. Not *quite* rancid, the bacon had been bought in cheaply by the village store from one of the colliers which used Pentuan harbour.

Sophie Piper wanted to complete the dress. Harriet, her

eleven-year-old, partly crippled daughter, needed it for the next day.

Sophie went outside. The two adjacent cottages were in darkness. Most households in Pentuan found it necessary to economise on lighting and heating, the families going to bed when darkness fell. The only blaze of light came from the Ship inn, a few paces beyond the second darkened cottage. Sophie knew there would be plenty of candles here. They would surely loan her one.

Tentatively, Sophie Piper pushed open the door of the inn. It was not busy inside: a couple of local fishermen, half a dozen seamen from ships in the small harbour, and two whores who had walked to the village from St Austell hoping to enjoy an evening's free drinking and maybe earn a shilling or two afterwards.

The two whores glared at Sophie Piper as she entered the inn. Unaware of their hostile glances, she approached one of the serving-women, with whom she occasionally passed the time of day in the village street.

Explaining the purpose of her visit, Sophie Piper added plaintively: 'Even a small piece of candle will do, just so long as I can finish off the dress for my Harriet. It's only an old dress, cast off by her sister, but she were some excited when I told her I'd have it ready for tomorrow. I don't want to disappoint her. She's a cripple, you see. She don't have much in life to look forward to, especially now, with her father gone . . .'

'Don't you worry, my dear. You won't need to disappoint her. There's a whole shelf piled high with candles in the store at the back. No one's going to begrudge you a couple.'

The serving-woman looked more closely at Sophie Piper. She observed her thin and threadbare dress, and her arms pimpled with cold.

'Wasn't your husband one of the men lost in the fishing-boat with Nathan Jago, from Polrudden?'

Sophie Piper's eyes filled with tears and she could only nod in reply.

'I thought as much. You come over here by the fire while I fetch the candles. You'll have little money to spare to heat your own house, I'll be bound. No, I'll hear no argument from you. We're quiet enough tonight; no one's going to mind.'

Seating Sophie Piper on a bench beside the roaring log fire that burned in the large fireplace, the serving-woman hurried away, to return a few moments later with a tankard, two-thirds full of cheap but warming gin. Ignoring Sophie's half-hearted protests, the woman said: 'You get this down and you won't notice the cold again tonight, I promise you.'

The gin was followed by a second, quite as generous as the first. By the time Sophie Piper made her unsteady way homeward, clutching half a dozen candles, the problems of her life were temporarily forgotten.

Maud Piper was the first member of the family to rise the next morning. She found the unfinished dress lying on the kitchen table, where it had been placed before her mother had left the house. When Harriet limped awkwardly downstairs, the dress was ready for her and Maud was busy preparing breakfast.

Two nights later Sophie Piper paid another visit to the Ship inn, this time to return the candles she had borrowed. There had been a full day's work at the Portgiskey fish-cellar. After purchasing the candles, Sophie had pence enough in her purse to buy a drink for herself and another for her new-found friend. The visit marked the beginning of a new pattern of life for Sophie Piper. From now on visists to the Ship inn became more regular. If she had money in her purse, she would buy drinks. If not, her friend gave them to her. Sophie Piper found herself looking forward to her evenings in the warm and friendly atmosphere of the Ship inn with eager anticipation.

In early March a fierce storm blew up in the English Channel and ships fled for the nearest shelter. One merchantman, homeward bound to London from the Mediterranean, put into St Austell Bay, and with considerable skill the captain managed to ease his ship alongside the quay at Pentuan. It was the largest vessel ever to dock in the small fishing village. The ship had been in foreign waters for many months, and long before nightfall both village inns were packed with thirsty sailors who had money to spend.

Sophie Piper, opening the door of the inn expecting to enjoy her usual evening drink and a chat with her friend, was overawed by the smoke, the noise, and the number of sailors crowded inside the usually quiet inn. She would have closed the door and returned to her home had not her friend spotted her.

Pushing her way to the door, the serving-woman pleaded: 'Sophie, we're rushed off our feet in here tonight. Will you help us out? Just serve drinks to some of the tables for me. There'll be a drink or two for you during the evening – and a sixpence when you finish.'

Sophie Piper closed the door behind her and followed her friend across the crowded room.

Sophie Piper was slower at serving drinks than the hard-drinking sailors thought she should be. However, when the sympathetic serving-woman explained her circumstances, they curbed their impatience, and free drinks came Sophie's way faster than she could down them.

Unused to heavy drinking, by the time the grandfather clock chimed the hour of midnight Sophie hardly knew what was going on about her. When two of the sailors suggested she leave the inn with them, she raised no objection. Once outside, the cold air hit her and Sophie stumbled. She would have fallen had not one of the sailors caught her. With an arm encircling her waist, he helped her along the road, whispering in her ear as they went.

Sophie Piper drew her head back indignantly, but she was unable to see the sailor's face in the darkness. 'A sh . . . shilling . . .?' The word came out badly slurred. 'Why should you give me . . . a shilling?'

Both seamen laughed, and the man with his arm about her waist whispered an explicit explanation of his offer.

Sophie Piper drew her hand back, fully intending to

remonstrate with the sailor for his lewd suggestion. Instead, the hand dropped to her side again and she began to giggle. She was still giggling when the seamen helped her up the gangway to the merchantman, holding her up between them as she stepped to the deck that heaved gently with the movement of waves driving in off the bay.

She giggled again when the men undressed her in the darkness of the between-decks mess, the sound provoking a sleepy complaint from one of the crewmen who slept in a hammock in a corner of the mess. One of the men who had brought her from the inn spoke sharply in return, and the grumbling ceased. Next, the seamen laid a thin hammock mattress on the lockers that doubled as seats around the edge of the messroom and laid Sophie back upon it.

The thin mattress did little to disguise the uncomfortable hardness of the wooden lockers as the seamen took Sophie in quick succession. It was an unsatisfactory experience. Sophie enjoyed it more when both men made love to her for a second time, and now it was her moaning and not giggling that brought forth a second complaint from the seaman in the hammock.

After no more than an hour on board the gently pitching merchantman, Sophie Piper was led back across the gangway and left alone on the quayside, two silver shillings clutched tightly in her hand.

The next day Sophie Piper had no recollection of making her way home and tumbling into her own bed; but Maud had heard her, and when the fifteen-year-old girl came downstairs in the morning she found the two silver shillings lying side by side on the kitchen table.

Maud would have liked to tax her mother about the money, but she had breakfast to make for the other girls before setting off to a nearby farm where she helped with the chores. The farmer's wife was a full nine months pregnant and unable to carry out the heavier duties on the farm.

It turned out to be a longer day than Maud had anticipated. The farmer's wife went into labour in mid-morning, although it was six o'clock in the evening before her child was born. The baby was a son, much to the delight of the farmer. After being presented with five daughters in the last six years, he had despaired of having a son to inherit the farm from him.

When Maud reached home, the cold house was in darkness, her sisters in bed and her mother already at the Ship inn.

The merchantman was still moored alongside the Pentuan quay, and when Maud came downstairs in the morning there were *three* bright new shillings lying upon the kitchen table.

At noon that day Maud left the farm and went home. She found Harriet alone in the kitchen. The crippled girl sat in front of a low-burning fire, her crippled leg drawn up beneath her, her eyes heavy-lidded, as though she had been crying. When Maud asked what was wrong the younger girl at first refused to give any explanation. Then, when Maud enquired after their mother, she saw the glint of tears in Harriet's eyes and knew where the trouble lay.

'Ma's still in bed.'

'Is that what's troubling you? That she's lying in bed most of the day?'

Harriet shook her head without giving her sister an answer.

'It *is* something to do with Ma that's upsetting you, I can see that. What is it, Harriet? You'd better tell me now because I'll find out, sooner or later.'

'It's folk in the village. They're talking about Ma. They say she's been going on the ship with the seamen and . . . you know.'

Tears were rolling down Harriet's cheeks now and she stood up awkwardly, balancing on her crippled leg, her fists clenched tightly at her sides.

'It isn't true, is it, Maud? Ma wouldn't do such a thing.'

'Of course she wouldn't,' Maud lied. She had half-guessed the source of the money her mother had been bringing home, but had not wanted to face up to the truth. Now she had no alternative.

Today was pay day for Maud, and the farmer had given her an extra shilling to celebrate the birth of his son. She handed the shilling to Harriet. 'Here, go to the store. Get some tea, and if Mrs Hunkin's baked any cakes today buy one and bring it home. It's a treat – from me. Go on now, before I change my mind and think of something else I should be spending the money on.'

Harriet gave Maud a warm hug and then limped from the house. Through the window Maud watched her sister's slow, painful progress for a few moments, then turned from the window and made her way heavily upstairs to the bedrooms.

Her mother's room was in darkness, and Maud wrinkled her nose in disgust at the smell of stale alcohol that assailed her nostrils as she opened the door. Drawing the curtains, she let the early-spring sunshine into the room before opening the window. The wind was still strong. It billowed out the curtains and rattled the window before she was able to latch it into place.

Sophie Piper stirred, but only to pull the eiderdown higher over her head.

Moving determinedly to the bed, Maud took hold of the bedclothes and peeled them from her mother.

Sophie Piper groped around her for the missing bedclothes. When she could not find them immediately, she reluctantly opened her eyes, blinking painfully at the light. Then she saw Maud bending over her and a groan left her lips.

'Ow! What are you doing here? Put the bedclothes back over me and get off to work.'

'I've been to work. Now I'm home again and it's time we had a talk.'

'I don't *want* to talk. Go away and leave me in peace.'

'No. I've just found Harriet in tears in the kitchen. *You* might not want to talk, but you can't stop the neighbours from gossiping about you and the sailors from the ship.'

Sophie Piper's attitude changed from irritable belligerence to abject self-pity. 'Folk in this village are quick enough when it comes to gossiping, but how many of them have come to see how I'm keeping, eh? Answer me that, if you can. They don't care about me struggling to bring up a family, with no man to help me and no one to talk to here in the house. I get lonely, Maud. That's why I speak to the men from the ship. It's *loneliness,* that's all.'

'Is it loneliness that makes them give you money?' Maud spoke very quietly. 'Oh, Ma! What would Pa say if he knew?'

'Your pa isn't here to help me bring up four children.' Sophie made the statement sound like an accusation. 'If he was, I wouldn't need to go out and earn money in the best way I can to feed you all.'

Stretching out an arm, Sophie Piper managed to take a grip on the bedclothes and pulled them up about her.

'Let folk in the village talk as much as they like. They've not offered me a penny piece to help feed you. Neither has her who puts on airs and graces up at Polrudden. "I'll give you work," she says. "Come and take fish whenever you want it," she says. But how much are her words worth? I've had hardly any work since your pa was lost, and no more fish than will keep us all skinny. Well, I've found a way to keep you fed and clothed. Damn the village and its gossip, I say. Now, leave me alone; I'm tired.'

Sophie Piper pulled the clothes over her head again. Maud remained in the room for some minutes looking down at the motionless form beneath the bedclothes, then she turned and walked slowly from the bedroom.

When Harriet returned to the cottage accompanied by her two younger sisters, Maud had bread on the table and plump mackerel frying in their own oil over the kitchen fire.

Harriet was in a happier frame of mind now and smiled at Maud as the two younger girls chattered throughout the meal. They had spent the morning in the nearby village of Mevagissey where they had earned twopence each for unravelling and repairing fishing-nets.

Maud did not eat with her sisters. When they had

finished the meal, she washed up their plates and suggested the three younger girls go to the foreshore in search of driftwood for the fire.

When they had gone, Maud had a wash and carefully combed her hair. Then she went to the room she shared with the other girls and took her best dress from a trunk in the corner of the room. Shaking out the creases, she looked at it critically. The dress was not new, but it contained no repairs or patches. Putting it on, Maud hoped she looked reasonably attractive. There was no way of checking. The only mirror in the house was in her mother's room.

Quietly letting herself out of the house, Maud made her way through the village towards the small harbour. As she went, it seemed to her that everyone in the village must be staring at her, aware of what she planned to do. But she looked neither to left nor to right, and soon she was on the stone quay, the cottages of the village behind her.

The stormbound merchantman was at the far end of the quay, where there was enough water for the vessel to remain afloat, even at low tide.

Only one man was on the deck. He was the ship's mate, a short, bearded man, dressed in blue jersey and dirty serge trousers. But Maud knew nothing of the hierarchy of a sea-going ship's crew. To her he was just another sailor.

Her heart beating alarmingly, she stepped on to the gangway that connected ship and shore. She had no idea of what she was going to say. Only a grim determination drove her on.

'Well, now, and what do we have here? Is there something I can do for you, my young beauty?'

Maud swallowed her nervousness and spoke as boldly as she dared.

'No . . . but Sophie Piper said I might be able to do something for you.'

'Sophie Piper? The woman from the Ship inn?'

Maud nodded. 'She's not feeling too well today. She . . . she said I should come along here.'

'You? Why, you don't look a day over fourteen. If you

ask me, you should be up at the chapel school right now.'

'I'm *seventeen*,' Maud lied indignantly. 'And you don't need book-learning to know what to do when you go to bed with a man.'

Maud had never received any schooling. The scornful reply she had given to the mate of the merchantman was the one given to *her* by her mother when Maud had wanted to enrol at the Methodist school.

The mate grinned, and Maud tried not to notice that many of his teeth were bad. 'Them's cheeky words, young lady. Can you prove you know what they're all about?'

'I know what they mean, well enough,' replied Maud defiantly, her heart pounding wildly once more.

'All right, then. Let's you and me go down to my cabin. How much do you charge?'

Maud was momentarily disconcerted, 'Er . . . the same as my . . . The same as Sophie.'

The mate grinned again. He knew well enough how much Sophie charged – but he doubted whether this slip of a girl did. Besides, London was only a few days away. He needed to have money in his pocket when he returned to his family.

'Well, now, you won't be as experienced as Sophie, so I reckon fourpence is a fair rate. Six if you're especially nice to me.'

Maud had no idea what being 'especially nice' entailed, and she did not dwell upon the thought. She nodded quickly and followed the mate down below decks to his cabin.

There was not much light from the dirty porthole in the cabin. Even so, Maud needed to steel herself before she could undress under the bearded man's gaze, and she knew a moment of sheer panic when his hands reached out to explore her young body.

'There's not much meat on you, girl; but they do say it's sweeter when it's close to the bone. Come on over to my bunk and we'll see . . .'

It was not as bad as Maud had imagined it would be. The

mate was rough with her, and she found the smell of his body sickening, but it was not so very different from the night when one of the village boys had seduced her in the heather behind Pentuan beach. That had been the previous summer, when the girls and boys from the village had adjourned to the beach with two gallons of rough cider, payment for helping to gather the harvest on a nearby farm.

Maud was in the cabin for no more than twenty minutes. As she dressed she tried not to look at the mate as he pulled a pair of trousers up over his nakedness.

Thrusting a sixpenny piece at her, the mate growled: 'Here. I'm not sure you've earned it, but no doubt you'll satisfy the men. Come on, you'll want to earn yourself some money while you can. If the wind continues to drop, we'll be leaving Pentuan on tonight's high tide.'

Hurriedly, Maud finished dressing. Then she followed the mate up a ladder and along the deck to the crew's quarters. Maud's arrival brought forth a great roar of approbation. It smelled even worse than the ship's mate in here. There was a firkin of St Austell ale in a corner of the messdeck and the men had helped themselves liberally in order to wash down the unpalatable midday meal.

'Quiet!'

The mate had a voice that could be heard in the rigging at the height of a storm. The bellowed order was tempered by a smug grin, and he draped an arm across Maud's shoulders.

'I've got a present for you before we sail – sent to us by Sophie. She hasn't as much meat on her as the whores we had on board in Naples and Gibraltar, and she's got a lot to learn; but Maud's eager to please, and her charges won't empty your pockets. Fourpence is all she's asking. Make the most of her – but remember she's to be off the ship before dusk.'

The eager shouts from the crew as the mate left the messdeck brought an expression of wide-eyed fear to Maud's face. She looked about her at the grinning faces, and suddenly she was frightened. These were rough, coarse men, of a type not often seen in a small fishing village like Pentuan.

At the far end of the mess a number of men sat playing cards at a table strewn with the debris of a meal. Peering above his cards at her, one of the men growled: 'She's no more than a child. Send her packing and let's get on with the game.'

'She's old enough.' A heavily built seaman with a week's growth of dark stubble on his chin rose from the table and took her arm roughly. 'When she leaves here she'll have my fourpence in her purse, and a fire in her belly, too, I don't doubt. Come on with you, girl, your arse will need to move faster than your feet if you're to satisfy everyone before sailing time.'

Feeling as though she was caught up in a bad dream, Maud allowed herself to be led to the darkest part of the mess, where the ship began to curve in towards the bow. There were blankets lying here, forming a hard bed on the seat-lockers.

'All right, get your clothes off and lie down.'

Maud looked aghast at the man. It was gloomy here, but there was sufficient light for the crew to watch her undress.

She hesitated, and the seaman gripping her arm hooted with delight. 'Well, I'll be damned! I believe we've found us a shy whore! She's in two minds about taking off her clothes. What do we do, lads?'

'Why, we takes 'em off for her, of course.'

The reply met with a howl of approval, and men resting in their hammocks swung to the ground to join the high-spirited frolicking. Maud's attempted resistance only provoked increased amusement. While the burly, stubble-chinned seaman held her fast in a painful grip, the others stripped her, at the same time subjecting her to a variety of coarse indignities. When Maud was quite naked, the seaman holding her flung her down on the blankets. Falling on top of her, he began making violent love to her, encouraged by his shipmates.

It was the beginning of a nightmare couple of hours for

Maud. At first, the seamen stood around watching and shouting encouragement, but as more and more men used her, with only an infrequent whimper breaking from her lips, interest flagged. Men returned to their hammocks, and the card game was resumed with only an occasional argument about who was next in line to take Maud.

To Maud, it seemed a lifetime elapsed before the mate's voice bellowed through the hatchway, ordering the men up top to make ready for sea.

At the sound, the man lying on Maud grunted for the last time and eased his bulk from her.

The seaman who had suggested she was no more than a child now called on the seamen to pay for their entertainment. As pennies rained down on the blanket about her, some men grumbled that they had not been given value for their money.

Maud sat up with some difficulty. The lockers beneath her were made of wood and the blankets had not been thick enough to cushion her sparsely fleshed body. She gathered up her clothing slowly and painfully, not looking at the men about her. Her mind was as numb as her body. It was as though the events of the afternoon had happened to someone else; but, as feeling gradually returned to her bruised body, she knew she would never be able to erase the memory of what had happened to her today.

The sympathetic seaman gathered up the coins from the rumpled blankets while she dressed. When she was more or less fully clothed, he held out the money to her.

'There's four shillings and fourpence here. I don't doubt there should be more, but we're putting to sea and not likely to see Pentuan again. You're lucky to be getting this.'

Taking her hand, the seaman placed the money in her grasp and held on for a few minutes longer. 'I don't know why you're doing this, and it's none of my business, but it's plain to see you haven't been a whore for long. I wasn't proud to sit back and do nothing about what was happening to you today, but if you're going to sell your body to seamen you can expect far worse treatment.'

His fingers tightened on her wrist. 'Think of what I'm saying to you, girl. I've a daughter of my own at home. I doubt she's any younger than you. If I were to learn she was a sailors' whore, I'd die of shame. If you've a father, then spare a thought for him . . .'

When Maud left the merchantman, hot tears were blinding her eyes and every aching step she took reminded her of the seaman's words. She was convinced that every fisherman's wife she passed in the village street must know how she had spent the afternoon.

By the time she reached home she had regained some of her composure. Her mother was in the kitchen, flushed and angry as she stirred the contents of a large pot hanging over the flames of the kitchen fire.

'Where do you think you've been? There's nothing done about the house and I've had to get the evening meal ready for everyone. This is your task. You know that well enough without me having to keep telling you.'

Darkness was falling outside, and Sophie Piper had not looked too closely at Maud when she entered the kitchen. Now she did – and what she saw made her forget the fish stew cooking over the fire.

'Just look at the state of you! Where have you been, our Maud? What have you been up to?'

'While you've been doing my chores, I've been doing yours.'

Maud placed on the table the money she had earned from the sailors. 'I've been on the ship and there's my earnings. If money needs to be made that way, then in future *I'll* be the one to earn it – not you. If Pa ever comes back and finds out about what I've been doing, he'll throw me out of the house. If he learned it was *you*, he'd murder you and swing for it. He doesn't deserve that.'

CHAPTER EIGHT

On the last day of March 1814 the Allied armies of Austria, Russia and Prussia entered Paris. A few days later Napoleon Bonaparte was forced to abdicate, by order of the marshals of France.

For many months the world had known that the downfall of Bonaparte was merely a matter of time. Yet the French public, firm in the belief that the little Corsican general was invincible, was stunned. Napoleon Bonaparte's leadership had brought France from anarchy to the glory of Empire in less than two decades. Now he was to be exiled to the island of Elba, off the west coast of Italy. Here he would rule over an 'empire' of peasants and mountain goats.

When the guards at Verdun military prison sullenly swung open the gates on an April day to admit officers of the victorious Prussian army, it was the first taste of freedom for ten years for some of the prisoners-of-war. Most were non-combatants. Fishermen and merchant seamen, they had been captured when plying the disputed waters of the English Channel. Many were Cornishmen, and among these were Nathan and his crew from Pentuan, captured only a few months earlier.

The released Englishmen were treated with great courtesy and generosity by their liberators, but Nathan found it desperately frustrating that the Prussians displayed no sense of urgency about repatriating the Englishmen.

The months of imprisonment had been hard for Nathan. He was a solitary man, in the manner of most men who accept command, and not used to discussing his thoughts with others. He missed Amy desperately and worried about her. But his concern was not only for Amy and his own family, but also for Pascoe Lanyon, the elder of the two brothers who formed part of his crew. Pascoe was a very sick man. For some months before his capture he had showed signs of the wasting disease, although he had always strenuously denied being unwell. However, prison life had worsened his condition alarmingly.

When May arrived without any progress being made to return the fishermen to England, Nathan announced his intention of making his own way home. Twenty Cornishmen, including the whole of his own crew, declared they would go with him. Pascoe Lanyon swore he would be able to keep up with the others despite his state of health.

The remainder of the prisoners, led by Nicholas Dunne, a staunch old Methodist sea captain from Mevagissey, preferred to await the arrival of an emissary of the British government. The Prussians were constantly assuring the Britons that this emissary would arrive from Paris 'in the very near future'.

The Prussians made no attempt to detain Nathan and his party when he told them of his plans. Indeed, they provided him with ample money to purchase food along the way, and letters from the Prussian commanding officer to ensure safe passage. The Britons were also offered horses commandeered from local farms but, as few of the fishermen were able to ride, the offer was declined.

For fifteen days the Cornishmen, led by Nathan, trudged through the French countryside on the road to Paris, slowed down towards the end of their long journey by the rapidly weakening Pascoe Lanyon. Along the way they saw many signs of battle. At the edge of one small town which had been almost flattened by a heavy cannonade, they passed the decaying remains of Russian infantrymen, laid out in lines at the edge of a months-old battlefield. Collected after the fighting was over, they had been abandoned and forgotten when the burial detail realised the town was being pillaged without them.

Eventually, the Cornishmen reached the wide streets of Paris. They found the capital city wearing the heavy grey mantle of defeat. Its tree-lined avenues were littered with all manner of filth and its surly people were too dispirited to care. The only splashes of colour to be seen were the uniforms of the victorious Allied forces.

Soldiers were much in evidence everywhere. Cavalry clattered through streets glistening with the rains of early summer, and off-duty infantrymen stood in the arcades, making 'arrangements' with the city's prostitutes, many of whom sported ribbons in the colours of the occupying powers.

There were a few British soldiers here, their role to clear the way for a diplomatic mission from Britain. Seeking out the colonel in charge of the small British detachment, Nathan told him of the plight of his own crew and of the British prisoners awaiting help in Verdun.

The harassed colonel promised to send an officer to Verdun, but stressed that no one could be spared immediately.

'I have no authority in France,' the colonel repeated for at least the eighth time. 'My orders are to arrange for the establishment of an ambassador at the earliest opportunity. Rumour has it that the ambassador will be the Duke of Wellington himself. As you will understand, mine is not a duty to be taken lightly with conditions in France so uncertain. Much of the country still refuses to believe Napoleon Bonaparte has been exiled. I won't be sorry when the new king, Louis XVIII, arrives in Paris to take over his throne. A country needs a figurehead to look to for guidance and stability. All this revolutionary nonsense has brought the country to the brink of total ruination.'

'When is the King due to reach Paris?' Nathan had plans of his own, but they could not be put into operation until it was safe to travel in coastal France.

'I wish to God I knew!' The colonel showed signs of exasperation. 'I wish I could believe that *anyone* knows. It might be today; it could be a year from now. The whole French administration is in utter chaos. Now you will have to excuse me; I have work to do. Come and see me again in about a week. Things might have improved by then. In the meantime I'll try to arrange for a doctor to see your sick crewman. Goodbye, Jago. Consider yourself lucky to have been freed from captivity. Take the opportunity to cele-brate.'

Halfway to the door of the spacious office, Nathan stopped and turned back to the harassed colonel. 'Is Louis, comte d'Argon likely to be with the King?'

For a moment, the colonel's indifference disappeared. 'You know the comte?'

When Nathan nodded, the colonel became less officious. 'Yes, d'Argon will certainly be accompanying King Louis. The comte is a very important member of the French royal household. Er . . . if you and your men find yourselves short of money, come back and see me again. I am quite sure I can requisition some for your purposes.'

Nathan and his fishermen spent a disturbed night in a barracks taken over by the Russians. Their room over-looked the parade ground where a regiment of Cossacks was in camp. The Cossacks were a thoroughly undisci-plined, uncouth and unattractive fighting force. It was said that the Russian officers had found it necessary to tell the Cossacks they were still in Russia, in order to prevent them breaking out of barracks on an orgy of rape, pillage and murder.

However, their officers had been unable to prevent the horsemen from the Russian steppes obtaining plenty of drink. The Cossacks spent their nights in wild celebration which frequently erupted in violent and bloody argument. The only Cornish fisherman who slept well was the ex-hausted and ill Pascoe Lanyon. His pain had been eased by a large dose of laudanum, supplied by a French doctor who treated him in tight-lipped silence.

The following morning, King Louis XVIII of France, latterly the comte de Provence, brother of the guillotined King Louis XVI, arrived in the French capital to reclaim the throne of France for the Bourbon family.

The King's party arrived at the gallop, his carriage

keeping to the centre of the wide Paris avenues. Escorted by gentlemen of his court, and with a strong detachment of Allied cavalry acting as outriders, the new monarch scorned the approbation of his subjects. Those Parisians who saw the cavalcade watched in silence as the procession sped past, *en route* for the royal palace of the Tuileries.

Nathan realised that everyone associated with the new king would be kept busy restoring the former power of the monarch in a land that had been a republic for twenty-four years, but he was determined to return to Cornwall quickly – and he had no intention of spending another night in the barracks occupied by the noisy and quarrelsome Cossacks.

While the other fishermen set off to explore the dubious pleasures of Paris, Nathan headed for the Tuileries palace. Fortunately for Nathan, Louis XVIII had not yet been able to muster even the nucleus of an army and his palace was guarded by Prussian soldiers. When Nathan made his enquiries for the comte d'Argon the letter given to him by the Prussian commander in Verdun ensured that immediate action was taken to locate the French nobleman.

Louis d'Argon did not wait for Nathan to be brought to him. He came to the guard commander's office himself. His face lit up with pleasure when he saw the Pentuan fisherman.

'Nathan! This is such a wonderful surprise. What are you doing in France – and so far from the sea? I do not flatter myself you are here seeking me – but, come, we will talk on the way to my quarters. The King has put a whole suite at my disposal, much to the disgust of his courtiers. Many of them are four to a room! Tell me your news. What of Polrudden and the beautiful Amy?'

'You know as much of them as I do,' declared Nathan ruefully. He told the Frenchman what had happened to *Sir Beville* after Louis had been safely landed.

By the time Nathan came to the end of his story, Louis d'Argon had stopped walking and was looking at Nathan in abject dismay.

'You have been a prisoner all this time and I did not

know? Why did you not try to send word to me?'

'I thought your mission was too important to be put at risk by my misfortune.'

'It was of the *utmost* importance, and entirely successful, thanks to you,' Louis d'Argon rested a hand on Nathan's shoulder. 'My friend, you have suffered on behalf of King Louis. It is fitting he should know of this. Come, here is my suite. You will rest in comfort while I speak with the King.'

'I'd rather you spent the time trying to get us home – or at least finding somewhere decent for my crew and a few fellow-Cornishmen to stay while we're in Paris. One of them is very sick. We spent last night sharing a barracks with a regiment of Cossacks. It's an experience I'd rather not have to repeat.'

'With *Cossacks*, you say? My God! I would rather share a bath with a family of crocodiles. Do not worry. I will have new accommodation found for your crew, and a good doctor for your sick. They will stay here, in the barracks of the King's Prussian guard. They speak neither French nor English, but they are well disciplined and clean. I can understand your anxiety to return to England, my friend, but the road is still uncertain. Even the King's personal despatches to the coast have been temporarily suspended.'

While they were talking Louis d'Argon ushered Nathan into a magnificent room that appeared to have been newly decorated. Handing Nathan a large bowl-shaped glass, the Frenchman filled it almost to the brim with brandy, the fumes from the drink quickly pervading the room.

'I shall be offended if I return and see your glass empty, my friend. All I have is yours. I am going to find the King now.'

Nathan had been seated in the room for at least thirty minutes when the door was flung open and a woman hurried into the room, words spilling from her angrily.

'Louis! We have a crisis. The duchesse d'Angoulème is being impossible. She demands that her suite be changed. She finds the noise of the Prussians changing their guard abominable. I have said you will –'

The tirade was in French, and suddenly the newcomer realised she was talking not to Louis, comte d'Argon, but to a stranger – a ragged stranger who stood up from his chair, a half-empty brandy-glass in his hand, and bowed to her.

'Who are you? Where is the comte d'Argon? What are you doing in his rooms?'

The woman, who must have been in her mid-thirties, was tall, expensively clothed and elegantly attractive. At the moment she was flushed and angry, the colour in her cheeks serving to heighten her beauty.

'The comte d'Argon is with the King. I am resting here, drinking the excellent brandy Louis has left with me.'

'You are English?'

During his months of captivity, Nathan had learned both to speak and understand French, but his accent was far from perfect and the woman put the question in English.

'I am, Madame. But your command of my language is greater than my knowledge of French.'

For a moment the woman's suspicions vanished. Then, as she looked again at his shabby, well-worn fisherman's clothing and boots that showed the effects of tramping hundreds of miles on French roads, her doubts returned.

'Does the comte know you are in his room, drinking his Cognac?'

'The comte, my dear Henrietta, poured the drink him-self. While Nathan is in this country, my room and, indeed, all my possessions are his.'

Louis d'Argon had entered the room unnoticed. Draping an arm familiarly about the woman's shoulders, he spoke to Nathan. 'I am sorry to have been so long, but I find you in beautiful company. No doubt Henrietta will have had many questions to put to you?'

The woman looked from Nathan to Louis d'Argon in blank confusion, and Nathan hurried to explain. 'The lady has only just entered the room. We haven't introduced ourselves.'

'A thousand pardons! Nathan, may I introduce to you

the lovely and delightful Henrietta, marquise d'Orléan. She is the half-sister of Charles Duvernet, and aunt to your Jean-Paul.'

Sudden enlightenment flooded Henrietta d'Orléan's face and she looked at Nathan in delight. 'You are the Englishman who saved Jean-Paul's life! M'sieur Jago, for this I kiss you.'

Matching the word to the deed, she kissed him quickly on the lips, then stood back from him, holding his hands.

'Jean-Paul is the only one left to bear the Duvernet name. Many were killed during the reign of the mob, in Paris. As for my brother . . .' She shrugged unhappily. 'It has been so long since there was news of him, I fear he, too, must be dead.'

'If the Duvernet name is to live on, it will be better for the existence of Jean-Paul to be known only to the three of us here,' warned Louis d'Argon seriously. 'The King is not yet secure on his throne and the people will not find him the most attractive of men. The young son of a Bourbon who served Napoleon Bonaparte with distinction is capable of bridging the wide gulf between republican and monarchist far more successfully. When to this is added the dramatic story of his rescue from the sea, and the tragic loss of his beautiful mother, his appeal becomes formidable. No king – certainly not Louis – would sit easily on his throne while such a threat exists.'

Nathan was looking from Henrietta to Louis d'Argon in astonishment. He was aware that Jean-Paul came from a good family, but Louis d'Argon had said nothing to him about the young boy's nearness to the throne of France.

Henrietta d'Orléan saw his bewilderment and squeezed his hands reassuringly. 'I am grateful only that you saved the son of my much loved brother, M'sieur Jago. His claim to the throne of France means nothing to me. However, Louis is right. It will be better not to talk of Jean-Paul when others are near.'

She released Nathan's hands and casually touched his rough-spun fustian jacket. 'I apologise for my earlier suspicions, but you are not dressed in the clothes one expects to see within the palace of a king.'

'Henrietta is right. We need to find new clothes for you – and quickly. The King wishes you to be brought to him this evening. For the moment, he has gone to bed, to rest. The ridiculous gallop to Paris has quite exhausted him.'

'King Louis wants to see me? Why?'

'You need to ask? You are a hero! There are very few heroes in the court of King Louis of France. I fear it is filled with arrogant scheming men and bored, complaining women, as Henrietta knows only too well.'

Reminded of her reason for coming to the room, Henrietta told Louis d'Argon of the complaint made by the duchesse d'Angoulême, daughter of the late King Louis XVI.

Louis d'Argon sighed in exasperation. 'She has the finest suite in the palace – finer even than those I have given to the King. If the duchesse thought of anything beyond her daily toilette, she would gain great comfort from the sound of Prussian guards beneath her windows. It is a sound that would have gladdened the heart of poor Marie-Antoinette. Very well, tell the servants to prepare the late Dauphin's suite for her.'

Henrietta's eyes widened. 'But those are rooms where all the maidservants were slaughtered by the mob at the time of the Revolution. It is said their ghosts cry out in anguish still.'

'So? No doubt they cry out in French. It should not disturb the duchesse.'

To Nathan, Louis d'Argon said: 'You will be pleased to know your fishermen have been allocated new lodgings. A servant has been sent to bring them to the palace. They will sleep in the guards' quarters. I can assure you they will be well cared for.'

'I trust we'll not need to impose upon your hospitality for very long. I'm very concerned about Amy and Polrudden. I was able to send no letters from Verdun. For all I know, Amy has given me up for dead.'

'No, not Amy. She will be scanning the sea every day for your return. But you will need to stay here for a day or two. A Bourbon king once more occupies the throne, but the citizens of France have not become monarchists overnight. Ruffians from Bonaparte's army roam the countryside in murderous, half-starved gangs. Small detachments of Prussian soldiers have been ambushed and killed not a mile from this palace. Travellers to the coastal regions need a strong escort, and soldiers are not always available, especially now the needs of the king take precedence over all others. We will talk more of this tomorrow. Today we need to find clothes for you if you are to meet King Louis. It will not be easy. Time is short, and I know no Paris tailors . . .'

'I can help,' suggested Henrietta. 'I have a house in Paris and many of my husband's clothes are there. They might prove a tight fit for M'sieur Jago across the shoulders, but the length should be right – and I know an excellent tailor who will come to the house and make the necessary alterations.'

'My dear Henrietta! When I recommended that King Louis should take you into his household, I informed him you were a woman without equal in beauty and resourcefulness. Your beauty is there for all to see. Now Nathan will learn of the other attributes that make you the most remarkable woman in France. Go with Henrietta, my Cornish friend. You will be in excellent hands.'

CHAPTER NINE

Nathan and Henrietta, Marquise d'Orléan drove through the streets of Paris in a small enclosed carriage. Henrietta scorned an escort, declaring she had survived the bloody excesses of the Paris mobs as a child and lived through the years of anarchy. She had seen Napoleon Bonaparte bring law and order to the country after his truly incredible rise from artillery captain to brilliant and victorious general and Emperor of France. Henrietta had never needed an escort during these turbulent years. She refused to accept one now a king had returned to rule France.

The carriage took them to a large house no more than half a mile from the Tuileries. Like the palace, the house overlooked the River Seine.

The door was opened to them by a servant, and it was apparent to Nathan that the house was lived in, not kept merely because it was fashionable to have a home in Paris. He followed Henrietta upstairs to a huge bedroom. The servant was with them and he proceeded to unfasten the shutters at the windows. When they were opened, there was a breathtaking view across the river.

Henrietta opened wide the numerous doors of a great wardrobe that occupied one whole wall of the room. Inside was an array of clothes, the like of which Nathan had never before seen.

Henrietta chose coats, breeches, shirts and hose, laying them out on the huge bed for his inspection. When the bed was completely hidden by clothing, she stood back, satisfied.

'I think these will serve while you are in Paris, M'sieur Jago.'

'You are very generous – but, please, my name is Nathan.'

'Nathan.' She repeated the unfamiliar name easily, pronouncing it with just a trace of accent, and smiled up at him. 'Thank you. And you will call me Henrietta. Marquise is somehow so . . . *formidable*.'

'Many things you may be, Henrietta. *Formidable* is not one of them.'

'M'sieur Jago – Nathan – I do believe you are paying me a compliment. I am flattered. It is my understanding that Englishmen never pay compliments to women unless they are protected from possible seduction by the virtue of age – be it their own or that of the lady.'

'That sounds the sort of remark that might be heard in the smart *salons* of London or Paris. I come from the country, from Cornwall. Men there are in the habit of meaning exactly what they say.'

Henrietta's eyes sparkled with suppressed humour as she said: 'Thank you, Nathan. A *sincere* compliment is a rare gift. I will treasure it always.'

Changing the subject hastily, Nathan asked: 'These clothes . . . Won't your husband mind me borrowing them?'

'My husband has been dead for two years. I should have got rid of his clothes long ago. Paris is full of ragged men who have need of them. Somehow, I never got around to throwing them away.'

'I'm sorry. I didn't know . . .'

'How could you? Please do not apologise. It does not upset me to talk of poor Henri. He was much older than I. It was a marriage of families, not of lovers. He died of cholera on a mission to Italy for Emperor Bonaparte. But we will talk of the future, not of the past. Tell me of Jean-Paul. Is he a clever boy? You would not know, of course, whether he favours his mother or Charles?'

'I took him from his mother's arms on the deck of *L'Emir,* but it was in darkness. I only saw her features in death, after her body had been taken from the sea. She was a beautiful woman, and Jean-Paul is a handsome child. Whether he favours his father, I couldn't say.'

'Poor Jean-Paul – and poor Charles. You know, he never saw his son, but he loved his wife very very much. He longed to have them both with him in France. If only they had all remained in Martinique . . .'

'Why did he leave them behind when *he* returned to France?'

'Charles was a soldier. A good soldier. He said he enjoyed fighting for *France*. He did not care whether the country was led by a king, emperor or citizens' committee.

He was a true patriot. For this, perhaps, a man might be forgiven many of the things he does in his lifetime.'

'You talk as though his death has been confirmed. Louis told me he is only missing.'

'His name appeared on none of Bonaparte's casualty lists, but such lists were deliberately incomplete. Had the people of France realised how many of their sons and husbands were dying for one man's ambitions, Napoleon Bonaparte would never have led another army –'

Henrietta's words were interrupted by a knock at the door. 'Ah! That must be the tailor. I will leave you and he together. When he has finished come downstairs. I will have tea ready.'

The tailor was a fussy little one-eyed Jew. In an outrageous English accent he told Nathan he had lived and worked in London for five years after escaping the excesses of the early days of the Revolution.

'Five years. Five long, long years,' he lamented, talking through a mouthful of pins as he adjusted a suit Nathan had been ordered to put on. 'I was making clothes for men who knew nothing of fashion. To save a penny they preferred to have their clothes made for them by charlatans. Your London tailors use inferior cloth and stitch a gentleman's waistcoat as though making a horse-blanket. It *pained* me to work among such people. I had to return to Paris. Every head that dropped from the guillotine to the basket was a blow to business, but at least my poor gentlemen had the comfort of knowing their life's blood was spilled on the best-tailored clothes in Europe.'

Nathan doubted whether such knowledge made dying any easier for the decapitated aristocrats of France, but he kept his own counsel. The little tailor was so volatile that a contradiction might have resulted in him swallowing a mouthful of pins.

During a lull in the little tailor's almost continuous chatter, Nathan admitted he had no money with which to pay for new clothing. The tailor spread his arms wide in a philosophic gesture.

'So? How would a tailor earn a living if a gentleman was required to show money whenever he wanted clothes? The marquise has said you are to be dressed fit to meet King Louis. Should I show disrespect to the King – and to France – by allowing you to meet him dressed in less than perfection, or as close as is possible for a man who wears another's clothes? No, for you, as for any other gentleman, I do my best. For the marquise . . . I do more.'

The garrulous little tailor was incredibly speedy at his work. No more than half an hour later, Nathan was walking downstairs to join Henrietta. He wore a pair of altered velvet breeches, white ruffled shirt and new hose and shoes brought to the house by the resourceful tailor.

Viewing Nathan's broad-shouldered elegance, Henrietta expressed her delight at this transformation from English fisherman to French gentleman.

Nathan grinned self-consciously. 'I feel I must look like a dancing master.'

Adjusting the cravat at his neck, Henrietta said quietly: 'Oh, no, Nathan. No one will mistake you for a dancing master. Not with shoulders like these.'

She rested her hands on his shoulders, and as he looked down into her green eyes he glimpsed an expression on her face that could only have been a reflection of his own thoughts.

Abruptly, Henrietta's hands dropped from his shoulders and she walked to a table near the window. Returning with a glass of Cognac, she handed it to him.

'You have already explained that you are not a courtier, but tell me something of your life in England.'

Nathan was aware that he *wanted* to impress Henrietta. Perversely, he deliberately chose not to.

'I'm a working fisherman, Henrietta. I earned the money for my boats in the prize-ring. Now I live in a manor-house because it's my son's heritage, and I'm working hard to keep it for him.'

'The prize-ring! Ah, that explains those shoulders. As for your manor-house . . . There are more poor aristocrats than rich ones in France. This was true even before the Revolution. Most possess only an excess of pride – and a manor-house. They, too, would feel lost in the court of a Bourbon king. You are a remarkable man, Nathan – and a handsome one. You will be much sought after by the ladies of King Louis' court. If this is what you wish, then your stay in Paris will prove pleasant and long.'

'I intend returning to Polrudden as soon as possible.' Nathan hesitated, seeking to phrase his next words carefully. 'There's nothing remarkable about me, Henrietta. I'm an ordinary man, with all the weaknesses of a man. If all the ladies of the French court are as beautiful as you, I fear my resolve may well weaken. If you see this happening, I beg you to remind me of what I've said here today.'

Henrietta looked at Nathan with an expression that combined delight and mock-regret. 'Subtle flattery *and* tact. You are a natural courtier, Nathan Jago. Very well. If I think you are succumbing to the charms of any other woman, I will speak to you as though I were your sister.'

It seemed Nathan's cravat still failed to please her. As she talked she moved forward to straighten it once more. Looking up at him, she rose to her toes and kissed his cheek gently, giving him a breath of her perfume.

'There. A sisterly kiss – to seal our "arrangement". Now, go back upstairs to that lazy, good-for-nothing tailor and tell him this cravat is not lying correctly. He must change it for you. Tell him also that we must be ready to return to the palace at five o'clock.'

When Nathan left the room, Henrietta walked thoughtfully to the window and looked out across the river without seeing anything of the Paris landscape. She had agreed to help Nathan remember where his duty lay, but it would not be as easy as he had made it sound. Standing close to Nathan had stirred unfamiliar feelings in her. She would do her best to help Nathan avoid the detaining embraces of the women of the court of King Louis. But, if she failed, Henrietta determined no *other* woman would have him for long.

By 5 p.m. a thoroughly transformed Nathan was handing Henrietta into her carriage before carefully seating himself beside her. Nathan wore a dark-blue velvet coat over a fine linen shirt that had lace at collar and cuffs. Nankeen trousers, fine silk hose, and shoes with buckles of worked silver completed the outfit. In his hand, Nathan carried a hat that bore an extravagant plume of ostrich feathers.

When the coach began to move, Henrietta leaned across from her seat and straightened the coat about him to prevent it from creasing.

'You look superb, Nathan. Fit to meet a king.'

'I would be happier standing on the deck of a fishing-boat in my working clothes, a pipe in my hand.'

'Do not worry. I have not forgotten my promise to send you safely on your way. But you have the remainder of your life in which to fish, if you so wish. Today is a very special day for you. One to live in your memory for ever. Forget your responsibilities and enjoy whatever comes.'

There were many more people on the streets now, and the carriage was frequently forced to slacken speed. Eventually, their slow progress began to cause Henrietta concern. It was unthinkable that they should be late for Nathan's meeting with King Louis XVIII. Leaning from the carriage window, she called to the driver, urging him to go faster.

Moments later the carriage swung off the main avenue in a bid to leave the crowds behind. It had not travelled more than a hundred yards when the carriage slewed to a sudden halt. Looking through the window, Nathan saw they were surrounded by a crowd of rough-looking men, many wearing tricolour cockades in their hats to denote they were republicans.

Fortunately, one side of the carriage was pressed too close to a nearby wall for the door to be opened on that side, and Nathan immediately placed himself between Henrietta and the other door.

He was only just in time. The door was wrenched open and the men outside crowded around the carriage doorway, demanding to be given money for food.

Nathan was relieved to see that, while the men carried sticks, none of them appeared to be armed. It was not so much a hold-up as a particularly aggressive begging.

'We have no money,' declared Nathan. 'Now, clear a path for the carriage, if you please.'

'Liar!' spat one of the Frenchmen, who wore the tattered remnants of an army uniform.

'An *English* liar at that, unless I'm mistaken,' shouted another beggar, as ragged as the first.

As the men surged towards the open carriage doorway, the coachman called: 'Clear a way for the horses. We have an appointment with the King.'

It was the worst thing he could have said. The men surrounding the carriage were followers of Napoleon Bonaparte. Some had taken to the streets to depose Louis XVI, years before, and had been present when a young National Guardsman held up that unfortunate monarch's head on the execution platform, in the Place de la Révolution.

'France acknowledges no Bourbon king.'

'We killed one fat pig. Louis XVIII will go the same way.'

'Pull the Englishman from the carriage. We'll turn him upside down and see if he sheds any good French money.'

This last suggestion met with the noisy approval of the men about the carriage. As they crowded closer, a voice shouted: 'Do the same with the woman. If she has no money, it will serve to brighten a dull day.'

A roar of coarse laughter went up from the mob, and a beggar who appeared to be their leader put a foot on the carriage step. Before he could climb inside, Nathan's fist hit him on the point of the jaw and sent him crashing back among his fellows.

The laughter changed to anger, and two men tried to enter the carriage simultaneously. This time two short, sharp jabs were sufficient to send them tumbling after

Nathan's earlier victim. From the doorway, Nathan saw that the men who had been standing in front of the horses had hurried back to see what was happening inside the carriage. The way ahead was clear.

Calling for the coachman to whip up the horses, Nathan avoided a vicious jab from a stick and sent another man tumbling back into the crowd.

The shouts of the coachman were accompanied by a sharp crack of his whip. The startled horses were galvanised into immediate action, sliding and slipping as they sought a grip on the smooth cobblestones. The carriage jerked forward and there was a final flurry in the doorway as Nathan dislodged a last would-be footpad and slammed the door shut.

The coachman drove along the narrow thoroughfare at breakneck speed. As the carriage bounced and lurched on the uneven surface, Nathan cradled Henrietta in his arms to prevent her being flung against the sides of the vehicle. The driver never slackened speed until the coach slewed from a narrow street into the wide avenue, almost opposite the Tuileries palace.

As Nathan's arms dropped away from Henrietta, she looked up and saw him grimace.

'Nathan, what is it? You are hurt?'

'No. It's this damned shirt. I knew it was too tight. It's torn apart, from collar to tail . . .'

For a moment Henrietta looked at Nathan blankly, then suddenly she started laughing. All the tension of the last few dangerous minutes poured out in her laughter, startling the Prussian guards who stood beside the palace gates, thrown open to allow the carriage through.

Wearing a new shirt, his clothes carefully brushed, Nathan waited outside the room where King Louis XVIII of France was holding court. He was kept waiting for almost an hour, with Louis d'Argon to keep him company. While they waited, Louis informed Nathan that his fellow Cornish fishermen had been brought to the palace and were enjoying more comfort than most of them had ever known before.

Nathan thought King Louis must be occupied with important affairs of state to keep them outside the room for so long, but when the great oak doors were finally swung open he could see the remains of one of the King's gargantuan 'snacks' being carried from the room by a small army of servants.

King Louis sat on a great chair occupying pride of place on a low carpeted podium at the far end of the vast room. Flanking him were many of the nobles of his court.

The King was talking to one of the noblemen when Louis d'Argon and Nathan were led before him. They were obliged to wait until he ended his conversation before they made their obeisances. The delay enabled Nathan to study the French king at some length.

Louis XVIII was not the most prepossessing of monarchs. Short and grossly overweight, each of his fat thighs was larger than the waists of the majority of the women of the court. His head was also large, with an exceedingly high forehead. Nathan had heard it said the King was so heavy he had difficulty in walking, needing to be lifted in and out of his carriage. Looking at the monarch now, Nathan could believe the rumours true.

Eventually King Louis ended his conversation and turned to the two men who stood before him.

Louis d'Argon bowed low, and Nathan followed his example.

'Sire, may I present an Englishman, Nathan Jago, Lord of the Manor of Polrudden, in Cornwall?'

It was the second time Louis d'Argon had introduced him in such a fashion, and Nathan's eyebrows rose slightly.

'M'sieur Jago saved many French lives, including my own, when our ship, *L'Emir*, was wrecked off the Cornish coast. He was later responsible for bringing me to France, in order to speak to the marshals and so facilitate Your Majesty's early return to Paris. As a result of this action he was captured by republicans and thrown into prison at Verdun. He and his crew were released by the Prussian army and are hoping to make their way home to England in the very near future. But Nathan Jago still serves Your Majesty well. Only today, on his way to the palace, he rescued the marquise d'Orléan from a mob of ruffians who had until recently served in Bonaparte's army.'

King Louis' glance rested on Nathan, and briefly there was something close to interest in his expression. Then the cold blue eyes turned to the comte d'Argon. 'We are well pleased with him. He should be rewarded. What was the honour instituted by Bonaparte – the one I have been urged to retain?'

'The Legion of Honour, Your Majesty.'

'Ah, yes!' The large king chuckled, and the action emphasised the flabbiness of his gross body. 'It will please me to award Napoleon Bonaparte's most coveted honour to an Englishman, a subject of the country that has contributed more to Bonaparte's downfall than any other.'

To Nathan the King said: 'Nathan Jago, you have served France well. We are pleased to acknowledge such service with this honour.'

The interview over, the King turned to speak to one of his noblemen once more. Louis d'Argon bowed, Nathan did likewise, and both men left the great room. Outside, Louis d'Argon offered his congratulations to Nathan on the award of the Legion of Honour.

'I'd rather have been provided with an escort to one of the Channel ports,' declared Nathan somewhat ungraciously.

'Oh, yes! I meant to tell you earlier. The King's personal jewellery is on its way to Le Havre from England. An escort of gentlemen and Prussian soldiers is being provided to convey it to Paris. I am to lead them. A number of fast coaches will be going along, leaving Paris tomorrow. You and your men can come, too. This pleases you?'

Of a sudden, Nathan seemed unable to stop grinning. In another twenty-four hours he would be on his way to

Polrudden. To Amy and Beville . . .

'Louis, your news means more to me than all the medals in the world. I must go and tell my men.'

'Of course. Then you will return to my suite. King Louis is having a ball tonight to celebrate his return to France. I am surprised there are enough aristocrats left alive to attend, but we have found them – and your medal is to be presented to you there.'

Nathan had thought the clothes given to him by Henrietta incredibly gaudy. Yet at the ball held in the Tuileries palace that night he felt almost dowdy. A great many men and women of noble birth had been beheaded during the years of terror following on the Revolution, but many more had fled the country to live in elegant luxury abroad. Moreover, Napoleon Bonaparte had established his own court, at which it was no longer a crime to be well born or titled and the fashions of the French were still a match for any court in the world.

King Louis appeared no less bored at his ball than he had been earlier in the evening. Too overweight to dance, he passed the time watching proceedings from the spartan comfort of a hard-stuffed *chaise-longue,* surrounded by men and women of the court.

Before the dancing began, Nathan was called to the royal presence. Here, applauded politely by the assembled aristocracy of France, he received the Legion of Honour from the King's hand.

Henrietta was the first to congratulate Nathan, and the enthusiastic manner in which she kissed him raised many eyebrows in the ballroom.

That evening Nathan enjoyed hero-worship such as he had not experienced since his prize-fighting championship days. There were congratulations from men of the newly restored aristocracy, but the vast majority of his well-wishers were women. Many dropped subtle hints that Nathan would be welcome to pursue his brief acquaintanceship with them elsewhere. On every occasion,

Henrietta was on hand to rescue him from the more persistent of his pursuers.

Nathan enjoyed the food, the wine and the flattery of the flirtatious French women. All helped to boost a morale that had been severely jolted as a result of his capture by the French authorities and the subsequent months of debasing imprisonment.

As time passed it became evident that the majority of celebrants at King Louis XVIII's ball would remain at the ballroom until dawn, but in the early hours of the morning a few of the guests made their excuses and left. Among their number was Henrietta, marquise d'Orléan.

She came to say farewell to Nathan, suggesting wryly that he, too, should leave if he wished to stay clear of scheming women and resume his journey to Polrudden on the morrow.

'I'll be with my men when they leave,' declared Nathan firmly. Looking behind Henrietta, he asked: 'Where's the escort to take *you* home?'

Henrietta rested a hand on Nathan's arm for a moment. 'I am going home alone, Nathan. The liaisons of the court are not for me.'

'You intend travelling the streets alone after what happened today?'

Taking Henrietta's arm, Nathan guided her to one of the great glass doors that opened out on to a small balcony. From here Nathan pointed to where the pale faces of onlookers could be seen pressed against the iron railings surrounding the palace.

'You see those people? Among them are the men who tried to rob us. They know your coach, and they have a score to settle. If they see you riding alone, you're certain to be attacked again.'

'I'll tell the coachman to stay away from dark and narrow alleyways,' declared Henrietta. 'But I am grateful to you for your concern.'

'At this time of night it matters little where you drive. There will be few *honest* people on the streets, and none willing to risk their lives to help you. No, Henrietta. If no one else is escorting you, *I'll* see you home.'

For a moment it seemed Henrietta might argue. Instead, she said: 'It is very kind of you, Nathan. I am grateful.'

Nathan looked about the room to see if he could catch Louis d'Argon's eye and explain where he was going, but Louis was nowhere to be seen. Then Henreitta took Nathan's arm, and he led her from the room, fully aware of the knowing smiles exchanged by those they passed along the way.

Henrietta was unusually silent in the carriage as it made its way along the darkened streets. Twice Nathan tried to make conversation, but after only the briefest of replies Henrietta lapsed into silence once more.

When the carriage arrived at Henrietta's house, the coachman opened the door then stepped discreetly back out of sight. Inside the carraige neither passenger moved and the silence between them became a slowly widening chasm.

'Well . . . we got you home safely.'

'Yes, Nathan. Thank you.'

'I'm the one who should be grateful – for your protection against all those designing women back at the ball!'

It was meant to be a joke, to stop the chasm from growing any wider. Instead, Henrietta said quietly: 'You have no one here to protect you from *me,* Nathan.'

'From you . . .?' As Nathan echoed her words, his throat felt very dry. Then suddenly her arms were about him and her mouth found his. For a moment Nathan held back. Then the feelings that had lain dormant during long months of captivity burst into new life.

The madness continued until her mouth slipped away, but Nathan still held her against him and he could feel her body trembling beneath his hands.

'Nathan . . .' Her lips brushed against his ear. 'You will come into the house with me . . .?'

Nathan knew what would happen if he went inside Henrietta's house – yet the knowledge tempted him sorely.

Henrietta was one of the most exciting women Nathan had ever met, and he had just suffered the enforced celibacy of a French gaol. Only the thought of Amy and all that awaited him at Polrudden caused him to hesitate – and suddenly it was too late.

Henrietta pushed him away. 'Take no notice of me, Nathan. I have drunk more than I am used to tonight. I am talking nonsense.'

'No, you're not . . .'

Clumsily, Nathan tried to pull her towards him once more. Managing to keep her distance, Henrietta put a finger to his lips and pressed it there. 'Sh! Say nothing more. You must go now. I *do* understand. Please . . . try to understand me also.'

The coachman moved forward once more to open the door which had swung shut in the slight breeze. He held it wide as Henrietta rose to leave. Before putting her foot on the step she turned and kissed Nathan very lightly on the lips. 'That is for my brother's son. Take care of him. If there is any news of his father, I will let you know. Until then it is safer for him to remain with you. Have a safe journey home, Nathan. If you think of me at all, may it be with affection, for be sure I will think of you – often.'

CHAPTER TEN

When Nathan set off with the Cornish fishermen early in the morning he had discarded his fancy French clothes in favour of more familiar fisherman's garb. The Cornishmen expressed good-natured disappointment. They declared that witnessing the arrival of Nathan in Pentuan wearing a French courtier's clothes would have made up for much of the misery of the prison they had left behind. Even Pascoe

Lanyon, looking increasingly frail, joined in the happy chaffing.

Nathan sat in a corner of one of the carriages with the fishermen, saying little. It seemed he might have left his sense of humour behind at the Tuileries palace. When Louis d'Argon reined in beside the coach and suggested Nathan might like to ride one of the spare horses brought along by the Prussian escort, Nathan accepted the offer readily.

As Nathan mounted the animal, Louis d'Argon reined in beside him. 'Your face is not that of a man who is going home, my friend. I trust you have not left your heart behind in Paris. I saw you leaving the ball with the lovely Henrietta.'

'I've left nothing behind in Paris,' Nathan snapped. 'I took Henrietta only as far as the front door of her home. Had I been able to find you, I would have left *you* to arrange an escort. I was anxious she should have protection against the footpads who attacked her coach earlier.'

'My apologies, Nathan. I should have known better.'

Something in Louis d'Argon's voice told Nathan his reply had been important to the French nobleman.

'You're fond of Henrietta, Louis. Does she know?'

'I asked her to marry me many years ago. I was an impetuous young man then, and her parents had just announced she was to marry the marquis d'Orléan. I told her she was much too beautiful to waste her life on an old man. She turned me down then, and has done so twice more since her husband died.'

Louis d'Argon shrugged his shoulders. 'It would seem I have a certain reputation with the ladies. None of them will take me seriously, not even when I propose marriage. Perhaps it is better so. I would not make a good husband.'

Nathan could not visualise Louis, comte d'Argon as a heartbroken swain, but he realised the Frenchman must be very fond of Henrietta indeed.

Nathan's mood improved with the ride, but it was only a temporary improvement. He had declared he was leaving nothing behind, yet there *was* something he was being forced to leave in France that he could ill afford to lose. His thoughts were of the fishing-boat *Sir Beville*, commandeered by the French fishermen of Raulet.

The small convoy made fast time to the coast, reaching the great port of Le Havre, at the wide mouth of the River Seine, with only one night stop. But even the rigours of such a hard and uncomfortable journey could not dampen the Cornish fishermen's enthusiasm at glimpsing the sea once more. Some of the men had been prisoners for five years, during which time they had never been allowed close to the sea.

Le Havre, guarding the great river that flowed through the heart of Paris, had been France's second-busiest port before the Anglo-French wars, but the British blockade on French shipping had brought ruination to the town. Now the war was over, Le Havre was determined to regain its earlier status in the quickest possible time. The harbour was crowded with ships of every description, many British men-of-war among them. Merchants' wagons piled high with produce and goods of every description jammed the roads leading to the dock area, and there was an air of rejuvenation that had not been evident in Paris.

The ship bringing Louis XVIII's personal treasure from England had not yet arrived, but there were many other English ships here. Eager to be home, the Cornish fishermen were in favour of finding a merchant captain willing to carry them to England on his return journey, but Nathan had other plans. While Louis d'Argon went off to find accommodation for his Prussian escort, Nathan called all the fishermen together and explained his idea to them.

'We've reached the coast safely, and there are ships here to take you to England – but they'll be going only to the Channel ports. You'll still have close on three hundred miles to walk through England before you reach Cornwall. You'll arrive home footsore, weary, and doubtless without a penny in your purses. I've got a much more satisfactory way of going home. When I and my crew were captured my boat was given to a fisherman in Raulet, on the Brittany coast. I'm going to get her back. I mean to travel back to Cornwall the same way I left. Any man among you who will help me recover my boat will arrive home the way a man with pride should – and he'll be five guineas better off. Who'll come with me?'

There was a silence as Nathan's words sank in. Then one of the fishermen shook his head. 'I was apprenticed to a ship's master as a boy. We sailed all along this coast. I know Raulet. It's as far from here as Cornwall is from the south-coast ports of England. The Frenchmen of Raulet probably aren't aware yet that the war's over. Besides, how will you get there? We needed an escort to reach here in safety. I say we find an English boat to take us across the Channel and shake the dirt of this damned country off our feet as quick as we can.'

There were a few murmurs of agreement, but old Obadiah Hocking, busily filling his pipe, said: 'I'm getting too old to spend my life tramping around the countryside, be it France, England or anywhere else. You got something in mind that'll save these legs of mine, Nathan?'

'Yes, but I'll need to make a few enquiries first. Those of you who are interested can meet me back here at dusk tonight – and, remember, *I'm* in a hurry to get home, too.'

Leaving the former prisoners-of-war arguing among themselves, Nathan set off along the waterfront to where he had seen English men-of-war secured alongside the harbour wall. There were a number of warships here, and they were well guarded. Nathan was still fifty paces from the nearest British vessel when he was challenged by a sentry wearing the uniform of a marine.

The marine was not a man of great intelligence. When Nathan introduced himself and began asking questions about the men-of-war and their duties, the sea-going soldier became increasingly agitated. Casting anxious glances back towards the ships, he saw a red-uniformed man wearing the crossed white shoulder-belts of a marine come to the side of a ship and look in his direction. Even from this distance Nathan could see the gold stripes of a sergeant on his arm.

'Sergeant McKinley! Will you come here, sir?' The marine pointed his bayoneted musket menacingly in Nathan's direction and said: 'You just stay here. Sergeant McKinley will deal with you.'

Nathan shrugged. He was getting nowhere with the marine. The sergeant might prove more helpful.

When the sergeant reached them, the marine explained: 'This bloke claims he's been held a prisoner-of-war by the Frenchies. He's asking a lot of questions about our ships.'

'Is he now?' The sergeant of marines looked Nathan over from head to toe and was not impressed with what he saw.

'Prisoner-of-war, were you? What's your rank and service?'

'I'm a fisherman, from Cornwall. Taken prisoner when I ran aground on the French coast.'

The sergeant's eyebrows rose mockingly. 'Ran aground on the French coast, you say. Weren't you a wee bit off course for a Cornish fisherman?'

The sergeant suddenly thrust his red face close to Nathan's own. 'I'd say you're more likely a deserter from one of the ships that's put in here from England recently. Keep him covered while I search him, Marine Tonkins.'

When Nathan protested, the marine stepped forward and brought the tip of his bayonet alarmingly close to Nathan's bare neck and Nathan fell silent.

'That's better. You just stand there quietly while I see what you have on you.'

The sergeant of marines stood behind Nathan and made a thorough search of his pockets. He found the gold coins remaining from the money given to Nathan at Verdun, and there was a dull clinking sound as they were transferred to the sergeant's own pocket.

Next the sergeant found the small silk-lined box containing the medal presented to Nathan by King Louis XVIII.

'What's this?'

Holding up the medal by its bright red ribbon, he read the inscription with difficulty, pronouncing each syllable as though it were a separate word: 'Re-pub-liqué Fran-caise. That's French! What you doing with a French medal? Don't tell me they're handing them out to British prisoners-of-war now the fighting's over!'

Even as Nathan opened his mouth to explain, the sergeant shouted: 'I know what you are. You're one of them deserters who went over to the French and fought against his own countrymen.'

Without warning, the sergeant's fist came down on the back of Nathan's neck. Nathan wheeled around, his fist raised to hit back, only to have the butt of the marine's musket crash against the side of his head.

Fortunately, the musket caught Nathan only a glancing blow, but it was of sufficient strength to drop him to his knees. Even so, Nathan jumped up and would have taken on both men had not the sergeant's next words brought him quickly to his senses.

'Get him on board, Tonkins. If he tries that again, shoot him! It'll save a trial and the waste of a useful length of rope.'

Aware that any further attempt at explanation was likely to have painful consequences, Nathan was prodded none too gently towards the ships.

They were passing a frigate, heading towards a much larger ship-of-the-line, when an officer standing at the top of the frigate's gangway called to the marine sergeant, asking what was happening.

The marine sergeant brought the small party to a halt, aware that the ships alongside the harbour quay were lined with interested sailors. 'I've caught a deserter, sir. Not only that, he's been fighting for Napoleon and got a French medal for doing it.'

'That's a lie, Commander Martingale.'

Nathan needed to shout to make his words heard above the jeers and catcalls of the sailors who had listened to the explanation of the sergeant of marines.

His outburst earned him a blow in the back from the marine's musket, but the officer had heard him and he came down the gangway now, wearing a puzzled expression. Peering closely at Nathan, he asked: 'Do I know you?'

'You did once – in *Victory*. You were a young midshipman then, and I was Coxswain Jago.'

'*Nathan* Jago? But you were honourably discharged from the service. Went on to become champion prizefighter of all England, as I recall. Of course, I recognise you now. Well, I'm damned! But what's all this nonsense about?'

The officer put the question to the sergeant of marines, who had listened open-mouthed to the conversation.

Holding out the medal, the sergeant said: 'He . . . he had this in his pocket.'

Taking the medal from the sergeant, Commander Martingale looked at Nathan for an explanation.

'It's the French Legion of Honour. It was presented to me a few days ago in Paris – by King Louis XVII of France.'

The naval commander's face registered disbelief, and Nathan said quickly: 'It's a long story, but it can be verified by the comte d'Argon. He's in Le Havre now with a Prussian escort, on a special mission for King Louis. There are also twenty Cornishmen here, among them the crew of my fishing-boat. They'll confirm everything I have to say.'

The naval officer frowned at the marine sergeant. 'I think you've made a mistake, Sergeant. Mr Jago will come on board *Blazer* with me. When I've heard his full story I'll be taking him to see the Admiral.'

'Yessir.' The sergeant of marines saluted and, without looking at Nathan, turned to go.

'Aren't you forgetting something, Sergeant?'

At Nathan's words, the sergeant stopped. Looking at Nathan's outstretched hand he flushed, then delved in a pocket and returned the gold coins he had appropriated during the search.

As the sergeant marched stiffly away, Commander Martingale shrugged apologetically. 'Unlike his fellow-soldiers on land, a marine sergeant has little opportunity to accumulate booty. Come on board to my cabin. I've a feeling you have an interesting tale to relate.'

An hour later Nathan was repeating his experiences to Vice-Admiral Sir Cuthbert Giles – and there was no one in a better position to help Nathan recover *Sir Beville*. An energetic and enterprising seaman, Vice-Admiral Giles had a reputation for unorthodox behaviour. It had resulted in both censure and honours vying with each other for supremacy during his long and colourful career. His current task was to ensure that the ports of northern France were opened to commerce as quickly as possible.

Beginning with the wreck of *L'Emir* beneath the cliffs of Polrudden, Nathan told the Vice-Admiral of Louis d'Argon's return, and the trip across the English Channel that had resulted in he and his crew being taken prisoner. He ended by telling of the recent stay in Paris, and of the journey of the fishermen to Le Havre.

'Remarkable story . . . quite remarkable,' mused the Vice-Admiral, fixing Nathan with an admiring look. 'Now, I suppose, you're hoping one of my ships will take you back across the English Channel and dump you and your men close to Cornwall?'

'No. I'm hoping you'll have a ship, heading westwards, to drop us close to Raulet. My fishing-boat is there. I intend taking it back and returning to Cornwall in the same manner I left.'

'I see!' Sir Cuthbert's eyebrows drew closer in a frown. 'My task is to *prevent* trouble along the French coast, not provoke it.' He cleared his throat noisily. 'However, I'm quite certain their Lordships at the Admiralty never intended me to turn a blind eye to injustice. Commander Martingale, take *Blazer* and the two other frigates for a little foray along the coast. Check and report on the current position at the port of Brest for me. As it's on your way, you might drop Mr Jago and his men off at Raulet – and give him whatever assistance may be necessary.'

*

HMS *Blazer* sailed on the morning tide the next day, accompanied by two other frigates. On board were Nathan and sixteen of the fishermen who had been released from prison in Verdun. Pascoe Lanyon and his young brother were among them. The remaining four men, none of them from Nathan's crew, had chosen to take passage to England in a merchantman.

The three warships arrived off Raulet after dark the following evening. Mindful of his own downfall, Nathan warned Commander Martingale to anchor well offshore until a lead-line could help locate a safe anchorage closer to the harbour in the morning light.

Nathan was on *Blazer*'s upper deck scouring the seas with a glass, hoping to catch a glimpse of the once-familiar shape of *Sir Beville* among the returning fishing-boats, when dawn broke. When *Sir Beville* did appear she was so low in the water, laden with fish, that for a second Nathan failed to recognise his boat. His search passed on – only to return again almost immediately.

'There she is!' Excitedly he pointed out the fishing-boat to the commander, and the naval officer took the telescope from his hands.

'Man the boats!' Commander Martingale shouted the order, and sailors came running to clamber down rope ladders to the two boats waiting at the ship's side.

Nathan went with the boats, taking with him all his crew, except Pascoe Lanyon.

The two boats from *Blazer* quickly converged on *Sir Beville,* but the fishing-boat showed no sign of heaving to. Not until a shot from *Blazer* echoed across the water, and a cannonball sent a spout of water high in the air, twenty feet off her bows, did the French fishermen hasten to lower the sail.

The speed of *Sir Beville* dropped away swiftly, and as she wallowed in the swell both boats from *Blazer* bumped alongside.

'What is the meaning of this? You have no right to stop me. Our countries are no longer at war. I shall make a complaint to the authorities . . .'

The French skipper of the fishing-boat suddenly saw Nathan and he knew immediately why he had been boarded.

Standing on the deck of *Sir Beville,* Nathan had difficulty controlling the jubilation he felt. Affably, he said to the fisherman who had taken *Sir Beville* from him: 'I'm glad you're aware that we're no longer at war. I'm sure you'll welcome the opportunity to return *Sir Beville* to its rightful owner.'

'*Rightful* owner, m'sieur? It is a French-built boat. No doubt it has been a spoil of war before.'

'Possibly. But I paid good money for her. Besides, the spoils go to the victor – and Napoleon lost the war for France.'

The Frenchman gave an expressive gesture of resignation. 'I cannot argue with you, m'sieur – not when your words are backed by the guns of three British warships.'

'Your wisdom does you credit. Tell your men to go on board the British boats. You will all be transferred to other fishing-boats.'

'That catch. . . . It is mine.'

'I'll accept it as payment for the hire of *Sir Beville.* If you've landed many catches like this one, you'll have enough money at home to buy a new boat of your own.'

The philosophic Frenchman smiled for the first time. 'I have done well. You have a fine vessel. If there is another war, please return with your boat to Raulet once more.'

Half an hour later, with seventeen excited men on board, *Sir Beville* nosed out into the English Channel and crowded on full sail. With a full catch and only a light wind, the fishing-boat would set no cross-Channel records, but Nathan knew that when the sun rose again over the horizon he and his crew should be looking upon the cliffs of Cornwall.

CHAPTER ELEVEN

It had been more than five months since *Sir Beville* vanished on her last voyage from Portgiskey, and it seemed to Amy the whole fabric of her life was finally falling apart.

The winter storms had caused damage to the roof of Polrudden and new slates needed to be shipped in from the great slate quarry of Delabole, close to Cornwall's north coast.

The two fishing-boats from Portgiskey had begun fishing again after storms had kept them idle, only to run into trouble with the Pentuan inshore fishermen. The Pentuan seiners accused the Portgiskey drifters of fishing too close inshore, thus preventing fish from reaching them. It was a dispute that had raged for generations, but it had grown no less bitter with the passing years. Nathan had been able to contain the dissension by dint of his personality, but he had been unable to find a solution. Now the argument had flared up again, and the inshore men were threatening to take matters into their own hands if local magistrates did not take action. Because of this, the drift-fishermen were reluctant to take the boats to sea.

Cracks were also appearing in the traditionally close-knit community life of Pentuan. Nathan may have denied to Louis d'Argon that he was Lord of the Manor of Polrudden, but it was becoming increasingly clear that in the absence of a strong man at Polrudden the heart had gone from the village.

There were two empty cottages in Pentuan now. One had previously been occupied by the avaricious Lavinia Hockin, the other was the Mitchell cottage. Mary Mitchell, wife of Nathan's crewman, Matthew, had sold up her furniture and left for St Austell, taking her three young sons and two-year-old daughter with her. She had been born in St Austell and hoped her relatives there would give the family a home.

Meanwhile, fifteen-year-old Maud had now become the sole source of income for the fatherless Piper family. She earned her money on board the grimy coal-boats trading between the ports of south Wales and Pentuan. The boats brought in coal for the mine engines in the Pentuan valley, returning to Wales with ore for the furnaces of Cardiff.

Maud Piper's behaviour deeply shocked and offended the villagers, but neither they nor the two Methodist preachers could persuade her to abandon the way of life she had so recently adopted.

Besides, the Methodist preachers had a problem of their own and it was likely to affect the community more than the young girl who had taken to prostitution in order to feed her family.

The Methodist movement had been born out of the mother Church of England in the previous century, spawned by the people's frustration with the Established Church. Now the Methodist movement itself was going through a similar crisis. Methodism had expanded rapidly, its amazing success due almost entirely to the ceaseless vitality of its founder, John Wesley, and a small band of dedicated pioneer preachers. Wesley knew exactly what he wanted from his followers and seldom failed to draw it from them. He was an unremitting autocrat. In a letter written in 1790, Wesley had stated: 'As long as I live the people shall have no share in choosing either stewards or leaders among the Methodists.' Yet, for all this, his followers loved him for his autocracy.

Wesley lived to a grand old age, but he could not live for ever and when he died the authority vested in him passed to 'The Conference', or 'The Legal Hundred' as the governing body was sometimes called. The new leadership structure proved unsatisfactory for many Methodists. They wanted local Methodist societies to play a more significant part in their own affairs.

Not surprisingly, Cornwall was in the forefront of the dissension. The country's history had not always been linked with the affairs of England, and its people resented any authority that was vested east of the River Tamar.

Some Cornish Methodist preachers were already advocating a break from the authority of 'Conference' and urging local management of their own affairs, together with greater freedom in their mode of worship. Preacher Jago was one of these.

Josiah Jago had been out of step with his Methodist superiors for many years. He was an evangelist who preferred taking religion to the people, rather than have them come seeking it from him. He now found himself drawn into increasingly bitter dissension with the man who had been appointed as his helper.

Preacher Jago remembered only too clearly the days when Methodist preachers were hounded, ridiculed and thrown into prison for preaching the message of the New Testament in their own way; but with dogged, unswerving and honest faith they had persevered until the movement was recognised as being 'respectable'. He felt that he and his fellow-preachers should be allowed to continue taking the word of God to the people.

The Reverend Damian Roach had been ordained by the Church of England, but had chosen to transfer his allegiance to the Methodist Church. Less parochial than Josiah Jago, Damian Roach knew that the 'toleration' granted to the movement was not yet fully accepted by either the church of the land, or 'the Establishment'. Josiah Jago and those preachers who insisted that all men were equal, within and without the Church, could bring about a backlash of opinion against Methodism. The memories of the slaughter that had taken place in France, brought about by such sentiments, were still fresh in the minds of men and government and were likely to result in new repression.

The Reverend Damian Roach believed the Methodist Church should be consolidating the considerable progress it had already made and taking steps to establish a hierarchy along the lines of the Church of England. An ambitious man, Roach believed he had an important part to play in such a hierarchy.

The issues facing the Methodist movement had split communities the length and breadth of the country. Pentuan did not escape the controversy.

It had become customary for Preacher Jago and the Reverend Damian Roach to divide the Sunday services in the little Pentuan church between them, leaving lay preachers to take care of the outlying communities. At first, the villagers attended the services of both men, enjoying making comparisons between the style and biblical knowledge of each man. However, since the preachers had found themselves treading different paths, the village had divided into those who loyally followed Josiah Jago, and others whose loyalty remained with Damian Roach and the official Methodist line.

It hurt Preacher Jago to have his congregation divided in such a manner. He expressed his thoughts to Amy one day in mid-May, after toiling up the hill to Polrudden at the height of an early summer heatwave. He stood in the kitchen drinking tea and watching through the open window as Beville and Jean-Paul played together on the smooth lawn behind the house.

Amy was making bread, pounding and turning dough. Without looking up, she said: 'I shouldn't have thought it mattered very much. Just so long as everyone finds God in the way that's best for *them*.'

'It *does* matter, Amy. John Wesley devoted the whole of his life to Methodism because God told him it was the right way to carry His word to the people. When Wesley came to Cornwall he drove out the Devil and brought a new way of life for miners and fishermen. Before his coming they had feared neither God nor man. We've got to continue Wesley's work. God's work.'

'I'm sure it can't be as serious as you believe, Papa Jago. Damian says that Wesley succeeded because he gave the people what they needed, at the time they needed it most. Times are changing. The Methodist movement must change with them. It's time for the Methodist Church to come of age.'

'Damian says! *Damian* says!' Preacher Jago began to stride back and forth across the wide kitchen, the cup still in his hand. 'Damian has not been a preacher for even a single year yet. I've been preaching for forty-five! I was given special dispensation by John Wesley himself to remain in one circuit instead of moving on, because I know my own people so well. Damian Roach can't begin to tell *me* what the people of this area want.'

'Yet there are many people who attend his services because they want to hear what *he* has to say,' Amy replied quietly. 'And he's read every word Wesley ever wrote.'

'He's leading them along the wrong road,' declared Josiah Jago vehemently. 'Before they know it they'll have strayed from Wesley's church – yes, *and* lost God, too.'

Preacher Jago stopped pacing and looked at Amy over the top of the cup as he took another sip of tea. 'I'd be happier if you didn't entertain Roach so much at Polrudden. I'd hate him to influence you and the boys in your thinking.'

'I'm the only one who'll influence the boys in their thinking,' declared Amy, thumping hard at the dough in front of her. 'And I don't "entertain" Damian. He calls in here occasionally to offer his advice and help – both of which I'm in sore need of these days. In case you haven't noticed, there's no fish being landed at Portgiskey. This means there's little money coming in. I've had to dismiss half the staff and the remainder are working for no more than their keep, to save them from the poorhouse. If it weren't for night-trading, I'd be in the poorhouse myself.'

'Smuggling is an *abomination*. John Wesley said so himself, on many occasions. From what I hear, Damian Roach needs to be reminded of Wesley's words.'

'*Words* won't fill empty bellies, or pay bills – and it doesn't matter whether they're John Wesley's words or anybody else's.'

'You could always sell Polrudden.'

Amy stopped kneading dough for the first time since Preacher Jago's arrival. 'I'll sell my body like poor Maud Piper before I give up this house. Nathan's worked as hard as any two men to keep Polrudden for Beville. I'll not be the one to undo all he worked for.'

Josiah Jago was not used to women being as outspoken and forthright as Amy. 'I don't like to hear you saying such things. Maud Piper is a disgrace to womanhood and to the community. She's a whore. Such a young woman is abhorrent in the eyes of the Lord.'

When the dough resumed its noisy assault on the scrubbed surface of the kitchen table, Josiah Jago's jaw took on a determined set.

'Nathan is dead, Amy. As his father it hurts me to admit it to myself, but I'm convinced that until *you* accept it, too, you're never going to solve the problems that face you and young Beville. That French child, too, if you intend keeping him.'

'Because you've held a memorial service for Nathan doesn't mean I have to believe he's dead,' declared Amy, carefully controlling her voice. 'Neither you *nor* your God have been able to convince me of that.'

'Don't blaspheme, child. God's ways are beyond the understanding of men and women. You must face the facts. Nathan has been gone for months now.'

Wiping her hands on the apron she wore, Amy turned away from the preacher. In a strained voice, she said: 'Papa Jago, I would never try to turn you aside from *your* faith because I know how much strength you gain from it. Please . . . please respect mine.'

With this, Amy fled from the kitchen, leaving Josiah Jago frowning after her.

Upstairs in her bedroom, Amy slammed the door shut and leaned back against it as though she feared pursuit.

Close to the door was a bedroom table, on which Preacher Jago would have been most surprised to see a large black Bible, on the cover of which was a crucifix traced in gold leaf.

Reaching out, Amy opened the Bible. Written on the fly-leaf were the words 'To my dearest Amy, for the faith that has made all things possible'. It was dated 'Christmas 1812'.

The inscription referred to the faith that had been strong enough for Amy to stake the whole of a considerable inheritance on the outcome of Nathan's last prize-fight. Nathan had been expected to lose, so the odds on him were exceptionally good. In fact Nathan won. With her winnings, Amy bought Polrudden and brought it to him as a dowry.

Suddenly, tears blurred the handwriting in the Bible and Amy began shaking uncontrollably. Clutching the book to her, she told herself fiercely that it was *still* as important as it always had been to maintain her faith in Nathan's return. But after so many months without a word it was no longer easy. Dropping to her knees, Amy leaned her forehead against the bed and whispered fiercely: 'Please, Nathan . . . Please come back to us.'

Josiah Jago's opinion that it was time for Amy to face the reality of her situation and sell Polrudden was one of the few views shared by both Pentuan Methodist ministers.

The Reverend Damian Roach arrived at the house when the sun was casting long shadows across the Polrudden gardens. Amy had just put the two boys to bed. Receiving her guest in the study, she poured the young preacher a smuggled brandy, pleased to have his company. She hoped that his amusing talk would chase away the upsets of the day, but it turned out that Damian Roach was not in a mood to be amusing. He, too, had been involved in an argument with Preacher Jago.

'It had to come,' he explained as he sipped the brandy appreciatively. 'I'm only surprised it took so long. He and I have never really agreed on how a preaching circuit should be run. I want more chapels built. Josiah says the chapels we already have are sufficient for local needs and that people who are unable to reach them are happy to attend open-air meetings, or gather in a neighbour's house. He is wrong. Informality is no longer the cornerstone of our movement. We are a responsible religion now. Build a church and it becomes a focal point for the whole area. People are attracted there.'

'It's strange, really,' mused Amy. 'Not many years ago Josiah Jago was saying exactly what you're saying today. He built most of the chapels in the villages hereabouts and was ready to go to prison when the old squire had one pulled down.'

'Preacher Jago is growing old,' said Damian Roach unkindly. 'His thinking is no longer reasoned. His way is the *wrong* way. The younger men – yes, and the younger women, too – can see this. They will follow me.'

Amy looked at Damian Roach sharply. 'You might *think* they'll follow you but, first, you'll need to prove you know where you're leading them. Even then you might find they'll prefer to follow one of their own – a Cornishman.'

'If the Cornish don't follow me, others will,' asserted the young preacher. 'I don't intend remaining a circuit preacher for all my life.'

Amy had occasionally wondered why Damian Roach had become a Methodist so soon after his ordination in the Established Church. Now she thought she knew. 'Does Josiah know of your ambitions?'

'Preacher Jago doesn't really matter any more. I have written to Conference, suggesting he be removed from this circuit.' Damian Roach rose from his seat. Refilling his glass without asking, he began pacing restlessly about the room. 'They'll probably act on my suggestion and find somewhere else for him to go. I realise it may cause some initial resentment here, but it will ultimately benefit everyone. Properly organised, our church can become a major force in this country. It will be so strong we'll be able to nominate our own candidates for Parliament – and provide voters to ensure they are elected. Who knows, one day we might even see a Methodist prime minister!'

'Where is your place in this powerful new Methodist Church, Damian?' Amy put the question almost casually.

'Wherever I am best fitted to serve – but it will be in the forefront of progress. I have ideas, Amy. Many, many ideas.' Putting down the glass he was holding, he turned to face her, his face animated.

'When the Methodist Church sent me here, to Pentuan, I was dismayed. I regarded Cornwall as an unproductive backwater. I wanted to reamin in London, to meet with all the progressive thinkers of our time. I would have been almost as happy in the Midlands where new industry is changing the lives of thousands. The people there are bewildered and confused, lacking strong leadership. The Methodist Church should be there to guide and counsel them; to give them new hope for *this* life, as well as leading them to the Kingdom of Eternity. But now I'm *glad* I came to Pentuan. Since I came here I've learned I can *lead* people, persuade them to listen to me . . .'

Unexpectedly, Damian Roach raised his hands and rested them on Amy's shoulders. 'Coming to Cornwall has given me something else, Amy. It has led me to you, and to Polrudden.'

Taken aback, Amy reached up to remove Damian Roach's hands from her shoulders, but he grabbed her wrists and held them tightly.

'Amy, sell Polrudden to *me*. I'll offer it to the Methodist Church as a college to train preachers. It will become the beating heart of the Methodist movement. We will be teaching the men and women who will guide Methodism through the nineteenth century.'

'We?'

'Yes. You and I, Amy. Such a generous gift will ensure that I remain here, as principal. I have the qualifications. I taught at Oxford for two years and was well thought of there.'

Damian saw the astonishment on Amy's face and totally misinterpreted the expression. 'You're wondering how I can afford to buy Polrudden? My father has money, Amy. He owns coal mines in the Midlands. He didn't want me to take up Methodism, but if he hears I'm to become the principal of a teaching college he'll think very differently about things. If he doesn't . . . Well, we'll still manage – with you here as my wife.'

'Damian, you don't know what you're saying. I'm already married – to Nathan.'

Damian Roach brought Amy's hands together in front of her body. 'Amy, I realise the loss of Nathan has been a great shock to you. You loved him dearly, as a good wife should. This, too, I accept. There is no virtue in a woman who is capable of withholding love from her lawful husband. But he is gone now. He's *dead*. The time has come for you to accept this and begin a new life. I am offering you that new beginning.'

The young preacher's words dismayed and horrified Amy. She had leaned heavily on his strength in the recent months, but it had been because she regarded him as an understanding preacher. Not as a prospective lover, or husband. The help given her by Damian Roach might have been supplied by Josiah Jago, had the older preacher not looked upon human problems as less pressing than his duties as God's errand-boy.

Damian Roach's words about marriage and his plans for Polrudden swept over her like a rising tide threatening the rock to which she was so desperately clinging.

'I can't, Damian . . . I can't.'

'You can, and you *will*.' Damian Roach was at his masterful best. 'I know you're concerned about Beville, but he'll benefit from my teaching. When he's older we'll send him off to one of the finest schools in the country. He'll grow up to be a fine young man of whom we'll both be proud.'

Amy was looking up at the young preacher in shocked

horror now, but he was too carried away by enthusiasm for his plans to notice.

'Does it surprise you that I've put so much thought into this? That's my way, Amy, as you'll learn. There's more. I think I can get a good price for Portgiskey.'

'Sell Portgiskey . . .?' Amy could not believe Damian Roach was saying all this.

'Yes, I was talking to Samson Harry – you remember him, the Preventive Officer at Fowey? He's not a bad chap, really. He's willing to buy the cellar and the boats and give you *more* than the going price . . .'

That day was the worst Amy had experienced since Nathan's disappearance. Nothing had been going right for her, or for Polrudden, in recent weeks. Now she had quarrelled with the two men who were closest to her.

Preacher Jago was bigoted and totally selfish in his religious outlook, but he cared for her as much as he was capable of caring for anyone outside the immediate circle of the Lord's intimates. He was also Nathan's father, and Beville's grandfather.

Yet Amy was somehow far more hurt by her quarrel with Damian Roach. Her accusation against him of unpardonable interference in her affairs was entirely justified, as was her demand that he leave Polrudden and not return. Nevertheless, he *had* been very kind to her when she desperately needed help, and she had grown fond of him.

What both quarrels *had* achieved was to force her to face facts. There was now little likelihood of Nathan being alive. She still refused to admit he was dead, but her faith was beginning to appear foolish, even to herself.

On this warm May night Amy felt all hope slipping from her grasp.

CHAPTER TWELVE

Sir Beville rode the tide into Portgiskey Cove at dawn, her arrival shrouded in a sea mist that hid the village from the view of the eager fishermen.

Nathan frowned when he saw both *The Brave Amy H* and *Peggy Hoblyn* tied alongside the quay. One boat, at least, should have been at sea, drifting. The weather was good and he had seen a number of drifters hauling well-filled nets not far out from Fowey harbour. Yet even this fact could not dampen the excitement he felt at coming home once more.

The feeling was shared by every man on board *Sir Beville,* crewmen and passengers alike. All had homes within ten miles of Portgiskey, and each man was determined to make it there in time for breakfast.

The only sobering aspect of the homecoming was the condition of Pascoe Lanyon. Showing incredible stoicism, he had complained no more on the cross-Channel voyage than he had on the long overland journey from the Verdun prison. But Pascoe was a very sick man.

When the goodbyes had been said at Portgiskey and the men had hurried off to their various homes, Nathan helped young Cornelius Lanyon to support his sick brother as far as the village.

They were still many yards from his cottage when Pascoe Lanyon shrugged off their supporting arms. 'I'll walk up to my own front door, thank you. It *may* be for the last time, but nothing is going to deny me this moment.'

Cornelius Lanyon bit back a protest. He and his brother were very close. No one knew better than he how ill Pascoe was. He stopped at the gate of the small cottage and allowed Pascoe his brief moment of triumph.

Leaving the Lanyon family to their reunion, Nathan set off up the hill to Polrudden. The mist was thicker here, swirling in off the sea. Nathan smiled; it was a 'smuggler's morning'. He did not doubt he would need to resume his night-trading activities at the earliest possible opportunity. Things could not have been easy at Polrudden during his absence.

Memories of his once familiar routine returned to him as he drew nearer to his home. One of the things he had forgotten was the steepness of the hill rising from Pentuan to Polrudden. Long before he reached the tree-lined drive-way that curved towards the house he was breathing heavily, his heart pounding alarmingly. Nathan was not certain how much of the latter was due to the almost absurd excitement he felt at the thought of seeing Amy once more.

It was about 5 a.m. now, and the sea mist was beginning to thin in the sun at the top of the hill. When Polrudden came into view Nathan felt a large lump rise in his throat. There had been many times when he feared he might never see the great house again.

He headed for the rear of the house. There were sounds from here, and Nathan knew at least one kitchenmaid would be up. The first to rise, her duties included laying the kitchen fires, removing the ashes and scrubbing tables and floors.

The kitchenmaid was a simple woman – almost an im-becile – but she had been at Polrudden for all of her working life. When Nathan entered the kitchen she was rising from the fireplace, her black-smudged face half-hidden by untidy, wispy hair. A bucket of ashes was held in each hand.

She took two paces across the room before seeing Nathan. As her slack jaw dropped and her eyes began to widen, Nathan held a finger to his lips in a futile gesture.

The kitchenmaid backed away from him until she came in contact with the kitchen wall. Dropping the buckets with a great clatter, she fled from the kitchen into the house, her screams echoing along the passageways ahead of her.

Upstairs, in her bedroom, Amy was in the languid, self-indulgent state that was neither sleep nor wakefulness. The screams of the kitchenmaid brought her awake with a cruel abruptness.

Leaping from her bed as the screams drew nearer, Amy opened the door as the kitchenmaid stumbled up the last of the stairs and dropped to her knees at Amy's feet.

'The Lord save us, Mistress Amy. 'Tis the Master's ghost. I see'd it with me own eyes. Down in the kitchen. I see'd 'n.'

'Mary, get a grip on yourself. What is it you think you saw?' Amy's mind was still scrambled by sleep and had not yet begun to function in an orderly manner.

'It were Master's ghost. I swear it.'

'No, Amy, I'm no ghost. If I were, seeing you dressed like that would make me flesh and blood again.'

Looking up from the terrified kitchenmaid, Amy saw Nathan standing at the foot of the staircase. All the blood drained from her face, to be chased back moments later by a feeling of sheer uncontrollable joy.

Oblivious now of the servant-girl who cowered on the floor, Amy stepped towards the stairs – then suddenly everything spun about her. As she stood swaying, Nathan bounded up the last few stairs and caught her before she fell.

When Amy came to she was lying on her bed. As memory flooded back, she started up. 'Nathan . . . .!'

'It's all right, my love. I'm here.'

'Oh, Nathan . . . Nathan! Thank God! I feared I'd been dreaming.' Then their arms were about each other and Amy was both laughing and crying, in happy confusion.

An hour later they tiptoed into the bedroom shared by Beville and Jean-Paul. Beville still slept soundly, but the young French boy was beginning to stir and they crept out of the room again, as quietly as they had entered.

Nathan said little as he and Amy made their way downstairs. Seeing Jean-Paul had reminded Nathan of Paris –

and of the marquise d'Orléan. He was not ready to be reminded of anything that had occurred in France. Not just yet.

Nathan had given Amy an outline of his capture, captivity and subsequent return. The details would wait for the evenings that now lay ahead of them.

When more servants were awake, Nathan sent one of them to the village to set the women to work on the fish *Sir Beville* had brought home from French waters. He intended spending the day quietly at Polrudden, learning what had been happening in his absence and getting to know his son again.

Beville was pleased to see his father at the breakfast table, but he was equally pleased to discover that the egg cooked for his breakfast had a double yolk and Jean-Paul's only one.

However, Nathan was left in no doubt about Amy's joy at having him home once more. Whenever the opportunity presented itself, she would grip his hand tightly in hers, resting her body against him when they stood close. If they were more than an arm's length apart, her eyes rarely left him and she smiled happily whenever he looked her way.

Immediately after breakfast, Nathan's father puffed into the house, out of breath and perspiring as a result of his hurried toil up the steep hill from Pentuan.

After embracing Nathan in a rare display of parental emotion, the ageing Methodist preacher held Nathan at arm's length and studied him critically.

'You're thinner, my boy, but Amy's cooking will soon put that right. When I was brought news of your safe return I fell to my knees and gave thanks to the Lord. I'd given you up for dead – indeed, so had the whole of Pentuan. The only one who refused to give up hope was Amy. She had a faith in the Lord's mercy that has humbled me. I don't mind admitting it to you. But now you're home again, and you've brought new hope to Pentuan already. The women are hurrying to work in your cellar and their men are going out seeking fish for themselves.'

Amy said nothing. No one would ever know how close she had been brought to abandoning hope by Preacher Jago and his young assistant. Today was not a day for recriminations, or to relive the nightmare memories of recent months.

But it was too soon to put aside *all* that had occurred as a result of *Sir Beville*'s capture by the French.

Shortly before noon a small boy from the village came running to the house, red-faced and important. He brought a message from Cornelius Lanyon. His sick brother had taken a sudden turn for the worse and wanted to see Nathan urgently.

Nathan had been playing with Beville and Jean-Paul on the main lawn at Polrudden. Ignoring their protests, Amy told them it was time to go inside the house for their midday meal. Nathan had told her of Pascoe Lanyon's illness and of his determination not to give in to it before he reached home. It sounded as though he had won a very narrow victory against time.

'Send Will Hodge for the physician,' Nathan called back to Amy as he hurried after the Pentuan boy. 'I doubt if he'll be able to do much for Pascoe, but he can at least ease his pain.'

Nathan was shown into the Lanyons' spotlessly clean cottage by Pascoe's pretty young wife, Rebecca. The cottage was part of the Polrudden estate. The Lanyons' father had rented it many years before and it had come to Pascoe when he reached an age to manage his own affairs.

Ducking inside the low doorway, Nathan half-expected Rebecca Lanyon to launch into a tirade against him for returning a dying husband to her. However, bitterness and anger were not ingredients of Rebecca's gentle Quaker nature. Instead, she thanked Nathan for bringing Pascoe back to Pentuan.

'Would that I might have brought a *well* husband home to you,' said Nathan gruffly, embarrassed by her genuine gratitude.

'Had you done so, you would have performed a miracle,'

replied Rebecca Lanyon surprisingly. 'Only the Lord could have made Pascoe well. He has been a sick man for a very long time. My only regret is that I haven't been allowed more years to show him loving care. He has had a hard life.'

'I've sent for the physician,' said Nathan. 'Perhaps he can do something.'

Rebecca Lanyon shook her head. 'Pascoe has lost a great deal of blood. His life rests in the palm of the Lord's hand now. When it is time the Lord will close his hand and take Pascoe to Him.'

Nathan made his way up the steep and narrow staircase to a small bedroom that was fresh and light, with pretty curtains billowing into the room at the open window.

Pascoe Lanyon lay propped up on a number of pillows in a large wood-framed bed. His eyes were closed, his face pale. He looked very very weary. Cornelius Lanyon was seated beside the bed, a blood-stained cloth in his hand. He stood up as Nathan approached the bedside.

Rebecca Lanyon murmured a quiet apology and hurried from the room with a bowl that had been standing in a corner. As she passed him, Nathan glimpsed a heavily blood-stained sheet soaking inside the bowl.

'How is he?' Nathan whispered the question to Cornelius Lanyon.

Close to tears, the young man held up the bloody cloth and shook his head. Seconds later, Pascoe's body tensed as though gripped by sudden pain and a trickle of blood escaped from the corner of his open mouth.

Cornelius Lanyon wiped the blood away gently, and his sick brother opened his eyes. He was looking directly at Nathan, but it was a few seconds before recognition came to his face.

'Nathan . . .'

There was no power in the voice, and Nathan said quickly: 'Don't try to speak. The physician will be here soon. Just rest until he arrives.'

'I must speak to you . . .' Pascoe Lanyon bubbled blood again. When his brother had wiped his lips once more,

Nathan leaned close to catch Pascoe's whispered words.

'The cottage . . . Let on three lives . . . I'm the third . . . Worried for Rebecca . . .'

Nathan's finger on the bloody lips cut off Pascoe Lanyon's laboured words. He understood the reason for the sick man's concern. It was common practice in Cornwall for the tenancy of a house or farm to be granted for the lifetime of three named persons, usually husband, wife and eldest son. Such a tenancy had been taken out on the cottage many years before by Pascoe Lanyon's father.

'Don't concern yourself with such things. I'll have another tenancy agreement drawn up to cover yourself, Rebecca and Cornelius. It will be done right away. You just work at getting well again.'

Pascoe Lanyon's eyes closed, but his hand found Nathan's fingers and squeezed them weakly.

When Dr Ellerman Scott arrived at the Lanyon cottage he spent fifteen minutes alone in the bedroom with Pascoe.

When he came downstairs his sombre demeanour paved the way for an equally grim prognosis.

Plunging bloody hands into a bowl of water placed on the kitchen table, he said: 'I'm sorry to tell you your husband is a dying man, Mrs Lanyon.'

Rebecca nodded acknowledgement of his words, her expression revealing none of her feelings. 'Can you tell me . . . how long it will be?'

Shaking water from his hands, Dr Ellerman Scott took the towel held out to him by a silent Cornelius Lanyon.

'It could be today, or tomorrow. A week at the most. He's had a massive haemorrhage of the lungs. I'm surprised it didn't occur before today. I'd say it was sheer willpower that brought him home, nothing else.'

'*God*'s will, too, Dr Ellerman Scott. I won't forget to give *Him* thanks for allowing Pascoe to spend his last days with me. If you'll excuse me, I'll go and sit with him for a while.'

When she had left the room, Dr Ellerman Scott said to Cornelius: 'I wish I could have done more for your brother, but he's too far gone for any curative known to me. I'll leave some laudanum for him, but give it to him only if he's in great pain. In his present weak state it might send him into a sleep from which he'll not wake.'

After asking Cornelius to keep him informed of his brother's condition, Nathan left the cottage with the physician. Standing by his horse, the doctor looked about him and shook his head sadly. 'It always depresses me to come here. Pentuan's dying just as surely as that young man back there. I find it very sad.'

The physician's words took Nathan by surprise. Pentuan appeared no different from the village he had left behind when he was taken prisoner. But he suddenly realised how the village must appear to anyone who did not live here. Two of the cottages stood empty and the roof of one was in urgent need of repair. At the far side of the square another heap of weed-covered rubble marked the spot where an earlier village chapel had once stood. Half a dozen fishing-boats, their timbers warped and rotten, lay against the walls of cottages. A number of fishermen were to be seen, squatting together in two separate groups, casually repairing long seine-nets and gossiping. Blue smoke from their clay pipes drifted lazily into the air to be snatched away suddenly by a light breeze. Women stood in doorways talking in loud voices to their neighbours, occasionally cackling raucously at something that was said. There were children, too, playing their own games in a number of spots about the village square.

'There's not a single cellar working,' said the observant doctor. 'It's as though the Pentuan fishermen have lost all interest in fishing.'

'They're waiting for the pilchards to arrive,' explained Nathan. 'It's what they've always done. I've tried to interest them in year-round drift fishing. I'll continue to try, but it's not easy to change a way of life that's gone on for centuries. Only a few of them go out looking for fish. The remainder prefer to sit here, waiting for the fish to come to *them*. If they don't arrive, the same fishermen swear it's the nets of drift-fishermen keeping them away.

While I've been in France things have gone from bad to worse between seiners and drift-fishermen. Now my crews won't take the boats out.'

'The Pentuan seiners will have no support from the Mevagissey fishermen for a while,' commented Dr Ellerman Scott. 'Two of the men you brought out of France are the sons of fishermen there. Right now you're everybody's hero. Take advantage of it while you can; it won't last.'

The doctor was preparing to mount his horse when the two men heard shouting coming from the direction of the square. The sound was followed by a woman's prolonged screaming.

As the villagers stopped what they had been doing, Nathan hurried to the square, closely followed by the doctor.

The screaming was coming from the home of Saul Piper. The big fisherman was notorious for his violent temper, and as Nathan drew nearer to the house he could hear Saul's voice raised in anger. The shouting was accompanied by crashing noises, as though someone was bumping heavily into furniture. The woman's screams had become sobs now, begging Saul Piper to 'Stop!'

It was evident from the continuing din that Saul Piper was not heeding his wife's pleas. Suddenly, Harriet Piper hurried from the house as fast as her crippled leg would allow. Seeing Nathan, she pushed her way through the small crowd that had already gathered outside the house and limped quickly towards him.

'Please . . . Please help. Pa's killing our Maud. Please stop him, Mr Jago.'

The noise was coming from a bedroom, and Nathan took the stairs two at a time. Sophie Piper was standing in the bedroom doorway, her back to Nathan. She had her hands up to her face and was wailing loudly.

Pushing her to one side, Nathan entered the bedroom. The room was in a shambles. A cheap wardrobe lay front down on the floor, its shattered door lying to one side. A chest of drawers had also been tipped over, and the contents were strewn about the floor. Two drawers lay in a corner of the bedroom, smashed to matchwood. There were a number of beds in the room, but not one stood upright. Clothes and bed-linen were draped everywhere.

In a corner of the room was Saul Piper. Beside himself with rage, he was cursing incoherently and kicking at a small figure who cowered behind a shattered wooden bed.

Diving across the wrecked room, Nathan wrapped his arms about the ranting fisherman and pulled him to the centre of the room.

'Calm down, Saul! Quieten down and tell me what this is about.'

'Calm down? *Calm down*?' Saul Piper struggled in vain as Nathan's hold on him tightened.

Not until Saul Piper's struggles had ceased altogether did Nathan cautiously release his grip. The big fisherman stood in the centre of the room, chest heaving, his face flushed and twitching like a madman's.

From the corner of his eye, Nathan saw a movement as Maud painfully pulled herself up from the floor, using a shattered bed for support.

'Look at her,' mouthed Saul Piper, froth forming at the corners of his mouth. 'You look at her and *then* tell me to calm down. She's brought shame and disgrace to this house.'

Saul Piper had been drinking, but he was not drunk, and his anger was all the more terrible for this.

Nathan cast a quick glance at Saul Piper's oldest daughter. What he saw both shocked and appalled him. Maud Piper had taken a dreadful beating. Her face was bloody and bruised, one eye already closing. There were marks on her body, too, clearly visible because her dress had been torn down the front, from neck to hemline.

Also clearly visible was the swelling of Maud's belly, curving from her breastbone to the loose elastic of the grey cotton drawers she wore.

'You see that? She's carrying a bastard that might have any one of a hundred fathers. Would you believe I never noticed it when I returned home? She kissed me then as though she were a loving daughter, happy to see her father returned from the dead. She even *cried*! I doubt if the tears were for me. They were because she knew full well I'd learn what she'd been up to while I've been away. I did, too. I wasn't in the Ship inn longer than half an hour when in walks a seaman from one of the boats alongside the quay, stinking with sweat and black with coal. He stands in the doorway and, for everyone to hear, calls: "Has anyone seen Maud today? She shared my blanket last night and I reckon she had her hand in my purse afore she left this morning." "Which Maud are you talking of?" I ask him, knowing but one hereabouts. At that, he laughs. "Why, the Maud as can lay sailors faster than a fish lays eggs," says he. "Maud Piper," he says.'

Saul Piper's hands were clenching and unclenching at his sides, the muscles in his arms standing out like rope.

'I hit him,' hissed the fisherman. 'Punched him in that dirty mouth of his. Then I punched him again. It took four men to hold me back. Then the landlord of the Ship inn told me the sailor had been speaking no more than the truth. While I've been away in a French prison, my daughter's become a whore. A *sailors*' whore . . .'

Saul Piper's voice broke. His face contorting with rage, he made a rush at Maud once more, but Nathan blocked his way. Fists flailing, Saul Piper tried to knock Nathan aside. A brief scuffle ensued before Nathan brought his fist up in a short, sharp punch. He caught the demented fisherman before he slumped to the ground.

'Oh, my dear Lord! You haven't killed 'n?' The cry came from Sophie Piper, still standing in the bedroom doorway.

'No, he'll be all right.'

Clearing a space with his feet, Nathan laid the unconscious form of Saul Piper gently on the floor and stood up to look at the battered girl who still clutched at the broken bed for support. 'I doubt whether Saul will be any less angry when he comes to.'

Sophie Piper wrung her hands in anguish. 'He'll kill her!

He's a good man, Mr Jago, as well you know, but when he's angry there's no reasoning with him.'

Looking from mother to pathetic, injured daughter, Nathan arrived at a quick decision. 'You'd best come up to Polrudden, Maud. We're short of servants. You can do some work for your keep until it's close to your time. We'll discuss what's best for you then.'

'Bless you, Mr Jago. You won't regret this kindness. Maud's a good girl, really – and she's not afraid of hard work.'

Sophie Piper's gratitude was coloured by more than a tinge of relief. Throughout Maud's beating Sophie had been terrified lest her daughter break down and give the true reason why she had taken to prostitution to support the family.

That night Nathan lay in bed with Amy as a summer storm grumbled out at sea, beyond St Austell Bay, and heard how close they were to financial ruin.

There was very little ready cash and the amount due from rents was negligible. They could expect no tithe-money from the fishermen of Pentuan until pilchards were seen off the Cornish coast once more. The returns from the Portgiskey fishing venture could be expected to improve a little now Nathan was on hand to order the reluctant fishermen to sea but it would be a slow and uncertain recovery, heavily dependent upon the vagaries of weather and fish.

Nathan thought it might be possible to extend his smuggling activities, but now the Royal Navy was no longer engaged against the French its ships would be used to prevent smuggling. The returns from night-trading would continue to be high – but so, too, would the risks.

Nathan and Amy had made love. Now, lying in each other's arms on the first night of Nathan's return, they should have been able to shut out the cares of the world that existed beyond the four walls of their bedroom. But they both knew the situation was more serious than it had ever been before.

'We could sell one of the boats,' suggested Amy hesitantly.

They both remembered their dreams of owning the largest fleet of drifters on the south coast. Each was equally reluctant to abandon the dream.

Nathan merely grunted by way of reply. He was thinking. It must have been twenty minutes later; Amy was about to drift off into sleep when Nathan suddenly turned and raised himself on one elbow.

'There *is* another way to earn money. A way that doesn't necessitate us giving up anything. One more prize-fight could bring in enough money to last another year.'

Fully awake instantly, Amy was horrified at the suggestion. 'You're *not* serious? You haven't fought for almost two years and have spent the last few months locked up in a prison. You're not fit enough to fight.'

'It would take no more than a couple of months' hard work to get fit again.' It seemed to Amy that Nathan was only half-listening to her. 'Two men are currently claiming the championship, Jed Kelly and Mick O'Rourke. Kelly's an old man. I beat him six years ago and could do the same again. I don't know O'Rourke. Most of his fights have been in Ireland, but he has an impressive record. If I keep clear of him and fight Kelly, I could command a purse of, say, five hundred gunieas. That should see us out of trouble for a year, at least. By then things should have improved—'

'*No*, Nathan! Remember how badly beaten you were in your last fight? You weren't recognisable for weeks.'

'But I *won*. Officially I am still the Champion of England. That's all that counts when it comes to deciding the size of a purse.'

Amy opened her mouth to argue further. Instead, she said: 'Let's not talk about it tonight, Nathan. I've longed to have you here, holding me close, ever since the night you sailed off with Louis d'Argon. Let the problems of Polrudden wait a little longer. Until morning, at least.'

Amy reached out and drew him to her, and for a long time Nathan was allowed to think of nothing but her. Later, when the storm outside had rolled away along the Channel and the only sound was Amy's deep and contented breathing, Nathan lay awake in the darkness and made plans for the recovery of Polrudden's failing fortunes.

CHAPTER THIRTEEN

Pascoe Lanyon died exactly one week after his return to his home village. For the last three days of his life he lay in a state of semi-consciousness, induced by the pain-killing opium-based laudanum.

The funeral for the unfortunate fisherman took place in St Austell church, a few miles along the Pentuan valley. Only one man from the crew of *Sir Beville* did not attend the funeral, even though most of them had been fishing the previous night.

After a brief graveside service, Nathan saw the young widow safely on her way back to Pentuan in the Polrudden gig with Cornelius, then he mounted his horse and set off on an errand of his own.

The only crew member of *Sir Beville* to miss the funeral of Pascoe Lanyon was Matthew Mitchell. Large-boned and cheerfully inoffensive, Matthew had set off for St Austell to find his wife on the day of *Sir Beville*'s return. No one from Pentuan had seen him since.

When Mary, Matthew Mitchell's wife, left Pentuan she told friends she was taking her family to relatives in St Austell, and it was to the home of Mary's father that Nathan went first.

The house was in a low-lying area close to the river, and Nathan wrinkled his nose in disgust at the summer smell coming from the water and surrounding mud. As he walked towards the door, a number of children detached themselves from a large group paddling in the dirty river and ran to the house ahead of them. While some stood at the doorway, looking wide-eyed at Nathan, others ran inside, warning the occupants they had a visitor, 'a man wearing a dark suit, and not from these parts'.

Mary Mitchell's father came to the door. Behind him a young woman no older than Mary peered at Nathan from behind a half-open inner door. There seemed to be children everywhere, crawling or running, or simply clinging to each other.

When Nathan put his question, Mary's father shook his head and looked embarrassed. 'Mary isn't staying here. She came to see me when her husband was lost, but I couldn't let her stay. Well, you can see for yourself, there's no room. I married again when Mary's mother died. Now I've got a new family to look after. We're six to a bed as it is. I had no room for five more. I sent her to her brother's house. He and I don't exactly see eye to eye and we haven't spoken a word to each other these seven years, but he's still her brother. They're the same flesh and blood. You'd best go and see him, but don't say I sent you or you'll be told nothing.'

The directions Nathan was given took him out of St Austell, to the moors north of the town, where two or three engine-house chimneys could be seen from every turn of the winding road. This was tin-mining country, and the dull thud of beam-engines and the clatter of whim and stamp were more familiar sounds than the song of birds.

These were not good times for the tin mines of central Cornwall. The demand for ore had dropped and, between the mines, bleached white heaps of spoil were rising from the open workings of china-clay diggings. The new industry already threatened to overwhelm the centuries-old tin-mining operations hereabouts. Nathan was given more than one scowling glance from dark-bearded miners as he passed on his way. They saw few riders dressed for funerals on these moors. Well-dressed strangers were more likely to be china-clay men than tinners.

146

The home of Mary Mitchell's brother was no more salubrious than his father's house. There was a similar predominance of children here, too; but, unlike his father, John Curnow would never reach a healthy middle age. Mary Mitchell's brother was suffering from lung disease, the illness that had killed the man Nathan had just seen buried.

'Mary?' The name came out as part of a hollow cough. 'I couldn't care for her here. I can't afford to keep *one* family in food, let alone *two*.' A prolonged fit of coughing interrupted the explanation, and a gaunt scarecrow of a woman appeared briefly in the kitchen doorway to look anxiously towards her husband.

When the coughing fit subsided, the man said weakly: 'We gave her and the children a meal and a bed for the night, then one of my boys showed her the way to the poorhouse. That's where you'll find her. I took no pleasure from sending my own sister to a place like that, but there was nowhere else for her.'

'Thank you . . .' Nathan hesitated for only a moment. Reaching out, he pressed a half-guinea into the sick man's hand, explaining: 'Matthew Mitchell is one of my crew, and a friend. That's for the kindness you showed in giving Mary and the family a meal and a roof for the night.'

The look of joy on the man's face as he looked at the gold coin would have been sufficient reward in itself, but as Nathan walked to his horse the man called: 'Wait! If it's Matthew you're seeking, you'll not find *him* in the poorhouse. I had news yesterday that he's lodged in the lock-up in Bodmin. He's to be taken before the magistrate and charged with an assault.'

'Matthew – an assault?' Nathan found the news hard to believe. Remarkably slow to anger, Matthew Mitchell was one of the most peaceable men Nathan had ever met.

'That's what I heard. I know no more than that.'

Wheeling his horse, Nathan guided it back to the St Austell–Bodmin road. He was undecided whether to return to St Austell or ride on to Bodmin. He chose St Austell. It was nearer, and Mary Mitchell might know something of the astonishing charges levelled at her husband.

The poorhouse in St Austell was as depressing a place as Nathan had expected it to be. Dark and airless inside, a stomach-churning smell of over-boiled cabbage hung on the air.

'Mary Mitchell?' The poorhouse master had been about to thumb through a large bound register, but he stopped when Nathan mentioned her name. 'Yes, I know her. She's working in the laundry right now. Who are you, and what's your business with her?'

'I'm Nathan Jago from Polrudden Manor. I'm here to take Mary Mitchell and her children home to Pentuan.'

'Home? She told me she has no home.'

'I own the house she lived in before coming here. She can have it back. I'm also hoping to offer her work in my fish-cellar.'

The poorhouse master's manner underwent a change. It was apparent that Nathan was a man of some substance.

'Ah! Well, there's money owing for her keep, you understand? It's not a great deal; she's a good worker. However, her two children have had to be fed. The five-year-old can be, ah . . . "prevailed upon" to unpick old rope, but there's little work can be performed by a girl of two, is there now, Mr Jago?'

'Two children? The Mitchells have four.'

'Ah . . . yes, there *were* four; but I have many mouths to feed here, Mr Jago, and more coming in every day. The two older children were old enough to make their own ways in life – under suitable supervision, of course.'

'Old enough? William Mitchell is eleven, and young Sam can be no more than ten!' Nathan was appalled.

'Eleven and *nine*, Mr Jago. Eleven and nine – and paupers. I'm responsible to the parish for what is spent here. Two healthy young lads are better in good apprenticeships than accepting the bounty of the parish. No boy can take pride in living in a poorhouse. A good apprenticeship now, that's something very different. They were fortunate; both boys were placed with the same tradesman. Not that I should take all the credit for that. The younger boy went on trial to a tannery, right here in St Austell, but whenever he stopped crying he ran away and returned here. Then Mr Furniss, blacksmith over to Bodmin, said he'd take them both. That doesn't often happen, as I explained to Mr Mitchell –'

'Matthew Mitchell's been here?'

'Oh, yes. And very abusive he was, too. I had to send for the constable to put him out. He wanted to take his wife away without paying what was owed for her keep. I told him he was lucky I didn't take him before the magistrate and charge him with failing to provide for his family. But I'm not a hard-hearted man, Mr Jago. I'm not one to add to the misfortunes of a man who's been a prisoner of the French. Half the women who apply to come here are widows of men who died fighting the French. I don't turn away any more than I have to. Ah! Here we are.'

While he was talking the poorhouse master had been thumbing through the pages of the large ledger on the table before him. Now he opened it out and ran a finger across the page. Picking up a quill pen, he dipped it in an inkwell and looked up at Nathan speculatively. Nathan returned the look with tight-lipped distaste. Sighing deeply, the poorhouse master put the quill down again.

'Mary Mitchell has paid her way, Mr Jago, but there's three pounds, seven shillings and fourpence halfpenny owing for the two boys.'

Taking out four guineas, Nathan placed the coins on the table before the poorhouse master and waited as change was carefully counted out.

'Did you tell Matthew Mitchell where his two boys had been placed?'

'Of course. It is not meant to be a secret. The whole thing was arranged in the proper manner, with the consent of the magistrate – and only a magistrate can undo it again, as I told Mr Mitchell. If he's got any sense, he'll leave the boys where they are. A good apprenticeship isn't easy to come by in these difficult times.'

Nathan doubted whether Matthew Mitchell had been any more impressed by the poorhouse master's comments on the state of the country than he was.

Taking his change, Nathan said: 'Have Mary Mitchell brought here straightaway, if you please. I have business in Bodmin today.'

'You'll not try to take the children from Mr Furniss? They are legally in his charge. Bound to him by the magistrate right here in St Austell.'

'But a magistrate can terminate the apprenticeship – with the agreement of all parties. Am I right?'

The poorhouse master nodded. 'Yes, but Mr Furniss won't allow them to leave. He needs them in his work. He's had no one since his last apprentice died.'

'I'll discuss that with Mr Furniss. Bring Mary Mitchell here, if you please.'

Mary Mitchell arrived in the poorhouse master's office hot and red-faced from working over the steaming coppers at the rear of the poorhouse. She brought with her the smell of unperfumed soap. Her arms were red to the elbow from being constantly immersed in hot water and the knuckles of her hands were worn raw by the ridges of the washboards. Clutching at her dress was Kitty, her two-year-old daughter.

When Mary Mitchell saw Nathan, her eyes lit up in pleasurable recognition. The expression was immediately replaced by embarrassment as she remembered where she was.

'I've come to fetch you out of here, Mary. Take Kitty and the boy to Polrudden. Tell Amy you'll be moving back in the empty house in Pentuan. She'll help you with some of the things you'll need. I've no doubt the neighbours in Pentuan will rally round, too. They usually do. I'm off to Bodmin to bring back William and Sam.'

Mary Mitchell's joy threatened to overwhelm her, but this, too, was fleeting.

'How will we live in Pentuan, Mr Jago? I can work with the best of them when fish are being caught, but there's not been much work lately and . . . and now that Matthew's gone again times are going to be hard. I couldn't bear to come back here again, not once I've got the boys back. I'd do away with them first.'

Tears began to course down Mary Mitchell's cheeks, and Nathan said: 'Matthew gone again? What are you talking about? He'll be back; I'll see to that.'

'No. Matthew came to see me, Mr Jago. After me thinking for so long he was dead. Suddenly, there he was. I was so happy, I cried all over him. Then, when I told him the two boys had been taken away he left me again – and I haven't seen him since. He blames me for losing the boys, Mr Jago. I know he does. But what could I do? I couldn't stop them being taken from me. I tried to, but they told me I was lucky to have bed and board for the two youngest . . .'

'Mary, get a grip on yourself.' Nathan shook the fisherman's wife gently by the shoulders. Mary Mitchell was not the most intelligent of women, but she adored her husband and children. 'Matthew hasn't left you. I thought you knew him better than even to think such a thing. He talked of nothing but you and the boys, all the time we were in France. When he left here he went to Bodmin to find the boys. There was some trouble. I don't yet know what it was all about, but he's in the lock-up there. I'm on my way to Bodmin now.'

'I knew it! I knew it!' the poorhouse master squeaked triumphantly. 'I knew he'd land himself in trouble if he went after those boys. I told him so, right here in this room. I know a violent man when I see one. I've seen too many in my time. If they want a witness over in Bodmin, I'll travel there and tell them. They'll need to pay me expenses, of course, but I consider it my bounden duty –'

'Your duty is to arrange for the release of this lady and her two children. I suggest you attend to it *immediately* – unless you've a mind to have another violent man on your hands?'

As the loquacious little poorhouse master scuttled away, Nathan reassured Mary Mitchell: 'Don't you worry; everything will be all right. Go to Polrudden first and let Amy take care of things for you. I'll be home with Matthew and the boys just as soon as I've got everything sorted out.'

Nathan knew he had been wildly optimistic when reassuring Mary Mitchell. Matters involving magistrates were never straightforward or swiftly resolved. The more he thought about things as he rode towards Bodmin, the more pessimistic he became about the outcome of his self-imposed task.

It had been Nathan's intention to go first to the lock-up, to learn from Matthew Mitchell why he had been taken into custody. However, he had hardly entered Bodmin Town when he espied a sign advertising *'Jankin Furniss, blacksmith and farrier'*.

Reining in his horse before the smithy, Nathan sat for a few moments, wondering whether or not to call here first. From within he could hear the ringing of a heavy hammer upon metal. Suddenly a boy backed out through the smithy doorway, struggling to drag a length of heavy linked chain after him.

The clothing worn by the boy was filthy dirty and in tatters. It was not until the child turned to line the chain up with a fathom length, marked on the wall, that Nathan recognised William Mitchell, Matthew's eleven-year-old son.

William looked up when Nathan called but, although he knew Nathan well, only the briefest flicker of recognition crossed his pinched face. It was immediately replaced by an expression that Nathan interpreted as fear. There was bruising on William's face, ugly dark bruising on the cheekbone beneath his left eye that even the grime could not hide.

'What's the matter, William? You know me, surely? I'm here to see about taking you home . . .'

William's reaction was not at all the one Nathan had expected. The boy backed away from him until he reached the wide doorway of the smithy, then turned and fled inside.

As Nathan dismounted and tossed the reins of his horse over a hitching-rail, he heard a man's voice raised in anger within the smithy.

It was both hot and gloomy inside Jankin Furniss's premises. As Nathan stood inside the doorway, allowing his eyes to adjust to the poor light, the blacksmith came towards him, wiping great hands on a stained leather apron. The blacksmith was a big man, judged by any standards. An inch or two taller than Nathan, he was at least three times Nathan's girth about the waist. His head was quite bald and glistening with perspiration. The lack of hair here was more than compensated by a thick curly beard that enveloped the lower half of his face, hiding his thick neck and much of his great chest.

'Good day to you, squire. What can I do for you? Shoes for your horse, is it? Or something for the house or farm? Whatever it is, you've come to the right place. There's no finer blacksmith in mid-Cornwall than Jan Furniss. William! Where *is* that damned boy?' The blacksmith's voice was as big as the man. 'Come here and dust off a seat for the gentleman. I crave your pardon, squire. William isn't used to my ways yet, and he's inclined to be lazy. He'll learn, as he gets more familiar with my belt. Boys always do, given time.'

'It's William I'm here to talk about – he and his young brother.'

'Oh?' The blacksmith's manner underwent an immediate change, his whole being bristling with belligerence. 'I've had their father here to "talk" about his sons. I'll tell you the same as I told him: there's nothing to discuss. One's a good-for-nothing young layabout. The other's a snivelling little brat who spends half the day and most of the night crying for his ma. But, whatever they are, they're mine now, and they'll both learn my ways, no matter how many strappings it takes. That's all I'm saying. Now you can get out of here, or you'll end up in the lock-up, same as their father.'

'I was on my way to see him when I saw your sign. I still can't imagine what he's doing in the lock-up. I heard he'd assaulted someone, but that doesn't sound like Matthew Mitchell. Who is he supposed to have assaulted?'

'Me. He assaulted me – and if you're calling me a liar, then you'll likely end up being charged with the same. The constable's a friend of mine.'

It was what Nathan had suspected ever since he first saw the blacksmith. Matthew Mitchell had refused to leave when ordered to do so by this bullying giant of a man. He had taken a beating in front of his sons and now faced a false charge of assault to justify the injuries the blacksmith had inflicted upon him.

'Matthew Mitchell never assaulted anyone in his life, as I'll be happy to inform the magistrate.'

'You'll tell him nothing,' the big man grinned. 'Unless to plead "guilty". You and the boys' father ought to be ashamed of yourselves, trying to snatch two young apprentices from their master, and assaulting me for doing no more than to rescue them from the poorhouse.'

The big blacksmith reached out for Nathan, but he was too slow and grabbed air. Nathan stepped out of reach and planted two good punches into the other man's midriff.

Either blow would have winded most men, but Jankin Furniss did no more than grunt, as much in annoyance as with pain.

He came on again, this time at a lumbering run. Once again Nathan landed two solid punches, but they were no more effective than before and he only just avoided being wrapped in the blacksmith's great arms.

Twice more the big man rushed at Nathan, and twice Nathan managed to step aside. Then the blacksmith seized a long bar of iron, one end of which had been buried in the coals of the furnace. It emerged glowing an angry red, spitting fragments of clinging ash.

Wielding the rod as though it were a spear, Jankin Furniss drove Nathan before him to the far end of the smithy until Nathan could retreat no farther. His back to the wall, Nathan dodged first one way and then the other as the red-hot bar was prodded towards him. Then Furniss made a determined lunge that singed Nathan's jacket and seared the woodwork no more than an inch from his body.

Lying on a shelf, near at hand, Nathan saw a newly made short-handled cobbing hammer. Snatching it up, he swung it through the air and brought it down on the iron bar with a metallic clang that jarred his arm to the shoulder and caused him to drop the hammer from tingling fingers. The blow had the same effect on the blacksmith, and Furniss loosed the fiery weapon.

Nathan came away from the wall punching hard and this time it was he who drove his strong opponent before him. They had reached the centre of the smithy before Furniss stopped retreating. Holding his arms wide, he took a quick pace forward and succeeded in trapping Nathan in a body-hug that squeezed much of the air from Nathan's body. Nathan fought hard to free himself, but the bearded smith was a skilled wrestler. Tucking his chin in tight to Nathan's shoulder, he shrugged himself into an advantageous position and began to increase the pressure on his opponent.

Unable to throw a good punch – indeed, scarcely able to breathe – Nathan knew he must take the initiative rapidly or lose the fight. Bringing up his arms with some difficulty, he tangled his fingers in the blacksmith's thick beard and heaved. For long, long seconds nothing happened, and it seemed Nathan's desperate bid to free himself had failed. Then, agonisingly slowly, Nathan began forcing the other man's head back.

The blacksmith was grunting with pain now, but not until he was staring back at the wall behind him did he ease his rib-crushing grip.

Sucking air into aching lungs, Nathan pulled his right hand free of the tangled beard and brought across two crashing punches to the blacksmith's throat.

Dropping his arms, Jankin Furniss staggered back, choking for breath. Giving the other man no respite, Nathan stepped in and delivered a barrage of blows, the like of which had felled better men than the blacksmith. Even the protection of the thick beard could not soften the effect of the punches. Rocked back on his heels, Jankin Furniss was floored by a straight right-hander. He dropped to his knees and when he tried to rise again Nathan felled him with a punch behind the ear that would have pole-axed a steer.

The blacksmith fell full-length on his face and lay twitching helplessly on the hard-packed earth of the smithy floor.

Looking about him, Nathan saw the wide eyes of William Mitchell staring up at him from beneath the blacksmith's workbench.

'You can come out, William; he'll not hurt you now. But where's your brother?'

'Down the cellar, over there. We'll need a light.'

Crawling out from beneath the bench, William Mitchell reached up and took a candle from a shelf. Lighting it from the blacksmith's forge, he handed it to Nathan. Crossing to a trap-door set in the floor against a side wall, William worked away at a stiff iron bolt and eventually pulled it free. With Nathan's help he swung open the trap-door to reveal a flight of granite steps. Only four steps were visible, the remainder disappearing beneath a sea of coal that reached the roof of the cellar farther back and sloped shallowly forward to the steps.

Lying on his stomach on the coal and blinking up at the candlelight in terror, was Sam Mitchell.

Nathan remembered the boy as a bright and cheerful nine-year-old, his mother's undoubted favourite, and spoiled by all the fishermen who worked from Portgiskey. The small boy in the cellar was covered from head to toe with coal dust, only his eyes and the paths carved down his cheeks by tears showing white. Sam's clothes were even more ragged than those of his brother. As the small boy crawled backwards farther into the cellar, as though trying to escape, Nathan thought he could see blood glistening through the dust and rags on the boy's back.

'It's all right, Sam.' William Mitchell was down the steps and in the cellar while Nathan was still taking in the boy's condition. 'It's Mr Jago, from Polrudden. He's come to take us home. To Ma – and Pa.'

Taking his young brother's hand, William hauled Sam forward until Nathan was able to lift him from the cellar to the smithy.

Sam Mitchell made no attempt to stand, or even to speak. He sat in the middle of the floor, tears coursing unchecked down his dirty face.

'How long has Sam been down there?' Nathan was puzzled by the small boy's unnatural silence and he put the question to William.

'Since the day before yesterday. He'd been beaten by Mr Furniss and he wet the bed during the night. Mr Furniss said if he couldn't behave no better than a little animal he ought to be treated like one. Sam cried most of the first day, and part of the night, but he hasn't made a sound since. I was scared he might have died, but when I tried to look Mr Furniss took his belt off to me.'

Nathan felt the anger rising in him as he crossed the smithy to where Jankin Furniss was beginning to stir. Taking the blacksmith beneath the arms, Nathan dragged him across the floor and propped him with his back against the smithy wall. Looking around, he found a bucket. Filling it with water from the barrel standing outside the door, Nathan dashed its contents in Jankin Furniss's face.

The blacksmith began spluttering and coughing, but when he made a move to get up Nathan flung him none too gently back against the wall again. 'You'll stay there until I've said my piece, Jankin Furniss.'

The blacksmith glared up at Nathan malevolently, but said nothing.

'I've come here to take these two boys home, where they belong.'

Furniss started to say something, but Nathan silenced him with a glance. 'Oh, yes, I realise they're bound to you as apprentices, but a visit to the magistrate will soon put that right. I suggest you make that visit, right away.'

'What if I refuse?'

Squatting down before the bearded blacksmith, Nathan said: 'If you refuse, three things are going to happen to you. First, I'm going to hoist you to your feet and give you a thrashing that Bodmin will talk about for years to come. Second, I'll take you before a magistrate and charge *you* with assault, both on me and on that nine-year-old boy over there. Third, just in case the first two don't put you out of business, I'll see that you never get another day's work from the gentry of Cornwall. If you doubt me, then you'll be calling Nathan Jago a liar, and I'll thrash you anyway.'

The threat to put Jankin Furniss out of business was an empty one, but the blacksmith was not to know this. In any case, Nathan had clinched the matter by the use of his own name.

'You're Nathan Jago? The champion prize-fighter?'

'The same. Now, go off and find your constable friend. I'm sure he'll take you to a magistrate right away, even though it is late in the day. While you're about it you can tell him you made a mistake when you charged Matthew Mitchell with assault. Make the excuse that you didn't realise all the circumstances of the matter when you laid your charge, or something similar, but that you'd now like to return the children to their father.'

Rising to his feet unsteadily, Jankin Furniss looked crest-fallen. 'I'm sorry we had to meet in such circumstances, Mr Jago. You've always been a hero of mine –'

Cutting the blacksmith's apology short, Nathan said curtly: 'Get on your way, Furniss – and don't dawdle. I intend bathing young Sam while you're gone. If his back is as bad as I fear it to be, I'm likely to forget all my promises and come looking for you.'

It was after midnight when Nathan reached home, having seen the Mitchell family reunited in their Polrudden-owned cottage in Pentuan. As Nathan had anticipated, once the plight of Mary Mitchell and her family became known, the villagers came forward with gifts of furniture, bedding, pots and other household items, some of them previously owned by Mary Mitchell and sold by her when she left the village.

Sam Mitchell's back was far worse than Nathan had realised at the time he made his deal with Jankin Furniss, and the boy would require a physician's attention at the earliest opportunity. His mental state had also caused some concern. He had not said a word all the way from Bodmin to Pentuan, even when his father held him in his arms on Nathan's horse along the way.

But then, when the party reached the cottage in Pentuan, and the small boy saw his mother standing in the doorway, he called out an agonised '*Ma!*' and, sliding from the horse, ran to her. Once in her arms he sobbed out his story, while Mary Mitchell held him to her and shed her own tears over the small boy.

Nathan rode home happy in the knowledge that the Mitchell family was reunited in its own home. He knew that time and love would one day heal the wounds that scarred young Sam's body and mind.

CHAPTER FOURTEEN

During the summer of 1814, the Portgiskey drifters caught enough fish to stave off the threat of imminent disaster and raise Nathan's hopes that better times were on their way.

One day in August, as Nathan eased *Sir Beville* slowly in towards the Portgiskey quay, the boat low in the water with a good catch of fish, Preacher Jago came from the fish-cellar and stood on the quayside. There was an onshore breeze blowing and, holding on his wide-brimmed hat with one hand, the preacher used the other to catch the mooring-rope thrown to him by Saul Piper. Looping the rope over a granite bollard, Josiah Jago greeted Nathan as he stepped ashore.

'You've had a good night's fishing. With what your other boats have already brought in you'll be able to keep the women in your cellar happy.'

Nathan nodded. 'All the boats are doing well. The seiners netted enough off Pentuan beach yesterday to keep them busy for the rest of the month. You'll have a happy flock, Father.'

'It's a sadly divided flock, Nathan. It distresses me greatly. You know how hard I've fought to maintain the circuit in the face of opposition from the Established Church, local landowners and magistrates. It seems I've won through only to have my efforts undone by the Methodist movement itself. I've had a letter of censure from Conference. They've ordered me to comply with their directives – most of which are impracticable here in Cornwall. I sometimes wonder whether Conference and those of us who preach on the circuits are occupying the same world.'

'You may have a valid point there,' agreed Nathan. 'But you didn't come to Portgiskey at this time of the morning to tell me about the troubles of the Methodist Church – and you certainly aren't here to see the sunrise.' He jerked his head to where thick grey cloud hid the sky from view.

'No, you're right, of course. I came seeking your aid, in urging one of your crew members to show a little Christian kindness and forgiveness to one of his family.'

Nathan might have argued that it was a pity no one had made the same plea to Josiah Jago when Nathan was a boy. The absence of these two attributes, together with the preacher's preoccupation with his church, had resulted in Nathan running away to sea when only fifteen years of age. Instead Nathan said: 'If you're talking of Saul Piper, you're wasting your breath. Maud is eating her heart out for her

160

pa, but he doesn't want to know her. At least, he says he doesn't.'

'I'm not talking of the Piper family,' declared Josiah Jago sharply. 'Maud Piper *chose* to become a harlot. She must bear the shame her way of life has brought upon her. My concern is for Lavinia Hockin, a staunch member of the Methodist Church all her life. She moved into Obadiah's cottage and gave up her own home when she thought him dead – as, indeed, we all did. Now he's treating her cruelly as a result.'

Nathan frowned. 'I heard she smashed much of his furniture, searching for hidden money. You can hardly blame him for being angry.'

'It's perfectly natural for a woman in a new house to want her own belongings about her,' replied Josiah Jago defensively. 'Obadiah is not justified in turning her out of the house and forcing her to sleep in his pigsty.'

Nathan repressed a smile at the thought of the prim and fussy Miss Lavinia Hockin bedding down in a pigsty. Maintaining a straight face, Nathan agreed that perhaps Obadiah Hockin's treatment of his sister was unduly harsh

'Then, you'll have a word with Obadiah about the matter? I've tried to talk to him, but he isn't a member of my church, and he told me it was none of my business.'

This time Nathan did smile. His father was inclined to be pompous and was not used to being told to 'mind his own business'. Obadiah Hockin was notoriously irascible and no respecter of another's standing in the community.

'It isn't often we see your father down here at Portgiskey,' commented Obadiah Hockin casually, as Nathan sat down on a pile of nets stacked nearby for repair, 'though I seem to remember he used to spend a lot of time with fishermen when he was gathering a following for Wesley. I'd say that either he's worried too many folk are listening to that new young preacher or he's wanting something. Would I be right?'

'On both counts, Obadiah. What he wants today is for

me to talk to you about your sister.'

'Ha!' Obadiah snorted, causing sparks to leap from his pipe. 'I thought that was the way of it. I gave him short shrift when he mentioned her to me the other day.'

'Is it true you're making her sleep in the pigsty?'

'And why not?' Obadiah Hockin took the pipe from his mouth and stabbed the stem in Nathan's direction. 'Let me tell you, it's no more than she deserves. I came home to find all my furniture broken up and thrown out for firewood. Even the feather mattress I'd had these forty-odd years had been ripped apart. That woman's lucky to have *any* roof over her head at night – and I've told her so.'

'Even so, Obadiah, she's not a young woman . . .'

Obadiah Hockin snorted again, before ramming the pipe back in his mouth. 'Lavinia would bite the head off anyone who told her she was getting old, especially if it happened to be a man. She thinks she's ageless. Happen she's right. The Lord must know that if He has her up there with Him she'll soon be telling Him His business – and she'd terrify the very horns off the Devil. No, Nathan, I reckon I've got things just about right. While I turn her out of the house at night I've got the whip hand over her. She'll cook my meals, wash my clothes and clean about the house – and all without exercising that sharp tongue, for fear I'll throw her out altogether. If I relent too soon and give her bedspace, she'll go back to her old ways. She's so domineering she'd soon drive *me* out to the pigsty. No, I'll bide my time; it'll do us all nothing but good.'

Nathan grinned. 'You know your sister better than I do, Obadiah. You will take her back in the house . . . eventually?'

Obadiah leaned over the side of the quay and knocked the plug of charred tobacco from his pipe into the sea.

'I'll have to. She mutters about me half the night and it's keeping my old sow awake. The sow's losing weight – and I've already taken orders for pork for Christmas.'

Obadiah Hockin came close to a smile. 'If Lavinia only knew it, she's a sight nearer to my money than she ever was when she smashed up my furniture. It's in a pot, buried not six inches under her bed, in the sty.'

Nathan was still chuckling when he set off from Portgiskey to go home to Polrudden. The tide was low enough to enable him to scramble over the rocks and take the short route, via Pentuan beach. Early-rising seine-fishermen were already here, preparing to put out in their boats. They would scoop in the fish that heaved and writhed in great shoals, held within the encircling nets secured just offshore.

The scene pleased Nathan as a fisherman. There was also the knowledge that as owner of the manor of Polrudden he would receive a tithe payment equal to one-twentieth the value of all fish caught. It was considerably less than the tithe imposed by the previous tithe-owner. Being a fisherman himself, Nathan was aware of the hardships brought about by tithes that were set too high.

When Nathan was halfway along the long Pentuan beach, Cornelius Lanyon caught up with him, out of breath as a result of running from Portgiskey.

'Do you mind if I walk to Polrudden with you, Nathan?'

'Of course not, but what business do you have there so early in the day?'

It was only a few minutes after seven o'clock.

'I'd like to have a talk with Maud – Maud Piper. That's if Mrs Jago won't mind.' The informality that Cornelius enjoyed with Nathan did not extend to the mistress of Polrudden.

'Amy won't mind,' said Nathan, curbing his curiosity. 'But I'm not certain Maud will be about just yet.'

'Oh, she will,' replied Cornelius confidently. 'She gets up early to feed the chickens, geese and pigs on the home farm. She enjoys that chore. The Pipers never kept any animals or chickens in Pentuan.'

Nathan became even more curious. Cornelius knew a great deal more about Maud's daily routine than he did himself. When he commented on this, the seventeen-year-old fisherman became aggressively defensive.

'I've known Maud since we were both children. Our homes were close and there's only a couple of years between us. She's *not* a bad girl, Nathan. No matter what Preacher Jago and the others say. I've heard rumours of why she did . . . what she did, but *she* won't tell the truth of it, so I've no intention of repeating village gossip. There's no sense causing more trouble than there's been already. Maud thinks the world of her pa. It broke her heart to have him turn her out the way he did. I've tried talking to him, but he says he doesn't want to listen – though I know he's as unhappy about things as she is.'

The aggressiveness seeped away from Cornelius Lanyon as he talked and, without looking at Nathan, he explained apologetically: 'Maud's not had much of a life, really. Being the oldest, she's always been expected to help bring up the others. As a matter of fact she's done a sight more than her mother, but *I* wouldn't tell Maud that. When we were both kids, she managed to get away from the family sometimes. We'd go up on the cliffs above Portgiskey and tell each other what we hoped to do when we grew up. She'd see a ship passing by offshore and tell me how much she'd like to sail off to somewhere exciting. Africa, the West Indies, Australia, the Americas – she didn't care much, just so long as it was a place where she wouldn't have the responsibility of her family. She envied Amy – Mrs Jago – when she was living at Portgiskey with her father. Mrs Jago enjoyed more freedom as a girl than anyone else in Pentuan. Some folk might have looked down on Ned Hoblyn as a smuggler, but Maud would have loved to be able to help him as Amy did.'

Cornelius Lanyon looked at Nathan self-consciously. 'It were all nonsense, of course. We both knew we'd never go far from Pentuan, or do very much with our lives.'

Cornelius Lanyon was silent for a while, frowning in concentration as he tried to find the words he wanted to say. 'Now poor Maud's gone and landed herself in a worse mess than she was in before. It's not fair, Nathan. She doesn't deserve such trouble. Now we're both more or less alone, I . . . I'd like to help her.'

'You're *both* alone?' Nathan looked at Cornelius sharply. 'What about Rebecca? I thought she was looking after you.'

'Not any more. Her parents came to see her when they heard Pascoe had died. They said it wasn't right for her to be living in the house with me. They persuaded Rebecca to go home with them. I think she really *wanted* to get back to that Quaker religion of theirs. She wasn't happy leaving it in the first place, but she loved Pascoe too much to give *him* up. When she realised the only way to get him was to leave her own church, she defied her parents and married him. This was the first time she'd seen either of them since. Perhaps her going home is for the best, really. She was a good wife to Pascoe. I wouldn't have wanted her to be unhappy for the rest of her life because of it.'

'I think you'd better look in at the kitchen for some breakfast when we reach Polrudden. I doubt if you'll cook any for yourself when you reach home.'

'I don't want no breakfast, Nathan,' Cornelius Lanyon said hurriedly. 'I just want to talk to Maud for a while, that's all.'

The two fishermen walked on in silence for a while. Then the muscles on Cornelius Lanyon's face began twitching nervously and suddenly he blurted out: 'I'm going to ask Maud to marry me.'

Nathan frowned. 'Are you quite certain that's what you want? Maud is only fifteen and she's carrying another man's child inside her. That's a lot of responsibility for a seventeen-year-old to take on.'

'I'll be eighteen in a couple of months – and what will happen to Maud when the baby comes if I'm not able to look after her? If she can't give the name of its father to the magistrate, she'll be committed to prison as a common whore, you know that. I won't see that happen to her. I'll take on the baby as my own. We'll be as happy a family as any other in Pentuan, you'll see.'

Deeply moved by Cornelius Lanyon's concern for the

pregnant girl, Nathan asked: 'Does Maud know of your plans?'

Cornelius Lanyon shook his head. 'I tried to talk about it when we were together the other evening, but she wouldn't listen. That's why I'm coming to Polrudden this morning. If I speak to her when she's carrying out her chores, she can't just run off. She's *got* to listen to what I have to say.'

They were in sight of Polrudden Manor now. The home farm was a little distance away from the road. Resting a hand on Cornelius Lanyon's shoulder, Nathan said: 'If you're quite certain you know what you want, then I wish you luck, Cornelius. Whatever happens, remember *I'm* on your side. Amy will be, too, when I tell her what you're doing. You have the cottage in the village to take Maud to, and I'll smooth things over with Saul if he tries to be difficult about a wedding. Away you go now – and come to Polrudden afterwards to tell me how you've got on.'

Maud Piper was already feeding the chickens by the time Cornelius reached the home farm. He stood watching her for some minutes, without being noticed. She was heavily pregnant now, the developing child seemingly grossly out of proportion to her young, thin body.

As she scattered grain for the hens and they pecked and quarrelled around her feet, Maud spoke to them constantly. Chiding the greedy birds, she ensured that her particular favourites did not go short. Suddenly she looked up and saw Cornelius watching her. Delight showed on her face before a more guarded expression took its place.

Maud knew he had been fishing and she asked: 'What are you doing up here, Cornelius Lanyon? Have you no home to go to?'

'I've got a cottage, Maud. But it's no home now.'

The look Maud gave him was filled with genuine sympathy. 'Poor Cornelius. You'll have to find some nice girl to look after you. There's more than one in the village would make you a good wife – or you can look to Mevagissey. They say there are two girls for every man there and they fight each other for husbands.'

'I've found the girl I want to marry, Maud, and it'll come as no surprise to your ma. I was five and you were three when I told her I'd marry you one day.'

Maud Piper's expression changed and she resumed feeding the chickens, scattering the seed unnecessarily far and wide. 'A lot has happened since then. *Too* much. *This,* for instance.' She patted the lump that distended her young body.

'The baby makes no difference to the way I feel, Maud. I told you that the other night.'

'You said a lot of foolish things the other night, Cornelius Lanyon. Things you'd best be forgetting. If I didn't have some man's bastard inside me, things might have been different. As it is . . .!'

Maud Piper upended the bucket, and the chickens fought noisily over the last of the grain. 'Come up to Polrudden and I'll see if I can beg some breakfast for you – or you can have mine. I'll not eat it. Just wait while I put this bucket away first.'

Home Farm was no longer occupied, although animals were still kept there. The farmhouse was a store for produce and hay, and it was to this building that Maud returned her bucket, placing it upon a nearly empty grain-sack.

The full sacks were piled high upon each other, and Maud asked Cornelius to pull one of them down for her to open, ready for the evening feeding.

Cornelius did as she asked. Cutting the string with his fisherman's knife he folded back the opening of the sack to make the grain more readily accessible.

He had closed the door behind him to keep the hens from the food-store and it was dark inside, sacks and hay being piled high against the small and dirty windows.

Slipping the knife back inside its sheath, Cornelius turned and bumped heavily against Maud. He put his hands out to steady her and unexpectedly found himself holding her. Maud laughed, but the sound died in her throat when she looked up into his face.

'No, Cornelius . . .'

Her protest ended as Cornelius's mouth came down hard upon hers. For some minutes she struggled against him, but the struggles grew gradually weaker and then her arms went about him, holding him to her.

There was a sound from the room above them and their mouths parted. Laughing shakily, Maud put her cheek against his. 'It's only an old rat. He lives up there. I've seen him once or twice.'

Cornelius Lanyon said nothing. Still holding Maud, he guided her clumsily backwards to the hay that filled half the room.

As Maud began to protest softly, she caught her foot against a small pile of folded sacks and fell back in the hay. Cornelius fell with her. He kissed her again, and for a few more minutes she responded. Then his hands began to explore her body and she stiffened against him. She made no move to stop him until his traversing fingers began to draw responses from her body.

Gripping her wrist, she whispered: 'No, Cornelius. Please don't.'

She tried to wriggle clear of him, but Cornelius was thoroughly aroused now. Breaking her grip, he pushed her back in the hay and rolled on to her, the weight of his body pinning her down.

Maud continued to struggle against him in silence for what seemed many long minutes – and then suddenly she began to cry.

Her tears proved more effective than all her struggles had been. Pushing away from her, Cornelius rose to his feet abruptly. He stood above her, tucking a rough shirt inside his trousers, a wide variety of emotions fighting for control of his face.

Maud rose awkwardly to her knees, straightening her dress about her. She looked up at Cornelius, and the tears on her cheeks shamed him. But it was she who apologised.

'I . . . I'm sorry, Cornelius. You have every right to

expect to take what you want from me. You can. You *still* can, if you want to. But please be kind. Don't *use* me. I've been used by too many men . . .'

As she bowed her head, Cornelius dropped to the hay beside her and his arms went about her once more. 'I'm the one who should be saying I'm sorry, Maud. I behaved like an animal, and you so big with child, too.'

She looked up again. Reassured by what she saw, she leaned against him. 'I'm only seven months gone. It will be all right, if you're gentle.'

Cornelius kissed the top of her head. 'No, Maud. I can wait – at least, until we're married.'

She pulled away from him then. 'Now you're being foolish again . . .'

Another kiss effectively silenced her, and he whispered against her cheek: 'I'm not being foolish, and I'll not take "No" for an answer. I know what you've done. More important, I know *why* you did it. The *real* reason. You see, the serving-woman in the Ship inn is a cousin of mine. She came to Pascoe's funeral and told me of serving drinks to your ma, after it was thought your pa and the rest of us were lost with *Sir Beville*.'

Maud looked up at Cornelius, her eyes wide with alarm. 'You haven't said anything about this to Pa?'

Cornelius Lanyon shook his head, and Maud's whole body sagged in relief. 'Thank God! You know Pa's temper. He'd kill Ma if he knew everything that happened while he was away. You promise you won't tell him?'

'I promise – even though it means *you* taking all the blame for what happened. But I'll not let you go to prison for having a bastard child. I'll promise to say nothing to your pa – but only if *you* promise to marry me.'

'Cornelius, it's madness. The baby . . .'

'The baby will know only one father – me. Isn't that better than have it grow up knowing the truth?'

Maud knew she should hold out against Cornelius. To build a marriage on such shaky foundations was a certain recipe for disaster. But Maud Piper was only fifteen years old. The thought of *having* a baby was frightening enough. What must inevitably follow the birth of a bastard terrified her.

'I love you, Maud.'

She nodded. 'I know. I love you, too. I always have.'

'Then, you'll marry me?'

She nodded, and suddenly it felt as though a great and terrible burden had been lifted from her. 'I'll make you a good wife, Cornelius. You'll never regret marrying me, I promise you.'

As Cornelius held her tight, Maud made a silent oath to keep her promise. She prayed also that Cornelius might still believe in her, and love her, when they walked together along the Pentuan street and met up with sailors who crewed the colliers from south Wales.

CHAPTER FIFTEEN

Cornelius Lanyon and Maud Piper were married in church in St Austell on the first day of September 1814. It was a quiet wedding. Even the church bells, customarily rung on such occasions, were silent. Maud's family did not attend the church, Nathan performing Saul Piper's duties in giving away the bride.

Saul Piper had been opposed to the wedding until Nathan pointed out the consequences to Maud if her child were born out of wedlock. The subsequent magistrate's hearing would bring disgrace upon the whole Piper family. Saul Piper had finally given his grudging consent, but he would not allow Maud's mother or sisters to attend the wedding. The remainder of the crew of *Sir Beville* was there, as were Amy and the two young boys from Polrudden.

Ignoring the sly looks and knowing winks occasioned by Maud's obvious 'condition', Nathan took the whole party into the nearby Queen's Head inn. Here, in a private room, he treated the newlyweds and their few wedding guests to as fine a wedding breakfast as they could have wished for. Afterwards Nathan let Cornelius drive Maud home to Pentuan in the fast gig while he followed on with the others, riding on a cart from the home farm which had brought produce to the town earlier in the day.

It was a happy family group which reached Polrudden at dusk, with Jean-Paul cradled in Amy's arms and Nathan holding a happy Beville. The young French boy was looked upon as one of the family by both Nathan and Amy now. As they approached Polrudden, Nathan and the boys were singing a song with mildly bawdy words which Nathan had learned in London some years before. Neither of the young boys understood the words, but the song had a catchy melody and they joined in with gusto, spurred on by Amy's amused disapproval.

The singing died away as the wagon turned into the Polrudden driveway. A large and impressive coach stood before the front door of the house. Only Jean-Paul, who had his back to the house, continued singing in a loud but unmusical voice.

'Who can that be?' Amy put the question to Nathan, but he was as puzzled as she was.

The maid who came out to meet the wagon was able to throw very little light on the identity of the visitors. 'They're *foreigners*, Master,' she replied, in answer to Nathan's question. 'They asked for you in English, all right, but they speak among themselves just like those French people we had here after the ship was wrecked down by the quarry.'

The servant's words broke the happy mood for the day. Both Amy and Nathan were reminded that Jean-Paul was *not* a Jago, but heir to a dukedom, with his roots in France.

'Take the boys to their bedroom,' Nathan said to the maid. 'We'll go in and find out who they are.'

The sitting-room where the unexpected guests had been left was in near-darkness, no servant having been in to light candles and ward off approaching nightfall. As Nathan and Amy entered the room, a man rose to his feet and advanced to greet them.

'M'sieur Jago. I am honoured to meet you once more. I am Armand, duc de Sauvigny. We last met in Paris, at the court of King Louis. And this must be your charming wife. The comte d'Argon has spoken often about her beauty. I must confess I have been eager to make her acquaintance.'

Bowing low over Amy's hand, the Frenchman murmured: 'I thought Louis must be exaggerating when he spoke of you. Now I can see he was unusually modest in his praise. I am delighted to meet you, Madame Jago. Allow me to introduce the two ladies who have accompanied me on my long journey from Paris.'

Nathan had been aware of two others in the room and realised they were women, but they were both seated well away from the windows and their faces could not be seen.

While the duc de Sauvigny was talking to Amy, Nathan took a tinderbox from a cupboard in the room and began lighting candles. His back was to the occupants of the room when the duc de Sauvigny began his introductions.

'This is my wife, Eleanor, and the other lady is Henrietta, marquise d'Orléan.'

At the mention of the name, Nathan swung round so quickly he dropped a number of unlighted candles to the floor.

Henrietta was standing before Amy, but she was smiling across the room at Nathan, in a manner that caused Amy to cut short her murmured words of greeting.

It was doubtful whether Henrietta noticed. Advancing across the room, she took both Nathan's hands in her own: 'Nathan, my dear, it is *wonderful* to see you once again.'

The ensuing embrace and the kisses Henrietta planted on each of Nathan's cheeks contained far more ardour than etiquette demanded, and her travelling companions both looked for Amy's reaction.

Nathan had also been taken by surprise by Henrietta's warm greeting, but when her lips were close to his ear she whispered urgently: 'Whatever is said, *do not allow Jean-Paul to leave Polrudden.*'

Before Nathan's astonishment could betray her, the marquise d'Orléan turned to the others, her hand linked with Nathan's.

'The debt owed by France to Nathan has been recognised by King Louis, but Nathan is also my special hero. When my carriage was attacked by a Paris mob he fought them off, and probably saved my life. I will always be deeply grateful to him.'

The duc and duchesse de Sauvigny murmured polite phrases, expressing admiration for Nathan and contempt for the lawless bands who still roamed France's capital city. Amy said nothing. Instead, she watched Henrietta. She wondered what form the French woman's 'gratitude' had taken when she and Nathan were together in France.

After a brief, awkward silence, during which Nathan tried once more to grasp the import of Henrietta's warning, he remembered his duties as a host. 'I'm sorry, I'm forgetting my manners. We've just returned from the wedding of one of the crew who was imprisoned with me in France. Please sit down and I'll have drinks brought in. You'll also be hungry. I'm curious to know why you're here, but questions can wait until later. You'll be staying at Polrudden, of course?'

Amid protests that it had not been the intention of the party from Paris to impose upon Nathan's generosity, a maid was summoned and instructed to prepare rooms. Will Hodge, the Polrudden groom, began to unload the carriage and attend to the horses, and suddenly Polrudden was the scene of more activity than it had known for very many months.

While the visitors were settling into their rooms, Nathan went in search of Amy.

He found her in the kitchen, supervising the servants who were in a fluster about preparing and serving food to nobility – albeit *French* nobility. A French maid was here, too, doing her best to overcome the barrier of language and explain what food the duc and duchesse de Sauvigny liked best, and how it should be prepared.

Nathan's presence in the kitchen was ignored by Amy until he said he wanted to discuss something with her. Giving him a look that would have frozen a fish, she told him she was too busy, adding: 'I've got to prepare a meal for our visitors. then perhaps your fine lady-friend will be "grateful" to me, too.'

Taking a bowl of batter from a servant-girl who was showing more interest in the conversation of the master and mistress of Polrudden than in her allotted task, Amy began beating the batter furiously.

Rescuing the bowl, Nathan handed it back to the servant. Taking Amy by the arm, he led her from the kitchen and through the back door, aware that everyone, including the French maid, was smiling knowingly.

Once in the garden, Nathan led Amy away from the house, saying: 'If I didn't know you better, I'd think you were jealous!'

Amy's derisive snort caused a panic-stricken fluttering among the birds settled for the night in a nearby dovecote. 'I'm not jealous,' she lied. 'I don't *care* what you did in France – but I don't want any of your French . . . *mistresses* here at Polrudden. This is *my* house, too.'

Driving all thoughts of the last night he had spent in Paris from his mind, Nathan brought Amy to a halt and swung her round to face him.

'Henrietta is not my mistress, nor has she been. I met her through Louis d'Argon; he's asked her to marry him on more than one occasion. Her greeting in there was an act. She passed on a warning not to allow Jean-Paul to leave Polrudden, no matter what is said. I don't know what it's all about, but I don't doubt it's of the utmost importance. Henrietta is Jean-Paul's aunt and has his interests at heart.'

Amy was shaken by Nathan's words. She had grown to love Jean-Paul and, until today, she had almost forgotten

174

the likelihood of his being claimed by relatives in France. Yet Amy had also seen the look Henrietta had given Nathan across the width of the sitting-room. No woman could act *that* well. Amy had no intention of losing her husband as well as her adopted son.

'We must learn what was meant,' said Nathan. 'I'll go to Henrietta's room while the others are changing for dinner.'

'No, leave this to me,' said Amy firmly. 'It will arouse no comment if the others come in while I'm in her room. It certainly would if *you* were found with her.'

Amy knocked softly on the door of Henrietta's room, and the speed with which it was opened told her the French woman had been expecting a caller. Amy also realised Henrietta was disappointed it was not Nathan who had come to the room, but this was not the moment to make the matter an issue.

The door was closed quickly behind Amy, and the two women stood looking at each other in silence for a few moments. Amy was thankful that her intuition had prompted her to come here in place of Nathan. Henrietta was dressed in a long white housecoat of a silk so fine it was possible to see she wore nothing underneath. Her long fair hair, piled high on her head in an elaborate arrangement earlier, now hung loose, reaching almost to her slender waist – and there was a subtle hint of perfume in the room.

Amy knew the other woman was examining her equally critically. For the first time in her life she felt self-conscious about her locally made clothes.

'Nathan says you gave him a warning about Jean-Paul,' explained Amy quietly. 'I'm here to learn more.'

'Please, won't you sit down?' Henrietta sat on the edge of the bed, and Amy moved to the only armchair in the room. As she did so she observed that the fabric of the chair was worn. She had never noticed it before.

'Jean-Paul, he is well?'

'He's very happy. He and Beville are great friends.'

'Beville is your son?'

Amy nodded. She was not going to explain to this woman that Beville was Nathan's son by an earlier marriage, and she gained comfort from the fact that Nathan had said nothing of it to Henrietta.

'I am delighted Jean-Paul is so happy here. It would please his father. You know Jean-Paul is the son of my half-brother? I am so excited at the thought of seeing him for the first time.'

'The danger . . .?' Amy urged. She was beginning to suspect the warning had been no more than a ruse to lure Nathan to Henrietta's bedroom, although there had to be a reason for this aristocratic trio's visit to Polrudden.

'Yes, the danger.' Henrietta clasped her hands in her lap and looked suddenly both vulnerable and unhappy. Amy was more certain than ever that she had been right to come to the room in Nathan's place.

'King Louis has learned that Jean-Paul is alive and living here with you. Louis – the comte d'Argon – and I were hoping it might remain our secret. I think one of the survivors must have said something on his return to France.' Henrietta paused, observing Amy's perplexed expression. 'You wonder why there should be so much interest in one small boy? My dear, in order to understand this you would need to know something of the intrigues of a French court, and also the complex character of the King himself – not to mention the full history of the Bourbon family. I am not certain I fully understand it myself. It will be sufficient for you to know Jean-Paul is descended from the Bourbons, the royal family of France, very few of whom survived the Revolution. This, of course, suits Louis. He is an unwanted and uncomely king. The people of France complain he was carried to the throne on the bayonets of France's traditional enemies. If another, more popular member of the Bourbon family could be found, to take the place of Louis, he would undoubtedly have the support of the vast mass of the French people. My brother was such a man. He was a Bourbon, but he also served Napoleon Bonaparte well. If he is dead, his son might prove a popular alternative. The

King is aware of this. He has expressed a wish that Jean-Paul be brought to Paris and raised at court.'

'But this is a wonderful opportunity for Jean-Paul. Would you be looking after him? He's a very lovable little boy . . .'

'You do not understand. Jean-Paul would not be in my charge. He is related to the King, too – and Louis XVIII makes the decisions at his own court. I believe that if Jean-Paul is taken to Paris his life will be in grave danger. Louis has waited a great many years to sit upon the throne of France. He is determined to remain there. Any threat to his ambition, however slight, will be swiftly eliminated.'

Seeing Amy's disbelief, Henrietta added: 'A lovable little boy with Bourbon blood in his veins would pose a very real threat to an aged and unpopular ruler.'

There was a long silence in the bedroom before Henrietta added: 'There is something else. My brother inherited a sizeable fortune; most is valuable jewellery that has been in the Bourbon family for many years. By taking Jean-Paul into his care, the King hopes to obtain Jean-Paul's inheritance. The French crown is in great need of money. The comte d'Argon is at this moment in Martinique, trying to ascertain whether my half-brother's fortune is there or elsewhere.'

'What sort of king is this Louis?' Amy was horrified by what Henrietta had told her. 'Do you really believe he would harm a small boy because he *might* pose a threat to him or *might* have some valuables that the King wants?'

'Louis XVIII is the *only* king France has. He is not good, but he is better than Napoleon Bonaparte. As to whether Jean-Paul might be harmed, the comte d'Argon believes he *would*. It was he who insisted I warn you. Please, I beg you, take my warning seriously. Keep Jean-Paul here with you. For a while, at least.'

'Jean-Paul has a home here for as long as he has need of one. He certainly won't leave if there's the slightest hint of danger.'

'To allow the duc and duchesse de Sauvigny to return

Jean-Paul to Paris would be placing him in *grave* danger. Please believe me, Madame Jago.'

'I believe you.' Amy rose from her chair with a natural grace that Henrietta envied. 'He won't leave Polrudden unless I'm satisfied such a move is in his best interests.'

'I am indebted to you . . . and to Nathan.'

Amy did not doubt the Frenchwoman's sincerity – but she was also a woman. 'That makes you *doubly* grateful to my husband, Marquise. I am curious about the first occasion, in Paris. Nathan made no mention to me of saving your life.'

'Your husband is a modest man, Madame Jago. Perhaps he is reluctant to talk of his deeds of courage.'

Henrietta found herself resenting this young girl. Although it was quite absurd, she, Henrietta, marquise d'Orléan, actually *envied* her! She envied her beauty, her natural, unaffected grace and charm, her youth – and she resented the hold she had over Nathan.

'We had been to my home to find Nathan some clothes from the wardrobe of my late husband. As we returned to the palace we were attacked by a mob. Nathan routed the attackers.'

'I see.'

The thought of Nathan accompanying this attractive and elegant woman to her home to try on clothes was a matter upon which she did not want to dwell. Amy had never before met a woman who possessed such poise and breeding, and such supreme confidence in herself.

At the doorway, Amy paused. 'Thank you for the warning – about Jean-Paul. Dinner will be ready in half an hour.'

Dinner at Polrudden began as a merry social gathering. Nathan and Amy rarely entertained guests at the ancient manor-house. Amy, in particular, had gone to great pains to ensure the meal was of a standard she believed her guests might have expected in their own country.

Before they ate, Nathan kept the glasses of the delegation from the French court well topped up with brandy. It was not the brandy of undoubted potency but dubious origin brought across the Channel for resale in Cornwall. This was estate-bottled Cognac, much prized throughout the civilised world. The Cognac had been given to Nathan over the years by Captain Pierre, master of the French smuggling vessel with which Nathan traded. Its excellence was immediately recognised by the duc de Sauvigny. He was mortified to find such a Cognac here, in this backwater of England. It was finer than any obtained by the royal servants for the palace of King Louis XVIII.

The wine served with the meal came from the same source. It was of equal excellence, and the dinner guests began to mellow. The duc de Sauvigny was an amusing *raconteur*. Amid the laughter that greeted his many anecdotes, no one appeared to notice that Amy never once spoke to Henrietta – and rarely said a word to Nathan.

Not until the main course of Fowey river salmon lay in pink steaks on their plates, surrounded by vegetables from the Polrudden kitchen garden, did the conversation turn to the real reason for the visit of the French king's emissaries.

'I have good news for you,' declared the red-faced and perspiring duc de Sauvigny abruptly. 'We are here to relieve you of a responsibility that was thrust upon you when you so bravely rescued the passengers of *L'Emir*. His Majesty King Louis has sent us here to fetch Jean-Paul Duvernet. He and the King are kinsmen. Since the boy is now an orphan, His Majesty has graciously decided to make himself the child's guardian and raise him in the royal court. It is a generous gesture in view of the adherence of the boy's father to the cause of Napoleon Bonaparte – and his marriage, which came as a shock to the whole Bourbon family. Most generous indeed.'

'You've had confirmation that Jean-Paul's father is dead?' The question was put by Nathan.

'Confirmation?' The duc de Sauvigny looked surprised. 'Confirmation is not possible. It will never be known exactly how many soldiers Bonaparte lost in his Russian campaign. The figure has been put as high as half a million –

and this by men not given to exaggeration. Of these poor wretches, not one in a hundred has been *confirmed* as dead. Nevertheless, their bones rot on the vast wastes of Russia just as surely as do those whose deaths are officially recorded. Charles, duc de Duvernet is dead, and no true subject of the King need shed a tear for him.'

Looking across the table at Henrietta, Nathan saw her face white and taut as she battled to keep her feelings in check.

The duc de Sauvigny followed Nathan's glance and started guiltily. 'My dear Henrietta, a thousand pardons! I beg your forgiveness. I forget the duc de Duvernet was your half-brother.'

'I prefer to believe Charles is *still* my half-brother. I share with Nathan a need for confirmation of the death of Charles before I begin to mourn his loss.'

'I understand your feelings, Henrietta. Regrettably, I cannot share your optimism. However, it matters little. His Majesty wishes to assume responsibility for the child, and I have been sent to take him to the palace in Paris.'

'I'm afraid it's not quite as simple as that,' said Nathan slowly. 'You see, the child's mother passed responsibility for Jean-Paul to *me,* shortly before she died. She begged me to care for him. You could say it was her dying wish. Amy and I have kept that trust.'

'Of course,' said the duc de Sauvigny, with a show of irascibility. 'His Majesty is aware you will have incurred considerable expense as a result. I am authorised to pay you a generous sum as recompense. Perhaps you will be kind enough to submit an account to me before we leave. It need not be in minute detail, of course.'

'I don't think you understand,' said Amy quietly. 'We have taken the trust placed in us by Jean-Paul's mother very seriously. Jean-Paul is part of our family now. We *love* him. We have no intention of giving him up to anyone – except his father, should he still be alive.'

The duc de Sauvigny greeted Amy's declaration with disbelief. 'Madame Jago, it is *you* who do not understand. I am here by order of His Majesty King Louis. It is his *command* that the child be taken to France and given the protection of the royal court. He is, after all, of Bourbon descent.'

'Louis is king of France. His commands mean nothing in England.' Nathan spoke firmly. 'Amy is right. Jean-Paul's mother passed him into my care. I'm not convinced it's in his best interests to be taken to the court in Paris. Unless something happens to change my mind, he'll remain at Polrudden.'

'What does the marquise d'Orléan think?' Amy asked the question looking directly at Henrietta for the first time since the meal began. 'After all, she is Jean-Paul's aunt.'

'I am also a subject of King Louis.' Henrietta spoke cautiously, aware that the duc de Sauvigny was watching her closely. Returning Amy's direct look, she said: 'Jean-Paul must return with us to Paris.'

'If you refuse to give the boy to us, I regret I will be forced to make an approach to your government,' added the duc de Sauvigny.

'Of course,' replied Nathan reasonably. 'But then a decision will need to be made in the courts of England. No doubt many things will come to light that are best forgotten, for the greater good of both our countries. Even if the courts were to order Jean-Paul to be given into your care – and it is by no means certain they would – the matter would not be at an end. Should anything happen to the boy at some future date – an unfortunate accident or a fatal illness, for instance – feelings in England would run very high. High enough to affect relations between our two countries, perhaps.'

The silence that followed Nathan's words was broken by the sudden explosive sound of choking from the duc de Sauvigny. The noise increased alarmingly, and the French duke rose to his feet, clutching his throat. '*Une arête* – a fishbone!' He croaked. 'Fetch a doctor. I am choking.'

'Let me see . . .' Amy came across the room to where the duc de Sauvigny was now reeling about dramatically, his hands clasped about his throat.

'No! Fetch a doctor. Quickly!'

Nathan nodded to a wide-eyed servant who stood in the doorway, paralysed with fear. 'Find Will Hodge. Send him to fetch Dr Ellerman Scott from Mevagissey. Hurry, girl!'

It was half an hour before the physician reached Polrudden, by which time the duc de Sauvigny was lying on the bed in his room, having been helped upstairs by Nathan. The choking had grown steadily more feeble. Now he lay gasping for breath between choking bouts, convinced he was dying. The duchesse sat at his bedside, attempting unsuccessfully to comfort her husband and occasionally lapsing into tears, bewailing the fact that her husband was dying in a foreign land.

Dr Ellerman Scott was brisk and businesslike. After taking a quick glance at his patient, he ordered everyone except Nathan from the room. The duchesse de Sauvigny demanded she be allowed to remain, determined her husband should not 'die in the company of strangers', but the physician brushed her hysterical arguments aside.

'He's lived for nigh on an hour with a bone in his throat. I don't doubt he'll survive a few minutes of my attentions.'

When the room was cleared, Dr Ellerman Scott leaned over the French nobleman, whose choking had suddenly become more severe.

'Hold his hands while I carry out an examination.'

Nathan had to force the duc de Sauvigny's hands from his throat, but he was able to hold them at the Frenchman's sides without too much difficulty.

The duc de Sauvigny opened his mouth in loud protest at the treatment he was receiving, only to have a large round ruler from a nearby desk instantly wedged between his teeth, preventing his mouth from closing.

As the French duke gagged and writhed, unable to vent his feelings in words, Dr Ellerman Scott suddenly removed the ruler and thrust a finger far down the choking man's throat. For a couple of seconds the duc de Sauvigny gagged in earnest, his heels drumming on the bed as he attempted to escape from the clutches of Nathan and the Mevagissey doctor.

Then the triumphant physician held up an object between his finger and thumb. It was the offending fish-bone.

'A very *small* object to have caused such consternation,' he commented wryly. 'Now I suggest you go downstairs and finish off your dinner. Wash it down with some of Mr Jago's excellent wine. By the morning you'll be laughing about this.'

CHAPTER SIXTEEN

There was little evidence of the good humour predicted by the physician the next morning. At breakfast the King's envoy had broken an uncomfortable silence to make one final plea for Jean-Paul to be handed over to him. When Nathan repeated his refusal, the duc de Sauvigny announced his intention to depart from Polrudden immediately after the meal.

Although the duc due Sauvigny had expressed concern for the welfare of the young French boy, neither he nor the duchesse made any requests to see Jean-Paul during their brief stay at Polrudden.

Henrietta visited Jean-Paul's room twice. The first occasion was soon after dinner had been brought to such an unexpected and dramatic end. Accompanied by Rose, the maid with responsibility for the two children, she tiptoed into the bedroom Jean-Paul shared with Beville and gazed down for many minutes at her sleeping nephew.

The second occasion was shortly before she left with the duc and duchesse de Sauvigny. Amy heard voices as she passed the boys' bedroom. Going inside, she found

Henrietta kneeling on the floor, trying to piece together two broken wooden models of fishing-boats, while the small boys handed her pieces of wood that seemed to belong to neither model.

Henrietta smiled up at Amy and held up the broken pieces of wood. 'Your son has told me I am not very good with fishing-boats. I think perhaps he speaks the truth.'

'You need to be born in a fishing village before you can understand fishing-boats – or fishermen,' retorted Amy, resisting an urge to warm to the attractive woman who smiled up at her.

'I doubt if such a premise is true.' Henrietta stood up, gently ruffling Jean-Paul's hair as she did so. 'A fisherman is no more difficult to understand than a soldier, a courtier – or a marquis.'

Henrietta was probably fifteen years older than Amy, and the mistress of Polrudden felt young and awkward in her presence.

'He was never my lover, you know.' The look Henrietta gave to Amy was as straight and open as the blunt statement.

'Should I *thank* you for that?' The words tumbled out before Amy could bite them back.

'I think not,' replied Henrietta with continuing candour. 'Your husband's love for you and your own great charm proved stronger than anything I or the ladies of the court of King Louis had to offer. You are a fortunate woman, Amy – and a beautiful one. I wish we might have been friends.'

Before Amy could reply, a loud wail went up from Jean-Paul as Beville tried to remove a locket from about the French boy's neck. Amy had never seen the locket before, but she guessed from whence it had come. However, by the time she separated the two small boys, the marquise d'Orléan had slipped from the room.

The locket was an expensive piece of jewellery. Obviously of gold, it was enclosed in a circle of diamonds and sapphires. Opening the locket, the small portrait of a handsome fair-haired man looked out at Amy. Coming to her side, Jean-Paul pulled down her hand and jabbed a finger at the portrait.

'Papa,' he said.

Life at Polrudden was unsettled after the envoys of King Louis XVIII of France had left. An air of uncertainty now clouded Jean-Paul's future. This in itself was sufficient to cast a pall of gloom over the household. Jean-Paul had endeared himself to everyone. Nathan did not doubt that the French king would make another attempt to gain custody of the young Bourbon heir to the titles and fortunes of the dukedom of Duvernet.

There were a number of questions Amy would have liked to put to Nathan about Henrietta, marquise d'Orléan and the time he had spent with her in Paris. Wisely, Amy bided her time, and gradually enough scraps of information came her way to enable her to build up a fairly accurate picture of how little *had* occurred between Nathan and the titled French widow. The knowledge came as a great relief to Amy. She had imagined far more. Yet she still believed she had come close to losing Nathan to the other woman.

In late August, at the height of the 1814 pilchard season, an event occurred to push the future of Jean-Paul Duvernet temporarily into the background and provoke a split in the Pentuan community that divided neighbour from neighbour.

As a direct result of the complaints made by the Reverend Damian Roach, the Conference, governing body of the Methodist Church, suspended Preacher Josiah Jago from his duties. They ordered him to London, to answer charges of conducting his services in an irregular and unacceptable manner. The letter sent by Conference stated that should the accusations prove to be without foundation Preacher Jago would be appointed to another circuit. It would be well away from Cornwall and the dissension surrounding him there. In the meantime, the Reverend Damian Roach would take over the Pentuan circuit.

Josiah Jago refused to accept the Conference directive. The 'irregularities' complained of were a reference to the increasing number of outdoor services he was conducting. Such meetings had brought many men and women to the Methodist movement, and he was not prepared to forgo them.

Cornish people had always enjoyed outdoor church services. John Wesley had realised this. A chapel was fine – it was a symbol of men's faith – yet nothing could improve upon God's own handiwork. Josiah Jago had been a great chapel-builder during his earlier years as a Methodist preacher, but he had come to realise that once a chapel was built too many preachers were inclined to sit back and wait for the faithful to come to them and find God. At his outdoor meetings, Preacher Jago took the Lord to the people. He was convinced his way was the right one. This was the way the Methodist movement had begun, and it had succeeded in bringing about a great religious revival throughout the land.

What Preacher Jago did *not* know was that similar services, sometimes lasting all day, and known as 'camp-meetings', together with other basic changes in the Methodist form of worship, were gaining considerable support in many parts of the country. 'Primitive Methodists', as advocates of the new reforms were becoming known, were causing Conference much concern. It had been decided that stern discipline was necessary if the Methodist movement was not to be torn asunder by dissension within its own ranks.

Josiah Jago knew none of these things. He knew only that the church he had served all his life had suspended him on the complaint of a preacher who had been with the movement for no more than a year.

It was a bitter blow, but worse was to come. Arriving at the Methodist church in Pentuan to preach in defiance of the ban, Josiah Jago found the building barred to him by supporters of the Reverend Damian Roach.

When Josiah Jago walked on to Polrudden to report this

latest indignity to Nathan, he stood before his son a defeated, dejected old man.

It hurt Nathan to see his father in such a state. Josiah Jago was a man with many faults but, although bigoted and impatient of others' shortcomings, he had always been a good servant of the Methodist movement, giving his faith precedence over his own family. He might have expected such loyalty to be returned.

As the embittered preacher sat sipping tea and relating his grievances, Nathan looked increasingly thoughtful. Eventually, he stood up and left the room without a word of explanation. When he returned some ten minutes later, he was waving a parchment document triumphantly.

'I thought I remembered the wording of the chapel deeds,' he said. 'This is a copy, made at the time the chapel was built. There is no way Damian Roach can keep you out of the chapel – although you can bar *him* if you wish. Look here . . .' Nathan jabbed a finger at the document.

'But the land was given by our Tom to the Methodist movement, as a gift . . .'

Tom Quicke was the farmer husband of Nathan's sister, Nell. A few years before, he had donated a small plot of land for the local Methodists to build their own church.

'Tom gave the land to the Methodist Society, yes,' agreed Nathan. 'But there's a clause in the deeds, decreeing it is to be held in trust for them by *you,* during your lifetime. For all practical purposes the chapel belongs to *you!*'

As Josiah Jago read through the document, Nathan left the room again. When he returned, he was shrugging on a coat. Looking at him questioningly, Josiah Jago asked: 'Where are you going?'

'With you, to remove the Reverend Roach from your church.'

Josiah Jago shook his head. 'I'll not interrupt anyone who's preaching the Lord's Word. I'll keep this copy of the deeds and speak to Damian Roach later. He's no fool; he'll not risk incurring the wrath of the law by continuing to deny me the use of the church. Indeed, I'm quite sure he'll be anxious that I don't lock *him* out.'

Rising to his feet, Josiah Jago said: 'I'm grateful to you, Nathan. I see the Lord's work in guiding the hand that compiled these deeds. It's His way of telling me I am still on the path He put before me.'

Laying a hand on his son's shoulder, Josiah Jago said 'I am holding an outdoor service this afternoon. Come with me. Tell me whether *you* think I am wrong.'

Nathan did not share his father's enthusiasm for religion, but Josiah Jago had never before asked his son to accompany him to a prayer-meeting. Nathan realised his father was feeling very much alone and uncharacteristically unsure of himself. He agreed to go.

The two men set off after an early lunch. Nathan was mounted on a horse, while his father rode the ageing and cantankerous donkey that had been his mount for almost as many years as Nathan could remember.

To Nathan's surprise, Josiah Jago headed inland, away from the fishing villages where the vast majority of his parishioners had their homes.

When Nathan enquired where they were going, Josiah Jago replied: 'To the downs beyond the Polgooth mine.'

'But that's now part of the new St Austell circuit.'

Josiah Jago shook his head. 'No, it *should* be on the St Austell circuit. Instead, it's the Devil's ground. I'm working to take it from him.'

Polgooth was no more than five miles from Pentuan. In less than an hour the two men were urging their mounts up a narrow path towards an area of broken and uncultivated ground. From here there was a magnificent view of the surrounding countryside. Centuries before, the land had been worked for tin. Nature had long since reclaimed it for her own, leaving only a series of grass-covered pock-marks, half-hidden by bushes and stunted trees, as evidence of the toil of the ancient miners.

On a nearby slope, the stark ruin of a more recent and

highly successful mining venture stood silent guard over a hidden skein of shafts and exhausted workings. Other mine buildings were silhouetted against the skyline to the west, and the steady, distance-muffled thud of a steam-driven beam-engine was evidence that the mineral resources of the area were not yet exhausted.

There was a cold wind up here, and Nathan wished he had worn his fisherman's jersey. He also wondered why his father had chosen such a bleak, out-of-the-way place to hold his meeting. It was not long before he had an answer.

As they swung to the right of the path to avoid a large thicket of sharp-needled gorse, Nathan saw a number of men standing in a group ahead of them. Their unsavoury appearance caused him to rein in ahead of his father, bringing both horse and donkey to a halt.

'It's all right.' Preacher Jago kicked back with his heels, and the ancient donkey edged past Nathan's horse. 'It's part of my "congregation", on its way to meet me.'

Nathan moved alongside his father and looked at him to see if he were joking. He should have known better. Josiah Jago had little sense of humour and rarely joked. Nathan looked more closely at the men moving along the path towards them. Two of the men wore shabby, torn great-coats, of a type worn by infantrymen of the British army. The others wore unidentifiable clothing that hung in tatters about their bodies.

One of the men, larger than his fellows, limped to where Josiah Jago had slipped to the ground from his donkey's back.

'We was beginning to think you weren't coming this week, Preacher. Some of the men were getting a mite restless.' The ragged man looked at Nathan suspiciously. 'Who's this?'

'It's my son Nathan. I'm sorry I'm late, but I'm in trouble with my church authorities, for what they call unorthodox behaviour.'

'Because you're preaching to us? If you didn't do it, no one else would.'

Extending a large hand to Nathan, the man said: 'It's an honour to shake your hand, Mr Jago. Fenwick Garland at your service. I did some prize-fighting myself, until I did this at Orthez . . .' He slapped the stiff leg that caused him to limp. 'I was *Sergeant* Garland then, of the 32nd Regiment – Cornwall's own.'

'Cornwall's *own*?' One of the men standing behind Fenwick Garland spat his disgust on the mud of the path. 'We'd have been better treated had we been taken prisoner by the French. See this . . .?'

The speaker turned his back. The cheap shirt he wore was cut to ribbons. The skin beneath it was a series of ugly weals, one or two of them darkened by congealed blood.

'They did that to me in St Austell only yesterday. I was whipped out of town by order of the magistrate. He told me I was a vagrant and would see the inside of the gaolhouse if I was to come back again. That wasn't what they said six years ago when the recruiting sergeant came round to the hiring fair, offering us the King's shilling to go off and fight for our country. Eleven of us joined the regiment that day. All puffed up like peacocks we were when folk said we were heroes and cheered us on our way. The ones who did the cheering then are the same ones who whipped me out of town. Eleven of us – and I'm the only one who came back. Now I don't know whether I'm the lucky one or not. No home, no family left alive, no work – and not a poorhouse in Cornwall will take me in.'

Josiah Jago rested a hand on the man's shoulder in a gesture of sympathy. 'There's a better world waiting for you, my friend, and one there who knows the pain of a scourging. Come, let's find the others.'

Accompanied by the former soldiers, Nathan and Josiah Jago continued on their way until they reached a large depression in the ground where once the extraction of tin ore had taken place on a large scale.

Standing or sitting in this great hollow was a veritable vagabond army. There were more than a hundred, a sprinkling of women among them. Some were common tinker women, others the wives or widows of soldiers. They had followed their menfolk across the battlefields of Europe, returning to share their fate in their native land. All greeted Preacher Jago with a respect that transcended both their dress and undoubted poverty.

Josiah Jago responded by conducting a stirring service, giving his tattered congregation a powerful sermon on the joys of the life hereafter. Nathan expected many of those present to be cynical, regarding the Methodist preacher's words as a mere sop, to make them more ready to accept their present state. Instead, the men and women gathered on the cold and windy downs hung on his every word, uttering frequent and fervent 'amens' to express their approval of the preacher's promises.

It was a moving experience for Nathan. During the two cold hours he spent on the downs above Polgooth he gained new respect for his father, both as a preacher and as a compassionate man.

When the service ended, the motley crowd of beggars crowded around Josiah Jago to thank him and extract a promise that he would return to conduct another service the following week.

While Josiah Jago conversed with the others, Nathan sought out Fenwick Garland and asked him how he had met the preacher.

'I heard him preaching in the open air over by Gorran,' explained Fenwick Garland. 'I wasn't the most sought-after man at his service,' he added ruefully. 'Everyone else was dressed in their Sunday-best clothes. I wore what I've got on today – the *only* clothes I have. Afterwards, your father came across to speak to me and I told him all about us forgotten old soldiers and the like, living up here out of folks' way, the best we can. The very next Sunday he's here to give us as good a service as you'll hear preached in the finest chapel in the land. He's given us new hope – and, God knows, we can do with all the hope we can get.'

'Unfortunately, there are those who don't share your enthusiasm for his outdoor services. The Methodist Conference is trying to have him moved away from Cornwall. He was even shut out of his own church this morning.'

'On account of us?' Fenwick Garland asked the question angrily, in a voice that caused a number of men standing nearby to turn and look in his direction.

'Not exactly,' corrected Nathan. 'They don't like the way he runs his circuit and are unhappy about such open-air services.'

'Are they indeed? Well, I promise you this, Mr Jago. If this "Conference" insists on your father leaving, we'll march up to London and make them send him back to us again. I may not be the old Iron Duke, but the men here will follow me, I promise you that – and we'd gain a few more along the road to London. As for locking him out of his own church . . .! You just say the word and we'll come along and mount guard on it for him. The boot would be on the other foot then, right enough. Nobody would go inside without Preacher Jago's say-so.'

Suddenly, Fenwick Garland had forgotten his rags and the humiliation of being hounded from towns and villages with the cry of 'Vagrant!' ringing in his ears. He was once more *Sergeant* Fenwick Garland of the Cornwall Regiment, ready to lead his comrades into battle.

'You remember my words, Mr Jago. If your father needs us, or is in any trouble, you come up here and call on our help. We'll gladly give it – to the death, if need be. Preacher Jago's given us new hope, if not in this life, then in the next – and there's many of us who won't mind getting there earlier than expected.'

CHAPTER SEVENTEEN

Sergeant Fenwick Garland was able to be of service to the Jago family far earlier than anyone could possibly have anticipated.

Although the war in Europe had come to an end, the ordinary people of Cornwall had little cause for celebration. At first, the cessation of hostilities had brought about an immediate rise in the price of tin. Miners who had been out of work for many months – years, in some cases – bought shovels, picks, black powder and candles on credit, confident they would be able to repay the mine merchants from their first quarter's profits.

Unfortunately, the upsurge in the fortunes of the tin-mining industry was of very brief duration. Suddenly there was no longer a market for tin. The mine-owners, the 'adventurers', had been hard-hit on too many previous occasions to risk waiting for another rise in the price of tin. They closed their mines.

Thousands of miners, most owing money and with families to support, found themselves without work yet again. In desperation they tramped from one mining area to another, hoping to find something – anything – to earn some money. Their paths crossed those of the returning soldiers of Wellington's army, and sailors recruited by the press-gangs, their services no longer needed.

Desperate for work, the ever-increasing brotherhood of the unemployed scoured Cornwall. They offered their labour to farmers in return for food for their hungry families. Sometimes they were taken on, displacing farm-workers who were themselves subsisting on a mere seven shillings a week. But it proved to be a bad year for grain. Food-prices reached a new peak, and there was barely enough for those who could afford to pay. Men who were forced to watch their families slowly starve became desperate. The incidence of crime increased alarmingly. Bands armed with sticks and bludgeons roamed the lanes, robbing many a hapless traveller or unfortunate wandering Jewish trader.

Before long, farmers feared to take their produce to market lest they be waylaid along the way, or on their return, when they had coins jangling in their pockets.

For the man with grain to sell, his only hope of getting it to market, or to a harbour for shipment, was to ask the local magistrate for an escort of militia – preferably militiamen from outside the hungry county.

Matters became so critical that the county authorities belatedly realised a disaster of alarming proportions was looming. Unless something was done rapidly, many Cornishmen and their families would starve to death.

In reality, many deaths indirectly attributable to the shortage of food had already occurred. In the mining districts where the situation was worst, epidemics of colds and fever had broken out earlier than was usual. Children and old people, already weak from lack of food, were falling victim, and many died.

It was not surprising that much of the unrest in Cornwall originated in these hard-hit areas.

By late September 1814 things were desperate in the mining area to the north of St Austell. Hardly a mine was working. Those few that remained open were employing a mere handful of men. As fever swept the district, leaving five young children dead in its wake, the hunger and frustration of the jobless miners erupted in violence.

It began when some unthinking adventurers, winding up the affairs of a mine in which they had shares, decided to spend some of the remaining profits on a feast for themselves and their mine captains.

Early on the day when the party was to take place, miners, together with their wives and children, began to gather outside the mine counting-house. They watched in sullen silence as food began to arrive and long trestle-tables were assembled in readiness.

Finally, shortly before the adventurers were due to assemble, bread, porter and ale were set out on the tables, together with cold meats and savouries. This proved altogether too much for a watching lad of no more than eight years of age.

Darting forward, he grabbed a handful of bread rolls and turned to run. One of the mine captains supervising the feast was too quick for him. Catching hold of the child, he lifted him easily in the air with one arm, belabouring him all the while with his free hand. Crying out in pain, the small boy still managed to stuff his mouth with bread as he kicked and struggled in mid-air, coming very close to choking himself.

Even now the situation might have been saved had the mine captain been content with thrashing the lad and setting him free. Instead, he called to two of the clerks who had been engaged in winding up affairs at the mine, and who were to share in the feast.

'Take this light-fingered young villain and lock him in the pump-house. When we're done here I'll turn him over to the magistrate.'

The mine captain's loud words provoked an increasing murmur of anger from the crowd. Before the boy could be taken away, a heavily bearded man stepped forward blocking the clerks' path. 'That's my boy you've got there. He's not had a bite of food in his belly for three days. I'll not see him sent to gaol for taking a handful of bread.'

'You should have taught him not to touch what isn't his, Solomon Bennett. Out of the way now, or you'll be in as much trouble as your boy.'

'Not on his own he won't, Cap'n.'

The remark came from one of two miners who stepped forward to flank Solomon Bennett. Now more miners began pushing their way through the angry crowd to stand with them.

Suddenly another small boy ran from the watching crowd to secure a loaf of bread from the half-laid tables. As though it were a signal, everyone – miners, their wives and families – surged forward to surround the tables and empty them of their fare.

There was only enough to satisfy the fortunate few. Minutes later, as the tables collapsed beneath the weight of the struggling crowd, cries went up of 'The counting-house kitchens . . . There's food there.'

The counting-house was stormed and within ten r̶ had been cleared of every item of food being pre̶ the adventurers. There was no stopping the ̶ their children now. The stout locks on the mine shop kept the pillaging horde out for a while, but soon the door itself was battered free of its hinges by a huge wooden tunnel-support and the looters spilled inside.

What little food was in the store soon disappeared, but still there were more empty bellies than full ones. However, success had aroused the passions of the miners. They declared they would not go to their homes while any of their number remained hungry. When one of the miners called for volunteers to follow him to the market-place in St Austell to obtain grain, he received a noisy promise of support from more than two hundred throats.

News of the miners' march and their earlier success went ahead of them. Soon many more, eager to express their own frustration and helplessness, flocked to join them. By the time they began to stream down the hill into St Austell Town their ranks had swelled to more than a thousand strong.

Wisely, when he saw the size of the angry crowd, the St Austell magistrate ordered the town's constables to remain out of sight. Brought up in a tin-mining area himself, he knew how easily a large group of miners could be transformed into a rampaging mob.

The miners marched upon the market which extended the length of the town's main street, and they caused chaos. The weight of numbers pressing forward against those in the lead upset stalls, and produce displayed on the pavement was trampled underfoot – but there was no grain to be found.

For some minutes the miners milled about aimlessly, not content to have their new-found solidarity founder so quickly. Then a cry went up from the head of the column. It was taken up and repeated along the street-market. Corn was being sent out of the country from the tiny port of Pentuan. There was a ship being loaded there at this very moment . . .!

Much to the relief of the residents of St Austell, the miners from the high downs poured through the town streets and marched along the valley road beside the river, heading towards Pentuan.

Long before they reached the small fishing village, their numbers had doubled. Miners from a few of the shallow Polgooth tin mines downed tools and joined them, as did tin-streamers working the river along the way.

Less welcome were Fenwick Garland and his ex-soldiers from Polgooth Downs, and a whole army of unsavoury vagrants who had recently moved into dense woods that covered both sides of the long Pentuan valley. Since these men had taken up residence, travelling at night had become a hazardous undertaking unless a man travelled with well-armed friends.

No one in St Austell was more relieved than the magistrate at the departure of the corn-seeking miners. For some weeks there had been a company of militiamen stationed in St Austell in readiness for just such an emergency as this. Two days before they had been ordered to the mining districts of western Cornwall where hungry miners were threatening to march upon the busy port of Falmouth.

Before the tail-end of the column marching upon Pentuan cleared St Austell, a rider on a fast horse was on his way to Bodmin. He carried a hastily scribbled note from the magistrate, requesting aid from a company of south Wales militia, newly arrived in the county.

Returning from a fishing trip spent fruitlessly seeking pilchards, Nathan saw the miners, and those they had gathered along the way, crossing the narrow bridge to the fishing village.

He lost sight of them as *Sir Beville* passed between high cliffs to enter Portgiskey Cove, but the women working in the fish-cellar quickly put him in the picture, their shrill voices echoing across the decreasing expanse of water between boat and quay.

'They'll find no more corn here than they can grow on a heap of mine waste,' growled Saul Piper. 'The only vessel alongside the wall in Pentuan is full of Welsh coal. The ship they've come seeking sailed this morning.'

'She left with no more than a ton and a half of grain on board,' said Obadiah Hockin, 'and that was bound for the fleet in Plymouth.'

'It's a pity the ship isn't still here. Had they learned the truth for themselves, they might have gone home peaceably,' commented Nathan. 'As it is, they'll be disgruntled and looking around for mischief.'

'Well, we're safe enough here,' said Obadiah Hockin complacently. 'And there's little enough in Pentuan to keep them there for long. After the landlords of the Ship inn and the Jolly Sailor have taken any money they might have, they'll go elsewhere – to Mevagissey, perhaps.'

'Perhaps.' Nathan was not convinced. 'All the same, I'll go across and keep an eye on them when we've tidied *Sir Beville*.'

Work on *Sir Beville* was almost completed when Nathan glanced up and saw a small boy scrambling down the steep hillside into the valley behind Portgiskey. Reaching the foot of the hill the boy tripped. Picking himself up, he began running towards the fishermen.

As the boy drew nearer, Nathan saw it was young William Mitchell, one of the two boys he had rescued from the Bodmin blacksmith.

Nathan's immediate thought was that something must be wrong with a member of Matthew Mitchell's family. However, when the boy reached the quay, panting heavily, he called to Nathan.

'Mr Jago . . . Ma sent me . . . to find you.'

'You'd better sit down for a while and give me your message when you've got your breath back.'

'No . . . Ma says it's urgent. She heard some men talking . . . not miners. Some of they vagabonds from the woods along the St Austell road. They were on their way to "the big house" . . . to Polrudden. They said there was likely to be pickings there. Ma said they were an evil-looking lot. You'd best get up there, Mr Jago.'

Nathan had caught occasional glimpses of the men who lurked in the shadows beside the St Austell road. He did not doubt there were magistrates' warrants in force for most of them.

Hurrying to the cottage beside the fish-cellar, Nathan lifted down an aged brass-barrelled blunderbuss which was kept loaded above the fireplace. The cottage had once been Amy's home, and Amy's father was a notorious smuggler. The formidable old weapon had sent Revenue men running for cover on more than one occasion. Nathan hoped it would not be needed at Polrudden, but he did not under-estimate the seriousness of Mary Mitchell's warning.

Leaving the cottage, Nathan found his five crewmen waiting for him. They were armed with a variety of weapons, ranging from a gutting-knife to a marlin spike.

'Where do you think you're going with those?'

'With you.'

Assuming an air of indifference, Saul Piper added: 'It stands to reason. If anything happens to you, we're out of a job. No one hereabouts would take an out-of-work drift-fisherman. We'd end up like that lot over at the village. Hungry, no place to live, and no one to give a damn whether we lived or died. I don't want that for me – or for my family. We'll be along to see you stay out of trouble.'

Nathan nodded, but to Obadiah Hockin he said: 'You'll stay here. See that no one harms the boat or the tackle.'

Obadiah Hockin was inclined to argue, but Nathan was already striding from the quay, the remainder of his crew-men close behind him. Obadiah Hockin was an old man. It was doubtful whether he could have climbed to the top of Pentuan Hill. If he did, there would be little fight left in him.

In the village, Nathan and his men needed to push a path through the throng which was now more than fifteen hun-dred strong. Some – a very few – were inclined to raise an objection when they were pushed aside. Invariably, the protest died on their lips when they saw the expression on Nathan's face and glimpsed the brass blunderbuss carried in the crook of his arm.

Halfway up the steep hill, Nathan's worst fears about the

situation at Polrudden were realised. A breathless, panic-stricken servant-girl would have fled past without recognising him, had Nathan not called sharply for one of the fishermen to hold her.

The servant-girl, Ann, was a simple-minded girl from Pentuan village and she struggled and screamed in the arms of her captor, beating against his arms with her fists.

'Ann . . . *Ann*! Get a grip on yourself. What's happening up at Polrudden?'

Nathan needed to repeat his words half a dozen times before they got through to the near-demented girl.

When she stopped trembling, the words tumbled out. 'I was working in the kitchen, sir, me and Jessica, when these men rushed in through the door. They was evil-looking, dirty men in ragged clothes. They left muddy footmarks all over the floor that me and Jessica had scrubbed twice today. Filthy 'twas, that floor.'

Nathan was unable to curb his impatience. 'What did they do . . . these men?'

Some of the fear returned to the girl. 'They grabbed us, sir. Me and Jessica. They pulled poor Jessica's skirt right over her head, and her screaming fit to bust. They'd have done the same to me, I don't doubt, but I bit the man who had hold of me. Bit him on the thumb, right through to the bone. When he let me go, I ran. I ran as though the Devil were after me. But I could hear poor Jessica's screams all the way to the lane.'

'Where is Amy – Mrs Jago – and the boys?'

'The Mistress went out a couple of hours ago, Master. Went up to Venn Farm, to see Mrs Quicke . . .'

Nathan's sister, Nell, was pregnant again. Her time for the latest was near, and Amy visited her as often as she could. Venn Farm was far enough from Polrudden for Amy to be safe – but Nathan's relief was premature.

'. . . the young master and Jean-Paul are up at the house. Last I saw, they were playing on the lawn with Rose . . .'

Rose Vincent was the girl who looked after the boys.

Nathan prayed silently that she might have had the sense to take the boys to safety before the mob reached Polrudden. But Rose was no more than fifteen years of age. He could not leave it to chance. 'How many men are there?'

Ann shook her head. 'I don't know, Master. It seemed the whole kitchen was full of 'em. Them as wasn't after me and Jessica was cramming food down their throats as though they hadn't eaten for weeks . . .'

Suddenly, Ann looked beyond Nathan and her eyes widened with fear. Turning quickly, Nathan saw some twenty men dressed in rags, coming up the hill towards them. Limping at their head, yet moving so fast the others were hard put to keep up with him, was Fenwick Garland.

'It's all right. Ann. They are friends. Go on down to the village now, and stay there until I send for you.'

The white-faced servant-girl waited until Fenwick Garland and his men reached Nathan before edging nervously past them. Lifting her skirts, she fled in the direction of Pentuan, without once looking back.

It was doubtful whether Fenwick Garland noticed her. When Nathan began climbing the hill once more, Fenwick Garland was at his side. Talking breathlessly, he said: 'I heard there was some trouble at Polrudden, Nathan. We thought we'd come up to see if you had need of us.'

'I'm obliged. Some of the men who've been living rough along the valley have broken into Polrudden. My wife isn't there, but I'm concerned for the two boys and my servants.'

'You've cause for concern,' said Fenwick Garland grimly, at the same time forcing the pace so that Nathan was hard put to keep up with him. 'There's some desperate men among them. Cut-throats, robbers, deserters and gaol-breakers. They're wanted by magistrates the length and breadth of England. Now they've reached Cornwall there's nowhere else for 'em to go.'

'Then, the sooner we clear them from Polrudden, the better.'

Nathan and Fenwick Garland reached Polrudden together, with the Portgiskey fishermen and Garland's ragged army strung out behind them.

There was a group of Polrudden servants gathered at the far end of the drive, keeping the distance of the wide lawns between them and the house. There was some sort of commotion going on among them, and when Nathan drew near he was dismayed to see Amy there. She was having a heated argument with Will Hodge.

Jean-Paul was here, too, gazing wide-eyed and frightened from Amy to the young Rose Vincent who knelt on the ground, sobbing and wringing her hands.

'What's going on? Where's Beville?'

At the sound of Nathan's voice, Amy turned away from the servants and ran to him. 'Those men have Beville in the house. I wanted to go in after him. Will Hodge stopped me.'

'Thank God for that! Will, do you know where they have Beville?'

'I saw him not ten minutes ago. He came to the window of his bedroom but was pulled back again. I think Jessica's in the room, too, with some of them vagabonds. One of the maids hid in an upstairs cupboard when they broke into the house. She escaped through the dining-room window just now and said that as she ran down the stairs she could hear Jessica crying. All the other servants are out of the house – except for young Robert. He put up a fight and was clubbed down in the hall.'

'How many men are inside?'

Will Hodge shook his head. 'I don't rightly know. Twenty or thirty, I'd say. Too many for us to take on – even if we'd been ready for 'em.'

'Is there a wine-cellar in the house?' Fenwick Garland put the unexpected question.

'Yes, a well-stocked one. Most of it was left by Sir Lewis Hearle, although I've added a keg or two of brandy. What's that got to do with anything?'

'Everything. Most of the men in there are former soldiers. If there's drink to be had for the taking, they'll find it. Napoleon knew that well enough. If ever our troops cap-

tured a château which had well-stocked cellars, he'd give
our men an hour to find the drink and pour it down their
throats, then he'd counter-attack. We lost many men that
way before our own officers learned their lesson and kept
the men from the drink.'

'We'll hope there are no officers among them today.
Amy, you'll stay here until this is over. Better still, take
Jean-Paul to Venn Farm and remain there with him.'

When Amy began shaking her head, Nathan spoke to the
Polrudden groom. 'Will, I'm making you responsible for
the safety of Amy and the boy. Do whatever you think is
necessary – but keep them well clear of the house.'

Nathan left Amy protesting loudly. With his crew and
the ragged former soldiers from Polgooth Downs at his
back, he sprinted across the lawns towards the house,
making for a little-used side door. Nathan carried the keys
in his pocket. He used the door whenever bad weather
caused him to return from fishing unexpectedly during the
night hours.

When Nathan and his men entered the house they made
straight for the cellar. On the way they could see the
house had been ransacked by the intruders. Drawers stood
open, their contents strewn about on the floor, but Nathan
was too concerned for Beville to be angry.

The door to the cellar stood open, the padlock forced
from its hasp. The noise from below proved that Fenwick
Garland knew the type of man with whom they were deal-
ing.

'Is there another door from the cellar?' Fenwick
Garland asked.

'No.' Even as he made the reply, Nathan was slamming
the door and driving home two stout bolts, top and bottom.
'And there's little else but wine down there for them. Now
we'll go and find Beville.'

Not all the intruders were in the cellar. As Nathan led his
men through the house a man came from the direction of
the dairy, a partly devoured ham in his hands. At sight of
Nathan, the thief let out a warning shout before the butt of

the heavy blunderbuss was slammed against the man's head, felling him to the floor.

Robert, the young Polrudden servant, was lying in the hall, showing signs of recovering consciousness, and two of the fishermen helped the dazed servant from the house.

While this was going on Nathan heard a sound from upstairs and he looked up in time to catch a glimpse of a bloated, heavily pock-marked face above a thick red beard, looking out from Beville's room. Then the door slammed shut and there was the sound of a heavy key being turned in the lock.

'Damn!' The element of surprise was gone. Nathan toed the unconscious vagabond. He fell off the bottom stair and sprawled grotesquely on the carpet in the hall. His tattered shirt was gaping wide, exposing skin stained by the grime of months of outdoor living.

Nathan looked around to see Fenwick Garland still gazing up at the closed door of Beville's bedroom.

When Fenwick Garland spoke again, his voice was filled with concern. 'We've got trouble, Nathan. *Bad* trouble. I know the man up there in the room with your son. He calls himself Jem Grubb, from the port of Liverpool. Some men say that isn't his real name. But he's a fugitive from the troubles in Ireland. Whatever his real name, he was *Corporal* Grubb when I knew him, recruited to the Army when he was too drunk to know what he was about. He was in the 32nd Regiment, though not in my company. It was said they had to make him a corporal because there wasn't anyone else in the company could give him an order. He was sent home in disgrace after receiving three hundred lashes. I was responsible for that, as well he knows. Even so, he got off lightly. I swear most of his musket-balls were fired at the backs of English officers and not at French soldiers. Once back in England, it seems he was arrested for killing a young girl. He escaped from the lock-up and has been on the run ever since. He's credited with more than one murder, and any number of highway robberies. He's a bad one, Nathan. Take my word for it.'

'Then, the sooner we get Beville away from him the better.'

Nathan took the stairs two at a time, but Fenwick Garland found them more difficult to negotiate. At the door to Beville's room, Nathan stopped. From inside he could hear whispering. There was another sound, too. It was difficult to identify with certainty, but it might have been the whimpering of a woman. After a moment's hesitation, Nathan hammered on the door with the butt of the blunderbuss.

'Grubb – or whatever you're calling yourself now – can you hear me?'

After a lengthy pause, a gruff voice replied: 'I can hear you.'

'I want my son, Grubb. The boy you've got in there.'

'Well, well, well. So it's Nathan Jago at last. I expected you long before this. So did your kitchenmaid. Never mind, there's been time for your son to learn a thing or two about life . . .'

'You're talking of a three-year-old, Grubb. Let him go. Send him out here to me.'

'Oh, you'd like that, wouldn't you? It would make it easy for you and your friends to burst in and take me prisoner. Oh, no, Jago. Your boy's in here, and here he'll stay, until I'm ready to let him go. He's a chubby little chap. Reminds me of a plump, plucked chicken . . .'

'Grubb! Either you let him go or I'll break down the door and heave you out of the window into the garden.'

'No, you won't, Jago. You'll stay where you are and listen to what I have to say. Do anything else and he'll wind up with his throat cut – ask *him* if you don't believe me.'

There was a sudden squeak from Beville and he began to cry. Nathan's anger flared, and he had actually raised the blunderbuss to blast away at the lock when he heard Grubb say: 'You tell him, girl, if you don't want to feel the edge of this blade, too.'

A moment later Jessica's querulous voice called: 'You'd best do as he says, Master. He's got a knife to Beville's throat.'

205

'You hear that, Nathan Jago? Do as I say if you want to see either your boy or the maid alive.'

'Don't be frightened, Beville. I'll soon have you out of there.' Nathan could hear Beville crying softly. 'Are *you* all right, Jessica?'

There was a derisive laugh from inside the room. 'So *that's* her name! Funny, I never thought of her as having a name. But you should be asking me that question, Jago, not her. Yes, she's all right. Mind you, I've had livelier wenches in my time, but she's "all right". Now, you just listen to what I have to say. If you want to see your boy alive again, you'll have a boat ready and loaded with enough food for me and my men, in an hour. Then you'll provide arms for us – and stand well clear when we come out of here. Do you understand?'

'You're asking the impossible, Grubb. The rest of your men are already under lock and key.' It was the truth, in a manner of speaking. 'There's no way I can have them released now. As for food, you've already stripped my house bare. There's fish at Portgiskey, nothing more.'

Nathan could hear a great deal of whispering from inside the room, indicating that one or more of Grubb's men were inside with him. Then a less cocksure Grubb asked: 'What about the boat . . . and guns?'

'There's a boat at Portgiskey and it's ready for sea now. The only gun I can lay my hand on is the blunderbuss I'm carrying with me.'

After more whispering from the room, Grubb called: 'That will have to do, but I want no tricks, Jago. I saw you coming to the house with a whole lot of men. Call them off. Clear the house and move them back across the lawns, where I can see them. You go with them, but leave the gun outside the bedroom door.'

Nathan hesitated, hoping to think of some way he might use the situation to his advantage, but Jem Grubb was becoming increasingly impatient.

'You hear me, Jago?' There was a sudden frightened scream from Jessica and she began to cry. 'Perhaps you hear "Jessica" better. I only nicked her then. Next time I'll slit her throat.'

'I hear you, Grubb. The blunderbuss is leaning against the wall, beside the door.'

'Right. Send someone to get that boat ready, then clear the house. Remember, no tricks. Not if you want your son to stay alive.'

'I'll do as you say, Grubb. But if I see so much as a bruise on Beville when you come out I swear you'll not live to set foot in my boat.'

Leaning the blunderbuss against the wall beside the bedroom door, Nathan backed away to the stairs, motioning for Fenwick Garland to come with him. When both men reached the hall, Fenwick Garland said in a low voice: 'You go outside, where Grubb can see you. I'll wait here and hope for an opportunity to get him when he's on the way out.'

'No,' said Nathan sharply. 'You'll help me clear the house. There will be no attempt on Grubb until Beville is safe. Do as he says, for now.'

It took ten minutes to clear the rooms, and Nathan was careful to close all the heavy wooden doors between the hall and the cellar, so that the sounds of the drunken prisoners would not be heard by Grubb as he left the house.

Jem Grubb came through the front door of Polrudden slowly and cautiously. The loaded blunderbuss was in his right hand. With his left, he firmly grasped the neckband of Beville's shirt. Another ragged man walked nervously behind him.

An angry murmur rose from a crowd of watchers, which now included many of the Pentuan villagers. The sound died quickly as Grubb pointed the wide muzzle of the brass-barrelled gun in their direction.

Nathan waited until Jem Grubb and his companion, with their young prisoner, were well clear of the house. Then he made his move. Walking from the group of fishermen, he headed towards the three slow-moving figures.

The gun barrel immediately swung to cover Nathan, and

Grubb's grip on Beville tightened. 'Keep away, Jago. If you come any closer, I'll blow your son in two.'

'No, you won't.' Nathan kept walking, hoping there was more confidence in his voice than he felt. 'If you use the gun on Beville, you'll have no chance at all of escaping. I'll kill you with my bare hands.'

'Wouldn't you rather use the gun on me, *Corporal* Grubb? You swore you'd kill me one day. Well, now's your chance . . .'

Nathan stopped some four paces from Grubb and Beville as Fenwick Garland left the anonymity of the crowd and limped towards the armed man and his companion from the other side.

'*Sergeant Garland!*' Jem Grubb spoke the name in a hoarse whisper.

'That's right, Corporal Grubb. Sergeant Garland. I had you flogged, remember? Then dismissed the regiment and sent back to England in disgrace. Now's your chance to even the score. Or do you value your freedom more?'

Grubb's grip upon Beville's collar slackened. In an instant the boy had broken free and was running to Nathan.

The barrel of the blunderbuss swung in Nathan's direction, then shifted back to Fenwick Garland.

'It's a trick. You're trying to trick me,' Jem Grubb sounded confused, uncertain what the two men were trying to do.

'There's no trick.' Nathan held Beville's hand tightly. 'The boat's waiting down at Portgiskey. All you have to do is walk down the hill and take it.'

Turning, Nathan began to walk away. He heard the click as the hammer of the flintlock blunderbuss was pulled back to the firing position. It caused the hair on the back of his neck to rise.

Fenwick Garland called to Grubb again. 'You're looking in the wrong direction, Corporal. All Nathan Jago wants is to take his son to safety. I'm the man you need to watch. You forgot that once before . . .'

Nathan walked steadily on towards Polrudden, tense in

the expectation of a shot. Beville was now walking at arm's length in front of him. He would be shielded by Nathan's body if a shot came.

Then Jem Grubb replied to Fenwick Garland, and Nathan realised, with a surge of relief, that Grubb was not about to shoot.

'You couldn't nail me when you had two good legs and with the whole of the British army behind you, Sergeant Garland. You'll not trick me out of my freedom today. Yes, I've thought of revenge. For all these long years I've hoped to meet up with you one day and take my revenge. It's not a thought that will bother me any longer. Seeing you crippled and dressed in rags is revenge enough. Why, I'd feel cheated if you *was* to die now. You live long, and let your heart bleed a little more every time you remember the man you used to be. Mind you, if you were to step a little closer I'm not saying I wouldn't put a dent in your head with the butt of this gun.'

A scornful smile on his bearded face, Jem Grubb backed away along the driveway, not taking his eyes from Fenwick Garland. His companion did the same. Because of this, neither man saw the mounted troop of militiamen enter the driveway from the lane outside.

Fenwick Garland saw them. He stood without moving a muscle. Then, when no more than thirty feet separated Grubb from the militiamen, the fugitive heard a sound. He turned to see the part-time soldiers fanning out as they advanced towards him.

Jean Grubb swung back towards Fenwick Garland again, the barrel of the blunderbuss rising. But the former sergeant of the 32nd Regiment had survived too many battles to be caught napping by Jem Grubb. He had already dived for cover behind a stump where a great oak had once stood.

A cry that contained rage, frustration and despair escaped from Grubb's throat. Before the lieutenant in charge of the militiamen could shout an order, the blunderbuss came up and Grubb's finger squeezed the trigger.

When the heavy pall of black powder-smoke cleared, the

horrified watchers saw Jem Grubb lying in the driveway. Half his head had been blown away by the charge from the aged brass blunderbuss. Grubb had known he would stand on the gallows if he allowed himself to be taken by the militiamen. Rather than face such a prospect he had chosen to end his life at his own hands. Beside him, his companion looked down at the dead man in slack-mouthed dismay, and Nathan turned Beville's head to hide the gruesome scene from him.

CHAPTER EIGHTEEN

Josiah Jago's decision to defy the dictates of the far-distant Conference brought him an unexpected flood of support from the Methodists of his circuit, many of whom had supported the Reverend Damian Roach until now.

Their switch of allegiance surprised only Roach himself. Preacher Jago's parishioners were behaving in a manner true to their own history. Cornish men and women had a long history of rebelling against arbitrary decisions made on their behalf by bodies beyond the Cornish border. So it was now. The chapels on his circuit were filled when Josiah Jago conducted a service, and his outdoor meetings attracted Methodists from all over the Duchy. Those attending were eager to meet the man who was challenging the authority of the ruling Methodist body.

Damian Roach contemplated barring Josiah Jago from the handful of chapels on the circuit, knowing he could call upon the magistrate to enforce his decision. He held back, aware that Preacher Jago would retaliate by closing the important Pentuan chapel to him. Instead, Damian Roach resorted to the pen, sending a series of complaining letters to the Conference in London, urging *them* to take action to implement their decision.

The Methodist Conference added Damian Roach's letters to the growing pile of reports reaching them from all parts of England. The cracks in the structure of the Methodist movement were growing wider all over the land. The unwieldy governing body of the Methodist Church could not agree on the best method of bringing the dissidents within their ranks to heel.

Such disaffection was, perhaps, inevitable. Until his death in 1791, John Wesley, founder of the Methodist Church, had ruled the movement with a rigid autocracy. Such was the magnetism of the man, his absolute authority was never seriously challenged as long as he lived. It was Wesley himself who decided that upon his death power should pass into the hands of a self-selected committee of one hundred preachers – 'the Conference'.

For a while the collective leadership worked reasonably well; but as those who had known and respected John Wesley died others came to the fore to take their places. Younger men, less inclined to adulate the memory of a man they had never known. Men who wanted to consolidate the gains they had already made and project an image of permanence and respectability.

The subtle change of emphasis within the movement both confused and dismayed many of the older circuit preachers. Men like Josiah Jago, who loved the evangelical aspect of Wesley's Methodism. Men whose great joy was in taking the teachings of the Son of God to those most in need of His message.

All over the country honest preachers weighed their beliefs against the directives of the Methodist Conference. Where conscience emerged the victor, preachers continued in their old ways and awaited dismissal. One day they would join together and be known as *Primitive* Methodists, but that day had not yet arrived. For the moment they were rebels, defying a church that had lost the momentum given

211

to it by its dynamic founder.

The bitter dispute between the Methodist Church and its errant preachers would continue for years, but as time passed it began to assume less importance in the life of the Pentuan fishing community.

While the two preachers waged theological warfare, the pilchards began running off the south Cornwall coast. They came in great shoals and, suddenly, there were more fish than had been seen in very many years. While they remained, every able-bodied man and woman was fully employed once more. So, too, were the children and old men who crowded the beaches and helped haul in the nets containing the bountiful harvest.

Nathan's days and nights had never been busier. Making the most of the sudden glut of fish he had taken on two additional crews. His three boats were working day and night, as was the fish-cellar at Portgiskey. So busy were they that local coopers could not keep up with the demand for barrels in which to pack the salted fish. A shipload of barrels was brought in from Bristol, but before they arrived Nathan found it necessary to take two of his drifters from fishing and send them to Plymouth for barrels to keep his business going.

For two weeks it seemed as though the sea's long-awaited bounty would never end. Eventually, of course, the pilchard run had to cease, but when the end came it was with a dramatic suddenness that left the small fishing community stunned.

The day had not gone well at Portgiskey. Hard work and incredibly long hours were beginning to tell on everyone's nerves. Foolish but bitter quarrels broke out frequently in the fish-cellar. During the midday break two young girls who were 'walking out' with the same fisherman suddenly began an argument, urged on by the older women about them. Before Nathan could bring it to a halt one of the girls lashed out with a fish-gutting knife. Its razor-sharp edge left a gaping bloody track across the other girl's face that would scar her for life. As she fell screaming to the ground,

Nathan took the knife from her assailant, who now stood back, pale-faced and aghast at what she had done.

When one girl had been sent post-haste to the doctor and the other to her home to face possible arrest and imprisonment, Nathan was called to the quay at Pentuan.

Two ships were tied up to load salted pilchards. One cargo was destined for the fleet lying at Plymouth, the other was being taken to Italy, where there was an assured market for the fish. The masters of the two vessels had got together and it was they who had sent for Nathan. His fish comprised almost half the cargo for each ship, but the two masters wanted him to lower the price that had earlier been agreed between them.

Nathan protested and the masters were apologetic – but they were also quite firm. There was more fish being landed than the market could possibly absorb. Therefore prices must drop. Either Nathan agreed, or they would buy from another source.

Nathan argued for an hour, but he knew he could not win. The ships' masters were right. If Nathan refused to lower his prices, other fish-cellars could be found, their owners anxious to sell. Eventually, Nathan was forced to settle for a price that would leave him with only a small profit. But it was better than none at all.

When Nathan returned to Portgiskey that evening he had to intervene in yet another quarrel, this time between young Cornelius Lanyon and his father-in-law, the explosive Saul Piper.

Since his marriage to Maud Piper, Cornelius had been working quietly to effect a reconciliation between Maud and her father. For a while it seemed he might be winning, but tonight a hint that he and Maud would welcome a visit from her father had unexpectedly enraged the quick-tempered fisherman.

'I've already said I want nothing to do with the girl. As far as I'm concerned, I've got only three daughters – and they're all living a decent life at home. Maud's yours now. She'll not see me in your home, and I don't want to hear she's been in mine. I'm bringing my girls up to be decent, clean-living Christians. I'll have no whore flouting herself and her ways in front of them. Not now, nor when she's delivered of that sailor's bastard she's carrying in her belly.'

'Maud's my wife, Saul. There's no call to talk of her like that. As for the child, it will be born with my name. Be it son or daughter, I'll be proud to be a father to it.'

Saul Piper spat over the edge of the quay. 'Them's brave words, boy. You keep on repeating 'em to yourself when you walk down the street in Pentuan and imagine the little bastard looks like every coal-heaving seaman you pass. You'll likely change your tune then. Happen if she has another you'll be looking even closer, just in case there's a likeness there, too.'

Cornelius Lanyon lunged angrily at Saul Piper, his thin arms flailing. Fortunately for the slightly built young man, Matthew Mitchell was close enough to grab him before any of the blows reached their target.

Effortlessly holding Cornelius clear of the ground, the slow-talking Matthew Mitchell remonstrated with Saul Piper. 'There's no call to talk about his wife like that. The two young 'uns are making a good go of things and they both deserve a bit of happiness.'

'Happiness?' There was a wealth of bitterness in the single word. 'The day Maud was born I was the happiest man in Pentuan. For years I could get through the worst night's fishing with the thought that in another hour or two I'd be seeing our Maud . . .'

For a moment Saul Piper's voice threatened to break, but he recovered himself with a visible effort. 'It was the same when we were in prison in France. When I worried about the family I'd console myself with the thought that our Maud was at home . . . that she'd look after things until I got back. Our Maud let me down. She'll do the same to him.'

Cornelius Lanyon had stopped struggling while Saul Piper was talking, and Matthew Mitchell lowered him to the ground. Without releasing his hold on the young man,

Matthew said quietly: 'She kept the family together for you, Saul, in the only way she could. Have you ever thought of what that's cost her. If you haven't then I think it's time you did. Maud's always been a good daughter to you. I don't doubt she'll make Cornelius a good wife.'

For a few moments Saul Piper appeared to be struggling for words. Then he turned and strode away towards the fish-cellar.

When Nathan heard of the incident later that evening, he thought it wise to separate the two men. Cornelius Lanyon went to sea that night in *The Brave Amy H* and Saul Piper in *Sir Beville*. As the night crew of *The Brave Amy H* was relatively inexperienced, Nathan sent Obadiah Hockin out with them.

It had been Nathan's intention to go to sea with one of his boats, but it was becoming increasingly important to find new markets for the fish they were landing and he intended travelling to Plymouth on the morrow.

Nathan saw the three boats off as darkness fell, before trudging home wearily. He had been fishing the previous night, and the afternoon spent bargaining with the masters of the merchantmen meant he had been unable to take any sleep.

At the top of the hill Nathan looked out to sea and frowned. A heavy bank of dark cloud was creeping up towards the moon and a strong offshore breeze was beginning to blow. It looked as though bad weather was in the offing. If so, it would mark the end of the pilchards' 'run'. Nevertheless, it had been the best pilchard season in living memory and had given a much-needed boost to the economy of the little fishing community of Pentuan.

Nathan was woken in the early hours of the morning by a deafening thunderclap that rattled the tiles of the roof of the house as lightning flickered all around. Before the next roll of thunder drummed out its violent message, Nathan heard the whining of the wind as it found gaps in the weather-warped window-frames on the seaward side of

Polrudden. There was a fierce storm raging outside, and the wind had backed to the east – the worst possible direction for the fishermen from Portgiskey.

Nathan's arm was trapped beneath Amy. As he eased it free she stirred, asking sleepily: 'What's the matter?'

'There's a bad storm. An easterly. I'm going to Portgiskey to make sure the boats are in.'

Amy sat up in bed, immediately awake, as another lightning flash illuminated the room. As a child she had lived with her parents at Portgiskey. No one knew better than she the dangers to boats and cellar in a severe easterly storm.

'I'll come with you.'

'You'd best stay with the boys. This storm might frighten them.'

'Rose is sleeping in their room. Jean-Paul had the snuffles last night, and she stayed with the boys. I know Portgiskey better than anyone else. I'll be of more use to you there.'

Amy was dressed and ready as quickly as Nathan, her slight figure lost inside a heavy fisherman's jersey and large waterproof coat. With a wide-brimmed hat tied down on her head, there was very little to be seen of her as they let themselves out of the house to brave the storm. Nathan took her hand affectionately as they headed along the long driveway together.

It was as severe a storm as either of them had ever experienced. Lightning sizzled and crackled across the sky, illuminating the way ahead and affording them glimpses of the sea, whipped to a frenzy by the storm. The wind was the worst of all, driving Nathan and Amy before it until they reached the protection of the high-banked hedges flanking the road.

In spite of the hour, lights were showing in many cottage windows. The Pentuan fishermen were removing their own boats from the threat of the storm.

The tide was too high for Portgiskey to be reached along the long, sandy Pentuan beach, and Nathan and Amy were forced to approach Portgiskey from the landward side. Making their way along the valley that led to the break in the cliffs where the fish-cellar was situated, Nathan and Amy battled in the teeth of the gale, frequently slipping on the wet grass as each tried to support the other.

When they drew nearer to Portgiskey, Nathan gripped Amy's hand more tightly and shouted something to her, at the same time pointing ahead.

Amy was unable to catch Nathan's words above the noise of the storm, but she knew what he was trying to say. There were lamps alight in both the fish-cellar and the adjacent cottage. Someone was already at Portgiskey. Amy prayed it might be the crews of their three boats.

One boat was certainly safe. The intermittent lightning revealed the two masts of a drifter, swaying wildly alongside the jetty as the boat was buffeted by wind and sea.

When they reached the shelter provided by the Portgiskey buildings Amy pulled Nathan to a halt. He brought his head down close to hers, and she shouted: 'The boat will need to be pulled well up on land, behind the quay. A big wave might take the boat with it and smash it to smithereens. I saw it happen to one of my pa's boats . . .'

Nathan nodded. He had already appreciated the danger to the fishing-boat. Gripping her arm in acknowledgement, he left her to make her way to the cottage alone, while he fought his way along the quay to the boat.

A few minutes later, as he slackened off the ropes securing the boat to the quay, he was joined by the crew of *Sir Beville* and the daytime crews who had made their way to Portgiskey. It took half an hour of back-breaking effort before the heavy fishing-boat was dragged to safety on the shingle behind the quay.

Afterwards, as Nathan stripped off his sodden outer clothing before a welcome fire, he asked the question that had been uppermost in his mind since his arrival at Portgiskey.

'Has anyone seen anything of *Peggy Hoblyn* and the *Brave Amy H*?'

All the men who had helped to drag *Sir Beville* to safety were also changing, their wet clothing steaming in the heat from the fire. A number of women who worked in the fish-cellar were here, too, preparing hot tea laced with brandy for their men. Under normal circumstances, the presence of women in a room where men were changing would have provoked a great deal of coarse banter. Tonight the men changed in a heavy silence and Nathan's question hung on the air for long minutes before Ahab Arthur, skipper of *Sir Beville,* answered him.

'We were fishing with *The Brave Amy H.* It was a bit rough, but I've known it worse. Then suddenly a squall blew up from nowhere. Next moment we were in a storm such as I've never known before, and hope never to witness again. I had the men cut the lines free and ran for home.'

Ahab Arthur looked at Nathan apologetically. 'I'm sorry, Nathan. I know nets and lines are expensive, but there was no other way.'

'You did the right thing; you saved my boat – and your crew. I wish to God the others had done the same. You saw nothing of them at all?'

When Ahab Arthur shook his head, Saul Piper, uncharacteristically subdued, said: 'I did. The lightning made it as clear as day out there at times. After we'd cut the gear loose and were on our way in I saw the crew of *The Brave Amy H* trying to haul in their nets.'

Saul Piper's words brought a moan of despair from the women in the room, most of whom were wives or mothers of the men who manned Nathan's boats.

Saul Piper's voice grew suddenly husky. 'I know it was them. I recognised young Cornelius, him as should have been with us tonight . . .'

Nathan winced as though he had been dealt a low body blow. To attempt to haul in nets in such weather was suicidal.

'How about *Peggy Hoblyn*? Did anyone see anything of her?'

Ahab Arthur shook his head. 'There were a lot of drifters

out tonight. Just before we put out the nets *Peggy Hoblyn* came past us. Someone called to say they were going farther out. Perhaps they've put into Fowey harbour.'

'Yes . . . That's probably what they've done.'

Nathan's true thoughts were hidden from everyone except Amy. She knew, as he did, that no fisherman in his right mind would try to take a fishing-boat through the narrow entrance to Fowey harbour with a fierce easterly storm raging.

By the time the sun cast its first slanting rays into Portgiskey Cove, many of the Pentuan villagers had begun to assemble on the small quay. They stood in small groups, talking quietly. The smell of disaster was in the air and it would affect a great many Pentuan families.

Within an hour of sunrise the storm had abated sufficiently for the fishermen of Pentuan to launch their boats and set off in search of *Peggy Hoblyn* and *The Brave Amy H.* Nathan was already at sea in *Sir Beville.*

Within minutes of the Pentuan boats putting to sea, the theory that *Peggy Hoblyn* might have reached the safety of Fowey harbour was cruelly dashed. One of the Pentuan boats picked up the body of a crew member and transferred it to Nathan's boat.

By mid-morning four more bodies had been found. Two, from the *Peggy Hoblyn,* had been recovered at sea. The others, both fishermen from *The Brave Amy H,* were found floating among the sea-washed rocks not a hundred yards from Portgiskey Cove. One of them was Obadiah Hockin. There could be no doubt now that both Portgiskey boats had foundered in the storm.

Nathan accompanied the body of Obadiah Hockin to his home, where the old fisherman's sister, Lavinia, was now firmly ensconced in the house, the pig once more enjoying sole occupation of its sty. Before leaving the house Nathan told Lavinia Hockin where her brother's savings might be found. To his surprise, she immediately burst into tears.

'Six months ago such news would have gladdened my

heart,' she sobbed. 'But since he came back from France me and Obadiah have grown to understand each other as we never had before. He was a good man, Mr Jago . . . a good man. I'd trade all his money – and my own, too – if I could have him back here again. I should have told him while he was alive because he'll never believe it from anyone else. No, not even from the lips of Our Lord Himself!'

Of all the searchers who scoured the sea and the foreshore about Portgiskey, none drove himself harder than Saul Piper. He was at sea for most of the day with Nathan. Then, when *Sir Beville* returned to Portgiskey, he joined one of the search parties scouring the foot of the cliffs for bodies from *The Brave Amy H*.

Not until long after dark did Saul Piper return to his home, weary and haggard from lack of sleep. Walking into the kitchen he startled Maud, who had been weeping by the fireside, surrounded by her sisters.

'Have you . . .?' Maud's moment of hope died as she saw the tortured face of her father.

'He's dead, isn't he? *You* killed him.' Maud screamed the accusation at her father. '*You* started the quarrel that had him sent to sea in *The Brave Amy H*, instead of crewing with *Sir Beville*.'

'Maud . . . I couldn't know. I wouldn't have done anything to hurt Cornelius . . . I *liked* the lad.'

'You *hated* him. You hated him because he married me. Because he'd made me happy again.' Maud's face was contorted with grief. 'I hate *you*! I hate you because . . . because you've killed all the love I've ever known.'

'Maud . . .'

Slipping past his outstretched arms, Maud ran out through the doorway and fled into the night, running awkwardly, both hands clutching the unborn baby that filled her belly.

'Pa, go after her . . . please!' The plea came from Harriet, who rose from a stool by the fireside and limped towards him.

Any other time Saul Piper would have been quick to take

some action, even if only to cuff his daughter for daring to tell her father what he should do. But he had endured a strenuous twenty-four hours. They had taken a toll on both his body and mind. Saul Piper was exhausted, too tired to think clearly. He could demand no more from his body and did not have an answer for his crippled daughter.

'Your father's had enough, Harriet,' said an unusually decisive Sophie Piper. 'He needs food and rest. Our Maud will be back, you'll see.'

Maud Lanyon *did* return to the Piper house in Pentuan.

She was carried there on a sheep-hurdle borne by a farmer and his two sons who owned land between Pentuan and Mevagissey – but not until her bloated body had floated in and out with the tide for forty-eight hours.

Cornelius Lanyon's body was recovered only hours later, not two hundred yards from where Maud had been dragged from the sea.

The bodies of the young couple lay side by side in the Pentuan chapel with those crew members of *The Brave Amy H* and *Peggy Hoblyn* whose bodies had already been recovered.

It was a brief reunion for the tragic young couple. The storm had claimed many victims along this part of the Cornish coast and the coroner was a busy man. He held an inquest in the chapel in Pentuan and took only forty minutes to arrive at a verdict on the eleven men and one woman.

The verdict in respect of the eleven seamen was 'death by drowning'; but when he came to Maud Lanyon the coroner recorded a verdict of *felo de se* – suicide. To this the busy coroner added a rider that Maud's body should be laid to rest during the hours of darkness, and that Christian rites should not be observed.

Both Nathan and Saul Piper jumped to their feet to protest at the coroner's verdict. Nathan argued that there was insufficient evidence to justify such a finding. He pointed out that Maud's body was found only yards from that of her husband. He suggested Maud might have seen her husband's body floating among the rocks and died in a vain attempt to bring it to shore. Saul Piper, shaken by the verdict, begged only that Maud be allowed a decent Christian burial.

The harassed coroner paid no attention to either plea. Neither man had said anything to make him change his mind. The verdict would stand. Five minutes later he was on his horse. Accompanied by the coroner's officer, he was heading for Mevagissey. Here there were seven fishermen who had fallen victim to the sudden violence of the recent storm.

Maud Lanyon was buried shortly before midnight. Her grave was beside a lonely crossroads on the high road beyond Polrudden, where the trees bowed their heads in permanent deference to the power of the wind that blew from the sea.

The burial had been planned for an earlier hour, but another storm had blown up. The handful of mourners had waited in vain for the wind and rain to abate. Far from improving, the storm grew steadily worse and so it was decided to go ahead with the grim proceedings.

The body was conveyed in a Polrudden cart to the crossroads. Frightened by the wind and rain that lashed the coastal road, the horse was skittish. In trying to control the frightened animal, Will Hodge used more swearwords than were customary at an interment.

Maud Lanyon's grave was not a deep one. Nathan, Saul Piper and Will Hodge took turns digging by the weak yellow light of a fretful lantern, but by the time they were down three feet they were standing knee-deep in muddy water. Another six inches and the gravediggers were forced to halt. The rain was falling more heavily now and the water-level in the grave rose steadily.

Clumsily, the three men slid the cheap coffin from the wagon, Will Hodge alternately cursing the rain and the horse which would not stand still.

The coffin was lowered into the shallow grave, displacing water. For a few uncomfortable moments the mourners stood around the open grave. Each was trying to think of the girl whose body was in the coffin at their feet, and not of the rain that trickled inside the snuggest-fitting coat – and there were few present who wore clothing that had not been bought to fit someone else.

Apart from Saul Piper there were three other members of the Piper family: Sophie, the crippled Harriet and the thirteen-year-old simpleton, Tess. Amy was there, too. She had grown fond of Maud during the brief time the Pentuan girl had worked at Polrudden and the two had often talked together of their hopes and fears.

After her marriage, Maud had slowly grown more confident of the future. Cornelius had been a kind, gentle and considerate husband. He had gradually restored Maud's faith and self-esteem. Of those about the graveside, only Amy did not doubt the accuracy of the coroner's verdict. She knew Maud Lanyon would not have wanted to live without Cornelius.

After Nathan said a brief prayer for Maud's soul, the small knot of mourners joined in a mumbled version of the Lord's Prayer. Then the men began the melancholy task of shovelling earth into the shallow, water-filled grave.

Nathan had tried to persuade his father to allow Maud's body to be buried close to her husband, in the little grave-yard attached to the Pentuan Methodist Church. Josiah Jago refused the request. Neither would he attend her interment, although he did lead his congregation in a prayer for her soul. To have done more would have placed his preaching licence at risk. The Reverend Damian Roach would have been delighted to lay the information before the Church licensing authority.

When the grave had been filled in, and the turf carefully replaced, Nathan led the horse and wagon to and fro over a wide area of grass verge around the spot. A body buried outside consecrated ground was not protected by the laws of the land. Grave-robbers or the morbidly curious could exhume such a body without fear of retribution. The only safeguard was secrecy. The only cross that would ever mark Maud Lanyon's last resting-place was provided by the meeting of two roads.

CHAPTER NINETEEN

The loss of two of his boats was a disastrous blow to Nathan. With only one boat working there was no hope of keeping the Portgiskey fish-cellar fully employed and earning enough money to maintain Polrudden Manor. All the profit he had made during the season, and the tithes from the Pentuan fishermen, would be needed to replace fishing tackle lost by *Sir Beville* and carry out essential structural repairs to Polrudden.

Nathan spent the next few nights fishing, while his mornings were taken up going through the accounts of both Polrudden and the fishing venture at Portgiskey. For a whole week Amy saw him only when he emerged from the study at Polrudden, haggard and weary, or before he set off for a night's fishing, tired and irritable, sleep kept at bay by worry about their future. Things were not improved when both the boys caught mumps, the illness demanding much of Amy's attention, by night and by day.

It was now November and the weather was uncertain. *Sir Beville* was moored alongside the quay at Portgiskey for more days than the boat spent at sea. With no money coming in on these days, Nathan worried more than ever. For Amy, the weather had certain compensations. It meant she had Nathan at home, where she could share some of his problems. Since the sinking of the two fishing-boats there had been little opportunity for talking.

One evening, when they were seated together for an

evening meal, Amy realised it was the first occasion on which they had shared the same table for longer than a month. It proved to be a difficult mealtime, almost as though they had become strangers. It was a feeling neither had experienced before, not even when Nathan returned after many months of imprisonment in France.

Amy made a determined effort to make conversation as they ate, but it was soon apparent that Nathan was not listening. Nor was he eating with anything approaching enthusiasm. He sat at the table pushing the food about his plate, his thoughts elsewhere.

'Nathan, I know you're worried about everything, but won't you at least *try* to share your thoughts with me? We can work something out between us. I *know* we can.'

It was as though she had never spoken. He continued to shift the contents of his plate from one side to the other, then moving it all back again.

'Nathan! I want to be able to *help*. I can't do that until I know how you're thinking. It's time we had a talk.' There was exasperation in Amy's voice.

'Uh?'

Nathan shook his head, as though waking from a dream, and Amy repeated: 'We've got to talk about things, Nathan. Work something out together.'

Nathan pursed his lips. '*Talking* isn't going to help. Something needs to be *done* – and very quickly.'

'All right.' Amy ignored the irritability in his voice. At least he was talking to her. 'Do you have anything in mind?'

'Yes. A return to the prize-ring.'

It was a reply Amy had been half-expecting. With only one boat they had been unable to step up their night-trading activities. In fact, smuggling was becoming increasingly difficult all along the Cornish coast. The Preventive Service had brought a second boat to Fowey and both were being assisted by men-of-war. The Royal Navy had time on its hands now Napoleon Bonaparte was enjoying enforced exile on the island of Elba. Two Cornish fishing-boats had already been captured. Nathan had used prize-fighting

225

winnings to buy his first boat, and betting on the outcome of another bout had gained Polrudden for them. It was hardly surprising he should turn once more to a proven means of raising money, now things were so bad.

Nathan had been a very good fighter, his career culminating in a bout that brought him the title of 'Champion of all England' and the promise of a good purse whenever he stepped inside a ring. But Nathan had not been in training for some years. He had lost the fitness and dedication that made all the difference between champions and losers.

All this went through Amy's mind, but she was careful to couch her objection to his proposal in more general terms. She did not want to hand Nathan a challenge he would feel obliged to take up.

Nathan listened to Amy with growing impatience. When she stopped talking, he said angrily: 'You've done your best to tell me what I *shouldn't* do. Perhaps you'll come up with some idea for making money to get us out of our troubles.'

'We could sell Polrudden,' replied Amy quietly.

Nathan looked at her as though she had struck him. 'Sell Polrudden? *Sell . . .?*' Pushing back his chair, Nathan stood up. 'Polrudden is Beville's birthright. He was born here. So was his grandfather, his great-grandfather, and generations of his ancestors before them. You'd throw all that away? No! If I have nothing else to give him, he'll have Polrudden. I swear to that.'

'Is that your *real* reason for wanting to hold on to Polrudden, Nathan? Or is it because you believe you owe a debt to someone else? To Beville's mother, perhaps? After all, this was *her* home, too.'

Amy's unexpected question took Nathan by surprise. He rarely thought of Elinor these days – and certainly not as Beville's mother. Beville had become *their* child – his and Amy's. Beville loved Amy as much as any child loved his mother, and Nathan knew she loved the small boy in return.

'You've never really liked Polrudden, have you? Any

more than you understand what it means to me to be able to give the house to Beville one day. *You* were left Portgiskey by your father. If I had to rely on mine, I would have *nothing*. I want more for *my* son.'

'I *do* know how important Polrudden is to you, Nathan. I knew it when I bought the house for us – for you, me and Beville. I love living here, but I don't think we should shape our lives around a house – any house. We should be doing whatever is best for us as a family.'

'Oh, yes. I'd almost forgotten it was *you* who saved Polrudden, *your* money that bought it for Beville.'

Amy knew the loss of the two boats and their crews had been a shattering blow for Nathan. She was also aware of the desperation he felt at his inability to make good the loss. Nevertheless, his words hurt.

'My money was riding on your skill and courage. If it hadn't been for you, Polrudden would never have become ours. Like everything else that's been done since then, we did it together.'

'You trusted my skill then. Trust it again.'

Amy's distress increased. 'Have you forgotten the beating you took in your last fight? You were unrecognisable for two weeks afterwards. You're *older* now, and out of training. You'd be fighting younger and fitter men. Men hungry to make their mark on the world. You've told me often enough of the tragedy of fighters who won't admit they're too old for the prize-ring. Yet now you're telling me you want to go off and do the same thing! It's senseless.'

'Nothing makes sense any more. You . . . me . . . our way of life . . . the hard work . . . even the plans we made – they were all wiped out in a single night.'

'It could have been much worse, Nathan. *You* might have been at sea in *The Brave Amy H* or *Peggy Hoblyn*.'

Nathan knew Amy was right, but the knowledge made him feel no less helpless. Nor did it go any way towards solving the problems that weighed so heavily upon him. Turning away abruptly, he left the room.

Behind him, Amy took a forkful of food to her mouth in

an automatic gesture, but when she tried to swallow it threatened to choke her. She felt she had somehow failed Nathan at a time when he most needed her, but she did not know what else to do.

Nathan was not in the house at bedtime, and Amy went to bed alone. But she did not sleep. The house had been quiet for a long time when she heard the sound of the heavy front door being opened and carefully closed again. It was followed by clumsy footsteps on the stairs. It sounded as though Nathan might have been drinking in one of the Pentuan taverns. Her suspicions were confirmed when he came into the bedroom and bumped against much of the furniture before seating himself heavily on the bed to remove his boots.

When Nathan slid in bed beside her, the heavy fumes of cheap brandy reached Amy even though he lay on his side, facing away from her. After waiting in vain for him to say something, Amy reached across and rested an arm on his cold body.

He did not move when she caressed his arm, and she stopped. For perhaps ten minutes they lay side by side in silence. Then Amy tried once more to arouse him. Putting an arm about him, she snuggled her body close to his.

'Nathan . . .'

There was no reply, but she tried again. 'Nathan. Can we talk, please?'

There was silence for a few more seconds, then the sound of drunken snoring filled the air.

Nathan was honest enough with himself to know that everything Amy had said made a great deal of sense. Selling Polrudden and investing the money in boats and equipment for Portgiskey was a certain way of overcoming their present difficulties. He had even begun to consider the idea in earnest, when something happened to change his thinking once more.

Nathan was preparing to leave for a night's fishing when a stranger rode up to Polrudden. Both his garb and the mount he rode showed signs of a long ride. From his bedroom window Nathan watched the rider approach the house and dismount. By the time Nathan finished dressing and made his way downstairs, the stranger had been shown into the study.

When Nathan entered the room, the man looked at his fisherman's garb uncertainly. 'Mr Jago? *Nathan* Jago?'

'Yes. You have business with me?'

'Ah . . . yes.'

Nathan's garb still appeared to disturb the man, and Nathan explained impatiently: 'I'm about to go fishing. I'll be obliged if you'll state your business as quickly as possible.'

'Of course, Mr Jago.'

The stranger's relief was evident, and Nathan realised he had assumed Nathan was going fishing for sport rather than to earn a living, but he did not bother to put the record straight.

'I have come from London. I travelled by coach as far as Plymouth, and took a coach from there. Your Cornish roads, you know . . .? They have a certain, er . . . notoriety. I've heard it said they are worse than the roads in Wales. I, ah . . . would hesitate before subscribing to such an opinion. However, I concede there *is* some truth in what they say . . .'

'Your *business*?' growled Nathan, but he was interested now, as well as curious. Why should anyone ride from London to see him? 'Who are you?'

'Of course, of course!' The man laid a document-case on the table. As he unfastened the leather strap with which the case was secured, he explained: 'My name is Edward Cottle. I am a clerk – a *senior* clerk, you understand – with Messrs Honey, Terrett & Forsyth, solicitors. I am here regarding the estate of the late Sir Lewis Hearle.'

'The *late* Sir Lewis Hearle?'

'Yes. Oh dear me! Am I to understand you have not heard of his demise? I thought . . . Well, he *was* your father-in-law, and you are living in Polrudden, the family home of the Hearles for very many generations . . .'

'Polrudden was purchased from Sir Lewis Hearle a couple of years ago. He and I have not met since then.'

'Ahem! I see . . . Yes, I see. Nevertheless, I am sorry to be the bearer of such sad news, Mr Jago. You will realise, of course, that your son, Beville, is now the fourth baronet? As his father and legal guardian you will be required to sign some papers on the young Sir Beville's behalf. I regret to tell you that Sir Lewis left more debts than possessions but there *is* a small trust fund in favour of Sir Beville. Messrs Honey, Terrett & Forsyth will administer the fund on behalf of your son, until he comes of age. There are also certain matters that require your presence in London at your earliest convenience. In the meantime, if you will be kind enough to sign these papers . . .?'

Nathan scarcely heard a word of the last few sentences uttered by the solicitor's clerk. He was far too excited at the thought of his son inheriting his grandfather's baronetcy. *Sir* Beville Hearle Jago . . . of Polrudden. There could be no question now of parting with the manor-house. Even Amy must realise this.

'Mr Jago, may I trouble you for your signature, sir? I have lodgings booked in St Austell tonight. I fear I shall lose the road in the darkness . . .'

'Of course. I have a quill here on the desk.'

Nathan put his signature to a number of documents, the contents of which were hurriedly explained to him by Edward Cottle. They were mainly to release money, to allow solicitors to meet the more pressing of the late Sir Lewis Hearle's debts.

Nathan also heard the circumstances of the death of the third baronet. A Member of Parliament for many years, Sir Lewis Hearle had collapsed and died while giving one of his rare speeches in the House of Commons. He was speaking against an anti-slavery clause in the agreement the Allies were making with France. The manner of his death had been immediately seized upon by anti-slavery campaigners as a sign of the wrath of God. Whether it was true or not, Sir

Lewis Hearle influenced more people by the manner of his death than he had at any time during his long parliamentary career – albeit *against* the cause he was espousing.

When the solicitor's clerk left Polrudden, Nathan went in search of Amy to tell her the news. He had promised the clerk he would come to London during the first week of 1815, to wind up the affairs of the late Sir Lewis Hearle.

CHAPTER TWENTY

When the coach exchanged the ruts and potholes of the country roads for the teeth-jarring cobbles of London Town, Nathan felt a return of the old excitement that always gripped him when he returned to the capital city of England.

One of the most crowded cities in the world, London contained itself with ever-increasing difficulty. It was beginning to spill out from its ancient boundaries, reaching out towards Paddington village and the little hamlets to the south and west.

It was dark when Nathan arrived, and the streets of the capital were beginning to fill with people. Most were working men and women, their worn clothing practical rather than colourful, their gait hurried as they made for home.

Others – army officers and gentlemen – were making their way more leisurely to or from their clubs. Their cutaway coats, beaver top hats and skin-tight pantaloons tucked inside shiny boots were dictated by fashion and not by vocation.

In the carriages cluttering the narrow streets, women sat facing each other, spencers fastened tight about their necks, the ostrich feathers adorning their hats bobbing with the movement of their transport.

It had been more than two years since Nathan was last in London, but very little had changed. The street-traders still advertised their wares in loud, hoarse voices, offering bread, meat pies, faggots, ribbons and trinkets. Crowds of urchins lurked around the entrances to clubs and salons, inns and coffee-houses, jostling each other whenever a carriage slowed and stopped. Opening doors and lowering carriage steps, the urchins offered exaggerated obeisance in the hope of a penny tip. Others waited in the shadows, ready to dart forward should an unwary man leave the corner of a purse or the chain of a gold watch protruding from an easily accessible pocket.

All this was as Nathan had always remembered London. So, too, was the smell that caused first-time visitors to wrinkle their noses in disgust. It was the unsavoury stench of the Thames, the river that served as a giant open sewer for London's populace, already nudging the million mark. It was a stench that the lowest drunken beggar shared with the Prince Regent and the peers in the Palace of Westminster. Here the smell was sometimes so overpowering that Parliament was forced to adjourn.

The late Sir Lewis Hearle's solicitors had offices in a courtyard just off Chancery Lane. Nearby was Carey Street and it was here, at the Plough inn, that Nathan found bed and board. The landlord of the Plough was John Gully, a prize-fighter who had shared the ring with Nathan on more than one occasion. Gully's inn attracted a clientele of former prize-fighters, and Nathan felt immediately at home.

'It's good to see you, boy,' declared Gully for the seventh time. The two men sat together in the low-ceilinged inn, close to a cosy fire, with a table laden with meat and ale between them. 'Since you left the prize-ring we haven't seen a champion worthy of the name here in London. Why, things are so bad, some of the gents of the "Fancy" have begged me to take up prize-fighting again.' John Gully chuckled. 'They'd need to put up a purse big enough to make the Prince Regent a pauper 'fore I'd enter the prize-ring again.' He suddenly stopped talking and looked questioningly at Nathan. '*You've* not come to London for a fight?'

Nathan shook his head. 'I've thought about it often enough, even though my wife says I'm too old to fight again. But I've come to London because my son has inherited a baronetcy from his grandfather. I need to clear up a few details with the solicitors.'

'A baronetcy, eh?' John Gully was impressed. 'You've done well with your life, Nathan. So have I. Now, instead of putting up my fists in a prize-ring, I put up money outside it. I've gambled well. It's knowing the fight game that's done it for me.'

Leaning across the table, John Gully lowered his voice. 'I'm a wealthy man now, Nathan. It's been suggested I stand for Parliament – and I've accepted. Can you imagine that? Me, John Gully, who'd once fight anyone for a guinea purse, a Member of Parliament! Why, I might even finish up a baronet, like that son of yours! We've come a long way, you and I – but there's many more who've gone the other way . . .'

John Gully emphasised his words by pointing a thumb downwards. 'Jed Kelly's one of them. He claims your title as "Champion of all England", but he's fought no one to earn the right to it. All it means for him is a night or two's free drinking at an inn where the "Fancy" gather. There are a great many men like Kelly in the prize-fighting game, and few like you and me. We've used the fight game to get what *we* want from life. Now we can afford to sit back and watch others making fools of themselves.'

During the course of a long evening, a number of former prize-fighters called in to say hello to the landlord of the Plough inn. All were given a free drink, and every one of them came to where Nathan sat, to shake him by the hand. Most had seen him fight, some had lost fights to him. By the time the convivial evening came to a close, Nathan felt like a champion once more. If he stumbled on a stair or two on his way to bed, it did not matter. There was no one to see him.

Nathan made his way to the solicitors the next morning, regretting the excesses of the previous evening. The feeling was heightened when the terms of Sir Lewis Hearle's will were explained to him.

Sir Lewis Hearle had never been a wealthy man, but he had made a number of wise investments during his lifetime and had used the proceeds to provide a trust fund for his grandson. When the young baronet came of age he would inherit a considerable sum of money, but the inheritance was conditional. The money would be Beville's *only if he were living at Polrudden*!

Sir Lewis Hearle had known better than anyone the high cost of running Polrudden. The upkeep of the ageing manor-house had brought the third baronet close to ruin. Now he had laid the burden squarely upon Nathan's shoulders. Should he fail, Beville would lose not only Polrudden, but his inheritance, too. It was a final act of malice from the baronet who had bitterly resented Nathan's marriage to his daughter.

That evening Nathan sat by himself in the Plough inn, staring moodily into a pewter ale-tankard. John Gully had sat with him for a while but, sensing his companion's mood, the landlord found an excuse to leave Nathan alone, giving instructions that his guest's tankard was to be kept filled.

Nathan had been drinking for about two hours when Gully returned to the table, his hand resting on the shoulder of a giant of a man who shuffled along amiably beside him.

'Nathan, here's a man I would like you to meet. We spoke of him last night. Jed Kelly.'

Nathan looked up, catching Kelly's sheepish grin. He had been thinking of this man far more recently than last night. It was almost as though fate had helped Nathan arrive at a decision by throwing the two men together like this.

Returning Kelly's smile with a scowl, Nathan ignored the other's proffered hand. Putting his tankard down heavily upon the table, he stared up at Kelly belligerently.

'So you now claim to be champion prize-fighter of all England?'

Kelly's smile disappeared, but only for a few moments. It was long enough for Nathan to see that dissipation and careless living had cost Kelly dear. He was at least ten years older than Nathan, and had fought with considerably less skill. Kelly was badly scarred about the eyes, and his nose was flattened and misshapen. His was the face of a loser.

'Well, Nathan, when you gave up the prize-ring there was no one else around to take the title, so I thought: Why not me? I've been a prize-fighter all me life, but I've never got much out of it. Not like you and Mr Gully, here.'

When Nathan said nothing, Jed Kelly's self-conscious smile returned once more and the self-styled 'Champion of all England' decided further explanation was called for.

'There didn't seem to be any other prize-fighter interested in the title, Nathan. I put it around that I was willing to fight anyone else who reckoned they had a right to the title, but there were no takers.'

Looking up at the other man's simple face, Nathan felt momentarily ashamed of what he was about to do. He dismissed the feeling as quickly as it had come. There was more at stake here than pride, be it his own or Jed Kelly's.

'There's a taker now, Jed. I'm here to take my title back – in the prize-ring.'

Jed Kelly's smile gave way to disbelief, which as quickly became dismay. Behind him, John Gully's bushy eyebrows came together in a puzzled frown.

'I . . . I don't want to fight you, Nathan . . .' Words eluded Jed Kelly as easily as did a good prize-fighter.

'You can please yourself,' declared Nathan bluntly. 'I believe Mick O'Rourke is also claiming the championship.

I'll fight him instead. Where will that leave you?'

Jed Kelly's slow mind turned over the implications of Nathan's words. If it got around that Nathan Jago and Mick O'Rourke were fighting for the championship of England, he, Jed Kelly, would slip back into the obscurity that had been his since he lost his last fight.

'Win or lose, you'll be able to boast that you once fought for the title. No one could ever take that away from you.'

Jed Kelly licked dry lips. 'I'm getting a bit old for prize-fighting, Nathan. Especially a championship fight.'

'So am I, Jed.' Nathan stood up. 'Do we have a fight? Or shall I approach O'Rourke?'

Jed Kelly was a head taller than Nathan and a great deal heavier. Much of his weight was flabbiness, but behind the fist of a man who knew how to throw a punch every pound counted.

'I'll fight you, Nathan. When?'

Nathan looked past Jed Kelly to John Gully, who had been following the conversation with bewildered interest. 'Can you arrange a prize-fight, John. A week from today?'

John Gully's expression was cold, and Nathan knew the wealthy innkeeper was remembering the conversation that had taken place between them the previous evening.

'I can arrange the fight, but the purse won't be high. Most of the "Fancy", including the Duke of Clarence, are enjoying the joys of France.'

'Get what you can. I'll leave it entirely up to you.'

Without another look at the man who would never again be able to claim he was champion prize-fighter of all England, Nathan walked from the room as the excitement of the prize-fighting clientele erupted behind him.

Later that evening, as Nathan lay fully clothed on his bed, staring up at the ceiling, there was a knock at the door. It was John Gully.

The coldness had gone from his face, but he was still puzzled. Entering the room, he straddled a chair and sat looking at Nathan.

'I thought you'd be out raising my purse money,' said Nathan drily.

'Time enough for that,' the innkeeper retorted. 'After the conversation we had last night I feel you owe me an explanation.'

Had it been any other man, Nathan would have told him to mind his own business, but he and Gully had known each other a long time. The other man was right. Nathan *did* owe him an explanation.

By the time Nathan finished telling Gully of the terms of Sir Lewis Hearle's will, and of the importance of Polrudden to the young Sir Beville, all the innkeeper's earlier friendliness had returned.

'I knew it had to be something like that, boy,' he said. 'But Jed Kelly is a nobody. You'll not earn enough from a fight with him to keep your precious manor-house for six months.'

'I realise that,' replied Nathan. 'But once I've beaten Kelly I'll be able to command far more money for a match with O'Rourke – enough, at least, to buy another boat.'

John Gully's eyebrows had shot up at mention of O'Rourke. Rising from the chair, he looked down at Nathan. 'So it's Mick O'Rourke next, is it? In that case you'd better come downstairs and put a man-size meal in your belly. We'll need to discuss your training – and some tactics.'

The day of the contest between Nathan Jago and Jed Kelly was as grey and dismal as the venue chosen for the championship fight. The ring had been erected on the mudflats of Wapping, only a bend of the river away from the high stone walls of the Tower of London.

As predicted, the absence abroad of so many members of the "Fancy", the gambling, sporting fraternity who supported the illegal sport of prize-fighting, had made it difficult for John Gully to organise the bout. However, the innkeeper had managed to get together a purse of 250 guineas. Two hundred would go to the winner, and fifty to the loser. It was a low purse by championship standards but, as Gully explained, neither fighter had been inside a ring for more than two years and the fight had been arranged at short notice.

As it was, the 2,000-strong crowd barely had value for their money. The hardy nature of Nathan's work meant he was reasonably fit. In addition, he had trained hard during the previous week, thanks to John Gully. Every day Nathan had run five miles through the London streets before most people were setting off to work. During the day there were exercises in the yard behind the Plough inn, and at least three bouts of sparring with the Plough inn's prize-fighting customers. Gully also ensured that Nathan had an abundance of good food, a minimum of strong drink, and a good rest at night.

Unfortunately, John Gully had no control over the training of Nathan's opponent. When Jed Kelly removed the heavy blanket coat that had been slung over his shoulders, and stepped forward to the centre of the ring, his stomach flowed generously over the tightened belt of his trousers. From the moment the fight began it was evident that Kelly was every bit as slow as his excess weight indicated. Looking slight in comparison, Nathan circled around Kelly, jabbing him at will with sharp, punishing punches.

The first round lasted seven minutes, by which time Kelly was already breathing heavily, perspiration streaming down his red face despite the raw cold of the winter's day.

When Kelly lumbered inside Nathan's punches and leaned on him, the crowd roared its disapproval, yelling for more action.

'Take it easy on me,' Kelly panted in Nathan's ear. 'I'm not as fit as I should be.'

Nathan's answer was to step back and land a flurry of blows to his opponent's flabby body. Jed Kelly dropped to one knee, and round one was over.

'I'd say Kelly's been training in half the tap-rooms of London,' commented Nathan as John Gully towelled his body vigorously. In the far corner his opponent leaned back heavily against the ropes, paying scant attention to the urgent advice of his cornermen.

'Drinking's always been Jed's weakness. That's why it was his tongue and not his fists that made him a champion.' John Gully gave Nathan's upper arms a final towelling as the thirty-second break came to an end. 'Go out and nail him quick, boy. You'll need to make the crowd want to see you fight again if you're to get the money you want for the next bout with O'Rourke.'

Round two lasted hardly more than a minute. After jabbing Kelly's head back with a straight left, Nathan brought over a right cross that left Kelly sitting in the Wapping mud, his head lolling stupidly.

Kelly's cornermen helped their heavy fighter to his feet and supported him to his corner of the ring, but the fight was almost over for the self-styled champion and the crowd felt cheated.

Had it not been for the boos and catcalls, Jed Kelly would have been allowed to accept defeat from the comparative comfort of his stool in the corner of the ring. Instead, alarmed that the angry spectators would become violent, the two cornermen prised Kelly from the stool and supported him to the mark in the centre of the ring. Here they deserted him, leaving him at the mercy of his opponent.

Kelly appeared to be so helpless that Nathan was reluctant to carry the fight to him. Nathan's hesitation almost proved his undoing. While Jed Kelly was still swaying, he suddenly produced a punch, swinging a huge fist up, seemingly from somewhere behind his back. Gathering momentum, the fist collided heavily with the side of Nathan's head sending him staggering backwards for three or four shaky paces.

Jed Kelly was not a good prize-fighter, but he *was* experienced enough to know he had landed a good punch. He moved in to press home the advantage – but he was too slow.

The same prize-fighting instinct had Nathan retreating rapidly from his opponent. By the time the lumbering Kelly caught up with him, Nathan's mind had cleared. The larger man walked into two punches that stopped him short and sent his world reeling about him. A fierce upper cut connected to his chin as he was dropping to his knees, and Jed Kelly's championship hopes pitched to the ground with him. When the thirty-second respite ended, he was still unconscious. Nathan had won.

The crowd who had been booing only minutes before went wild. Although cheated of a lengthy entertainment, they had seen a knock-out that would be talked of in prize-fighting circles for years to come. Nathan Jago could once more claim to be 'Champion of all England'.

CHAPTER TWENTY-ONE

Nathan began his return journey to Cornwall the day after the prize-fight. His win had been impressive enough for John Gully to promise Nathan a purse that should be close to a thousand guineas for his meeting with Mick O'Rourke. It would be a while before the necessary arrangements for the prize-fight could be made. O'Rourke was an Irishman with a home in County Wexford. Someone would need to travel there. Gully advised Nathan to spend the intervening weeks training hard. O'Rourke was reported to be a strong fighter. Skill alone would not suffice against such an opponent.

The fight with Jed Kelly had left Nathan unmarked, and he decided to tell Amy nothing of the prize-fight or of his future plans. She would not approve. She might even try to stop the fight – and Nathan was in desperate need of the money.

Both Beville and Jean-Paul were now fully recovered from the mumps, and Nathan had to try to tell Amy what had occurred at the London solicitors above the excited chatter of the two small and excited boys.

'I suppose this means you'll not consider selling Polrudden.'

'Of course.' Nathan swung Beville high in the air before putting the giggling boy on the carpet beside Jean-Paul. 'We have a baronet in the family now. Sir Beville Hearle Jago –of Polrudden. What's more, when he comes of age he'll have enough money to live in a style befitting his rank – but only if he has Polrudden.'

'Beville won't come of age for almost eighteen years. How do we keep Polrudden *and* live until then?'

'We'll manage.'

Nathan had been leaning down, prising Beville free of his leg. Looking up, Nathan caught Amy's unguarded expression of concern. 'Don't worry, I'll be returning to London in a few weeks' time. There are some more documents to be signed. I've also arranged a loan – to buy another boat.'

'A loan? Who'd loan money on a venture as uncertain as fishing?'

'John Gully,' replied Nathan glibly. Unused to lying to Amy he had practised his story all the way home from London. Even so, he was glad he did not have to look into Amy's face when he spoke. 'You remember John Gully, landlord of the Plough inn? He's a wealthy man now and intends standing for Parliament soon.'

'Aren't there enough foolish men there already?' retorted Amy sharply.

'What *is* it you want, Amy?' Nathan spoke in angry exasperation, the anger fuelled by his own ridiculous feeling of guilt at having lied to her. 'You don't want me prize-fighting. Perhaps you'll tell me how to earn the money to live? Nothing I suggest seems to suit you.'

For a moment it seemed Amy might reply. Instead she shook her head. 'You must do whatever you think is best, Nathan. I don't doubt you will anyway.'

With this enigmatic remark Amy turned and hurried away, leaving Nathan looking after her in surprise.

Later that night, as they lay side by side in bed, Nathan could sense the tension and unhappiness in Amy's body. They had hardly spoken to each other all evening, sharing an unhappy meal and afterwards undressing in silence in the darkness of their bedroom.

Turning towards Amy suddenly, Nathan put an arm about her. 'Does the thought of keeping Polrudden make you so unhappy, Amy?'

'No, of course not.' She turned to him, her body pressed against his. 'It's . . . it's knowing we'll need to make so many sacrifices to keep it, that's all.'

'We'll manage. Things will be easier when we have a second boat.'

'Yes,' Amy agreed. While Nathan had been away in London *Sir Beville* had landed some excellent catches. Two boats would have fetched them in a handsome profit.

'I'm sorry if I upset you by talking about Polrudden, but keeping it will be very important from now on, you know that.'

'Yes.' Amy's hand caressed his shoulder. 'I'm sorry, too. It's just . . . I've *missed* you, Nathan.'

'I've missed you, too.' He pulled her to him and for a long time all thoughts of Polrudden and the problems they would have to face in the future fled from the room.

Much later, as Amy stirred, she felt Nathan's arm about her and turned her face up towards him.

'Nathan . . .?'

'Um?'

He felt deliciously drowsy. Sleep was not far away.

'Polrudden is Beville's heritage, we both agree on that. What if we have another son . . . you and I? What would we give *him*?'

'Portgiskey and the boats. Does that make you happier?'

Amy snuggled in closer. 'Yes, that makes me happier. I think it will please our son, too.'

Nathan had returned to Pentuan at a time when Josiah Jago and the Reverend Damian Roach were engaged in yet another of their bitter wrangles. Much to Roach's disgust, although the Methodist Conference had officially suspended Josiah Jago from his preaching duties, they had stopped short of expelling him from the movement. The result was that Josiah Jago continued preaching and the vast majority of the Methodist congregation attended his services, even though most of those outside Pentuan continued to be conducted in the open air.

In a final desperate attempt to bring his colleague into disrepute, Roach laid information before the magistrate that Preacher Jago was preaching sedition to large numbers of vagrants on Polgooth Downs.

The very mention of the word 'sedition' was sufficient to stir any magistrate to instant action. This occasion proved no exception.

Josiah Jago was preaching on Polgooth Downs in a grey, damp mist that chilled his ill-clad congregation to their very bones, when a shout went up that horsemen were approaching along the narrow pathway. For the vagrant host, any happening out of the norm invariably spelled trouble for them. They quickly dispersed – only to find that the St Austell magistrate had laid his plans carefully. Under the cover of the mist, militiamen called in from Bodmin had completely surrounded the depression in the ground where the service was being held.

'Josiah Jago' – the magistrate knew the Pentuan preacher well – 'a complaint has been laid before me. A most *serious* complaint. It is alleged you are preaching sedition . . .'

'That he is *not*.' Fenwick Garland stepped forward. His whole being bristled with anger, and one of the militiamen lowered his rifle until the point of the long sword-bayonet was only inches from Garland's stomach.

Fenwick Garland brushed bayonet and rifle aside scornfully. 'I've not flinched from bayonets held by *fighting* men, laddie. I'm not scared of this one.'

Taking another limping pace towards the magistrate who was seated on his horse, Fenwick Garland continued as though nothing had occurred to interrupt him. 'I repeat. Preacher Jago has preached no sedition here – or in any other place, I'll wager. If he had, I'd have brought him to you myself. Ay, and so would any man here. Paupers we may be, and vagrants, too, but we've all fought for King George, and for England. We'd do so again if the need arose – even though our only thanks is a whipping if we so much as show our noses in your town.'

Drawn by the tone of Fenwick Garland's voice, the captain of the militia drove his horse through the ragged congregation to confront the angry man.

'What's going on here?' Peering down from his horse, he pointed a finger at Fenwick Garland. 'You've come to my attention before, but I'm damned if I can remember where.'

'Then, my memory's better than yours, Captain Geach. I served in your company in Portugal and Spain. The last time we met was when I carried you from the field at Vittoria. There's half a dozen of us here as was with you then.'

'*Sergeant* Garland! I'll be damned! I tried to find you when the regiment returned home, but they told me you'd been wounded at Orthez and discharged as a result.'

To the surprise of everyone, not least the magistrate, the militia captain swung down easily from his horse. Using his left hand, he grasped Fenwick Garland's hand warmly. Now Preacher Jago could see that the militia captain's right hand was missing.

To the magistrate, Captain Geach explained: 'Sergeant Garland saved my life at Vittoria – and at considerable risk to himself. The man was a damned good soldier. A hero!'

Turning back to Fenwick Garland, Captain Geach looked with horror at the rags the other man wore. 'What has happened to bring you to this sorry state? Your pension should have lifted you above such a way of life . . .'

Fenwick Garland spat in the mud at his feet. 'What pension, Captain? Soldiers are being discharged in thousands – no, *tens* of thousands. Where would the money come from for pensions? There are more than a hundred of us living a miserable existence here, and but two with ninepence a day each from the Chelsea Hospital. If it weren't for Preacher Jago warming our souls and sending us the occasional wagonload of fish from his son's fish-cellar, we'd all have perished long ago.'

The magistrate had listened with growing impatience to the exchange between the two former soldiers. 'Captain Geach. You may discuss the fortunes of your one-time comrades-in-arms another time. I brought you here to perform a duty.'

'It was as well you did so, Mr Hawke,' said the militia captain briskly. 'It's saved you from making a damned fool of all of us. Sergeant Garland has said there's been no sedition preached here. I believe him. What's more, I'll stand up and vouchsafe his loyalty in the highest court in the land. As it is, I'll be making a personal application to the Duke of Wellington for Sergeant Garland to be granted a pension. My advice to you is to apologise to the preacher for disturbing his service. Then my men will escort you to your home.'

'Apologise . . .?' The magistrate bridled angrily. 'I'm damned if I'll apologise to any *Methodist.* I'm sorry if I've wasted your time, Captain Geach, but my information came from a most reliable source.'

'Your information came from another Methodist preacher,' retorted Fenwick Garland, 'but a lesser man than Preacher Jago. There's a move to have Preacher Jago removed because he thinks the souls of soldiers are as important to the Lord as the souls of those who let others do their fighting for them. You're here doing the work of the Methodist Conference, Magistrate. This Preacher Roach must be a clever man indeed.'

The magistrate's face turned an angry scarlet. 'I didn't come here to bandy words with any ragged . . . *vagabond*. Captain Geach, escort me back to St Austell. *Now*, sir, if you please.'

The magistrate wheeled his horse away angrily. Captain Geach knew better than to antagonise him any more. He ordered his men to form an escort, but before riding to their head he said to Fenwick Garland: 'I meant every word I said about obtaining a pension for you. However, these things take time. In the meantime come and see me at my home, just outside Fowey. I'll find something for you to do there.'

Fenwick Garland patted his wounded leg ruefully. 'I still have French lead lodged in my leg, Captain. Some days it troubles me enough to stop me doing a full day's work – and I'll accept no man's charity. Besides, if I show myself on the King's highway I'll likely be whipped out of sight on the orders of your magistrate friend. There's more than one old soldier of the 32nd carrying scars inflicted by the "cat" on the orders of the likes of him. I'm grateful for your thoughts on a pension. If it comes through, you'll find me up here easily enough. If it doesn't . . . well, I'll think kindly of you for trying, and for accepting my word against the magistrate's informant. It's made me feel a man again.'

'You'll get your pension, Sergeant, and no old soldier was ever more deserving of one,' declared the militia captain. Pulling a cloth purse from his pocket, he emptied the contents into his hand and held the gold coins out to Fenwick Garland. 'Take this, Sergeant. It's only a few guineas, but it will buy warm clothing and medicines. If not for you, then for the others of the regiment, and the women.'

'Thank you kindly, Captain.' Fenwick Garland touched a finger to his forehead in salute. 'There are some here in need of help to see them through the rest of the winter. We'll send a prayer your way next time Preacher Jago comes along.'

*

Word that Damian Roach had tried to have Josiah Jago arrested spread quickly around the district. As a result, the following of the official representative of the Methodist Church grew even smaller.

In view of the situation, Nathan was most surprised when he brought *Sir Beville* in after an unsuccessful day's fishing to find the Reverend Damian Roach waiting for him on the quayside at Portgiskey.

After an inquisitive glance down into the boat, Damian Roach said to Nathan: 'I hear things aren't going well for you. That you've been fighting a losing battle for survival since the loss of your boats.'

Nathan shrugged non-committally. He had no intention of discussing his business with this man. 'Fishing is like your work, Reverend. Some you net, others slip through. I'm doing better than most.'

This, at least, was true. Most fishermen had caught nothing at all for a week. Nathan's boats usually returned with a basket or two of fish.

'You need to get yourself another boat. Two, maybe, the same as you had before the storm.'

'If you've nothing better to do than stand here making foolish statements and opening up old wounds, I'll thank you to leave Portgiskey, Reverend Roach. I'm tired and I'm hungry. My replies are likely to be less than polite.'

Jumping ashore, Nathan added: 'If you'll excuse me, I have some tidying up to do.'

Nathan moved along the quay and began spreading out nets as they were dumped on the quay by the crew of *Sir Beville*. The Reverend Damian Roach moved with him.

'There *is* a way to get money for new boats – *and* still have enough in reserve to survive a bad season or two.'

Amy had told Nathan about Damian Roach's plans for Polrudden, without giving Nathan any hint of the Methodist preacher's plans for *her* future. Because of this, Damian Roach's next words came as no surprise.

'Sell Polrudden to me.'

'Polrudden is not for sale. It never will be.'

'You're being foolish. Polrudden is an unnecessary mill-stone around your neck – Amy's, too. Life would have been much easier for her had she not had Polrudden to worry about while you were in a French prison.'

When Nathan made no immediate reply, Damian Roach persisted. 'I want to open a college for Methodist preachers here, Nathan. It would be of great benefit to everyone and bring tremendous prestige to the area. There would be work for the men and women of Pentuan. The arrival of the pilchard would no longer be a matter of life and death for the community. You would have a guaranteed market for much of your locally sold fish. Such a project would benefit everyone – not least the Methodist Church itself.'

'But most of all it would benefit you, Reverend.'

'I would be proud to be principal of such a college if Conference so decreed,' agreed Damian Roach defensively.

'What of my father? Where does he fit into this new and prosperous Pentuan?'

'Your father is getting on in years, Nathan. He finds it difficult to change with the times. But he's performed wonderful service for the Methodist movement; I don't doubt Conference will show its gratitude with a small pension.'

'You're a great one for change, Reverend. Since coming here you've managed to split the Methodist following and set neighbour against neighbour. Yet I don't believe you've even *begun* to show what you're capable of. Your thinking and that of my father isn't so very different. You both think that to have a committee of a hundred men managing the affairs of the Methodist movement is impractical. You *both* want it changed. The only difference is that *you* plan farther ahead than my father. You can see the day coming when the movement has a single leader, just as it did in John Wesley's time. When that day comes you hope to be in a strong position to make your bid for power. What could be better than to be head of the movement's teaching college – the one to *found* such a college? You'd be able to teach preachers your own ideas on Methodism *and* be the best-known member of the movement when it's time to vote for a new leader. You're clever, Roach. Far too clever – and ruthless, too – for a simple old man like my father. He believes all preachers are as selflessly dedicated to their calling as he. But he's taken on the might of the Established Church in his time, and won. There are many men like him in the Methodist movement. They'll see through you, long before you've achieved your ambition, and then you'll be finished. When that day comes I've a feeling my father will still be preaching in Pentuan. Now I've work to do, and then I'm going home. To Polrudden.'

CHAPTER TWENTY-TWO

A letter from John Gully, landlord of the Plough inn in London's Carey Street, reached Polrudden in mid-February. It should have arrived a week earlier, but snow had caused considerable disruption in the hilly counties that lay between London and Cornwall.

The letter was brief, but to the point. The championship prize-fight between Nathan and Mick O'Rourke was arranged for the tenth day of March. O'Rourke was already in London. John Gully had watched him in training and his advice to Nathan was to get to London as quickly as possible in order to intensify his own preparation.

It was evident from the tone of the letter that Kelly thought O'Rourke was good – very good. It was with increasing pessimism that Nathan made his arrangements to go to London.

He could not tell Amy the true reason for leaving but, as it happened, Amy asked few questions. She believed the letter had to do with the estate of the late Sir Lewis Hearle.

Amy had become strangely taut and withdrawn in recent weeks, her mind seemingly on other things. Nathan believed it was a result of the strain of trying to run Polrudden with insufficient money. It was this situation he hoped to remedy.

Nathan had been spending much of his time away from Polrudden, sometimes taking *Sir Beville* out to sea for as long as three or four days at a time, in a bid to find more fish. When he *was* home he spent long hours on the cliffs out of sight of Polrudden, training secretly for the forthcoming prize-fight.

On his arrival in London, Nathan was given no time to settle into his room at the Plough inn. He had hardly stepped from the coach before John Gully was leading him towards the yard at the rear of the inn.

When Nathan protested that he should at least have a meal before beginning training, John Gully said firmly: 'You've got ten days to reach peak fitness. Eat now and you'll want to rest afterwards. You need to get used to having little rest 'twixt dawn and dusk if you're to stand a chance against O'Rourke. Remember, I've watched him train. O'Rourke's good – and he's hungry for the title. What's more, he's ten years younger than you.'

Stripped to the waist in the yard, Nathan shivered in the chill, moist air, but it was not long before both cold and hunger were forgotten. The yard of the Plough inn was a well-known training-ground for up-and-coming young prize-fighters. Two of those present were detailed to spar with Nathan.

For the first time in his prize-fighting career, Nathan donned a pair of the padded gloves recently adopted for training and teaching purposes. The unaccustomed weight of the gloves, coupled with the fact that each of his opponents was a lighter, faster man, made Nathan feel lumbering and slow. He grew increasingly frustrated at the ease with which his sparring partners avoided his punches.

John Gully looked on in silence. This was exactly what he had planned. He had brought in two of the fastest young fighters in London for the purpose. Eventually, exasperated by the elusive opponent of the moment, Nathan mounted a two-fisted attack that took the other fighter by surprise. A jolting left caught him on the point of the chin. Despite the heavy padding on Nathan's gloves, the lighter prize-fighter crashed heavily to the hard-earth ground, and remained there.

As Nathan knelt anxiously by his unconscious sparring partner, other fighters gathered round. They were less interested in the unfortunate prize-fighter than in the punch which had laid him low. The designer of the padded gloves had declared they would prevent a man being 'knocked out'. Nathan had just proven him wrong.

John Gully was well pleased with the outcome of the sparring bout, but he was careful to keep his satisfaction from Nathan.

'It's a relief to know you can still throw a punch,' he said in an off-hand manner, 'but you'll need to move a lot faster if you're going to plant one on the chin of Mick O'Rourke. He has a powerful punch *and* speed. He also has the stamina of a brewery horse. He went sixty-three rounds to win the championship of Ireland.'

Nathan's sparring partner was sitting up now. As two men helped him inside the inn, John Gully called for the second sparring partner to take his place, at the same time waving other prize-fighters out of the way.

On the fourth day of his stay at the Plough inn, Nathan was sitting down to his evening meal, grateful for the opportunity to rest his aching muscles, when suddenly there was a commotion in the doorway. A surge of excitement ran through the room as a well-built young man with black curly hair picked his way through the crowd.

Stopping at one of the tables, the newcomer asked a question. He had to repeat it twice before the customer pointed a finger in Nathan's direction.

With a nod of thanks, the curly-haired young man pushed his way between the intervening tables and stood looking down at Nathan.

'Are you Nathan Jago, the prize-fighter? The man who beat Ned Belcher for the Championship of all England?' The accent was that of an Irishman from County Wexford.

Nathan looked up at the tall young man. Apart from a pair of square, broad shoulders there was little that was exceptional about him. He had pleasant features and gentle eyes, but Nathan remained cautious. He had met more than one young man of deceptive appearance whose ambition was to throw a punch at a prize-fighting champion.

'I am. Who's asking?'

The face split in an infectious grin as an unusually large hand reached out to grasp Nathan's own. 'Mick O'Rourke. The man who'll be taking the title back to Ireland next week.'

Nathan's hand was held in a powerful grip. As it was shaken vigorously, the Irishman added: 'I don't enjoy punching hell out of someone I've never met. Not even a Protestant Englishman, so I always make a point of meeting my opponents first. Would it be disturbing your dinner if I were to sit down with you for a while?'

'Not at all. Have a drink with me. What will it be?'

'Thank you kindly. I'll have a pint of porter, if it's all the same to you. English ale's a mite too gaseous for my liking and, much as I enjoy a drop of "the cratur", I'll not be taking whiskey until the fight's over.'

John Gully came across the room, wiping wet hands on a cloth. When Nathan introduced the two men, O'Rourke rose to his feet respectfully.

'I watched you training the other evening,' admitted Gully. 'I'm thinking it should be a good championship fight.'

'I'm honoured to hear you say so,' said the young Irishman. 'I've seen *you* fight, too. I was no more than ten at the time. My father took me to Dublin to watch you beat Pug Allen. That was the day I decided *I* was going to be a champion like you. I never thought I'd one day be shaking your hand and hearing you say you'd enjoyed watching *me* fight. This is a moment I shall always treasure.'

John Gully smiled. 'You're not short of blarney, Mick

O'Rourke, but you'll need more than words if you're to beat Nathan.'

'I wouldn't be doubting you for a single minute. He's been a grand champion and is a well-respected man. That's why I'm happy to be paying my respects – while he's still champion.'

Nathan laughed out loud, and John Gully's eyebrows jumped in acknowledgement of the supreme confidence of the young Irish prize-fighter.

'It hasn't crossed your mind you might just lose?'

Mick O'Rourke looked at John Gully with unfeigned surprise. 'It's to be my last fight. I won't lose.'

'Your *last* fight? But you're a mere youngster, and you're fighting for the Championship of all England. It's a *beginning*.'

Mick O'Rourke nodded his dark curly head seriously. 'Yes, it marks the *beginning* of a new life for me – but not in the prize-ring. I've saved all the money I've made from fighting and it's taking me to Rome, to train as a priest in the Holy Mother Church. I leave next month. I want to take the championship with me, as a gift to Him.'

After Mick O'Rourke's visit, Nathan's training was stepped up. He fought tough stevedores, punch-drunk coal-heavers and blasphemous Thames lightermen, but still John Gully was never satisfied. Every evening the innkeeper personally supervised Nathan's eating in one of the inn's small, private rooms, ensuring he had the best beef and steaks, and did not drink more than was good for him.

One night one of Nathan's regular sparring partners brought his sister along to the inn to meet Nathan and they were asked to stay and have dinner with him.

They both accepted the invitation with alacrity, but no sooner was the meal over than the sparring parnter made an excuse to leave his sister and Nathan alone.

It became immediately clear that the girl had engineered both the meeting and the early departure of her 'brother'. A pretty girl from the 'East End' of London, it was her ambition to make a career for herself in the theatre, but many other girls were of a like mind – far more than would ever succeed. To gain entry to the world of the theatre a girl needed to be noticed by the right people – and there were many of the 'right people' among the gentlemen of the 'Fancy'.

Nathan's dinner companion suggested, quite bluntly, that she should be seen in Nathan's company as often as possible before the fight. In return, she would accord Nathan certain 'favours'.

The girl never received an answer from Nathan. Before she had finished talking, John Gully entered the room. The bow he gave to the girl was polite, but there was no warmth in his manner.

'I trust you will pardon the intrusion, but I would like a word with Nathan – in private.'

Nathan laughed. 'What John means is that I am in very strict training, and it's past my bedtime.'

The girl looked from Nathan to the landlord of the Plough inn. 'Your bedtime? Blimey! It's only ten o'clock! You're joshing me, ain't you?'

Not certain of the girl's standing, John Gully remained acidly polite. 'To be a champion prize-fighter a man needs discipline. He has to train hard, especially against a fighter like Mick O'Rourke.'

'My age and the Lord are both on the side of O'Rourke,' Nathan grinned at the girl. 'Besides, John Gully's the man to introduce you to men of the "Fancy". Give her a drink and fifteen minutes of your time, John, and you have my promise I'll be asleep by the time you're done.'

To the young girl Nathan said: 'Goodnight, young lady. I've no need to wish you well in your chosen career; you have enough cheek and determination to get you there without any help at all.'

The girl smiled. 'Thank you, guv; you're a gent. When I tried the same thing on that Irish git you're fighting, all *he* did was tell me he'd pray for me soul, then he had me escorted off the premises.'

CHAPTER TWENTY-THREE

March 10th, 1815 was the day of the fight and it began in a frenzy of activity for Nathan. He rose late and was about to tuck in to an impressive breakfast when John Gully hurried through the door of the Plough inn dining-room and threw a heavy outdoor coat at him.

'Quick. Get into that and come with me. A coach is waiting outside.'

'I'm just about to have my breakfast.'

Gully snatched up the plate and a loaf of bread. 'You'll need to have it inside the coach on the way to Moulsey Hurst.'

'Moulsey Hurst? But that's miles away. I'm supposed to be fighting on Hampstead Heath.'

'You *were*. The magistrates got wind of the fight. Half a regiment of volunteers has been called out to see the fight doesn't take place. We'll lose a lot of spectators by switching to Moulsey, but they will be no more than rag, tag and bobtail. The "Fancy" will know where to come – and my bets have already been placed.'

'Will *we* make it to Moulsey Hurst on time?'

'Yes. The fight's not due to start until noon. We don't *want* to be there before then.'

On the way from the inn to the carriage, Nathan grinned to himself. John Gully was a sly old campaigner. He would deliberately make Mick O'Rourke wait for as long as he dared, knowing a fighter's muscles took a while to warm up after a wait in the cold. Yet Nathan thought such an inconvenience would matter less to Mick O'Rourke than to most other fighters John Gully had known.

The coach was met a mile from Moulsey Hurst by one of

the prize-fighters with whom Nathan had trained. He was mounted on a horse that would have looked more at home between the shafts of a brewer's dray.

'We've drawn a goodly crowd, John, but word's going about that the magistrates are out to stop the fight here, too. We'd best waste no time getting started.'

'Damn the magistrates! Why are they suddenly being so uncommonly prissy?'

'It's being said they're trying to exert their authority while the Duke of Clarence is out of the country. If he were here, they'd never dare venture within five miles of Moulsey Hurst.'

The prize-fighter's mount executed a tight circle at the edge of the coach, causing its rider to hang on tightly to the pommel. Then, with equal suddenness, the horse took off along the road from whence it had come. As it went, the hapless rider called back: 'I'll tell them you're on your way . . .' The remainder of his words were lost as he bounced along the road, arms and legs flapping wildly.

Mick O'Rourke was already in the ring when they arrived. As Nathan had anticipated, the Irishman was not in the least perturbed at being kept standing in the cold. He waved cheerfully to Nathan and raised a roar of laughter from the crowd at the ringside by quipping: 'Tell the driver to wait for you, Jago. You'll be leaving again before he's due payment for extra time.'

'Don't let him rile you,' growled John Gully as he helped Nathan off with his coat. 'O'Rourke's a great man with words. He's used them to his advantage before now.'

'His words don't bother me,' replied Nathan as he stripped to the waist. 'I hope I'll be able to say the same thing for his fists at the end of the fight.'

'Do your best to keep away from him in the early rounds. O'Rourke doesn't enjoy a long fight. He'll be out to end it quickly. Back away and let him do all the work.'

John Gully kept up a barrage of advice until the referee called both prize-fighters and their cornermen to the mark scratched in the earth at the centre of the ring. Here he satisfied himself that the men understood the rules of prize-fighting. As he talked, a number of pugilists, especially employed for the purpose, cleared the outer ring of all spectators except those who had paid for the privilege of viewing the prize-fight at close hand.

The rules of the contest were few. A round would last until either man was knocked down. Then a thirty-second rest period would be allowed. If either man was unable to come to the mark in a condition to defend himself at the end of a rest break, his opponent would be declared the winner. Two cornermen for each prize-fighter would remain inside the ring to support their respective men, but must not interfere with the progress of the bout.

There were no other restrictions. A fighter could hold and hit, butt, throw his opponent to the ground or gouge his eyes, as the mood or opportunity moved him. Between rounds he was free to partake of whatever alcoholic beverage was best suited to his needs.

There was no disagreement about the rules for the fight. These had been accepted by John Gully and Mick O'Rourke's men days before.

It was bitterly cold standing in the centre of the ring while the referee spoke, and Nathan was anxious for the fight to begin. When the referee finally ordered the commencement of the bout, both men circled warily about each other for a full half-minute, feinting rather than fighting. Then, as the crowd called impatiently for action, Mick O'Rourke darted in with a speed that belied his weight and delivered three good punches upon Nathan's ribs. Nathan retaliated with a good right to the side of the Irishman's face, and the crowd howled its delight.

Neither fighter was hurt by the brief exchange of blows. Indeed, O'Rourke actually grinned. Feinting once more, he slipped inside Nathan's guard and held on for a moment. 'You're still fast, Jago, but you'll need to do better if you hope to beat Mick O'Rourke.'

Having delivered this advice, O'Rourke butted Nathan in the face, grabbed him about the neck with his left arm, and began pummelling him about the face with his right. So hard were the blows that Nathan's legs buckled beneath him and he fell to his knees on the frost-hardened turf of the ring.

Back in the corner, Nathan had cold water thrown in his face until he gasped for breath and fought off the enthusiastic cornermen.

'Keep him at a distance,' John Gully hissed urgently. 'Use straight lefts. Trip him. Do *anything*, but keep him at arm's length. He's expert at the throw and delights in the "head in chancery", as you've just learned to your cost, but he doesn't like being taken any distance. Keep him going for an hour and he's yours, Nathan boy.'

Eleven minutes and two rounds later, Nathan suggested that John Gully should toe the mark with O'Rourke and put his theories into practice.

Nathan had successfully kept the Irish prize-fighter at a distance, only to be caught with hard, straight punches that proved Mick O'Rourke had a reach equal to Nathan's own. He was a very fast and very strong opponent – and always there was the Irishman's cheerful grin.

In the fourth round, Nathan had a moment of revenge. Ignoring Gully's advice, he carried the fight to his opponent and suffered the penalty. Mick O'Rourke retreated half the width of the ring then suddenly stepped forward. Reaching out powerful arms, he wrapped Nathan in a bone-crushing bear hug.

Mick O'Rourke was still grinning when Nathan hooked a foot behind the Irishman's legs and brought him crashing to the ground. Nathan's full weight fell on O'Rourke, winding him and forcing him to release his grip.

Nathan was on his feet in an instant. Mick O'Rourke, intent on resuming the fight, began to rise from the ground when a blow from Nathan to the side of the head sent him sprawling to the ground again.

There were howls of protest from O'Rourke's two cornermen, but the referee ignored them. He shared Nathan's belief that O'Rourke was rising to his feet intent upon resuming the fight.

It had been a good punch, and the grin had not returned to Mick O'Rourke's face when he came to the mark for the next round. The Irish prize-fighter was no fool. Now it was his turn to keep his opponent at a distance. He succeeded for two minutes before another flurried exchange ended with O'Rourke dropping to one knee on the hard Moulsey turf.

For Mick O'Rourke this was more in the nature of a tactical knock-down, and round five was to be the last taste of victory for Nathan.

Round six lasted an incredible eighteen minutes and had the spectators yelling themselves hoarse as the two prize-fighters stood toe to toe in the centre of the ring, exchanging punches, blow for bloody blow. When Nathan eventually stumbled to the ground it was a butt from the Irishman's rock-hard head, and not a punch, that put him there.

For two more rounds Nathan stood his ground. To the enthusiastic spectators it seemed he was more than a match for the younger challenger, but Nathan knew otherwise. His back felt the frozen Moulsey turf at the end of the eighth round and he returned to his corner with blood streaming down his face from a cut eye. For the first time in more than ten years of fighting, he faced defeat in the prize-ring.

Nevertheless, Nathan was not giving up his title easily. In the ninth round he mounted a fierce attack that took Mick O'Rourke by surprise. A good right visibly staggered the younger Irishman. But O'Rourke was both strong and skilful. He did not go down. Keeping constantly on the move, he successfully evaded Nathan's continuing attack. When the round was in its fifteenth minute, the Irishman's smile returned. Through swollen and bloody lips, he said: 'You'll need to run faster if you want to catch me, Jago. The years have put lead in your legs. Never mind, the load on them will be lighter without that championship crown.'

As he reached the end of his taunt, Mick O'Rourke suddenly stopped retreating and launched his own attack.

Taken by surprise, Nathan was struck in the face by a flurry of hard punches. He staggered, but did not go down, and the Irishman pursued him relentlessly across the ring, raining punches on Nathan's face and body. Eventually, Nathan's back was pressed against the rope that marked the outer limit of the 25-foot ring. He tried to fight his way out of trouble, but Mick O'Rourke had become a human battering-ram. A blow struck the side of Nathan's jaw and it was quickly followed by another. Nathan's legs refused to support him and he slumped to his knees before toppling forward on to his battered face.

Awareness returned to Nathan with a desperate urge to escape from the foul odour beneath his nose. As he fought against the smell, he became aware of a fierce roaring in his ears. At first, Nathan thought the sound was a result of O'Rourke's punches. As his senses cleared he realised the foul stench came from a fistful of feathers being burned beneath his nose, and the noise was the appreciation of an uproarious crowd.

'Is it over? Have I lost?'

Nathan gasped out the words, at the same time knocking the evil-smelling feathers aside.

'Not yet,' replied John Gully grimly, 'but it will be the end if you don't make it to the mark . . . *now!*'

Nathan rose to his feet by himself, but he would not have made it to the centre of the ring without the help of his cornermen.

When the referee called for the two combatants to 'fight on', John Gully hissed in Nathan's ear: 'Get through this round *whatever happens!* It's vital . . . for both of us.'

Then Nathan was on his own as Mick O'Rourke hurried in for the kill. Now it was Nathan's turn to display his ringcraft – and he had not become Champion of all England without learning all the prize-fighting tricks of his chosen profession.

For three and a half minutes he ducked and weaved and retreated, using all four corners of the ring. When retreat became impossible, he moved in close and clung to

O'Rourke, preventing the eager challenger from landing the blow that would bring the contest to an end. Finally, when O'Rourke had him trapped in his own corner, Nathan went down to a blow that he would have shrugged off only minutes before, and so earned a welcome thirty-second break.

A jubilant John Gully towelled him down, and Nathan asked: 'What was so important about the last round?'

'I backed my faith in you with hard money, Nathan boy. The odds were three to one against you lasting beyond the tenth round. I bet a thousand guineas that you would – and I put down a hundred for you. There's not a man in London has backed you to win. You've been away from the ring too long. Now you can go out there and do whatever you like.'

'But the purse . . .?'

'It's all here. A guaranteed eight hundred guineas. Five to the winner, three to the loser. Given the wager you've just won, you'll take home a winner's purse, win or lose. Go out there and stay out of trouble before you take a drop. Your face already looks as though it's escaped from a butcher's block.'

The referee called the fighters to the centre of the ring – and Nathan arrived at the mark filled with anger. He was angry with Gully, angry with his opponent, and angry with the prize-fighting fraternity. He, Nathan Jago, was the Champion of all England, yet his skill had been held in so little esteem that the odds against him lasting beyond the tenth round were rated at three to one, with no one believing him capable of retaining the championship! Well, he intended showing them he was still the champion. If Mick O'Rourke wanted to wrest it from him, the Irishman would need to earn it the hard way.

Nathan's unexpected onslaught brought the huge crowd to its toes, roaring encouragement. For more than five minutes Nathan harried Mick O'Rourke around the ring, landing many good punches. Yet when the round came to an end it was the Cornishman and not the Irishman who stood up from the ground.

Nathan fought the twelfth round on the defensive once more, eventually going down to a punch that felt as though it had sunk to the elbow in the pit of his stomach.

As Nathan rose to his feet for the next round, the prizefighter who had met Nathan and John Gully on the road to Moulsey Hurst forced his way through the crowd in the outer ring. He reached Nathan's corner, leaving consternation in his wake.

'It's the magistrates,' he gasped to John Gully. 'They're on their way here and look to have half the constables in England with them.'

John Gully hurried across the ring to the referee. Within seconds they had been joined by the cornermen from O'Rourke's corner and a fierce argument broke out. It ended when the referee ordered Gully and the others back to their respective corners and called on the fighters to come to the mark.

'He won't believe me,' hissed Gully angrily. 'He and O'Rourke's cornermen think it's a ploy to gain time for you to recover. The man's a fool. We'll all end up in gaol . . .'

The remainder of his complaint went unheard as Nathan took his place at the mark and set about defending himself once more.

The assumption made by Mick O'Rourke's cornermen was not altogether surprising. Nathan was in a bad way. His left eye was swollen so badly he could not see from it. There was a bad cut above the bridge of his nose, he was bleeding from both mouth and nose, and most of his face was badly contused.

Despite his injuries, Nathan was still prepared to stand in the corner of the ring and exchange blows with his opponent. Both men were throwing heavy punches at each other when Nathan became aware that the cries of the spectators were now registering alarm rather than approval. He and Mick O'Rourke exchanged glances, and both men abandoned their fighting stances.

'It seems your man was right,' said the Irishman, his disappointment apparent. 'You've been saved by the magistrate, Jago. Another three rounds and I'd have had the championship from you.'

'Perhaps . . . but I think it would have taken you another seven, at least.'

Suddenly the familiar grin returned to O'Rourke's face, hardly less battered than Nathan's own. 'Oh, well, it's the Lord's decision, I'm thinking. Had I won the championship, I might foolishly have decided I was too important to answer His call. He's probably saved me from the folly of my own pride.'

The crowd was fleeing before the magistrate and his constables now, threatening to carry away the ring as they ran.

'The purse . . . What shall I do with it?' The referee stood in the centre of the ring uncertainly, a heavy bag of coins held in each hand.

'Halve it.' Taking one bag, Mick O'Rourke passed the other to Nathan. 'I believe this is your last fight, too, Jago. You've been a good champion. It's been a joy to meet up with you in the prize-ring – but I'd have beaten you for sure had the magistrate not interfered, you can be sure of that. Now you'd best get to running, or he'll have that lot off you in no time at all.'

Even as he was talking, Mick O'Rourke was shrugging himself into his coat. Moments later Nathan was doing the same and then he was running with John Gully to where the coach, one of many, was trapped in a sea of fleeing prize-fighting fans.

He and John Gully were still yards from their coach when Nathan heard a voice calling his name.

'Jago! Over here. Quickly, man!'

Turning his head painfully, Nathan saw a large kerchief being waved from the window of a light carriage which had wheeled away from the others and was making slow headway against the tide of prize-fighting fans.

'Hurry, man, or the magistrate's men will be here.'

Nathan recognised the occupant of the carriage as one of the 'Fancy'. So, too, did John Gully. 'It's Lord Cecil. In the carriage with you, Nathan boy. He'll get you out of this, if anyone can. I'll see you later.'

'Where are you going . . .?' Battered, bloody, and barely able to see, Nathan knew a brief moment of panic.

'I've money to collect from men who aren't above using a little disturbance such as this to slip away and welch on their debts.'

Lord Cecil was one of the most influential and experienced members of the 'Fancy'. He followed the sport of prize-fighting throughout England and had survived more than one magistrate's raid. Instead of following the routes taken by the vast majority of prize-fighting enthusiasts, he took Nathan in the opposite direction, to the River Thames. Here he had a boat waiting. An hour and a half later, Nathan was being led to his room at the Plough inn.

Nathan had taken a bad beating at the hands of Mick O'Rourke and he was glad to stretch his aching body on the bed. His head throbbed as it never had before and when, after about an hour, he tried to raise it from the pillow he experienced a painful roaring in his ears.

Nathan lay back with a groan, hoping John Gully would soon return. But the innkeeper had still not returned by the time Nathan's failing sight told him darkness had fallen. Twice more he had tried to rise from the bed, but each time the noise and pain in his head forced him to lie back again.

Nathan's senses seemed to be playing tricks on him now, too. He lay on the bed imagining sounds – voices – only to have them disappear again, leaving him anxious and confused.

He heard knocking at his door, but ignored it, accepting the sound as just another manifestation of his delirium. He knew he was right when the sound ceased. But then – and he had no idea how much time had elapsed – the knocking returned and this time it was more insistent.

Then he imagined there were people in the room. Men and women – *a* woman. She had a voice he thought he recognised from another time, another place. It was a voice full of concern, and he imagined she was talking to him.

'Nathan, I am going to take you away from here. To my house. You have taken a dreadful beating. You need a doctor . . .'

The voice faded again, and he had the impression of much confusion in the room. As though from a great distance he heard another voice, that of a man this time.

'Come along there, don't just stand around doing nothing. Help me lift him. You heard what the marquise said.'

CHAPTER TWENTY-FOUR

In an elegant house in London's fashionable Manchester Square, Nathan lay back in a bathtub filled almost to the brim with water to which had been added fragrant herbs. As he relaxed, a doctor treated Nathan's battered face, applying salve to the bruises, cleaning up the cuts and checking the leeches attached to the swelling about his eye.

The doctor was not a member of the 'Fancy' and he viewed Nathan's injuries with undisguised disapproval, as he had during every one of the five days he had been treating him. He grumbled that a man who willingly submitted himself to such punishment should be considered for a place in a lunatic asylum.

Nathan only grinned stiffly. Henrietta had expressed similar sentiments when Nathan regained his senses and found himself in a bed in the house she was renting during a visit to London.

'That's as much as I can do for you,' said the doctor as he skilfully removed his leeches from Nathan's cheek and returned them to the small pewter pot, half-filled with water, carried with him for the purpose. 'I see you carry the scars of earlier fights. I'll no doubt be wasting my breath by telling you to give up prize-fighting, but I'll say it just the same. You have suffered severe concussion. Another fight like this last one and you'll run the risk of permanently damaging your brain. *Two* more and you'll likely lose your sight. I know what I'm talking about, Mr Jago, believe me. I've certified the deaths of two prize-fighters in recent years. Both were directly attributable to the prize-ring.'

'Thank you for the warning, Doctor. I can assure you that I've fought my last fight.'

The physician snorted derisively. 'I wonder how many prize-fighters have said the same to their doctors. How many times have *you* "retired"?'

Nathan ignored the question. The fights against Kelly and O'Rourke marked his second return to the prize-ring. 'Thank you for your concern and your treatment. How much do I owe you?'

'I was called here by the marquise d'Orléan. I will submit my account to her Ladyship in due course.' Gathering up his lotions and medical paraphernalia, the physician placed them carefully in a leather bag, inclined his head to Nathan, and left the bathroom.

When the surgeon had gone, Nathan sank his aching body deeper in the bath, until only his battered face was showing above the water. The prize-fight had been a salutary lesson for him. He could no longer meet the very high standard of fitness and skill demanded of a prize-fighting champion. Only the intervention of the magistrate had saved him from defeat and an even more severe beating. He would not fight again in a prize-ring. His guaranteed purse, plus the wager placed for him by John Gully, meant he could buy another boat and have money left over to put towards the upkeep of Polrudden.

Nathan heard Henrietta's voice somewhere in the house as she talked to the doctor, and he came back to the present.

He had every reason to be grateful to Henrietta. It was even possible she might have saved his life, if the physician were to be believed. She had been at a salon where the men were talking about the fight. One of the men had spoken of the battering Nathan had taken. He had seen Nathan being led inside the Plough inn and suggested he might have been permanently blinded. Thoroughly alarmed, Henrietta had learned from the speaker where Nathan was staying. She had taken a carriage to the Plough inn and there found Nathan lying alone in his room in a state of delirium and had him removed to Manchester Square.

As the water in the bath began to cool, Nathan climbed stiffly from the bath, dried himself and donned the dressing-gown thoughtfully placed for him on the bed in the next room. He still ached in every limb, and there was scarcely a square inch of body above the waist that had not been bruised by Mick O'Rourke's fists.

Nathan smiled when he remembered the Irish fighter. He had no doubt O'Rourke would transfer the dedication he had shown to boxing to the Catholic Church. He would make a good champion in either calling.

Nathan was still smiling when Henrietta knocked at the door of the bedroom and came in before he had time to call out for her to enter. She asked why he appeared to be so happy. When he explained, she looked at him in astonishment. 'You can think kindly of a man who has given you such a beating? I do not believe this!'

'Why? I did my best to do the same to him.'

Henrietta's bewilderment was real. 'Occasionally I am ready to believe the English are the most civilised people in the world. At other times . . .!' She shrugged. 'The doctor has told you it would be wise to give up prize-fighting? I think you should heed his words.'

'He had no business saying anything to you.'

'He had every right – for your own good. You will not fight again?'

'I don't have to think about it for a while. I've won enough from this fight to buy a boat and take care of most of my problems.'

'Excellent! This makes me very happy. But what of your immediate plans? Shall we dine here tonight?'

'Now I'm getting better I should return to the Plough inn and make arrangements for my journey to Cornwall – Ah!'

Nathan let out an involuntary gasp of pain as he turned towards the dressing-table. Clutching a rib, he sat down heavily on the bed. Some of Mick O'Rourke's hardest punches had been to Nathan's ribs, and turning awkwardly caused him sudden pain.

'What is the matter? Something is wrong?'

Nathan eased his body to a more comfortable position. 'It's nothing. Only bruising. O'Rourke could throw a good punch.'

'You are certain it is nothing more serious? Should I ask the doctor to return?' Henrietta sat down on the edge of the bed beside him, looking anxious.

'I'm all right. You mustn't worry about me.'

'How can I help it when you do such *stupid* things?'

Henrietta spoke the words fiercely – *too* fiercely. When she made as if to rise from her seat on the bed Nathan's hand stopped her.

'Why are you so concerned for me, Henrietta?'

'That is a foolish question. We are friends, it is natural that I should be concerned for you.'

'Only *friends*, Henrietta?'

Slowly, Nathan pulled her to him and she offered no resistance. Her body was soft and pliant, and there was a delicate fragrance about her. As his mouth found hers he had a brief feeling of unreality, as though this were happening to someone else, and not to him. Then the sheer physical pleasure of holding Henrietta's body close overcame all rational thought. Moving farther back on the bed, he pulled her down beside him . . .

Many hours later, Nathan was brought out of a state of drowsy exhaustion by the spluttering of the wick in the lamp at the bedside as the last of the oil burned. He moved, intending to pinch out the flame before the wick began smoking, but his limbs and Henrietta's were inextricably entangled. When he tried to move away she gave a low moan, half contentment, half complaint, and drew him back to her.

'The lamp . . .'

Henrietta tightened her grip on him. 'Is a lamp more important than I?' Her teeth found the lobe of his ear and succeeded in distracting him from the dying lamp.

After they had made love once more, Nathan lay in the large, soft bed with Henrietta nestled in his arms. The aches from the beating he had taken at the hands of Mick O'Rourke were effectively dulled.

'What do we do now, Henrietta?' He put the question quietly, not certain whether she was awake.

'You wish to make love to me *again*? But you do not have to ask . . .'

Nathan's arm tightened about her, not certain whether she was mocking him. 'I'm talking about the future.'

Henrietta nestled closer to him. 'Why, you will return to Polrudden, to Sir Beville, Jean-Paul . . . and your Amy. Sometimes you will come to London and I, too, will come to London. We will meet again . . . like this. You will find me a demanding mistress only when we are together. I do not think *this* should prove any embarrassment to you.'

When Nathan made no immediate reply, Henrietta stroked his face gently in the darkness, her fingers lingering on the swelling about his eyes. 'My poor darling. I am your first mistress?'

'Yes.'

'Ah! That makes me very happy, Nathan. It means I will always hold a very special place in your heart, always. But for you . . .? I fear it will be an experience that is touched with pain. For this I am sorry. I have no wish to cause you pain . . . ever.'

'Have you had many lovers, Henrietta?'

Her hand stopped stroking his face and she rose to one elbow and looked down at him, unseeing in the darkness. 'I will not answer you, Nathan. A *Frenchman* would never ask such a question. A man in bed with his mistress should neither talk about his wife nor question her about other lovers.'

There was a long silence before Henrietta settled down beside him again and said: 'There *have* been other men in my life, but very few. No one to whom I have given myself as I have to you. But we will talk of other things. Tell me what it will mean to your son to be a baronet.'

Nathan's arm tightened about Henrietta and he told her of Sir Lewis Hearle, of Elinor, Beville's mother, and of the terms of Sir Lewis Hearle's will. In return, he learned that Louis d'Argon had come back from Martinique empty-handed. No one there knew the whereabouts of the sizeable fortune that had been in the possession of the unfortunate Duvernet family. Rumour had it that Jean-Paul's mother had taken the jewellery with her to France.

'Then it's probably still in the wreck of *L'Emir,* lying at the bottom of the sea, just off the Polrudden cliffs,' mused Nathan. 'It will stay there until the ship rots and breaks up.'

Henrietta shrugged in Nathan's arms. 'Good. It means King Louis has one less reason for wanting to gain control of Jean-Paul. The boy should be safe with you now – at least, until he is of an age to question Louis' right to the throne of France. But tell me more of your reason for returning to the prize-ring once more.'

Lying beside Henrietta, Nathan told her of the storm, and of the loss of his two boats. She was a sympathetic listener, and he found it easy to talk to her.

'My poor, dear Nathan,' she murmured. 'It would seem that Beville's baronetcy is the only good thing to have happened to you since we last met. It is *too* awful. It is because of these things that you had to fight again?'

'Yes. Income from one boat won't keep Polrudden. With two boats and a lot of hard work, I can manage. *Three* boats would probably make enough during the season to see us through the bad winter months.'

'Fate has been very unkind to you, my dear. Perhaps I can help? I am a very wealthy woman. I would *like* to give you some money.'

Henrietta could not see the expression of hurt pride which crossed Nathan's face, but she felt his body stiffen and guessed the reason. 'If you would prefer it, allow me to *loan* you some money. You need repay nothing until you are able. No, Nathan, please do not refuse immediately. Think *very* carefully. I can give you – *loan* you – money enough to buy three, four – *ten* boats if you want them. Please do not think me foolish, although I have every right to be foolish if I wish. Look upon it as a business venture. Such is my confidence in you, I *know* it will succeed.'

Henrietta suddenly hugged him. 'Perhaps I could become a *partner* in this great fishing venture. I would like that, Nathan. I would like it very much.'

When Nathan did not respond to her enthusiasm Henrietta sighed and rested her head on his bare chest. 'Ah! No, perhaps you are right. I do not think Amy would be happy to have me as a partner.'

Henrietta was struck with another idea. 'But of course! Why can Jean-Paul not become your partner? It would be an investment for him . . . for his future. What would be the price of such a partnership? Two boats?'

Henrietta's suggestion opened up very exciting new prospects for the Portgiskey fish-cellar, but still Nathan held back. 'I don't know, Henrietta. I need the money for Polrudden. If I had to give half my profits to a partner . . .'

'It is not my intention that you should give Jean-Paul *half* your profits. That would be asking too much. No, Jean-Paul has been accepted by you as part of the Jago family; the profits should be shared equally between you. Say, a *quarter* share? The first payment due on his seventh birthday. Will that give you time to secure the future of your beloved Polrudden?'

Nathan turned towards her, as excited as Henrietta. 'It could lay the foundation of the largest drifting fleet anywhere in Cornwall. I could even think of buying a larger boat. A brigantine, perhaps – to take salted fish to Italy.'

'Why not? You can do *all* these things. You *will* do them. My darling, you can do *anything*!'

*

Nathan awoke with a start. A frame of light about the heavy curtains told him it was well past dawn. Then he heard the sound that had brought him back from sleep. Someone was hammering on the street door, seemingly determined to break it down.

Beside him Henrietta stirred, and then suddenly she, too, was wide awake.

Nathan's first thought was that the noisy visitor was somehow connected with his illicit sojourn in Henrietta's bed. Then the knocking ceased and the sound of a raised voice from the hallway reached the bedroom.

'My God! It's Louis!'

Henrietta's words were spoken in rapid French. Even as she spoke she leaped from the bed. Grabbing her dress from the floor, Henrietta fled naked from the room.

Nathan was in a quandary, undecided what he should do. Then he heard footsteps pounding up the stairs, followed by an urgent knocking at a door farther along the hallway. In the background, the shrill protestations of a maid went unheeded.

Swinging his legs from the bed, Nathan was reminded of how much his limbs still ached from the drubbing he had received. As he dressed quietly he could hear raised and excited voices coming from the direction of Henrietta's bedroom, but he was unable to make out what was being said in the rapid and indistinct flow of French.

When he was dressed he sat on the bed, unhappy at skulking in the bedroom while a man he regarded as a good friend was only a few yards distant. But to disclose his presence would compromise both Henrietta and himself. Nathan also remembered that Louis, comte d'Argon had confided in him that one day he hoped to marry the marquise d'Orléan. Nathan had betrayed not only Amy, but his friend, too. Of a sudden he felt both betrayals keenly.

For more than half an hour Nathan sat with only his conscience for company in the semi-darkness, not daring to open the curtains lest the sound bring someone to the room. Then he heard voices in the corridor outside. It seemed Louis d'Argon's departure was every bit as hurried as his arrival.

A few minutes after Nathan heard the front door slam shut Henrietta hurried into the room. Dressed only in a satin dressing-gown, cut provocatively low, she was pale and shaken.

'Nathan, I have to return to France immediately – and you must go back to Polrudden. Special care must be taken of Jean-Paul. His life is in danger once more.'

'Why? What's happening?'

Highly agitated, Henrietta paced back and forth across the room, seemingly unable to make up her mind on a particular course of action.

Nathan took her by the shoulders, forcing her to stand still and look at him.

'Henrietta, just stop moving for a moment and tell me what's happening. Why must you return to France – and why is Jean-Paul in danger?'

Suddenly Henrietta was clinging to Nathan and he could feel her shaking. He held her for some minutes before she pushed herself away and looked up at him with regained composure.

'Thank you, Nathan. I needed someone to hold me, just for a few minutes.' Taking him by the hand, Henrietta led him to the window and drew the curtains.

Below them in the square the day had long since begun. Hackney carriages trundled briskly along the cobbled road, or stood waiting hopefully in line opposite the elegant houses. Shawled servants hurried by, armed with capacious baskets, making their daily trip to Covent Garden market – once the 'Convent garden' of Westminster Abbey, more than a mile away. Here they would purchase vegetables brought in from the surrounding countryside and hurry back to receive a scolding from the household's cook for taking so long. Other servants, less well placed in the strict hierarchy of the servants' hall, scrubbed steps or cleaned windows, mindful of the whistles and catcalls of passing apprentices and tradesmen's lads.

'London is a wonderful city, Nathan.' Henrietta spoke wistfully. 'No matter what is happening elsewhere in the world, life goes on here as it always has. I hope it always will.'

Henrietta took Nathan's other hand and looked up at him with a serious expression. 'Napoleon Bonaparte has escaped from Elba. He landed in France with an army and is advancing on Paris. Most of the King's regiments have already gone over to his side and King Louis is preparing to flee the country once more. I do not think Great Britain and the Allies will allow Napoleon to take the throne of France, but with a French army behind him it is possible he will be able to dictate who *shall* take the throne. Jean-Paul is an obvious choice – with Napoleon Bonaparte acting as Regent. Louis believes this possibility has already occurred to the King. He will be more anxious than ever to have the boy out of the way.'

'Then, I must return home immediately. But you will remain here, in London?'

Nathan was remembering the mob who had attacked Henrietta's coach when he and she were returning to the Tuileries from her Paris home. These men would come into their own in the turmoil caused by the flight of King Louis XVIII and the advance through France of Napoleon Bonaparte.

'I must return to Paris. Everything I have is there. The comte d'Argon – Louis – has arranged a passage for me from Dover tonight. He will return here for me in an hour. It will be better if you are gone by then. I think he guessed I have a lover in the house, but I would rather he did not know it is you.'

Henrietta studied Nathan's battered face and was satisfied by what she saw there. 'Do not concern yourself about me, my darling Nathan. I promise not to travel in a carriage through the streets of Paris without an escort – and remember, I have lived in France through darker days than these. But thank you for caring.'

Minutes later Nathan left the house in Manchester Square and hailed a hackney carriage. Across the square, secure in the shadows of a closed carriage, Louis, comte d'Argon watched Nathan leave Henrietta's house. An expression akin to pain crossed his face. Then, when Nathan's hackney carriage had passed by, Louis called out of his carriage window for the coachman to return him to the French embassy.

CHAPTER TWENTY-FIVE

It was ten days before Nathan reached Polrudden. He travelled homewards only as far as Brixham, in Devon, some sixty miles short of Pentuan. From here he sent a rider to Amy with a letter detailing the happenings in France and the danger they posed to Jean-Paul. He asked Amy to ensure that the child was never out of sight of the house unless accompanied by an armed escort.

Meanwhile, in Brixham, Nathan went to the boat-builder who had built the very first drift-fishing boat Nathan had owned, *The Brave Amy H*. The yard was renowned for building the finest luggers found anywhere along the south coast of England. For most fishermen hereabouts, this meant the best anywhere in the whole of the British Isles.

It had been Nathan's intention to order a new lugger for drift-fishing, but the boat-builder was able to show him a lugger built by himself some years before. It had recently been bought back from a local fishing enterprise which had gone broke.

'I'll need to put in a bit of work on her,' said the slow-talking, pipe-smoking boat-builder, 'but she's a stout boat. One of the best I ever built. Too heavy for a tiller, though. I need to take it out and put in a wheel, then she'll handle with the best of 'em.'

Nathan looked at the drifter speculatively. It was a large boat, much larger than any of his others had been. He would need extra crew to man her, but with the vessel's wide, flat stern he could sail farther in search for fish. Perhaps venture as far as the Irish fishing-grounds – even to the profitable Italian markets with a cargo of salt fish, perhaps.

As though reading his mind, the boat builder said: 'She's a good deep-water boat. Her last owner spent a season fishing the North Sea for herring and cod.'

'I don't doubt she's a good boat. The last one you built for me was the best drifter in Cornish waters. But I haven't enough money for a boat this size.'

The boat-builder, sensing he was about to make a sale, removed the pipe from his mouth. 'She came back to me cheap. I'll pass her on for very little more. Give me four hundred and she's yours.'

'Guineas or pounds?' Either represented a lower price than Nathan had anticipated, but he, too, was a business-man.

'Pounds – and she'll come to you with a full set of fishing gear.'

'In that case you've got a buyer. There's my hand on it.'

Nathan remained at Brixham for six days while the boat-builder fitted a wheel instead of a tiller and carried out a series of minor repairs. During this time Nathan thoroughly familiarised himself with the vessel, and his delight with her grew with each passing day. When he was finally able to take *Successful* out on a trial run, the way she handled thoroughly justified the praise of her builder.

The following day, crewed by four Brixham men taken on for the single voyage, Nathan proudly sailed his latest acquisition into the tiny cove at Portgiskey.

Sir Beville was not alongside the small quay, and Nathan guessed the boat was out fishing, but all the women who worked the fish-cellar were there to witness *Successful's* arrival and soon they were joined by the Pentuan fisher-men, always quick to pick out an unfamiliar vessel. Ahab Arthur, Matthew Mitchell and the other members of Nathan's night crew were quickly on the scene, too. Called from their beds, they were almost as excited about the new boat as Nathan himself. Treading the unfamiliar decks of the large drifter, they pried into lockers and holds with a proud, proprietary interest.

When Nathan had been at Portgiskey for about an hour, Amy came along the valley behind Portgiskey. Clutching her hands was Beville on one side, Jean-Paul on the other. Behind them was the burly figure of Will Hodge, the Pol-rudden groom, accompanied by a strong young farmhand. Both had pistols tucked in their waistbands, proof that Amy had taken Nathan's warning seriously. This was a meeting Nathan had anticipated with conflicting emotions, pleasure vying with apprehension.

The children had no such inhibiting problems. When they saw Nathan they freed themselves from Amy's grasp and ran to the quay, to be scooped up, one in each arm, and hugged happily.

Amy, too, was elated because Nathan was home, and also because he had returned with a new fishing-boat. Her pleasure lasted only until she was close enough to see Nathan's face clearly. The swelling had long since gone down, and the worst of the cuts were healing well, but they could not be disguised. Neither could the heavy dis-coloration about his eyes and on his badly bruised cheek-bones.

Putting both boys to the ground, Nathan moved to greet Amy, but she stepped back from him in order to see his face better.

'You've been prize-fighting!' There was hurt in the accu-sation.

Amy looked pale and unwell. Nathan felt an urge to take her in his arms and tell her everything was going to be all right now he was home again. He did neither.

'I fought again, and here's what I have to show for the

fight – another boat. Large enough to stay at sea when every other fisherman in Cornwall is stormbound. I've also made enough money to keep Polrudden running until *Successful* begins making money for us. Come on board and have a look around. She's a beautiful boat, built in Brixham at the same yard as *The Brave Amy H.*'

'You had the fight arranged before you went to London?' Once more Nathan had the impression that Amy was more hurt than angry. 'Why didn't you tell me, Nathan?'

'Had I told you, you'd have worried.' Nathan spoke more irritably than he intended. He had secured a good purse and returned to Portgiskey with a new boat and money to spare. Amy should be grateful.

Amy suddenly changed the subject, but did not give Nathan the respite for which he had been hoping.

'I received your letter about guarding Jean-Paul. Tell me what's happening.'

'Napoleon Bonaparte is back in France and King Louis has fled the country. It's thought Napoleon will try to replace Louis on the throne with another Bourbon. One more sympathetic to him than Louis. Someone like Jean-Paul. If he's successful, Napoleon will suggest he act as Regent, in the hope that by so doing Britain and our allies will accept his return.'

'Who told you all this?' Amy looked Nathan in the eyes as she asked the question, and he had an uncomfortable feeling she already knew the answer.

'The marquise d'Orléan . . . Henrietta.'

Amy sucked in her breath involuntarily. 'You saw *her* in London?'

This was the moment Nathan had been dreading. 'She was in London and heard about the fight. She arranged for a doctor to treat me. I have much to thank her for . . .'

'So *now* you and your marquise are grateful to each other. I'm quite sure she finds that *very* satisfactory!' Suddenly Amy's self-control cracked. 'Oh, Nathan! It's bad enough knowing you've had a prize-fight without telling me. Why did you allow *her* to become involved?'

Aware that some of the villagers were listening to their conversation with undisguised interest, Nathan said: 'Look, can we continue this conversation somewhere in private? In the cottage, perhaps?'

Amy shrugged, trying hard to contain the hurt inside her. 'There's little more to be said . . . unless you have something to confess to me?'

Amy did not want to look at Nathan's face, fearing what she might see there; but she *had* to look, and his confusion was an icy dagger that chilled her to the heart.

Not trusting herself to speak, Amy turned and hurried back the way she had come, leaving Nathan standing on the stone quay with two small boys clinging to his hands, all three looking unhappily after her.

'Is something wrong, Nathan?' The question was put by Josiah Jago, who had just arrived at Portgiskey. Amy had passed him along the way and failed to return his greeting.

'No,' Nathan lied. 'I think she's feeling unwell, that's all.'

'Amy hasn't looked well for some weeks,' agreed Josiah Jago, accepting Nathan's reply. 'The two boys keep her busy, and she's concerned about the upkeep of Polrudden. Don't worry, she'll be all right now you're home again.'

Nathan knew better, but he said nothing to his father, or to anyone else. He took the two boys and his father on board *Successful,* spending an hour showing them around the boat, in company with those villagers who were able to crowd aboard the large drifter.

When Nathan returned home to Polrudden at dusk, he was breathing heavily after toiling up the steep hill from Pentuan with a noisy and active small boy perched on either shoulder.

There was no sign of Amy. Passing Beville and Jean-Paul into the care of Rose, their maidservant, Nathan went in search of his wife.

He found Amy sitting alone in the gloom of their bedroom, looking out of the window, across the high cliffs to the sea. It was almost dark outside now, with only a pale glimmer on the horizon to indicate where darkening sky met darker sea. She did not turn around when the door opened behind her – did not so much as move. Walking across the room, Nathan stood beside her chair. Even in the faint light from the window he could see tears glistening on her cheeks and he was ashamed. Kneeling, he found her hand. Her fingers were ice-cold and unyielding.

'Amy . . . I'm sorry. I knew you were against me fighting again. Had I mentioned the fight, you'd have tried to stop me, and we desperately needed money. I *have* money now – and a new boat. I've also been made an offer that can secure our future.'

'It isn't the fight that's upset me, although it *does* hurt to know you would take part in a prize-fight without telling me. It's knowing that she – your French marquise – was there to care for you afterwards. *She* was able to comfort you, to nurse you . . . I could see by your face that you'd taken a beating. It's . . . it's as though she's somehow taken my place. *She* was there when you needed someone, while I stayed here, looking after your house, your children and your business. Can you realise how that makes me feel?'

Glad that the darkness of the room hid his face from her, Nathan said: 'A physician provided the comfort for my face. She just happened to know one of the best in London.'

'You've already told me how "grateful" you are to her.' Amy's voice was still chilly, but her fingers were returning the grip of his hand now. 'All right, let's forget your marquise for a while. Tell me about the offer that's going to end all our money problems.'

'Well, actually, that's Henrietta's idea, too . . .'

Amy's fingers released their grip, and Nathan added hastily: 'It's a scheme involving Jean-Paul, not her personally. She's offered to put up money, a *lot* of money, to give Jean-Paul a share in our fishing business . . .'

Abruptly, Amy withdrew her hand from his. Had there been more light in the room he would have seen her clutch the arm of her chair so tightly the veins in the back of her hands stood out from the pale skin.

'What did you tell her?'

'I said I thought it a wonderful idea. I still do. We can use the money to buy more boats – a whole fleet of them. Henrietta's idea is that Jean-Paul will take no profit from the venture until he's seven. Then she'll take care of his interests until he's of an age to take them on for himself . . .'

Amy stood up, almost knocking over the chair behind her. In a shaky voice she said: 'Have you forgotten so soon the promise you made to me when you returned from your *last* visit to London – after you'd learned Beville had inherited his grandfather's title and you swore you'd keep Polrudden for him?'

'What promise?' Nathan's mind worked rapidly, but he could think of nothing he had said that had any bearing on the offer made by Henrietta.

'You *have* forgotten. It seems you don't recall what's said when you're in bed with *me*.' Amy spat the words at Nathan venomously. 'You promised that Portgiskey, the boats and the cellar would be your gift to *our* son, yours and mine.'

Now Nathan realised the trap into which he had blundered so incautiously. He tried to fight his way free. 'Polrudden needs to be saved for Beville because he's part of us *now*. He's real. You're talking of a problem we may never have to face. Even if it does arise, it might not be for years yet.'

'Wrong again, Nathan Jago. Your child is weighing heavily in my belly, for all there's only four months of life in him – and it *will* be a son, I promise you. I haven't told you before because I thought you had enough to worry you. It seems I was wrong. Your mind should have been occupied with thoughts of *all* your responsibilities.'

Leaving Nathan kneeling on the floor open-mouthed, Amy fled from the room. He reached the corridor in time to hear the door of the guest-room slam shut and the bolt on the inside being thrust home.

CHAPTER TWENTY-SIX

Across the English Channel, Napoleon Bonaparte was once more ensconced in the royal palace of the Tuileries in Paris. His army had swollen to well over a hundred thousand men, most of them experienced soldiers. He was already boasting that before the end of the summer it would number half a million; but it seemed the brilliant Corsican general was not to be given the time he needed. Already the armies of Europe were on the march against him. The Duke of Wellington, architect of Napoleon's earlier downfall, had arrived in Brussels to take command of the combined armies of Britain and the Low Countries.

The army which had carried Wellington to one brilliant victory after another in his Portuguese and Spanish campaigns was no more. Many of the battle-hardened regiments of the British army had been sent to North America, to combat the threat from the United States when the war in Europe was thought to be over. Others had been disbanded, or drastically reduced in size. Many of Wellington's seasoned old soldiers had been turned loose upon an ungrateful country and forced into vagrancy, in the manner of the recent heroes who lived among the ancient tin-workings of Polgooth Downs.

Now an urgent call went out from the disastrously under-strength regiments for recruits. In particular demand were those men who had already experienced the discipline and hardships of war. There would be no time to train raw recruits. Wellington wanted *soldiers,* and he needed them with the utmost urgency.

For the men leading an aimless life on Polgooth Downs, the new war came as an unexpected means of escape. The plea for the men to return to the Army and serve their country came from none other than Fenwick Garland, who had finally left the Downs to work for Captain Geach, the officer in whose company he had once served.

Captain Geach accompanied Fenwick Garland to the Downs. Unable himself to fight, because of the wounds he had received in the Peninsular Wars, Fenwick Garland now proudly wore the uniform of a recruiting sergeant for his old regiment, the 32nd. Every man recruited by Sergeant Garland was to receive a uniform provided for him at the expense of Captain Geach, and he would enter the barracks with a guinea in his pocket.

The news of the departure of the ragged army from Polgooth Downs was brought to Pentuan by Sergeant Fenwick Garland himself. He had come to find Josiah Jago, carrying to him the thanks of the re-enlisted men for the succour the preacher had given them during the miserable months spent in the damp heights above Polgooth.

Preacher Jago was away, riding his unofficial Methodist circuit, and so the recruiting sergeant sought out Nathan.

Nathan was working on the quay at Portgiskey, with Beville and Jean-Paul nearby, when Sergeant Garland arrived. Both boys stopped what they were doing, filled with awe at the sight of Fenwick Garland's uniform. They peeped wide-eyed at the scarlet-coated sergeant from around Nathan's legs as he explained the purpose of his visit.

Delighted at the changed circumstances of the reluctant vagrants, Nathan commented that Fenwick Garland was a different man from the one he had last met at Polrudden.

'Ah! That's what being a soldier does for a man, Nathan. Put him in the King's uniform and he'll stand taller, able to look the whole world in the eye. It's a grand life for a man. Don't you two boys think so now?'

Crouching down beside Nathan, Sergeant Garland spoke to Beville and Jean-Paul. Taking off his tall dark serge shako, he tried it on both boys, holding it so it would not fall down beyond their ears.

When he straightened up again, Fenwick Garland said:

'They'll make likely enough soldiers one day, Nathan. Officers, I've no doubt.'

The recruiting sergeant frowned as he looked from one boy to the other, and then back again at Nathan. 'I can see that one boy is the spitting image of you, but the other . . . Does he perhaps favour his mother?'

Nathan smiled sadly. 'He does indeed, but she lies buried in the chapel cemetery up the hill. His father *was* an officer – with Napoleon. It seems likely he left his bones in Russia when Bonaparte retreated from Moscow.' Nathan went on to tell Fenwick Garland the story of the loss of the French merchantman and of Jean-Paul's dramatic rescue.

'So the little chap's an orphan.' The recruiting sergeant looked at Jean-Paul in sympathy as the two boys 'helped' a Portgiskey fisherman to lay out a torn net on the quay. 'He has my sympathy, Nathan. My envy too. I was an orphan boy, but *I* was brought up in a parish workhouse. There's precious little joy to be found inside one of them places, I can tell you. Soon as I was big enough to see over the poorhouse wall I was off to join the Army. I was a drummer boy before I was old enough to be a real soldier. I'd say the lad was lucky to be rescued by the likes of you. He'll have a good life here in Cornwall, living at Polrudden.'

'I hope so, Fenwick, but we need to keep an eye on him for a while. He's related to some important people in France. There are those who'd like to have control of him – one of them being Napoleon Bonaparte himself.'

'Is that so?' Fenwick Garland looked at Jean-Paul with renewed interest. 'Well, you'll soon be able to stop worrying about old Napoleon, once and for all. My old regiment's sailing from Plymouth next week to join the Duke of Wellington's army. Napoleon hasn't had the beating of them in the past; I doubt if he's learned any new tricks while he was on Elba.'

'I hope you're right.'

'I am, Nathan, you mark my words. But I've wasted enough of your time with my idle chatter. Before I go I've got a couple of shiny buttons in a pocket here. I'm sure they'll give pleasure to two small boys.'

Nathan watched Fenwick Garland limp away from Portgiskey, marvelling at the change in the man.

Left alone to his tasks, Nathan wished he could find an equally satisfactory solution to his own problems. For two days after his return from London, Amy had remained locked in her room, refusing to come out when Nathan was in the house. She emerged only when he threatened to break down the door. But she would not speak to him, and Nathan slept that night in the cottage attached to the Portgiskey fish-cellar.

He was back at Polrudden now, but relations between himself and Amy were strained to near breaking-point. Nathan accepted that the blame was his and he felt his guilt keenly. At a time when Amy should be happily anticipating parenthood, she was probably more miserable than she had ever been before.

That evening a heavy silence hung over the dining-table like a pall, as it had during every meal since they had resumed eating together. Suddenly, Nathan put down his knife and looked across the table. Amy was pushing food about her plate, lacking all enthusiasm for eating. She was having an uncomfortable pregnancy, and her face was pale and thin.

'Amy, we can't go on like this. I'm sorry for taking the fight in London and not telling you. I'd do anything to undo what has happened, but it's too late for such thoughts – and it *did* give us some desperately needed money.'

'It isn't the fight that's upset me, Nathan. You know that.'

It was the longest sentence Amy had spoken to him since the night of his return and it gave him new hope, in spite of her words.

'I've already said we'll forget about Jean-Paul having a share in Portgiskey. Henrietta won't mind. I suspect she only made the offer because she thought it would be a help to us.'

'Thought it would help *you*, perhaps. I doubt if *I* figure in her schemes.'

'You're being foolish. Henrietta is a marquise, a member

of the royal household of King Louis of France. I'm . . . just a fisherman.'

'You were "just a fisherman" when you married the daughter of Sir Lewis Hearle of Polrudden. Now you're master of this house, your son is a baronet, and the nephew of your marquise is living as one of our family. You are no longer "just a fisherman".'

'Amy, it wouldn't matter if I were a royal duke. *You* are my wife and you're carrying *our* baby. You're the most important thing in my life right now.'

Pushing her chair back from the table, Amy stood up and looked at Nathan coldly. 'If I thought your marquise believed that, things might be different between us. Now, if you'll excuse me, I'm going to bed. I'm very tired.'

Later that evening, from the shadowed window of her bedroom, Amy watched Nathan setting off along the driveway on his way to Portgiskey and a night's fishing. Had he been able to see her, Nathan would have been astonished at the tender expression on Amy's face as she watched him trudge away from the house. There was all the love there he thought had been lost to him.

As Nathan reached the lane at the end of the driveway, he turned. Amy's hand came up as though she would wave, but she stopped herself. It would not have mattered; the evening shadows were deepening and he could not have seen her. Amy did not know whether to be relieved or sorry.

She smiled sadly. Poor Nathan! He was a relatively unsophisticated man. A woman like Henrietta, marquise d'Orléan was capable of turning heads more worldly-wise than Nathan's. Amy knew she was being hard on him. Perhaps tomorrow she would relent a little. She *needed* Nathan and wanted the last few months of her pregnancy to be a happier time than she had experienced until now.

Amy went to sleep that night content that the morrow would see happiness return to her life at Polrudden.

Nathan did not return to Portgiskey the next day, and Amy

waited in vain for the anticipated reconciliation. Not until she walked down the long hill to Portgiskey and spoke to the crew of *Sir Beville* did she learn that Nathan had sailed *Successful* to the rich fishing-grounds off Ireland. He had told his men he intended fishing the well-stocked fishing-grounds for herring. If the fishing proved good and local markets were available, he would probably remain away for about a month. Nathan had told Amy of his plans more than a week before, but she had been ignoring him at the time and the matter had not fully registered with her.

Amy was deeply disappointed that the quarrel between them was not to be resolved as quickly as she had hoped, but she determined not to waste the time until Nathan's return. Ten days after his departure *Sir Beville*, fishing well offshore, discovered a large and unseasonably early shoal of pilchards. It was a rich bonus not to be missed, and the fishing-boat made regular trips between the shoal and the Portgiskey fish-cellar.

At the same time, a merchantman limped into Mevagissey harbour and beached there to repair a serious leak. The ship was bound for the Mediterranean, but the crew had been forced to throw much of the cargo overboard in their desperate bid to stay afloat. Amy successfully negotiated with the ship's master to load salted pilchards for Italy when repairs to his vessel were completed.

Extra women were called in from Pentuan to help fulfil the order and they worked hard and noisily, their happy chatter reflecting the pleasure they felt at having an unexpected boost to their meagre incomes.

Amy spent her days at Portgiskey, supervising the salting and pressing and packing of pilchards into fifty-gallon barrels, or 'hogsheads' as they were known. It was necessary to buy in more hogsheads from the coopers in St Austell, as well as ship in a large quantity of French salt. This was brought in by night from an unlighted ship standing out in the bay, thus evading the crippling duty of fifteen shillings a bushel placed on salt by the British government.

Beville and Jean-Paul went with Amy to Portgiskey on

most days. They would play in the sand which at low tide extended beyond the rocks at the foot of the cliffs, to link up with the wide expanse of Pentuan beach.

Amy had no qualms about allowing the children to play here. The beach was gently sloping and not subject to the great waves that often swept the north Cornish coast. Besides, the children were rarely out of sight of the women working in the fish-cellar.

On the day before the hogsheads of fish were due to be loaded on the newly floated merchantman, the women in the cellar, led by Amy, were working at full stretch to complete packing the cured fish and secure the hogsheads. It was not until mid-afternoon, when it became apparent that the order would be completed on time, that Amy guiltily remembered she had not seen the children for a couple of hours.

Walking out on the quay, she saw a small figure at the water's edge, at the entrance to the cove, close to the rocks. She looked about the cove for a second little boy but she could not see him. She was not unduly concerned. He was probably behind the rocks, only a few feet from the child she could see.

'Beville! Jean-Paul!' Amy called, but the small figure continued to prod at something in the sand that had caught his attention. The surf, breaking against the shore not six feet away from where he was playing, would effectively prevent him hearing her voice, but the other child was still nowhere to be seen.

Frowning in annoyance, Amy carefully made her way down the slime-covered steps to the sand and began walking towards the tiny figure at the water's edge. The boy suddenly stood up, and now Amy could see it was Beville.

She covered half the distance towards him before Beville saw her. He waved, but still there was no sign of Jean-Paul. For the first time, Amy felt a twinge of uneasiness.

'Jean-Paul! Where are you?' Amy called loudly, looking about her and expecting the small French boy to emerge from a hiding-place among the rocks.

No one appeared, although the sound of her voice finally caused Beville to leave his place at the edge of the sea. He ran towards her holding something in the palm of his hand, held out in front of him.

'Look. A crab.' Beville identified the tiny creature in his hand when still twenty yards from her. It was no larger than a half-guinea coin.

'Where's Jean-Paul?' Amy repeated the question twice before Beville's attention was diverted from his newly acquired pet crustacean.

'Gone.'

Beville's matter-of-fact reply filled Amy with more apprehension than any detailed explanation.

'Gone? Gone where? Beville, do you hear? Answer me.'

The urgency in her voice finally filtered through to the small boy. Dropping the crab on the ground, he rubbed sand from his hands.

'Jean-Paul went for a ride. On a horse. The man said I couldn't go.'

Now Amy knew very real fear as she recalled the threat to abduct Jean-Paul. Events in France were so far away from the remote Cornish fishing village that it had seemed foolish to continue having the small boy escorted wherever he went. She had ordered Will Hodge and the farmworker to resume their normal duties.

'What man, Beville? Did you know him?'

Beville shook his head as he bent to retrieve the tiny crab which was lying helplessly on its back in the sand, legs kicking vainly at the air. 'Was *two* men. They only gave Jean-Paul a ride, not me. It isn't fair . . .'

Leaving Beville crouched over the crab, Amy ran to the sea end of the cove. She hoped desperately that she might see Jean-Paul being returned to Portgiskey by a friend whom Beville had failed to recognise.

She could see along the empty length of the Pentuan sands. There was only the tracks made by two horses. Twin tracks coming towards Portgiskey – and two returning again, towards Pentuan.

Amy hurried back for Beville, the sheer horror of the situation driving her to panic. When she took Beville's hand she twice set off towards the fish-cellar – and twice turned back, heading for Pentuan, uncertain what to do.

Seeing one of the older women watching her with much interest from the Portgiskey quay, Amy managed to regain control of herself.

She called out instructions that would enable the women to have the hogsheads ready for collection. Then, without further explanation, she picked Beville up in her arms and ran with him to Pentuan village. She arrived gasping for breath, her heart beating alarmingly and a painful ringing in her ears. She asked everyone she met whether they had seen Jean-Paul. One astonished villager after another shook his head. Then Harriet Piper, the crippled daughter of Nathan's crewman, remembered seeing two riders come from the Pentuan sands and head towards St Austell along the valley road. One was holding a small boy in front of him on the horse. She added that she thought at the time the boy resembled Jean-Paul.

Now Amy knew there was no hope of the whole dreadful nightmare turning out to be some simple mistake. Jean-Paul had been kidnapped!

How Amy struggled up the long steep hill to Polrudden with Beville she never knew. At times she put the small but stocky little boy down, but he would walk only a few yards at an agonisingly slow speed before complaining that his legs ached, and Amy had no alternative but to pick him up and carry him.

By the time she arrived at Polrudden, Amy was in a state of collapse, the world swinging wildly about her. She was also suffering great pain. It was a pain that began in her belly and swept up like an all-consuming flame to engulf her chest and even her head.

Amy was aware of the alarm she caused when she eventually stumbled inside the house. Near-hysterical, she refused to rest until Will Hodge had been sent for and she had told him incoherently what had happened to Jean-Paul.

Amy extracted a promise from Will Hodge that every able-bodied man employed at Polrudden would be provided with a horse and sent out to scour the countryside in search of the missing French boy. Not until this was done did Amy give way to the pain that racked her body, and allow herself to be half-led, half-carried to her bedroom.

CHAPTER TWENTY-SEVEN

It was dark when *Successful* eased into Portgiskey Cove. The fish-cellar was silent and empty, *Sir Beville* somewhere out in the bay. Nathan had been away for more than three weeks, and the trip had proved highly profitable. Fishing within sight of the Irish coast, he had found an eager market for his heavy catches in the hungry garrison town of Wexford. He had taken full advantage of his good luck until heavy seas brought the fishing to an end.

Calling a cheery 'Good night!' to his crew members in the darkened street of Pentuan, Nathan set off to climb the hill to Polrudden. He wished he knew what his reception would be from Amy; whether she would be talking to him once more. His thoughts made the hill seem even more steep than usual. By the time he turned into the long drive leading to the house, his pleasure at the success of his long fishing trip had almost drained away.

Nathan was startled to see a great many lamps still burning in the house. It was after ten o'clock. Amy and the servants were usually abed by this hour.

As he drew nearer to the house, Nathan saw a light carriage and a saddled horse standing in front of the door. He frowned. It was unusual to have visitors at Polrudden –

and almost unheard of for them to stay until such an hour.

The front door was standing open, and Nathan hurried inside. In the hallway he met two grave-faced men taking their hats and cloaks from a Polrudden servant. One of the men was Dr Ellerman Scott, the other a stranger to Nathan.

'What's going on? Who's ill? Is it one of the boys . . . or Amy?' Fearfully, Nathan put the questions to Dr Ellerman Scott.

'Mr Jago, I would like you to meet Surgeon Isaacs. I sent for him to attend your wife.'

Surgeon Isaacs shook hands with Nathan, his expression grave. 'Your return is timely, Mr Jago. I fear your wife is a very sick young woman.'

'Is it something to do with the baby . . .?'

Surgeon Isaacs nodded. Still grasping Nathan's hand, he said: 'It *was*. I regret to tell you she lost the baby yesterday.'

The surgeon's words dismayed Nathan. The baby had meant so much to Amy. She would be heartbroken. He looked towards the stairs, anxious to go to her, but the surgeon was still talking.

'Your wife is causing me much concern at the moment, Mr Jago. She is still losing a great deal of blood and growing weaker by the hour. I have tried all I know to staunch the bleeding, but without effect. I fear she may have ruptured a blood vessel when she foolishly overstrained herself.'

'What happened?'

'The French boy – the one you rescued from the ship that sank off the cliffs – someone went off with him while your wife was working at Portgiskey. It seems she *ran* all the way back to Polrudden for help, carrying your son for most of the way.'

This latest revelation staggered Nathan. Somebody had taken Jean-Paul! Suddenly, Nathan knew the dreadful anguish Amy must be suffering.

'Can I see Amy now?'

'Leave it for an hour or two.' The reply came from Surgeon Isaacs. 'I have given her a mild opiate. Hopefully, rest will help. I can think of nothing else. There is a maid with her at the moment. I am spending the night at Dr Ellerman Scott's house and will return to see your wife again in the morning.'

Resisting an urge to peep into Amy's room after seeing the medical men on their way, Nathan sent for Will Hodge, to check on what was being done to find Jean-Paul.

The weary ostler told Nathan he had learned that the two men who were believed to have made off with Jean-Paul had been seen about Pentuan for two days before the boy had been taken. Much of their time had been spent in the Jolly Sailor inn, where they had taken a room. They were known to have ridden in the direction of Portgiskey Cove on more than one occasion. The men had left the Jolly Sailor inn without settling their accounts, but nothing left behind in their room gave any clues to their identities or the direction in which they might be heading. Will Hodge had sent men out on all main roads seeking the kidnappers and Jean-Paul. He had himself checked the road towards Falmouth, the great sea-port to the west.

Neither Will Hodge nor the men he sent out had met with any success. The last hope lay with *Sir Beville*. The vessel was not fishing, as Nathan had thought, but was scouring the coast, searching for any foreign vessel that might be anchored close inshore, awaiting delivery of the young captive.

Will Hodge had also informed the magistrate in St Austell, but when the magistrate had learned Jean-Paul was a French orphan he had refused to instigate a hue and cry.

Nathan admitted that the ostler had done as much as he might have done himself. Unless *Sir Beville* was able to discover something new it would appear the kidnap had been successful.

It was midnight before Nathan went up the stairs to see Amy. She was in the large bedroom she and Nathan had shared before his trip to London, not in the small room she had used since then. Opening the door quietly, he caught the maid dozing in a chair at the bedside. She started up when Nathan stood over her, but he held a finger to his lips before she could speak. Amy lay still in the bed, her face as pale as the linen pillow on which it lay, her breathing shallow but regular. Nathan signalled for the frightened maid to leave the room. He would sit with Amy through the night.

He sat slumped in the easy chair beside the bed for many hours, thinking, his mind far too active for sleep. As the grandmother clock on the mantelshelf ticked away the hours, Nathan thought of how much unhappiness he had caused Amy by his brief interlude with Henrietta. The whole fabric of their life together had been ripped apart, and he wondered if it could ever be repaired.

Nathan realised how tragically guilty Amy must have felt when she realised the small French boy had been carried off. She loved Jean-Paul, and he returned her love. Yet Nathan was every bit as guilty. He should have ensured that vigilance was maintained to guard the boy against those who sought to harm him; but, somehow, the renewed state of war between England and Napoleon Bonaparte had an air of unreality. There was no threat to fishermen from French men-of-war; no press-gangs preyed on the coastal villages, snatching men to crew British warships. It was hard to realise that a small boy's life was in danger as a result of a war that had such little effect on life inside Cornwall.

Henrietta would have to be told of the kidnapping, of course – but Nathan put the thought away immediately. He had no means of communicating with her.

He looked again at Amy. She had not stirred since he entered the room. Only the faint rise and fall of the bed-clothes showed she still breathed.

Light could be seen beyond the curtains now. A new day was dawning. Nathan wondered what it would bring. Easing himself from the chair he drew the curtains quietly. It was a fine morning, the sun beginning to climb clear of the ribbon of mist that bound the horizon. Its reflection spread in a sparkling rose-pink carpet on the calm grey water. It was a dawn like so many Nathan had viewed from this very window. The sort of morning that made him happy to be a fisherman. He had shared many such moments with Amy.

Turning back into the room, it was a second or two before Nathan realised that Amy's eyes were open and she was looking at him.

'Amy, my love . . . .!' Nathan dropped to his knees beside the bed and took Amy's hands. As she looked at him, her eyes filled with tears.

'Nathan, I'm sorry . . . about Jean-Paul . . . the baby . . . everything.'

'Sh! Don't try to talk – and you mustn't cry. You've nothing to be sorry about. *I'm* the one who should be apologising. I ought to have been here when you needed me.' Suddenly, Nathan's relief overwhelmed him. Choked with emotion, he put his arms about her. 'Amy, I love you very much.'

'I love you, too, Nathan. I've missed you.' She began to cry noisily, and Nathan rocked her gently to and fro, making soothing noises, as though she were a baby.

When Surgeon Isaacs and Dr Ellerman Scott arrived Nathan was having breakfast and Amy was sleeping peacefully and naturally.

Washed and fed, Nathan felt more confident about facing the day ahead, but when the two medical men returned from visiting Amy the surgeon warned him of entertaining undue optimism.

'She's still losing a lot of blood,' he explained grimly. 'Your return has *improved* her chances of recovery, no more.'

'But she's so much better this morning. Her maid says so, and there's colour in her cheeks.'

'I'm giving you an opinion as a surgeon, Mr Jago, not as a maid. She's a very sick woman and there will be no improvement until she stops worrying about this young boy who's gone missing. True, she's also grieved about the loss of the baby she was carrying, but women get over such things. No, it's this other business that's playing on her mind. Find the boy and you'll be setting her on the road to recovery.'

Both doctors left soon afterwards, Dr Ellerman Scott promising to return the next day.

Amy went to sleep again after the visit of the two medical men, and Nathan played for a while with Beville before going to bed for a couple of hours. Everything possible had been done to find Jean-Paul. It needed a miracle to bring him back now, and Nathan knew of only one man who was a believer in miracles. That man was his father.

When Nathan reached Pentuan village early that afternoon, he found the Methodist preacher's home empty. One of the Methodist class-leaders told Nathan the preacher had gone to Plymouth with Recruiting Sergeant Fenwick Garland. The men recruited to bring the 32nd Regiment up to strength were due to embark from the Devon port, to join the remainder of the Cornwall Regiment in Belgium. Among them were the men who had lived so close to starvation on Polgooth Downs. They had requested that Josiah Jago hold a prayer-meeting for them on board the transport before it set sail.

From Pentuan, Nathan went on to Portgiskey. Here he helped the crew of *Successful* to prepare the large drifter for a night's fishing, but he could not settle down to work and the return of *Sir Beville* came as a welcome diversion.

As the fishing-boat manoeuvred in the confines of the cove, edging slowly towards the quay, Nathan called across the intervening space, asking for news of Jean-Paul. There was none.

Ahab Arthur and his tired crew had scoured the inlets and harbours of south Cornwall, sailing as far eastwards as Plymouth in their search. They reported a great many foreign ships in Plymouth harbour – far too many for a watch to be kept on each of them – and none was openly flying the tricolour of France.

After thanking the men for the many hours they had put

into the search, Nathan made his way homeward. He felt thoroughly detected. As he reached the driveway to Polrudden, he heard the sound of singing coming from farther along the St Austell road. There was more than one voice, and one of them belonged to a child. The song was innocently bawdy, being one sung by soldiers of Wellington's army when on the march. One of the singers held a note for longer than his fellow-choristers, and Nathan thought he recognised his father's voice. But Nathan had never heard the Methodist preacher sing a song such as this before. In fact, Nathan had never heard him sing *anything* that was not a Methodist hymn.

Nathan stopped for a while and listened as the singers came closer. Now there could be no doubt at all. One of the singers *was* Josiah Jago.

Before long three figures came into view around a bend in the narrow road. The first was Josiah Jago, his legs dangling down on either side of his dejected-looking old donkey. Limping along happily beside him was Recruiting Sergeant Fenwick Garland. On the sergeant's shoulders, and proudly wearing his soldier's hat, was Jean-Paul Duvernet!

As Nathan ran to meet the trio, the singing faltered and stopped, Jean-Paul waving wildly from his perch on Fenwick Garland's shoulders. He wriggled so much in his excitement that the recruiting sergeant was compelled to grasp Jean-Paul's ankles to prevent him from falling to the ground.

'Jean-Paul . . . Thank God! Where have you been?' Nathan swung the excited boy from Fenwick Garland's shoulders and held him close.

'I've been with Grandpa Jago and Sergeant Garland. We've been singing soldier songs – and I can *march*.' Listening to the boy talk, Nathan marvelled that anyone would have believed him to be a French boy. His accent was most certainly Cornish.

Nathan hugged the boy to him so tightly that Jean-Paul gave a squeal of protest. Over the boy's head, Nathan spoke to the two men. 'How does Jean-Paul come to be with you? We've scoured the whole of Cornwall, and beyond, looking for him.'

'You might well ask,' replied Fenwick Garland. 'We were on the Devon side of the Tamar, Preacher Jago and me, waiting to cross the river to Cornwall. The ferry pulled in and there on board were two men – and Jean-Paul with 'em. As soon as he recognised your father the boy called out "Grandpa! Grandpa Jago!" and he runs to us. The two men didn't stop to give us any explanations. They jumped their horses ashore and were away before we even got a good look at 'em, leaving us to bring the boy home to Polrudden. We got as far as Looe last night and came on the rest of the way today, as quick as we could. I don't doubt Mistress Jago will be nigh out of her mind worrying about him.'

Nathan told the two men what had happened as a result of Jean-Paul's abduction. 'But Amy's going to get better again now,' he added, hugging Jean-Paul to him yet again. 'This is the miracle I've been praying for, and you've brought it to us. Come up to the house and see for yourself the difference it will make to Amy.'

The return of Jean-Paul marked the turning-point for Amy, but her recovery was slow and she bitterly mourned the loss of her baby. Nathan expressed his concern at her slow progress when Surgeon Isaacs accompanied Dr Ellerman Scott on a final visit to Polrudden.

'She was a very sick young woman,' explained the surgeon. 'Had the return of the young French boy not rallied her, I doubt if she would have survived. However, there's nothing physically wrong with her now; all she needs is to have something to take her mind off what's happened. My advice to you is to make your wife pregnant again, Mr Jago. The sooner the better. You'll find it a more effective cure than any physic Dr Ellerman Scott or I can prescribe.'

The surgeon's suggested 'cure' for Amy might have been

medically sound, but it was totally lacking in sensitivity. Amy was not yet ready to resume a full married life, and Nathan made no attempt to implement the surgeon's advice.

CHAPTER TWENTY-EIGHT

In the early summer of 1815 the European allies were mustering their armies to oppose Napoleon Bonaparte. A million men had been promised, and all across the Continent marching men were converging on France. In Belgium, 80,000 troops under the command of the Duke of Wellington were deployed to guard the approaches to Brussels, with 150,000 Prussians extended on their flank.

Napoleon knew that given time he, too, could raise a million men, but time owed no allegiance to the tricolour of Republican France. The newly returned Emperor was forced to resort to a course less familar than soldiering. He tried his hand at diplomacy.

Promising to abide by the decisions made by the Allied 'Council of Europe', formed since his enforced abdication, he despatched trusted couriers bearing letters of conciliation to the courts of Europe.

To England.

One Sunday in May, Amy ventured out of doors for the first time since the loss of her unborn child. An armchair was placed on the lawn for her to enjoy the warm sunshine, and she and Nathan watched the two boys playing together.

The sound of horses on the road at the end of the driveway provoked little interest. Wagons frequently plied between St Austell and the tiny harbour of Pentuan, even on a Sunday. But when Nathan heard the shout of a coachman he looked up, surprised to see a coach turning from the roadway into Polrudden.

Owing to the poor state of most of the county's roads there were few coaches in Cornwall. Nathan could remember seeing *none* resembling this great carriage with polished maroon-coloured coachwork and pulled by four magnificent matched horses. Behind the carriage rode six cavalrymen, wearing the scarlet and gold uniforms and elaborate plumed helmets of the Royal Life Guards.

The two small boys stopped their playing and stood together on the lawn, struck dumb by the sight of the smartly attired cavalrymen.

Within moments of the carriage rolling to a halt before the main door of Polrudden, Nathan had forgotten the presence of the soldiers. A footman leaped to the ground and opened the carriage door to lower the step. Then he handed out a passenger whom Nathan had never expected to see at Polrudden again. It was Henrietta, marquise d'Orléan.

As Amy drew in a sharp breath, a tall, fair-haired man of about Nathan's age also stepped to the ground. The left sleeve of his jacket was neatly folded and pinned to the shoulder. There was something very familiar about the man's face, but it hardly had time to register with Nathan before Henrietta called his name excitedly and ran to him.

'Nathan, my dear! I am so happy to see your face has healed and left no scars.' Taking both his hands in hers, she kissed him warmly. 'You are looking *so* fit!'

Then Henrietta saw Amy seated in the armchair, looking pale and distressed. 'Amy, you are not well! What is the matter?' Crouching by Amy's chair, she embraced the mistress of Polrudden almost as warmly as she had her husband.

'Nathan, what have you been doing to this poor girl?'

Amy was struggling to gather her scattered wits when suddenly, and wordlessly, the attention of everyone on the lawn became focused on the one-armed man who had been a fellow-passenger in the carriage with Henrietta. Forgoing all introductions, the stranger knelt beside the two boys who had now moved closer to the dismounting guardsmen. Speaking softly in French, he was trying to persuade Jean-Paul to come to him.

Henrietta's whispered, emotional explanation was unnecessary. The man was Charles, duc de Duvernet, Henrietta's half-brother. The father of Jean-Paul.

The small boy eventually moved close enough for Charles Duvernet to put his arm about his son. However, when spoken to in French, Jean-Paul moved away again and the hurt on the face of his father was clear.

Looking about him, Jean-Paul saw Amy. Running to her, he clambered on her lap. Ignoring the man who was his father, the small boy pointed to the horses.

'Soldiers!' The word was uttered with the lisp of a three-year-old.

'You will need to teach your son to speak French, I am afraid. He has been with us for a long time.' Nathan's explanation broke the painful silence.

'Of course. I should have realised. But he looks so like his mother. My poor, dear Marie-Louise. Not to talk to him so . . . it was impossible.'

The Frenchman had a good command of English, but he spoke carefully, in the manner of a man unused to the language. 'Pardon me, my manners are unforgivable. Madame. M'sieur. I am Charles Duvernet, the father of Jean-Paul . . .'

Amy's smile served only to show how close to tears she was. 'Introductions are not necessary. You see only your wife in Jean-Paul, but he is very like his father also.'

Bowing low over Amy, who still held Jean-Paul, Charles, duc de Duvernet brought her hand to his lips and held it there.

'I thank you, Madame Jago. From my heart, I thank you for so much . . .'

Choked with emotion, Charles Duvernet straightened up. In a matter of moments he had control of himself once more and looked around for Nathan. 'M'sieur Jago. To you I owe far more than gratitude. I have heard so much about you and your bravery . . .'

Nathan saw Amy's gaze shift to Henrietta – but Charles Duvernet was still talking. 'The comte d'Argon talks of you with so much pride, one would almost think *you* were French. I think he holds you in more respect than he does his king.'

'You've met Louis recently?' Nathan was surprised. Louis d'Argon was a King's man, a member of the King's household. Charles Duvernet was a republican and an officer in the army of Napoleon Bonaparte.

'It surprises you? We met in London recently. Poor Louis, he does not know whether his duty compels him to hate me or to love me. I am an enemy of his king – but I am also the closest relative of the woman he is to marry.'

When Charles Duvernet's words sank in, Nathan swung around to seek confirmation from Henrietta. She was facing away from him, crouched in conversation with Beville. Something in her stance told Nathan she had heard her half-brother's words but had no wish to face him.

'Louis and Henrietta are to be married?' Nathan put the question to Charles Duvernet.

'You did not know? Of course, how could you? Henrietta, I apologise for spoiling your surprise. Stand up and accept the congratulations of your friends.'

Nathan's good wishes were more puzzled than enthusiastic, and Henrietta did not meet his eyes in acknowledging them.

The duc de Duvernet did not notice the embarrassment he had caused. Without removing his gaze from Jean-Paul, he said: 'M'sieur Jago, is it possible for a servant to provide the horses with water – and the soldiers, too, perhaps. I regret they are not an escort, but a guard. There is so much I have to say to you and your beautiful wife, but before Henrietta and I seek an inn I would like a few minutes alone with Jean-Paul. You understand?'

'Of course, but there is no question of either of you

seeking an inn, even if there were an appropriate one nearby. You'll stay here.'

A few minutes later Nathan and Henrietta helped Amy inside the house, the marquise expressing great concern at Amy's weak condition.

Amy had believed herself well on the road to recovery, but she felt weak and helpless, in the presence of this elegantly beautiful woman. Henrietta's sympathy merely served to make matters worse. Amy's eyes burned as she held back the tears that threatened to make an utter fool of her.

The next few hours were busy ones for Nathan. He and Amy lived a quiet life at Polrudden. Now they suddenly had two well-born guests in the house, together with Henrietta's personal maid, coachman and footman, and the six Life Guards, whose presence had yet to be explained.

By late evening the house was settling down to a busy but orderly routine. Amy felt better after a rest in her room, and Charles Duvernet had finally succeeded in establishing an early, tentative relationship with his son. Jean-Paul had gone to bed proudly declaring that he now had a papa, 'just like Beville'.

Over dinner that evening, Charles Duvernet told the story of his missing years, when he had been presumed dead. It was a harrowing tale of suffering, infused with courage and an indomitable determination to survive.

A captain in Napoleon's army in Martinique when he met and married the most sought-after beauty on the island, Charles Duvernet was soon afterwards recalled to France. His orders 'to join Napoleon Bonaparte's Grand Army'. Marie-Louise, now pregnant, expected to follow when the baby was born. Unfortunately, before this came about, British forces occupied a number of French Caribbean islands, Martinique among them.

However, before setting off with Napoleon Bonaparte on the conquest of Russia, Charles Duvernet managed to smuggle a message to his wife. She and his unseen son, together with a number of other citizens of importance, were to be ready to leave Martinique at a moment's notice. A ship had been found to bring them to France. Unfortunately, owing to the vigilance of the British navy, it was not possible to give even an approximate date for the ship's arrival. It might be within three months – it could take a year. In fact, the ill-fated *L'Emir* did not reach the island until August 1813, by which time Napoleon had retreated from Russia, leaving the bones of almost half a million Frenchmen behind.

Charles Duvernet had begun the Russian campaign as an officer of Napoleon's General Staff. During the advance upon Moscow he was promoted colonel and given command of a regiment of élite cavalry. Always in the van of battle, Colonel Duvernet and his cavalry led the great army into Moscow, only to find the city deserted, the storehouses empty. Worse was to come. The next day the magnificent Russian city went up in flames.

The 'Grand Army' of 600,000 soldiers was deep in the heart of a hostile nation. Bonaparte waited in vain in the burned-out city for the Russian Tsar to offer his country's surrender. It never came, and finally Bonaparte ordered his army to retreat, intending to sweep southwards on the return march to France. Instead, the French retreat was checked by the tenacious Russian army and Napoleon was forced to retrace his steps through countryside already stripped bare by pillaging French soldiers.

Starvation was now a very real threat, and the retreat would have become a headlong flight had the weather not taken a hand. As it became colder, so mists rose to envelop the hungry army. Platoons, companies, even whole regiments became separated from the great army. They were never heard of again, most being killed by the Russians harrying the flanks of the floundering French army, bent on vengeance. Then, when the morale of the French had reached a new low, the wind howled down from the vast Arctic wastelands to the north, bringing snow such as the French soldiers had never before experienced.

Ordered to delay the Russian pursuit of Bonaparte and

his General Staff, Colonel Charles Duvernet did his best to hold his regiment together, even ordering the execution of four starving French infantrymen who killed one of his cavalry horses for food.

In a fierce skirmish near Borodino, where only a few months before the French had inflicted a crushing defeat on the Russian army, a Cossack sword sliced Colonel Duvernet's left arm to the bone. Still his ever-dwindling regiment of cavalry fought its way westward, opposed now by the vengeance-seeking Russians, the terrain and the ever-worsening weather. Five days later, his wounded arm as black as the frost-encrusted mane of his mount, Charles Duvernet was abandoned in a derelict barn, left for dead by the cavalrymen who killed and ate his horse.

Within an hour Charles Duvernet was a prisoner of the Russians. It was not their practice to spare French soldiers, but Duvernet was fortunate. He was found by Russian officers seeking a temporary billet. A general was with them. He recognised Charles Duvernet's rank, and it transpired that he and the French duke had actually met in better days, when Napoleon Bonaparte was seeking an alliance with the Tsar.

Charles Duvernet was spared, the Russian general himself heading the escort that took the Frenchman to the Tsar. Fortunately, the party fell in with the Tsar's own surgeon within twenty-four hours of leaving the front. After only a cursory examination of the wound the surgeon amputated Charles Duvernet's arm at the shoulder. The operation undoubtedly saved the French colonel's life, but for many weeks he hovered in the strange, unreal world of those who are barely alive yet refuse to acknowledge death's victory.

Charles Duvernet survived and spent long months of convalescence in the glittering surroundings of the Tsar's court. Here he was forced to remain, a lone, tragic, yet romantic figure, until Napoleon Bonaparte was deposed and sent to Elba.

Released by the Tsar, and scorning the delights of a

capital city once more ruled by a French king, Charles Duvernet took a ship to Martinique, seeking his wife. He was told of her passage in *L'Emir* and given details of the vessel's tragic end. He met a survivor who had seen Marie-Louise Duvernet's body laid out in death in the tiny Pentuan chapel, but the survivor knew nothing of Charles Duvernet's son. He must have perished like so many of *L'Emir*'s passengers whose bodies had never been recovered.

Seeking the fortune in jewellery that had been left with Marie-Louise, Charles Duvernet succeeded in locating the woman who had been Marie-Louise's personal maid. She informed him that his wife had taken every piece of jewellery with her on board *L'Emir,* locked inside a casket of iron-bound leather.

With little left to live for, the one-armed ex-colonel made his way to Elba to join his former emperor, believing his family and fortune had been lost at sea.

Charles Duvernet arrived on the island of Elba in time to take a part in Bonaparte's return to Mother France. Charles Duvernet rode beside Bonaparte as regiment after regiment of King Louis XVIII's army came to do battle with Napoleon Bonaparte, only to change sides, falling in behind their late emperor and marching with him to Paris. So many of the King's men swelled Napoleon's ranks that one morning King Louis awoke to find a banner attached to the railings outside the royal palace. Purporting to be a message from Napoleon to the King, it read: 'Please do not send me more of your soldiers. I have enough already.'

Yet no matter how many soldiers joined his army, Napoleon Bonaparte knew it was too few. Allied armies were crowding the borders of France. They *could* be defeated. Given time he could raise a *new* Grand Army. But always there was that one word that meant so much: 'time'. It was an old enemy, yet one Napoleon had out-witted before.

Even as France's ex-emperor was making a triumphant return to his former capital, Charles Duvernet, duc de

Duvernet was on the road to Calais. He carried with him a letter from Napoleon Bonaparte to Lord Liverpool, Prime Minister of Great Britain. Napoleon declared he had learned the error of his former ways. He was no longer obsessed with territorial expansion. All he wanted now was an opportunity to rebuild his beloved France, within its own borders. He owed a debt to his nation and his sole ambition was to see that debt repaid. Alternatively, Napoleon Bonaparte hinted that he might be prepared to accept a regency . . .

In London, Napoleon Bonaparte's letter was returned, unopened, to Charles Duvernet. The personal plea of Bonaparte's envoy fell on equally stony ground. Great Britain and her allies wanted no more of the scheming little Corsican. He must surrender to the Allies or it would be war.

Charles Duvernet sent Lord Liverpool's reply to France with his aide. In London he had been reunited with Henrietta. From her he heard the incredible news that his son was alive and well, living in the home of a modest squire in Cornwall.

Through Henrietta's influence, Charles Duvernet was granted permission to remain in England for fourteen days after the end of his mission. Before the end of that time the French boat that had brought him from France would come to Portgiskey to return him to his homeland. Lord Castlereagh, the Foreign Secretary, accepted the word of Charles Duvernet as a nobleman that he would return to France as he promised. Nevertheless, the British Foreign Secretary was taking no chances on a man so close to Napoleon Bonaparte. He sent an escort along to ensure that Charles Duvernet caused no mischief.

This was the story told to Amy and Nathan over dinner that evening.

When Charles Duvernet ended the account of his life in the service of Napoleon Bonaparte, he added: 'You can have no idea how often I dreamed of my first meeting with my son, before I was told he and my wife had perished . . .'

The sympathetic silence that followed his words was broken by Henrietta. 'You did not tell me you would be returning to Bonaparte, Charles. Does the comte d'Argon know?'

'Ah! Poor Louis.' Charles Duvernet was content to change the subject. 'Yes, he knows. He does not approve, of course. But, then, *I* do not approve of his king.'

'What of Jean-Paul in all this?' The question came from Amy. 'Will you take him away with you when you go? We'll miss him. He's been like another son to us.' Nathan knew Amy was thinking again of the son she had lost.

'France is not a good place for a small boy. There will be war. Henrietta could take him to London with her, of course; but Jean-Paul is very happy here. It would please me greatly if you would allow him to remain with you for a while longer. I will pay for his keep, of course – and for a servant.'

'No payment will be necessary,' said Nathan firmly. The joy shown by Amy at Charles Duvernet's words was worth more than money. 'Jean-Paul has brought much pleasure to Polrudden and he's a good companion for Beville. He's welcome to remain here for as long as you wish – and I can promise you he will not forget his father.'

'What if there should be another kidnap attempt?' Amy asked the question anxiously.

Charles Duvernet shook his head. 'The King will make no more attempts to take Jean-Paul. *I* am the threat to his throne now, not my son.'

It was not until the third day of the visit that Henrietta and Nathan were able to talk, away from the company of others. They met in the garden one evening as Nathan returned from Portgiskey and Henrietta was admiring the flowering shrubs that bordered the driveway.

Henrietta greeted Nathan with an enthusiasm that made him wonder whether the meeting really *was* accidental. He could not know she had been examining the same shrubs for longer than an hour.

'Nathan, my dear! I was beginning to fear I would *never* have you to myself before I left Polrudden.'

'Isn't that better for everyone?'

Henrietta took a couple of paces along a path that disappeared among tall flowering shrubs. When she realised Nathan was not following, she turned to face him. 'You did not think that way in London.'

Nathan wondered whether she was mocking him. He could not know that Louis, comte d'Argon had watched him leave the house in Manchester Square and returned to confront Henrietta with his knowledge. Louis had caused a noisy scene, reminding Henrietta that she would be barred from the court of King Louis if the truth ever reached the King's ears. Louis swore he would not allow Henrietta to throw away her future and her reputation for an Englishman – not even one whom Louis admired and was proud to call a friend. The liaison must come to an end. The only certain way would be for Henrietta to marry again. He, Louis, had asked her to marry him on more than one occasion before. He asked her again – and warned Henrietta of the consequences of another refusal.

It was not the most romantic of proposals, but Louis repeated it many times during the course of the next few days, as he and Henrietta journeyed through France to Paris. He repeated it once more at the royal palace, before fleeing from France with King Louis XVIII. It was here, much to Louis d'Argon's surprise, that Henrietta accepted him. Since then she had not seen Louis again.

'When we were together in London, Amy had not lost a baby – and you were not to be married to Louis.'

'I am truly sorry about the baby, Nathan, especially for what it has done to Amy. She desperately wants to have a son for you.' There was no mockery in Henrietta's voice now, only an unexpected wistfulness.

'Did you know you and Louis were to be married when . . . when I was in London for the fight?' The question was blurted out awkwardly, almost rudely.

'In my heart I think I have *always* known I would marry

dear Louis one day. But if you are asking whether I had *agreed* to marry him at that time the answer is "no". Why do you ask such a question? Is it because you believe it is all right for you to deceive Amy, but *not* for me to do the same to Louis?'

'That isn't what I meant. I . . . it doesn't matter. Shall we walk to the house now?'

'No.' Henrietta had been watching his face and suddenly she took his hand. 'That is not what you are saying, I know. You would like me to tell you that what happened was more than a passing excitement for me. I cannot say such words, Nathan. For the sake of Amy, and Louis – yes, and for you, too – I *must* not say them.'

She squeezed his hand. '*Now* we will go to the house.'

Henrietta did not release Nathan's hand until they were walking along the driveway towards the house. They walked on in silence until they reached the door. Here Henrietta paused and said softly, 'Thank you, Nathan. Thank you for letting me know that what happened between us was more than an easy conquest for you.'

Before Nathan could reply, Henrietta hurried inside the house and Charles Duvernet, his son on his shoulder, was hailing Nathan from the lawn.

From the window of her room, Amy had watched Henrietta and Nathan walking together, and the irrational fear she had of the Frenchwoman returned tenfold.

Amy was acutely aware that she had been unable to satisfy Nathan's physical needs for many months now. She believed this beautiful French aristocrat was quite capable of taking Nathan from her, if she wished. When tears blurred the scene before her she turned from the window, not wishing to see the two of them together.

Amy did not come down to dinner that evening, pleading that she did not feel well enough.

When Amy also failed to put in an appearance for breakfast the next morning, Henrietta made her way to Amy's room after Nathan had left for Portgiskey. She had seen a movement at Amy's window the previous evening, when she and Nathan were together, and felt she knew what ailed the mistress of Polrudden.

When Henrietta entered the room she felt a pang of envy for the youthfulness of the girl seated in a wing-backed chair by the window. Amy was now twenty-two years of age, but her illness had pared every ounce of fat from her body and she was as slim as any young girl in her early teens.

Henrietta did not miss the wary expression adopted by Amy when she entered the room, but Amy invited Henrietta to sit opposite her and Henrietta took her place, remarking politely on the fine view from the window.

'Yes, I like this room. I can see all the comings and goings along the driveway.'

'Then, you'll have seen me walking to the house with your husband yesterday evening.' Henrietta made the statement so matter-of-factly that even Amy was unable to read anything into her words. 'It is the first opportunity he and I have had to talk together since I arrived here. He is a hard-working man – and he has need of you, Amy.'

'I'm sure your company is ample compensation for him,' Amy retorted. Then, half-afraid of the answer she would receive, she asked: 'What *did* happen in London . . . between you and Nathan?'

'What has *Nathan* told you?'

'He'll tell me only what did *not* happen. I am left to imagine the rest.'

'You must believe your husband, my dear.' Henrietta felt infinitely older than this unhappy young girl. 'There is nothing for either he or I to tell you. He is my friend, a very wonderful friend; but I pose no threat to your marriage, I assure you.'

Amy looked at the Frenchwoman. She sounded so sincere, so honest, and yet . . . 'I wish I could believe you,' she said fiercely, angry at the weak state which had left her incapable of taking the initiative with this woman.

'You *must* believe me, Amy.' Henrietta leaned forward and rested her hand on Amy's arm. 'Your marriage is too important for you *not* to believe.'

The two women sat looking at each other, saying nothing for a long time. It was Amy who broke the silence.

'Whose idea was it that you should buy into the fish-cellar?'

'Does it matter?'

Amy shook her head, but her whole tense being gave the lie to her words. 'It did. It doesn't matter now.'

'Putting money into Nathan's venture was my idea, a way of thanking him – of thanking you both – for what you have done for Jean-Paul. But Charles has returned now. He will assume responsibility for his son and my reasons for wanting to become involved with Nathan's business have fallen away. But I would still put money into the business if it would help you.'

'Portgiskey belonged to my father. When he died I ran it with my mother until Nathan became a partner. It's a *family* business. One day I hoped – I *still* hope – it will go to Nathan's second son . . . when Beville has Polrudden.'

'I understand.' Henrietta stood up. 'I am happy we have had this talk. I will be leaving Polrudden soon and I doubt if we will ever meet again. Recover your health soon, Amy. One day you will have a son to take over Nathan's fishing-boats – but do not look upon having a child as your life's mission. Nathan has need of you, too.'

When Henrietta left the room, Amy sat without moving for a very long time, trying to gather thoughts together in her aching head. She could not make up her mind whether or not she liked the French marquise, but one thing *was* certain. Henrietta was very fond of Nathan.

CHAPTER TWENTY-NINE

The ship that was to return Charles Duvernet to France dropped anchor at the entrance to Portgiskey Cove three days earlier than expected. Not wishing to excite the local inhabitants, the captain of the vessel did not fly the tri-colour ensign of Napoleon Bonaparte, and he kept his crew confined to the ship. Nevertheless, there was not a fisher-man in Pentuan who did not know that a vessel belonging to 'the Little Corporal' was lying at anchor off the Portgiskey fish-cellar.

That evening, as Nathan and the captain of the flagless vessel walked through the village on their way to Pol-rudden, sullen glances were cast in their direction. Many of the villagers had friends and relatives in Wellington's army. These soldiers might be facing Bonaparte's army any day now. There were also those fishermen who remembered sufferings, real and imagined, resulting from the long years of war between France and Great Britain.

However, the French vessel carried good Armagnac and Cognac on board, and the diners at Polrudden later that evening paid little regard to the feelings of the residents of Pentuan. Even Amy seemed to enjoy herself, although as the hour grew later she began to tire. Because of this, Henrietta announced she was going to bed early, enabling Amy to make her excuses and leave the men to their carousing.

The Armagnac brought to the house by the French sea captain was of an excellent quality, and the men drank vast quantities. At midnight, when men of more sober habits were in their beds, the drinking men sent an invitation for the sergeant of Charles Duvernet's escort to come and join them. The sergeant accepted with alacrity, and he and Charles Duvernet were still discussing the respective merits of French and English cavalry at 2 a.m., when the French captain announced he was returning to his ship. Nathan suggested that the captain should remain at Polrudden for the night, but the Frenchman declined the offer. His place of duty was on board his ship. He had a dinghy moored at Portgiskey and his ship was less than a hundred yards offshore. It would take only a few minutes' energetic rowing to reach the ship.

Nathan could not have detained the Frenchman, had he wished to do so, and he was certainly not sober enough to make the return walk between Polrudden and Portgiskey with him.

When Nathan awoke in the morning his head felt as though the brain was making a fight for freedom. When Nathan put his feet to the ground the throbbing in his head felt even worse than when he was in the horizontal position.

Groping his way to the washstand, Nathan bowed over the large pewter bowl and poured a jug of cold water over his head. Gasping from the sudden shock, he made his way to the window and drew back the curtains.

The bright sunshine outside caused Nathan to wince. The sun had risen many hours before and was reflected in the mirror-like surface of the sea. Nathan was about to turn away when something caught his eye, close to where Portgiskey Cove was hidden by tall cliffs. A ship was lying at anchor outside the cove and a boat – no, *two* boats were heading inshore.

Nathan snatched up the leather-bound telescope he kept on his dressing-table. Putting it to his eye, he focused on the scene of the activity.

The ship was a British man-of-war, the 32-gun frigate *Calliope,* which had recently taken up station at Fowey, as part of the government's determined bid to eliminate smuggling along the coast. What was more, the vessel's starboard guns were run out, all of them pointing inland towards Portgiskey.

Swinging the telescope slightly to the right, Nathan saw that one of the smaller vessels was a longboat from the frigate, manned by armed sailors and marines. Leading the longboat was the Fowey Revenue cutter. Nathan had no difficulty picking out the squat, powerful figure of Revenue Officer Samson Harry at the helm.

Nathan's headache was forgotten immediately. Dressing hurriedly, he ran downstairs and out of the house. He had almost reached the road when a troop of men wearing militia uniform turned in at the gate. Out of breath and out of step as a result of hurrying up the steep hill from Pentuan, they were perspiring freely.

'You'll be Jago, I'm thinking?' The question was asked in the sing-song accent of south Wales. These men were from the Monmouth militia, stationed in St Austell, brought in to reinforce their Cornish colleagues in the unlikely event of Napoleon Bonaparte falling upon England from across the Channel. They were also available should the starving Cornish farmworkers finally rise in revolt, the Cornish militia being more likely to support their countrymen than fire upon them.

The man who spoke the words was the captain of militia, and he was perspiring more than any of his men.

'I'm Nathan Jago, and this is my land. What are you doing here? Has it anything to do with the warship anchored out beyond Portgiskey?'

'One thing at a time, Mr Jago. First of all I am placing you under arrest.' Turning to the sergeant who had moved to his side, the captain snapped: 'Seize him and secure his wrists.'

The sergeant stepped forward, and Nathan promptly knocked him to the ground. The two militiamen who came to their sergeant's aid would have been treated in the same manner had Nathan not heard the hammer of the officer's pistol being drawn back. The officer stood only a couple of paces away, and the click sounded ominously loud.

'Raise a hand to another of my men and I'll be fully justified in shooting you, Mr Jago. It's well known that you're handy with your fists, I believe.'

Protesting loudly, Nathan allowed himself to be pinioned by two militiamen, while a third secured his wrists with manacles that pinched his skin.

'I demand to know the reason for this outrage,' Nathan snapped when the captain had inspected his wrists and the two militiamen had released their hold on him.

'You can put your questions to the magistrate. He's down in the village right now. First, we'll search your house and see if you have any Frenchmen hidden here.'

So that was it! Someone had alerted the authorities that there was a French ship at Portgiskey. Nathan breathed a sigh of relief. This could all be explained away as an error on the part of the magistrate. But who at Pentuan had laid the information?

'There *is* a Frenchman at the house – a Frenchwoman, too – but there is a perfectly innocent explanation . . .'

'Save your explanations for the magistrate. I'm merely carrying out my duty. But I don't mind telling you I have nothing but contempt for a man who makes money from illegal trading with the French. They are probably killing our countrymen in France at this very moment . . . Who is that standing by the door of the house?'

'It's your Frenchman, captain. The duc de Duvernet. The lady standing with him is the marquise d'Orléan. She's a member of the household of Louis XVIII, King of France.'

The captain of militia looked sharply at Nathan. 'This is no time for jokes, Jago.'

It took only a few moments for the militia captain to realise Nathan was not joking. Dismay crossed his face as realisation came that he had probably made a dreadful mistake.

'The household of . . . King Louis of France?' The militia captain seemed to be having difficulty in speaking.

'Only the marquise. The duc de Duvernet is one of Napoleon Bonaparte's staff officers. But here's a man who

316

will be able to explain everything to you.'

The sergeant of the Life Guards was coming from the direction of the stables, accompanied by one of his troopers. The sergeant had seen the militiamen arrive and summed up the situation as being one where full uniform was called for. He and the trooper with him were the first to be dressed. The others were still donning their elaborate scarlet uniforms.

Ignoring the volunteer officer, the cavalry sergeant addressed himself to Nathan. 'What's going on, Mr Jago?' Is there something my men can do to help?'

Nathan held out his shackled hands. 'They think I'm harbouring enemies of the King, Sergeant. I said you'd be able to explain the situation to them. They won't believe me.'

'The duc de Duvernet may well be an enemy when he's back in France, but while he's here on a peace mission he's under the protection of the Foreign Secretary, Lord Castlereagh. I have a copy of my orders from the Foreign Secretary here. You may wish to see them.' The sergeant addressed himself to the militia captain, adding: 'First, I suggest you remove those darbies from Mr Jago's wrists . . . sir.'

The sergeant's last word was a grudging concession to rank. The militia captain was an amateur soldier, not liable to service outside the country. The sergeant was a professional soldier, a veteran of the Peninsular Wars. Furthermore, he was a *cavalryman* contemptuous of all soldiers, part-time or professional, who marched on foot.

The militia captain, Hywel Hughes, was all that the cavalry sergeant believed him to be. A successful shopkeeper, Hughes had expanded into merchandising during the late war. More recently he had developed a taste for social life. Believing that a commission in the country's militia would gain him entry to Monmouth society, he had offered his services. His timing was near-perfect. Many of the experienced militia officers had accepted regular commissions in the Duke of Wellington's army and been sent to Belgium. Hywel Hughes was accepted by the militia and given the rank of captain.

His appointment *had* succeeded in making Hywel Hughes more socially acceptable. He was now on the fringe of Monmouth society, his two daughters receiving invitations to balls at which they were meeting eligible young men of good families – the families with which Hughes would dearly love to be linked by marriage one day.

It had taken many painstaking years for Hywel Hughes to achieve the social standing he now possessed – years during which he had been careful to offend no one who might be considered his social superior. Now, in a tiny fishing village in this backwater of England, the Monmouth merchant felt the fabric of his tiny pinnacle begin to crumble beneath his feet.

'There would indeed appear to have been some mistake. You there, release Mr Jago immediately. Please accept my sincere apologies, Mr Jago. But I was only carrying out orders, you understand?'

'The orders of the St Austell magistrate?' Nathan stood rubbing his wrists, chafed by the forged-iron manacles.

'Of course. I merely placed my men at his disposal. Perhaps you'll come and speak with him. He's down at the small harbour with the rest of my men. They're helping the Navy and the Revenue men capture a French smuggling vessel.'

Full enlightenment suddenly illuminated Hywel Hughes's face. 'Would the ship have something to do with your French guests, too?'

'It would. We'd better get down there before someone does something foolish. The guns on that man-of-war are run out ready and they're aimed at an armed merchantman sailing under Lord Castlereagh's protection.'

'You come down to the village as quickly as you can, Mr Jago. I'll go ahead and try to prevent a most regrettable incident from happening.'

Without waiting for a reply, the captain of militia scurried away along the driveway, heading for Pentuan village.

By the time Nathan and Charles Duvernet arrived at Portgiskey accompanied by the six cavalrymen and the remainder of the Monmouth militia, the action was over. On the quayside a grim-faced St Austell magistrate stood listening alternately to Captain Hywel Hughes and Samson Harry, the Revenue officer from Fowey.

Nathan deduced from the graphic movements of his arms that the Monmouth militia officer was denying all responsibility for the events of the day. Samson Harry, red-faced and blustering, appeared to have adopted an attitude of defensive belligerence.

Farther along the quay, a small group of men surrounded by armed militiamen complained bitterly in rapid French. Closer to the cellar, two men with bloody clothing sat with their backs to the wall of the building. A third lay unmoving on the ground nearby. All three wore the uniform of the Royal Navy. Nearby, standing in excited groups and taking in all that was going on about them, were some of the women from the Portgiskey fish-cellar.

Addressing the magistrate, Nathan said: 'I'm trying to run a business here. I suggest you take your men away before you make bigger fools of yourselves than you have already.'

The magistrate flushed angrily. 'I acted in response to a request for help from a Revenue officer. So far I have been given no proof that my actions are unjustified. The captain of a French vessel was arrested by Revenue men last night, right here on your quay. The ship has been searched and found to contain a quantity of wine and brandy. I also understand you have been entertaining French guests in your house. As we are once again at war with France my duty is perfectly clear.'

'The captain was arrested? By Samson Harry? If he's been harmed there will be trouble . . . serious trouble. He's been guaranteed safe passage between England and France by Lord Castlereagh himself.'

'You have proof of this?' Thin white lines appeared

about the magistrate's tight mouth.

Stepping forward, the sergeant of Charles Duvernet's cavalry escort handed two envelopes to the magistrate. 'These letters are signed by Lord Castlereagh, sir. One gives permission for the duc de Duvernet to remain in this country so long as he's accompanied by an escort. The other is an order for all British vessels to guarantee safe passage to the French vessel *Quebec* whilst in British waters or on the high seas. I understand a copy of the letter was given to the captain of *Quebec* when the vessel was in the Pool of London.'

'No one showed *me* any letter,' declared Samson Harry defiantly. 'All I saw were more kegs of brandy and wine than any ship going about legitimate business has any right to carry.'

'*Quebec* is a *French* ship. Frenchmen like to drink. Possibly you do not understand the ways of Frenchmen, m'sieur? Had the captain been on board his ship I am quite certain he would have showed you the letter. I am surprised he did not explain his business when he was arrested.'

Samson Harry rounded on Charles Duvernet angrily. 'I spent five years in a stinking French gaol. You can tell me nothing about the habits of the French. The captain said many things when we arrested him, but none of them made much sense.'

Without raising his voice, Charles Duvernet said: 'I was a prisoner of the Russians, m'sieur – I left my arm in that country – but I know little more of them now than I did before my capture.'

The magistrate handed the letters back to the cavalry sergeant and spoke to Nathan. 'I regret this misunderstanding. However, I must repeat that my actions were dictated by the information given to me. I could have done nothing else. I will be submitting a report through official channels, of course.'

The magistrate was passing responsibility for the morning's work to Samson Harry – and the Revenue officer was well aware of the consequences. He had a well-paid position and did not intend losing it without a fight.

'Before you make out that report you ought to know *all* the facts. Like you, I, too, rely on information I'm given. That's what happened in this case. I was told there was a French smuggler anchored here, waiting to offload a cargo of spirits and take on French spies who'd been staying at Polrudden.'

'You'll need to do better than that, Officer Harry. Such information should be thoroughly evaluated before you involve the Navy, militia and a district magistrate. If I paid attention to tavern chatter, I could fill every gaol in the country.'

'This wasn't tavern chatter. It came from a source I wouldn't think of doubting. After all, if you can't trust a Methodist preacher, especially one who's been ordained, then who *can* you trust? If you want to put your report in, then you go ahead. But make certain you lay the blame where it belongs. At the door of the Reverend Roach.'

The captain of the French merchantman *Quebec* was released none the worse for his sojourn in a Cornish lock-up and he shrugged the whole matter off as a huge joke. Sheepishly, he even suggested to Nathan that the Revenue officers might have saved his life. By the time he reached Portgiskey he had realised he was hopelessly drunk. Had he attempted to take a boat out to his ship it might have proved to be his last voyage.

There were no more incidents involving *Quebec,* and Charles Duvernet used the time before she sailed gaining the confidence of his young son.

From the time he rose in the morning, until bedtime, Jean-Paul rarely allowed his father to stray from his view. Nathan remarked on the relationship the two had achieved, when he and Charles Duvernet were walking with the two boys along the cliff-top behind Polrudden. It was the last morning of Charles Duvernet's stay and the Frenchman was trying hard to hold his emotions in check. He and Jean-Paul had formed a strong bond during their ten days together, and today it was difficult to hide the anguish he felt at parting from his son.

Above the old quarry at the edge of the bay, Charles Duvernet paused and looked down to where a gentle swell broke on ragged black rocks.

'This is where the ship carrying Marie-Louise and Jean-Paul was lost?'

Nathan nodded. 'Oddments from the ship are still washed ashore in rough weather.'

'You were the last one to talk to my wife?'

'Yes. Her thoughts were of Jean-Paul. She begged me to take care of him.'

'Poor Marie-Louise.' Remembering his late wife, Charles Duvernet squeezed Jean-Paul's hand so hard the boy squeaked in pain.

The Frenchman picked his son up quickly, kissed him and placed him back on the ground.

'Marie-Louise would be happy to know how faithfully you have kept the trust she placed in you, Nathan. For this I will be for ever in your debt.'

'Jean-Paul has been one of the family. Amy loves him as a son. It's going to be a dreadful wrench when she has to let him go.'

'Ah, your lovely Amy. It is sad she should have lost her own child so recently. She has taken it very badly. Yet she is young; she will recover.'

Turning back to the sea, Charles Duvernet asked: 'Where does the wreck of *L'Emir* lie?'

Nathan pointed to a line of sharp-toothed rocks, just off the entrance to the quarry. 'She'll be lying on the sea-bed, just beyond the farthest rock.'

Charles Duvernet watched the swell throwing waves upon the rocks and shuddered as he thought of what had occurred on that dark, stormy night.

'You swam out there to rescue my son – in the darkness and with a storm raging?' The Frenchman grasped Nathan's arm briefly. 'You are indeed a brave man, my friend.'

Looking suddenly thoughtful, Charles Duvernet asked: 'What is the depth of the water out there?'

Nathan shrugged. 'No more than six or seven fathoms at low tide. Ten at the most.'

'So little? Yet in the heart of a sunken ship it might as well be a mile beneath the water . . .'

Nathan looked at Charles Duvernet curiously, waiting for him to explain.

'Marie-Louise was bringing a fortune in jewellery with her from Martinique. Much of it has been in the Duvernet family for generations. Some had been taken from Spain. The remainder . . .' The French nobleman shrugged. 'One of the Duvernets was a well-known pirate.'

Charles Duvernet gazed at Nathan speculatively. 'I make you an offer, Nathan. It is also a challenge. Recover the jewellery and half is yours. The remainder will go to Jean-Paul. There is enough to make both you and my son very rich indeed.'

Putting a friendly hand on Nathan's shoulder, Charles Duvernet said ruefully: 'There! I have presented you with a fortune – yet I have given you nothing at all, while you have returned my son to me. No man has ever given me more. But I would like to return now. I wish to visit Marie-Louise's grave just once more. Then I fear it will be time for me to leave Polrudden.'

When it was time for Charles Duvernet to return to France, Nathan and the two boys accompanied him to Portgiskey. The parting between father and son was a sad wrench for both of them. Jean-Paul cried that he wanted to go with his 'papa', while Charles Duvernet promised he would return as soon as possible. Nathan and the two boys waved vigorously until *Quebec* cleared the cove, then they climbed the hill to Polrudden and watched the vessel sail out of St Austell Bay and disappear in the distance.

Henrietta also left that day, with the six troopers who would escort her to London. Amy emerged from her room and watched in silence as the marquise d'Orléan kissed and embraced Nathan warmly.

'Goodbye, my very dear Nathan,' Henrietta said softly. 'I doubt if we will ever meet again, but I will think of you often.'

Over his shoulder, Henrietta could see Amy watching them impassively. Taking a pace back from him, but still holding his hands in hers, she said even more softly: 'Take good care of Amy. She is more sick than you realise – and she has great need of you.'

Nathan was momentarily startled by her words, but Henrietta was already being handed into her carriage by her coachman.

As the carriage crunched off along the driveway, Amy came to stand beside Nathan. The two boys, tired of waving, ran off in a game of chase across the lawns.

The carriage swayed from the driveway to the rough, rutted lane, and Amy unexpectedly put an arm about Nathan's waist and smiled up at him.

'I'm glad she's gone.'

'You didn't like her?'

'I don't know. It's just . . . Polrudden didn't seem to be mine while she was here. It was as though she belonged here and I didn't. I had an uneasy feeling the house thought so, too.'

Nathan hugged Amy to him, relieved that she seemed so much better than she had of late. 'I must ask Dr Ellerman Scott to mix a tonic for you. It's high time you returned to your old self once more. Polrudden is *ours* – yours and mine, and Beville's. *We* belong here, no one else. But if we're to decorate the east wing the pilchards will need to start running soon. If they don't, I'll need to take *Successful* back to Irish waters again.'

'Poor Nathan. You have so many problems and I am being no help to you at all. I'll try to improve quickly, I promise.'

Nathan saw tears that were born of weakness well up in Amy's eyes. He hugged her to him again. 'Don't worry. You'll soon be fully recovered. Why, I've seen an improvement in the last couple of *minutes*. Before you know it, you'll be running things at the fish-cellar again. Then perhaps we'll sail up to Bristol. Do you remember when we last went there? You couldn't have been more than seventeen at the time . . .'

Nathan led Amy inside the house to the sitting-room. They spent the remainder of the day relaxing, and that evening when the children were in bed the house seemed strangely quiet. They were able to chat in an easy familiarity they had not known for many months.

When the sky outside began to darken and the room was in deep shadow, Nathan said: 'I think it's time you were in bed. I'll go up and see if your room is lit.'

'You're not going fishing tonight!'

It was a plea, and Nathan recognised it as such.

'They can do without me for one night. For all we're catching it's a waste of time *any* of us going to sea.'

'Then, don't bother with the lights. Will you see me upstairs, please, Nathan.'

It was too dark to see Amy's face properly, but this was the first time she had asked Nathan to accompany her upstairs since his return from the fight with Mick O'Rourke.

It was even darker on the stairs, and Amy took his arm. Outside the door to her room Nathan hesitated before kissing her gently on the mouth.

'Good night, Amy.'

Instead of releasing him, she clung on. 'Nathan . . . come to bed with me. But be gentle, please . . .'

Closing the door behind them, Nathan followed Amy to her bed. The curtains had not been drawn, and as Amy removed her clothes in the faint light Nathan felt the stirring of desire that the sight of her slim, naked body had always aroused.

Sliding in bed beside her, he could feel the trembling of her body beside him. He kissed her, and as she clung to him he felt the fire in her.

As his kisses and caresses became more demanding, Amy began to sob with desire. At least, Nathan *thought* it was desire; but when he tried to take her she suddenly went rigid. With unexpected strength she pushed him from her and a wail of anguish left her lips.

'I can't, Nathan. I can't! I can't! I'm not ready . . . not yet. Oh, Nathan, I'm so sorry . . . Please go. *Please!*'

Removing the weight of his body from her, Nathan tried to soothe her; to tell her it didn't matter – that there would be other times. His efforts to placate her seemed only to upset her the more, until her pleas for him to leave bordered on hysteria.

Slipping from the bed, Nathan dressed in silence, while Amy lay on the bed sobbing. Outside the door he waited until her crying had died away to an almost inaudible weeping before making his way slowly to his own room. He felt drained of energy, as though he had just returned from a long and weary journey.

CHAPTER THIRTY

Soon after dawn on 16 June 1815 the British 5th Division set out from Brussels. They moved southwards along a road that would take them through the villages of Waterloo and Genappe, and thence to a rendezvous at Quatre Bras. Marching as part of the 5th Division were battalions from the regiments of Gloucestershire, Derbyshire, Essex and Scotland, as well as a Hanoverian brigade – and the 1st Battalion of the 32nd Regiment from Cornwall.

The soldiers laughed and joked as they marched out of the Belgian capital. At their head Lieutenant-General Sir Thomas Picton raised his hat to the friends he passed, jovially exchanging banter with them. The night before, the commanders of the British army had attended a ball in the capital. Few officers left before 2 a.m., in spite of the ever-increasing number of messengers who presented themselves at the ball, seeking out the Duke of Wellington.

The light-hearted mood of the 5th Division remained with them until they emerged on the wide plains south of Brussels and were sobered by the sound of heavy cannonading some distance ahead.

Word travelled quickly along the lines of marching men. Napoleon Bonaparte's army had advanced from France in strength and was pushing back the able but aged Prussian commander, Field-Marshal Prince von Blücher, and his soldiers. Quatre Bras, their destination, was a vital crossroads linking the battered Prussian army and the combined Dutch, Belgian and British forces. If Napoleon succeeded in driving a wedge through here, the road to Brussels would be open to him. His troops would break through behind the Allied lines and overwhelm them. Quatre Bras *must* be held, whatever the cost.

The Duke of Wellington was at Quatre Bras early. He spoke with the confident young Prince of Orange, who was strongly positioned with a sizeable force of Dutch and Belgian troops. All was quiet, but when the Duke returned in mid-afternoon after visiting Blücher's headquarters the situation had deteriorated alarmingly.

The young prince had allowed the wood in front of his position to be heavily infiltrated by French troops without being aware they were there!

It was Wellington himself who first saw the French soldiers and realised the imminent danger they posed. Before he could take any action the French attacked in great force and the troops commanded by the Prince of Orange broke. Fortunately for the day, and for the course of the more famous battle that was to follow, Picton and his division reached Quatre Bras at that critical moment. Although his force was outnumbered by three to one and the French were being supported by four thousand cavalrymen, the British soldiers were flung into battle as each regiment arrived on the scene.

Wellington was under no illusions about the importance

of this battle and had sent out orders for the whole of his army to make for Quatre Bras at all possible speed. In the meantime, the men who were already here *had* to hold the crossroads.

The men of the 32nd Regiment were among those who bore the brunt of the attack. Against seemingly over-whelming odds they reeled under the weight of the on-slaught – but they held.

The Duke of Wellington was to be seen wherever the fighting was fiercest. If a British line appeared to be in danger of collapse beneath the sheer weight of the enemy forces, he was there to rally them. Once, when venturing too far ahead of his troops, he was almost captured by French cavalry. He escaped only by jumping his horse over a line of Highlanders, who held back the French cavalry-men with musket and bayonet.

For six hours of confused and bloody fighting the men of Picton's division held out, cheering wildly whenever men of newly arrived British regiments filed forward to fill the gaps in their thinly defended line.

By the end of the day Wellington's army had grown sufficiently for him to take the initiative and launch a counter-attack. He had judged his moment perfectly. After some fierce and bloody fighting the French army drew back in disarray.

Wellington had succeeded in his bid to hold Quatre Bras, but the cost had been high. In the Cornwall Regiment especially, there were many casualties. Almost half the men who had lived among the ancient mine workings on Polgooth Downs were dead.

Any hopes that the gallant soldiers of the weary 5th Division held out for a well-deserved rest were quickly dispelled. Wellington knew that a decisive battle with Napoleon Bonaparte was imminent, and too many of his troops were untried recruits. He could not afford to rest even a single company of Picton's battle-hardened veterans. The Prussians had been soundly defeated, although the tough old Prussian, Field-Marshal Blücher, promised to bring what remained of his army to Wellington's assistance. However, the Duke of Wellington had received many empty foreign promises during his long military career. He planned the forthcoming battle relying on the men under his immediate command.

With the remainder of those who had won the victory of Quatre Bras, the survivors of the 32nd Regiment retired in good order along the highway towards Brussels on the day after their victory at Quatre Bras.

Darkness came prematurely to the Belgian countryside on that June day, hastened by rains that quickly turned the fields and roads into a quagmire. That night the British army encamped on the ridge of Mont St Jean, a scant twelve miles south of Brussels, and a mile and a half south of the small village of Waterloo.

Rain fell on the weary troops as though the Gods were emptying the skies, intent upon gaining a clear view of the impending battle. Soldiers new to campaigning pulled sodden blankets about their shivering bodies and huddled in miserable, complaining groups. The veterans of the 32nd made pillows of straw, smeared their blankets with clay to keep out the heavy rain and lay down to get what sleep they could on what might be the last night their souls would spend on earth.

When daylight came, the men of Lieutenant-General Picton's division were given the task of holding a vital part of Wellington's line. Riflemen, infantrymen from Gloucestershire, Cornwall and the Highlands of Scotland, all were veterans of the Peninsular Wars.

They had to wait until early afternoon before their mettle was put to the test. The battle was already raging all about them when a column of 8,000 French soldiers, also veterans, struck at the positions held by Picton's division, at the same time driving before them the raw, inexperienced army of Belgian General Bylandt.

Not a man in the British division opened fire until the French column was twenty yards away. It was a devastating volley. Then, without pausing to reload their muskets, the

British troops surged forward and attacked the French infantry with their bayonets.

No army in the world could have withstood such a determined and disciplined charge. After offering momentary resistance, the French column broke and fled. It was a glorious victory for the British division, but one which Lieutenant-General Picton did not witness. At the very moment the tide of battle turned, he was killed by a musket-ball which struck him in the head.

Picton was escorted to eternity by the few survivors of those men who had once known hunger and privation on the downs above the Polgooth mine.

The day was won by the Duke of Wellington, and the hopes and ambitions of Napoleon Bonaparte were shattered for ever. Yet not a single one of Fenwick Garland's former comrades survived to celebrate the great victory.

Recruiting Sergeant Fenwick Garland was in the barracks in Bodmin, at the very heart of Cornwall, when the 32nd Regiment's casualty lists were received from Quatre Bras and Waterloo. Outside, in the streets of the town, people were dancing in the streets, celebrating the final downfall of Napoleon Bonaparte.

Sergeant Garland's finger moved down the handwritten pages, trembling to a halt whenever it touched upon the name of a man with whom he had once shared the lot of a vagrant. Six hundred and sixty-two men of the 32nd Regiment had done battle for their country, and for Wellington. By the time the sun had quitted the bloody hillside of Waterloo, 370 of their number lay dead or dying – and Recruiting Sergeant Fenwick Garland was the man who had sent them there. Wielding only a pen, he had been responsible for more deaths than ever he had as a sergeant of the colours.

Of a sudden, Fenwick Garland felt a need to get away from the celebrating crowds. He wanted to sit alone on a cliff-top and watch the ever-changing yet constant sea as it broke against the shore – the sea that lapped the coasts of both England and France.

Fenwick Garland took a horse from the stables of the Bodmin garrison and rode first to Pentuan. Here he met Preacher Josiah Jago, the man he had come seeking, as a Catholic seeks confession. But Fenwick Garland had chosen his moment unwisely.

When the recruiting sergeant told Josiah Jago of the deaths of his late comrades, the Methodist preacher was surprisingly unsympathetic. The men had died in the service of a Christian king. Their place in the Kingdom of God was assured.

In truth, Arthur Wellesley, Duke of Wellington was not the only man to have scored a notable victory that June day. Preacher Josiah Jago was also enjoying the rare taste of a battle won. In a remarkable volte-face, the Methodist Conference had recalled the Reverend Damian Roach to London. It was due, in the main, to the embarrassing incident involving the French merchantman; but, in a surprising move, they had also asked Josiah Jago to resume responsibility for the Pentuan Methodist circuit.

Preacher Jago was still out of step with the mainstream of Methodist thinking, but in the face of an alarming loss of membership the hierarchy of the Methodist Church had been forced to make a reappraisal of its narrow policy. It was decided that a new approach was called for, a policy of healing rather than one of division. If Preacher Jago remained within the Church, then so, too, would his congregation – and there were a hundred preachers with similar views throughout the land.

Full of the momentous events in his own life, the Pentuan preacher was not the man to give Fenwick Garland's conscience the reassurance it so sorely needed.

When the recruiting sergeant rode away from Pentuan he headed along the Pentuan sands and around the rocks to Portgiskey. Here he found Nathan. The whole world may have been celebrating the victory of the Duke of Wellington, but Nathan had nets to repair and the quiet of the fish-cellar gave him the opportunity to think. He wondered how Charles Duvernet had fared in the battle that was said to have ended with almost 50,000 casualties, among them one in every three of the British soldiers engaged.

Nathan had many things to think about. He was still barred from Amy's bedroom. Although physically well now, Amy alternated between forced gaiety and long periods of deep depression. When in this latter mood, the slightest incident could provoke a deluge of tears. In desperation, during one of Amy's particularly bad periods of depression, Nathan had ridden to Bodmin to seek the advice of Surgeon Emmanuel Isaacs.

The surgeon was a busy man. He was trying to put his affairs in order before setting off for London. Soon many hundreds of wounded men would be returning from Waterloo, many having had limbs amputated in hasty battlefield operations. Most would need additional surgery to tidy up the field surgeons' work. The Bodmin surgeon had been asked to assist in this task.

Emmanuel Isaacs listened to Nathan impatiently. He had examined Amy less than a month before. Nothing had changed since then.

'There is nothing at all physically wrong with your wife, Mr Jago,' he declared curtly. 'She has undergone an unfortunate experience, that is all – one that is by no means unique, even in these days of advanced medical care. Such matters are within God's own province and we surgeons are but mortal men. However, you have come here seeking my advice, so I feel at liberty to say what I think. Go home. Ignore the protests of your wife. Give her another child. When she finds herself pregnant again you will have a different woman on your hands, you mark my words. It may sound an insensitive solution, but at times such a course is necessary, in the best interests of everyone, not least the patient.'

So far Nathan had done nothing to put the surgeon's

advice into practice, although he thought much about what had been said.

Seeing Sergeant Garland riding towards him through the shallows at the entrance to the cove, Nathan temporarily forgot his troubles and called a greeting.

'I'm surprised to see you out here today, Fenwick. I expected you to be on the streets of Bodmin, celebrating the great victory. They say the Duke of Wellington has annihilated the French army. It seems there weren't enough soldiers left to escort Bonaparte from the field – even had they been able to keep up with him.'

Putting his horse to the ramp at the end of the quay, Recruiting Sergeant Fenwick Garland dismounted awkwardly and tied the reins to one of the iron mooring-rings.

'It wasn't only Frenchmen who died at Waterloo, Nathan. Englishmen died there, too, and the 32nd was in the thick of the fighting. There's many a fine man will never see Cornwall again.'

'Men you know, Fenwick?'

'Men we both know. All my old comrades you met up by Polgooth. They're dead . . . every one of 'em.' Sergeant Garland's lip trembled uncontrollably. 'Not a single one survived.'

Nathan was shocked by the news. Men died in battle, and the odds were such that more than one man who had gone to war from Polgooth Downs was destined not to return. But *all* of them! It was inconceivable.

'You're certain of this?'

'I read the casualty lists with me own eyes. Every one of 'em is as dead as yesterday's praise – and I'm the one who persuaded them to re-enlist.'

'I'm sorry, Fenwick. I really am. Come inside the cottage. I've something in there to raise to their memory. I doubt if anyone else will drink a farewell toast to them.'

Inside the Portgiskey cottage, Nathan reached into a dark corner where a blackened wood beam rested on an outside wall. He pulled out a squat stone flagon.

Pouring generous measures into two pewter tankards, he said: 'I thinks it's highly appropriate to drink to their memory in best Napoleon brandy.'

With the sea coloured a reflected gold, the two men drank toasts to the dead of the 32nd Regiment; to the Cornish survivors; to those who had led them into battle; to the Duke of Wellington, and another to the men of the victorious British army.

When the slanting rays of the sun picked at the weather-beaten sails of a squadron of men-of-war on the horizon, the two men drank to the memory of Admiral Lord Nelson; to the sailors of the Royal Navy; to comrades Nathan had lost during his naval days; to the ships they sailed in, and to the men who built them.

In flickering candlelight, Nathan and Sergeant Fenwick Garland drank to the fishermen of Portgiskey; to the Duchy of Cornwall; to the sergeant's horse; to Preacher Jago's old donkey; to each other – and to Polrudden.

Then, in the light of a half-moon, Nathan led Fenwick Garland out of the cottage. Together they waded thigh-deep into the receding tide in order that Nathan might point out the old manor-house, outlined against the night sky at the top of Pentuan hill.

'There's Polrudden,' he said drunkenly. 'The finest house in Cornwall. My son's family home. The house that goes with his baronetcy. Sir Beville Hearle Jago, of Polrudden. It's his heritage – yet he's coming damned close to losing it. D'you know why?'

Sergeant Garland shook his head vigorously, but Nathan was not even looking at him. 'I'll tell you why. Because down there at the foot of that cliff is a fortune in jewellery. A fortune that no more than sixty feet of water is keeping from me. Sixty feet of water between my son and his heritage. Is that fair? I ask you, is that fair?'

'You need a . . . a "diver". I spoke to one in Plymouth, when I saw the regiment off. A Prussian named Schlee . . .' Sergeant Garland slurred the word horribly and had a second attempt. 'Hans Schlee. He said he could work deeper than a *hundred* feet.'

'A *diver*, named Schlee? Never heard of him. Who is he?'

'I don't know.' Fenwick Garland shook his head sadly. 'Just another crank, I expect.'

Nathan nodded his head in agreement. Then, with his arm about Fenwick Garland's shoulders, he said; 'Let's go back to the brandy. I've thought of another toast . . .'

It was well after midnight when Nathan made his way home to Polrudden, leaving behind him an irregular pattern of footsteps in the wet sand of Pentuan. Recruiting Sergeant Fenwick Garland was snoring loudly on a bed in the Portgiskey cottage, his horse turned loose in the grassy valley behind the fish-cellar.

Polrudden was in darkness when Nathan let himself in through the kitchen door. He stumbled through the doorway and cannoned off the table before falling against the pots and pans that hung on hooks beside the great stone fireplace. Calling on them loudly to 'Sh!' Nathan tried to stop their noisy clatter. He succeeded only in sending more pots and pans bouncing across the flagstone floor.

Nathan escaped from the kitchen as quickly as he could, but not without kicking aside more of the pots.

The stairs to the bedrooms seemed steeper than usual tonight and Nathan missed his footing a number of times. At the top, he tried unsuccessfully to tiptoe past Amy's door where a plant stood on a table against the wall. Nathan thought he was the width of the corridor away, yet somehow he managed to bring the plant crashing to the floor.

'Nathan! Is that you?' Amy's querulous voice reached out from the room.

'It's all right . . . just the plant-pot.'

Nathan was on his hands and knees trying to scrape earth, foliage and pieces of broken pottery into a heap when Amy opened the door and held up a lighted candle.

Rising from the floor with difficulty, Nathan reached out for the wall, miscalculating the distance by no more than a few inches.

'Nathan Jago, you're drunk! You've been celebrating in the village.'

Nathan shook his head emphatically. 'I've not been celebrating. Fenwick Garland's friends . . . all killed at Waterloo. Been helping him to forget. He's at 'giskey, asleep.'

Nathan's words were not as clear as they might have been, but Amy understood and accepted his reason for coming home in such a drunken state.

'I'm sorry. Fenwick will have taken that badly. But you must go to bed now.'

'Yes . . . I'm going.'

Belying his words, Nathan tripped over the heap of earth, pot and foliage and dropped to one knee.

Helping him up, Amy said: 'You'd better lean on me, or you'll be back downstairs before you know it.' Guiding Nathan along the corridor to his own room, Amy opened the door, placed the candle on the table just inside the room, and led him to the bed.

Releasing his hold on her, Nathan lay back on the bed, breathing deeply as he willed the room to stop spinning about him.

As she removed his boots, Amy said: 'You're going to feel awful in the morning, but there are many celebrating Wellington's victory who'll feel far worse. Goodnight, Nathan . . .'

As she leaned over him to kiss him, Nathan reached up and caught her by the shoulders.

'Amy . . . Don't go yet.'

She tried to pull away from him, but he held her fast.

'Stay with me.'

'Don't, Nathan. You're hurting me. Please let me go.'

Nathan pulled Amy to him and tried to kiss her, but she turned her face away, first one way and then another.

'Please let me get up, Nathan. *Please*!'

He pulled her down to him and felt the lines of her body through the thin nightdress. One arm went about her, while the other hand moved to her breast in a clumsy caress.

'No, Nathan . . . *No!*'

The words of Surgeon Isaacs were stamped upon Nathan's mind: 'There is nothing at all physically wrong with your wife . . . Ignore the protests . . . give her another child . . . Give her a child . . .'

Shifting his weight on the bed, Nathan brought Amy down beside him. He held her with one arm while he fumbled with the fastenings of his trousers.

'Nathan . . . I beg you . . .!'

The trousers were loose now, and Nathan pushed them down and kicked them free. Then Amy was beneath him and the brutal pressure of his knee was forcing her legs apart.

She fought him now, her hands alternately pummelling and clawing at his back.

Ignoring her futile struggles, Nathan arched his back and claimed the right accorded him by divine law. He remembered the words from the marriage service even now: '*Submit yourself unto your own husband* . . .'

As the fighting and the clawing ceased, a wail left Amy's lips that would have chilled the blood of any sober being.

But Nathan Jago was not a sober man.

CHAPTER THIRTY-ONE

On Wednesday, the twenty-sixth day of July 1815, a 74-gun ship of the line sailed into Plymouth Sound and dropped anchor well out from the town and the wooded slopes of the surrounding hills. The great ship was no stranger to the famous south-western port. Ten years before, after the sea-battle of Trafalgar had immortalised the greatest admiral the world had known, the ship had limped into Plymouth Sound under makeshift masts and jury sails. Splintered and scarred, the warship had suffered more casualties than any other man-of-war in Admiral Lord Nelson's fleet.

Today, her ensign proudly waving from a tall mast, HMS *Bellerophon* was enjoying a moment of less exacting glory. Crowds lined the harbourside and surrounding hills. Every available boat had been hired out to those with money to pay. Eventually the patience of those who waited was rewarded with the sight of a short, portly man, dressed in a green greatcoat. His appearance on the deck of *Bellerophon* brought forth an escape of breath from the watching crowd. It sounded like the whisper of the wind in the trees about the harbour.

The man was Napoleon Bonaparte, the brilliant and ambitious soldier who had almost succeeded in his bid to fly the tricolour of France on the flagstaffs of every country in Europe.

Twelve days before, Bonaparte, who still insisted on being called 'Emperor', had surrendered himself to Captain Maitland, RN, on board *Bellerophon*, when the man-of-war was on station in the waters around Rochefort.

As a prisoner, Bonaparte was a considerable embarrassment to the government of Great Britain. However, to the boatmen of Plymouth, he was an unexpected and welcome source of income. On shore visitors flocked to the busy sea-port, clamouring for boats to take them out to the Sound, in the hope that they might glimpse the man who had changed the map of Europe.

With so many boats toing and froing between ship and shore, nobody took any notice of a young naval lieutenant who stepped ashore and hired a fast horse for a journey to Cornwall.

The young lieutenant from *Bellerophon* reached Polrudden after dark and handed Nathan a letter from Charles Duvernet. It contained an urgent request for Nathan to bring Jean-Paul to Plymouth as quickly as possible, and told Nathan and Amy of Charles Duvernet's plans for his son.

The lieutenant suggested that, in view of the uncertainty of Napoleon Bonaparte's future, it might be as well if they left Polrudden at dawn. A decision on what to do with the former emperor was expected to be reached very quickly. *Bellerophon* was standing by to sail immediately orders were received.

Lights burned at Polrudden until late into the night. All the possessions Jean-Paul had accumulated since the shipwreck were carefully packed for him. He had a surprising wardrobe of clothes and many toys that had been made for him by the Polrudden servants. There was a strong breeze blowing from the south-west, and Nathan suggested they should sail to Plymouth in *Successful*. They would be there in three hours. Meanwhile, the Polrudden groom would return the horse hired by *Bellerophon*'s lieutenant.

The naval officer agreed readily. Few sailors felt at home on a horse, and he was no exception.

At dawn the next morning a sleepy Jean-Paul left Polrudden in Nathan's arms. Clutching a rag doll, the three-year-old boy waved to a heartbroken Amy and the assembled servants until he passed from sight.

Nathan was well aware of the effect Jean-Paul's departure would have on Amy. He would not have been surprised to learn that, the moment she could no longer see Jean-Paul, Amy rushed inside the house to her room and refused to open the door to anyone for two days. Nathan had spent most of the night reassuring her that Jean-Paul would be happy with his father. Amy agreed he was probably right, but that made no difference to her own heartbreak.

Since the night of Nathan's drunken spree, he had gone to Amy's room on a number of occasions. She no longer fought him off, accepting his lovemaking with a total lack of emotion, but she would not move back to the bedroom they had shared after their marriage. Nathan found her present attitude almost as difficult to accept as her earlier rejection of him. Amy had begun to live her whole life now as though it were a chore that had to be endured, rather than enjoyed. She went about the house as though she were a ghost belonging to another age.

At first, the servants had been concerned for her, but when she grew neither worse nor better they began to relate cruel jokes about her and made signs to each other behind her back. Inevitably, Amy became aware of their ridicule and withdrew farther into the lonely world she had made for herself.

In a little less than four hours after leaving Polrudden, Nathan sailed *Successful* into Plymouth Sound. Had they left any later in the day it would have taken the fishing-boat almost as long to edge through the thick phalanx of boats gathered about *Bellerophon*. As it was, only a handful of spectator boats had assembled in the hope of seeing Napoleon Bonaparte appear on the deck of *Bellerophon* for a pre-breakfast stroll.

Bonaparte would not appear for another hour, but Charles Duvernet was waiting at the foot of the ship's gangway when Jean-Paul was lifted over the side of the Portgiskey fishing-boat to be hugged enthusiastically by his father.

Nathan wished Amy could have been present to witness the reunion of father and son. It would have removed any lingering doubts she might be entertaining about the right-ness of allowing the boy to sail off to share the exile of his father.

'We were worried about you,' said Nathan when Charles Duvernet, still carrying his son, led him to a cramped cabin below deck. 'When we heard of the number of casualties at Waterloo, we feared you might be among them.'

The Frenchman's face clouded. 'It was a close-fought thing, Nathan. For most of the time the battle might have gone either way. As it was . . .!' Charles Duvernet shrugged his shoulders. 'Napoleon had never personally fought a battle against British infantry. He would not listen when told of their tenacity. Many Frenchmen died for nothing, but that is war. Mercifully it is over now. France is back in the hands of the Bourbons and almost a whole generation of brave young men have been lost to her. However, time is a great physician. It can heal most things.'

Yet again Nathan thought of Amy. He hoped Charles Duvernet's homily would prove true in her case.

After a while Charles Duvernet, still carrying Jean-Paul, escorted Nathan aft. They walked below decks to a huge panelled cabin with windows opening over the stern of the ship. Here Nathan met Napoleon Bonaparte. The introductions were made as a valet dressed the former emperor in preparation for his first appearance of the day on the deck of *Bellerophon*.

Napoleon Bonaparte was smaller than Nathan had visualised him, although his shoulders had the width of a powerful man. It was evident, too, that Napoleon Bonaparte was used to eating and drinking well. He had a bulging midriff that even the most expert tailor could not disguise.

While Charles Duvernet made the introductions, Bonaparte scrutinised Nathan closely, but when he spoke his first words were for Jean-Paul. Unfortunately, he spoke in French, and Jean-Paul did not understand a word. Charles Duvernet was obliged to act as interpreter.

Napoleon Bonaparte raised his eyebrows, but patted Jean-Paul on the head with the comment that the boy had a lifetime ahead of him in which to learn his native tongue. He added with a faint smile that he, Napoleon Bonaparte, might find employment as the boy's tutor.

When numerous French men and women began to assemble in the cabin, Bonaparte spoke to Nathan for the first time.

'So . . . you rescued the son of the duc de Duvernet and brought him up an Englishman?'

Bonaparte again spoke in French. Nathan understood him well enough, but he had to search for words in reply. 'I brought him up as a small boy . . . as my own son.'

'Ah! And now you have given him into the care of his father. Would that my own son might be returned to me as willingly.'

For a moment, Bonaparte was no more than a rather sad little man, approaching middle age. The impression was a fleeting one. Moments later Napoleon Bonaparte was once more his imperious self. He snapped an order to his valet, who promptly scurried away to a trunk standing in a corner of the cabin, returning with a military-style hat to which was affixed a short tricolour plume, set in a small gold button.

Removing button and plume from the hat, Bonaparte proffered the insignia to Nathan.

'I can no longer give medals to men who perform a service for me, or for the members of my entourage, but here is a bauble for your son. He can wear it in his hat at play and pretend to his English friends that he is Emperor Napolean Bonaparte. When he is of an age to understand you can point to this and tell him Napoleon Bonaparte possessed little more than a cockade in his hat when he first set out to win glory for France. Goodbye, M'sieur Jago. May your son bring you all the pleasure that has been denied to me.'

With a nod of his head, Napoleon Bonaparte strode from the cabin to expose himself to the view of the waiting British public. Behind him his entourage jostled each other as they sought their rightful places in the strict order of precedence demanded by their deposed emperor.

Nathan remained on board *Bellerophon* for two hours without meeting Bonaparte again. As Jean-Paul led the two men on an exploration around the British man-of-war, Charles Duvernet told Nathan what he knew about Napoleon Bonaparte's exile.

A number of possible island homes had been suggested. The one most favoured by the British government seemed to be St Helena, no more than a speck in the vastness of the Atlantic Ocean. It would be a lonely and isolated life for the man who had enjoyed all that the palaces of Europe could provide. The prospects were less bleak for the young Jean-Paul. There was an active community established on the rocky island, comprised mainly of employees of the East India Company. There were schools, and the island had a surprisingly busy sea-port. Besides, Charles Duvernet envisaged sending Jean-Paul back to Europe to complete his education when the boy reached the age of twelve or thirteen.

Charles Duvernet enquired whether Nathan had made any progress towards retrieving the jewellery that was somewhere in the sunken French merchantman *L'Emir*. It reminded Nathan of what Sergeant Garland had told him, of the man in Plymouth who had been experimenting with diving suits and chambers. He repeated the conversation to Charles Duvernet, but the Frenchman was sceptical.

'Schlee, you say? I have never heard of him. Augustus Siebe, yes. Kleingart also. The Emperor was interested in their underwater experiments for a while, but he eventually decided that Siebe was nothing but a harmless lunatic. The General Staff were very relieved.'

'So you think it would be a waste of time to talk to Schlee?'

'Yes.' Charles Duvernet shrugged his shoulders. 'But can you recover the jewellery without any help?'

'No.'

'Then there is nothing to lose. Offer this man a high reward for success. Nothing if he fails.'

None of the crew of *Successful* minded spending the night in Plymouth. Charles Duvernet had given each of them five guineas for their part in bringing Jean-Paul to him, and there would be free ale in many a tavern for men who had stood on the deck of *Bellerophon* at the same time as Napoleon Bonaparte.

While the Pentuan fishermen set off to discover what Plymouth Town had to offer them, Nathan went in search of Hans Schlee.

He located the Prussian 'diver' in a ramshackle wooden

hut close to the Cremyll Passage at Stonehouse, beside the River Tamar. When Nathan pushed open the creaking door he walked into a scene of incredible chaos. Cut and uncut leather and canvas lay strewn about the floor, or piled in heaps in the centre of the hut. In one corner a blacksmith's forge roared noisily as a thickset, almost bald man swung a heavy hand-hammer, at the same time working large leather-hinged bellows with his foot.

As Nathan moved closer, the working man raised a charcoal-smeared face and looked in his direction. By way of a greeting, he said: 'You will hold this.' The accent was so strong that Nathan immediately knew he had found his man. For five minutes he held a strange, globe-shaped object in his hands while the Prussian diving pioneer repaired a thin split at its base.

When the work was completed, the Prussian took the strange object from Nathan and placed it in a large barrel filled with water. Holding it beneath the surface for a while, he gave a grunt of satisfaction and placed the object on a nearby bench. Wiping his hands on a filthy cloth, Schlee gave his attention to Nathan for the first time.

'I am Hans Schlee. You wish to speak to me?'

'Yes; but, first, what *is* that?' Nathan pointed to the globe-shaped object rocking on the bench.

Schlee's response was to lift the item in question and place it over his head, looking out at the world with dark, lively eyes through a small, round aperture. 'It is a helmet,' he explained, his voice echoing strangely inside his creation. 'A diving helmet.'

'You go underwater in that?'

'Of course.' Hans Schlee removed the helmet and looked at Nathan indignantly. 'I fit glass in the front, in order to see. I also wear a suit. It is almost perfected.' The Prussian inventor pointed to a shapeless heap of canvas and leather lying on the bench. Suddenly he rounded on Nathan. 'But who are you? Why have you come here?'

'My name is Nathan Jago. I came here looking for someone who might be able to recover something for me, from beneath the sea.'

'Who told you of me?'

'A friend . . . Fenwick Garland. He's the recruiting sergeant for the Cornwall Regiment.'

'Ah! The soldier. Ja, I remember him. He must be a proud man. His soldiers fought well. But they had Prince von Blücher and the Prussians with them, of course.'

'Of course . . . But the diving?'

'How deep is the water where you wish me to dive?'

'About eight or ten fathoms, fifty or sixty feet.'

'Bah!' Hans Schlee spat his contempt. 'You do not need a diver. Go to a fishing village and speak to any fourteen-year-old boy. He will *swim* down to such a depth for you.'

'The object I want is in a cabin inside a sunken ship. It might even be hidden.'

Hans Schlee looked at Nathan shrewdly. 'You think you know of treasure? Perhaps you have a map, too, drawn by a dying buccaneer?'

'What I seek is a box of personal possessions. I have a letter of authorisation from the rightful owner. I know where the sunken ship is lying. I can even tell you in what cabin you should look. What's more, if you're successful I'll pay you . . . five hundred guineas. On the other hand, if you're not, I won't be able to pay you at all.'

'Five hundred guineas . . . or nothing? This is an offer of work? You want a gambler, not a diver.'

Nathan nodded towards the items heaped on the work-bench.

'Having seen these, I'm not certain that isn't exactly what I'll be getting.'

Hans Schlee's chin came up immediately and he glared at Nathan angrily. 'You doubt my word? You think I am a foolish schoolboy who *plays* at diving? I tell you, I worked with Herr Kleingert of Breslau for three years. No man knows more about diving. You want me to dive? Very well, I *will* dive. When?'

345

'My boat's in Plymouth harbour right now. I'm ready to leave when you are.'

Hans Schlee was taken aback by Nathan's reply. 'We are talking of carrying out work under water – not swimming for pleasure. Do you think I have no more to do than don my suit and leap into the water? First, I need to know *where* I am to dive . . . how close to land . . . more about the ship . . . Only when I know all this can I prepare my equipment.'

'I'll answer all your questions here and now. In return you can tell me when you'll be ready to leave.'

When Nathan left the decrepit shack at Stonehouse, it had been agreed that Hans Schlee would be ready to take passage in *Successful* in three days' time. Now Nathan was going in search of the Polrudden groom who had returned the horse hired by the lieutenant from *Bellerophon*. Nathan would send him back to Polrudden on the Cornwall coach to inform Amy what was happening.

CHAPTER THIRTY-TWO

Hans Schlee's preparations for the dive were meticulous, and it was five days before Nathan guided *Successful* through the busy harbour of Plymouth, the deck piled high with diving equipment. On the way they passed *Bellerophon*, still surrounded by boats laden with sightseers. It had now been confirmed that Bonaparte was being exiled to the lonely island of St Helena. When the news was broken on board *Bellerophon* one of the ladies of Bonaparte's entourage had hysterically attempted to throw herself into the sea. The sensation-seeking onlookers were hoping she might repeat the performance.

Nathan tried to hurry Schlee, only to be met with the curt

rejoinder that each time he dived the Prussian put his life at risk. Careful preparation reduced the possibility of a piece of equipment failing at a crucial moment. He would leave only when he was fully satisfied.

When *Successful* docked at Portgiskey, Hans Schlee refused to leave his diving equipment in the fishing-boat. Neither would he allow it to be stored in the fish-cellar where it might be picked over by curious fisherwomen. Every item, including a bulky two-man pump, had to be locked inside the Portgiskey cottage and the key handed to the Prussian diver. Furthermore, he intended sleeping here.

When all this had been resolved, Nathan hurried off to Polrudden. He had been told that a servant had been to Portgiskey Cove twice, asking about his return. It seemed Amy was causing the household some concern.

In the hallway at Polrudden, Nathan was greeted by Beville. The child seemed both happy and relieved to see his father. He clung to Nathan, reluctant to let him go.

'Poor little mite,' said the maid who looked after Beville. 'What with you being away and the Mistress not wanting anything to do with him, he's been that confused he hasn't known where to turn.'

'Mrs Jago hasn't wanted him?'

'The Mistress hasn't left her room for two days. She won't let anyone in, neither. We're all worried about her, Master. She can't have eaten a single thing these past three days.'

Nathan extricated himself from his son's grasp with some difficulty, telling him: 'You stay with Rose for a while. I'll be back soon, and then I'll tell you what we're going to do tomorrow.'

When the maid led her mildly protesting charge away to prepare him for bed, Nathan hurried upstairs to Amy's bedroom. He tried the handle, but the door was bolted on the inside and he knocked loudly.

'Amy, it's Nathan. Open up.'

He thought he could hear the sound of movement inside

the room, but there was no reply to his call and he hammered hard on the door once more.

'Amy, I know you can hear me. Open up this minute or I'll break down the door.'

Again he heard movement inside the room, but Amy did not reply. He was about to put his shoulder to the door when he heard the bolt being drawn.

Opening the door, Nathan stepped inside the room. It was dark in there, the curtains closed. Striding to the window, Nathan drew the curtains, allowing sunlight to flood the room.

Amy sat on the edge of the untidy bed blinking at the bright light. She was dressed in a nightgown.

Distressed at what he saw, Nathan crossed to the bed and tried to take her in his arms, but she cringed away from him.

'Amy, what's the matter? The servants say you've been in here for two days. What's wrong with you? Do you feel ill? Shall I send for the doctor?'

Amy shook her head, but said nothing.

Moving an arm about her gently, Nathan could feel her whole body shaking. She was so thin that he doubted whether she had eaten since he left Polrudden to sail to Plymouth. Hearing a sound from the doorway, Nathan saw an anxious servant peering into the room.

'Go and bring some soup here – and tell the cook to prepare some food.'

'I'm not hungry,' exclaimed Amy, speaking for the first time since Nathan entered the room. 'I don't want to eat.'

'You must. You've been neglecting yourself while I've been away. Now I'm home we'll get you well again in no time. Beville will be going to bed soon. Would you like to see him for a while before he's tucked down for the night? He's been very worried about you.'

'Where's Jean-Paul?' asked Amy abruptly.

'He's safe on board *Bellerophon* with his father. They'll be heading for St Helena soon, by all accounts. They both send their love to you.'

'I love Jean-Paul. I love him as much as I would have loved my own son.'

'I know. We both do.'

'No! You already have a son. Beville is yours. Jean-Paul was *mine*.'

At that moment the maid hurried into the room carrying a bowl of steaming fish soup. It had been drawn from the huge pot hanging above the kitchen fire, ready for the servants' supper.

'Here, Mistress Jago. This will put some strength back in you.' The maid set the soup down on the table beside the bed and pulled out a chair.

She looked at Nathan, and he nodded. 'Thank you. Leave it there. I'll see to everything.'

When the maid had left the room, Amy said: 'I don't want the soup, or anything else. Food makes me puke.'

'I'll send for Dr Ellerman Scott. He'll give you something to settle your stomach.'

'There's no physic to aid what ails me. I'm pregnant again.'

'Amy! That's *wonderful* news.'

'Wonderful? To know I'll probably lose another child? To suffer again as I have since then?'

'You won't lose this one. You were very unlucky before. Too many things were happening about you.'

Amy shook her head. 'No, not *things* – places. At least, one particular place. Polrudden. The house is telling me that a child of mine doesn't belong here.'

'Amy, it's easy to imagine all sorts of things when you're not feeling well. Polrudden is our home – yours, mine, Beville's . . . and the baby's. We've been happy here in the past and we'll be happy once again, especially now there's a chance that our money worries may soon be over.'

'You're not going prize-fighting again?'

'There's no need. I've brought a man from Plymouth who's made a special suit that enables him to remain under-water for long periods of time. He's going to try to locate the jewellery-box belonging to Jean-Paul's mother.

Charles Duvernet says we can divide the contents equally. But have your soup before it gets cold and I'll tell you all about Hans Schlee.'

Much to Nathan's surprise and relief, Amy did as she was told. While she supped the soup, he related all that had occurred in Plymouth.

Later, Nathan and Amy went to Beville's room together and bade good night to a sleepy but now contented little boy. Afterwards they went downstairs together and tackled a meal the cook had hurriedly prepared for them. Amy merely picked at the food on her plate, but Nathan was satisfied that her fast was over. The obvious relief of the servants who cleared the meal showed that they, too, believed the mistress of Polrudden was on the mend.

However, after dinner, as they sat in the small drawing-room, their favourite retreat when they had no visitors at Polrudden, Amy suddenly said: 'Can we go to live in the cottage at Portgiskey for a while – until the baby is born?'

Nathan sighed. 'I thought we'd settled all that nonsense earlier. *No*, Amy, it just wouldn't be convenient. With two boats working I need all the storage space I can find and there's a great deal of tackle stowed there. Besides, I've handed the cottage over to Hans Schlee for the time being. If he's successful, we'll buy new boats and carry out all the work that needs to be done at Polrudden. We'll brighten the rooms and decorate one especially for the baby – *our* baby. You'll feel differently about Polrudden then.'

'What if this man doesn't find what you're looking for?'

Nathan shrugged. 'In a few months' time we might *have* to move into Portgiskey and even put Polrudden up for sale if nothing else comes along.'

Amy did not mention Polrudden again that night, but when bedtime came she insisted upon returning to her own room, saying she was exhausted after her fast of the past few days.

When Nathan was left alone he set about depleting the contents of a decanter of brandy and dreamed of the future.

Hans Schlee began work the next morning. With all the

350

Prussian's diving gear loaded on board, Nathan sailed *Successful* to the spot where *L'Emir* had gone down. Anchored fore and aft, the fishing-boat rose and fell on the low swell, only yards from the rocks which had claimed so many lives on a stormy November night two years before.

Eager to begin the salvage attempt, Nathan was impatient with Schlee's attention to detail, but it made no difference. The Prussian continued to work at his own speed, allowing neither threats nor pleas to influence him. He laid out fathoms of tubing, made up from canvas with leather reinforcing and small wood and brass rings stitched in at intervals to hold the tube open. This was the line which would carry air from the surface when he was working underwater.

Following a near-mishap when the heavy two-man pump was almost lost over the side owing to the swell, Hans Schlee insisted that the pump be securely fixed to the deck. This necessitated hailing an inquisitive young lad in a small boat and sending him ashore to Polrudden, to fetch a hammer and heavy iron staples of a type used in gate-hanging. When all was ready for the Prussian to carry out his first dive, Hans Schlee immersed his diving-suit in water for a test – and discovered it had developed a leak.

It was late afternoon when the Prussian made his slow and cautious way down a ladder lashed to the side of the boat. Weighted down with heavy lead ingots at his belt, he eased his bulk into the water as a rope looped about his waist was steadily paid out by Nathan.

The helmeted head had not completely submerged before Schlee rose again, waving an arm in a frantic signal to Nathan. For a few minutes Nathan was at a loss to explain the diver's strange behaviour. Then, turning around, he discovered that the two fishermen manning the pump had become so engrossed in Schlee's progress they had stopped pumping!

'Get to work on those pump-handles – quickly! Unless you keep pumping he'll have no air inside his suit and will suffocate.'

The two men resumed their work vigorously, and Hans

Schlee descended into the sea once more. This time he did not reappear and Nathan paid out the line, counting each small piece of canvas plaited in the rope at one-fathom intervals.

When eight had gone there was a slight pause and Nathan knew Hans Schlee must be on the bottom of the bay. He contained his excitement at the thought that he might be no more than minutes away from more riches than he had ever known before.

The rope began paying out again. Nine fathoms . . . ten . . . eleven . . . twelve . . . fifteen. Nathan tried to imagine what Schlee was doing. Could he be inside the wreck of *L'Emir*? Searching the cabin once occupied by Marie-Louise Duvernet and her son, perhaps?

The rope went slack in Nathan's hands and he began pulling it in, allowing it to fall in a coil at his feet. Hans Schlee had said the rope was a signal and needed to be kept taut. Two tugs meant he wished to be pulled up. Three indicated an emergency. Nathan pulled in all the rope that had been used on the second phase of Schlee's underwater excursion – and then it began paying out once more. Three times the sequence was repeated and Nathan became even more puzzled.

Suddenly, the water beneath Nathan erupted in a noisy turmoil of bubbles. At the same time Nathan felt a violent tugging on the rope. Once, twice – *three* times!

Calling to the fishermen standing nearby, Nathan shouted: 'Quick! Help me pull Schlee in.' Even as he made the call, Nathan was heaving on the rope. Hand over hand he hoisted the diver towards the surface, helped by *Successful*'s crewmen – and still the sea bubbled as though water was boiling in a great cauldron.

The metal helmet of Hans Schlee broke clear of the water, and Nathan could immediately see the reason for both the disturbance and emergency. The air-tube had split where it joined the helmet.

Removing the helmet was a time-consuming procedure, but Nathan completed it in record time. Little more than a minute after being pulled from the water, Hans Schlee was lying on the deck of the fishing-boat, alternately gulping in life-saving air and retching out the sea-water that had invaded his lungs.

It was evident that the air had won when Schlee began gasping jubilantly: 'It works! My suit *works!*'

'It works . . .?' Nathan was horrified. 'You mean you've never *tried* it underwater before?'

Hans Schlee grinned sheepishly. 'No. I have been unable to persuade anyone to loan me a boat and crew. But *they* are the fools, not you. Between us we have proved that a man wearing one of my suits can remain underwater for as long as he wishes. He can *work* underwater. Do you realise what this means, my friend?'

'It means you're damned lucky to be alive. This settles it – the attempt to locate the Duvernet box is over. I'll take you back to Plymouth tomorrow.'

'No!' Schlee shouted the word as though Nathan had inflicted a mortal wound on him. 'We cannot stop now. Not when we have proved beyond all doubt the box *can* be recovered – that is, if we can find the ship.'

'You never found *L'Emir*? What were you doing down there for so long?'

'Searching, my friend. Walking on the sea-bed, looking in every direction. I was as much at home beneath the sea as the lobsters scuttling about around my feet. It was wonderful. *Wonderful*! Please, we must not give up now. I will search for this treasure for less than the five hundred guineas you promised. I will search for *nothing,* but we must not give up.'

'*If* we resume the search, the fee stands. Judging by what's already happened today, you'll earn it three times over. But the air-tube . . .?'

Hans Schlee was holding the heavy helmet in his hands. He pointed to the split. 'Faulty canvas, no more. I should have reinforced it with leather. I will next time. But we need to look somewhere else for the ship. It is not down here.'

Nathan turned to Ahab Arthur, the oldest and most experienced fisherman in the crew. 'The French ship went down right here, but she can't be found now. Any ideas?'

Ahab Arthur nodded. 'Ay – and I had 'em when you first said what you were about, but it's not my place to speak my mind without being asked. I'd have started looking about a hundred yards over there.' Ahab Arthur pointed northwards to where there were many rocks protruding from the water. 'The bottom's flat here. The bad storm we had last winter would likely have pushed a wreck out beyond those rocks. There's a deep spot there, maybe ten fathoms deeper than here, and rocks enough to hold a ship. I know. I used to put out lobster-pots there some years back. Best spot for miles. That's where *I'd* look if I wanted to find the wreck of *L'Emir*.'

'All right.' Nathan made his decision and turned to Schlee. 'Will you have your air-tube mended by tomorrow?'

'It will be ready in an hour if you wish me to go down again.'

Nathan shook his head. 'We've done enough for one day. Let's go home. We'll try again tomorrow.'

Amy complained of feeling unwell at the breakfast table the next morning. She looked very pale, and Nathan suggested she went back to bed. He would send a servant to fetch Dr Ellerman Scott.

'Will you stay at home and be with me when he comes?'

'I can't, Amy. We hope to locate the wreck today.'

'Do *you* have to be there?'

'Yes. There's a fortune in jewellery involved. So much that I daren't trust anyone else to take charge. Just think, this time tonight all our money troubles might be over for ever. We will buy a fishing fleet –'

' – and *Polrudden* will be secure,' finished Amy with great bitterness. Suddenly she flared into anger. 'I *hate* Polrudden. I wish I'd never heard of the place. Go, then. Find your fortune. I only wish I had a husband who needed no more than to earn a living for his family.'

Rising from the table, Amy stormed out of the room and up the stairs. Nathan hurried after her, but he was only halfway along the corridor when her door slammed shut behind her and he heard the bolt being driven home. Nathan knew it was futile to attempt to talk her out of her present mood. Besides, there was work to be done.

The wreck of *L'Emir* lay upright, exactly where Ahab Arthur had suggested it would be. They were working within sight of Polrudden now. Nathan could see faces at the windows of the manor-house and he waved, hoping that Amy or Beville were watching.

It was unfortunate that no sooner had Hans Schlee found the sunken ship than he had to return to the surface because the repair to his air-tube was dribbling water. Half an hour's work binding it with leather proved sufficient, and Schlee descended into the sea once more, this time with the intention of entering *L'Emir* for the first time. Nathan had told the diver where the cabin was situated. It was the fourth or fifth cabin on the right, along the passageway from the rear passenger hatchway.

Hans Schlee was under the water for so long that Nathan became concerned for his safety. Then the rope began to slacken slowly as the Prussian diver slowly returned towards *Successful*.

The whole of the fishing-boat's crew lined the side to watch Schlee come to the surface. He rose from the water empty-handed, and a sigh of disappointment went up.

'I searched both cabins, but found nothing,' wheezed the tired diver. 'I will go down again. Perhaps I have missed something. But the work is tiring. I almost fell against the broken stump of the mast at the top of the hatch. Had I done so, it would have ripped my suit open. I must rest for an hour.'

'You've worked well.' Nathan rested his hand on the diver's shoulder, hiding his disappointment. There was still a chance that something would be found. The jewellery-box would be fairly large, but there was a possibility it had tumbled beneath a bunk. It may even have fallen from the cabin into the passageway outside.

Nathan's remaining optimism disappeared when Hans Schlee was brought to the surface for the second time late that same afternoon. The diver was not only exhausted, but was also shivering violently with cold. He managed to get out only one word before the fishermen led him away to wrap a blanket around him and force brandy between his chattering teeth.

The word was 'Nothing'.

Nathan knew the diver had done his best. Although their reasons were not the same, locating the Duvernet box of jewellery was as important to Hans Schlee as it was to Nathan. It would ensure that the world took his underwater 'diving' seriously.

Nevertheless, the fact remained. The treasure could not be found. The one chance of securing Polrudden for the future had gone. Nathan's feeling of despondency deepened when he returned to Polrudden and found Dr Ellerman Scott waiting for him.

The physician was checking the time on a large 'turnip' watch when Nathan entered the Polrudden library.

Declining the offer of a drink, Dr Ellerman Scott said: 'I'm already late for a dinner in St Austell, so I'll come straight to the point, Mr Jago. I confess that I'm concerned about your wife. Very concerned indeed . . . But do you mind if we walk outside while we talk? I've asked a servant to bring my horse round to the front door of the house.'

As they walked through the house, the physician explained his concern, and his words echoed what Surgeon Isaacs had once told Nathan.

'In the physical sense your wife is a perfectly healthy young woman, but the present state of her mind is most worrying.'

Startled, Nathan said: 'You're not suggesting she's . . . insane?'

'Oh, no, no, no! Nothing as serious as that. In fact, there's nothing that time will not cure by itself . . . But we now have the added complication of the baby.'

'But Surgeon Isaacs said that having another child would be the best thing that could happen to Amy!'

The two men were outside the house now, and Will Hodge was standing nearby, holding Dr Ellerman Scott's horse.

'For most women Surgeon Isaac's advice would be perfectly sound, but I fear there are other factors here. Some things I knew nothing about until today.'

'What sort of things?'

Dr Ellerman Scott looked at Nathan seriously. 'I'm talking about your wife's hatred for this house. I'm aware that it is totally illogical, but it's real enough. However, that is something that needs to be settled between the two of you. I can concern myself only with the medical problem.'

'And how do you propose solving that?'

'I'll be coming to see your wife again in a day or two. If she hasn't improved by then, we'll need to think of giving her something to rid her of the child.'

Dr Ellerman Scott rode away along the driveway to the lane, leaving Nathan staring after him, deeply disturbed. Nathan knew more than anyone how much it would cost Amy to lose this child.

Had either man looked up to Amy's bedroom, almost directly above the doorway, they might have seen Amy standing close to the open window. The expression on her face would have frightened them both.

CHAPTER THIRTY-THREE

Amy was already at the table when Nathan came downstairs the next morning. She looked calm and more assured than she had for many days. It gave Nathan a renewed hope that Surgeon Isaacs had been right after all: that having a child really would bring her back to normality, and Dr Ellerman Scott's gloomy forecast be proved wrong.

Nathan was in no hurry to leave for Portgiskey. Hans Schlee had been thoroughly exhausted the previous evening. He deserved a rest.

'You had no luck yesterday?' Amy's words were as much a statement as a question.

'No.' Nathan could not keep his disappointment from showing.

'What will you do now?'

'I really don't know yet. Spend more time fishing away from Cornwall, I suppose. If that doesn't work . . . Well, then I'll need to make a decision about selling Polrudden, inheritance or not. But that's only if all else fails.'

Nathan did not miss the expression of delight that crossed Amy's face. It hurt him. He had pushed himself hard for the last couple of years to retain the old manor-house. He told himself it had been as much for Amy's sake as for Beville's. But this was not the moment to provoke an argument about the matter.

'I'll probably return the diver to Plymouth today. There's a whole lot of equipment that can only be taken by sea. He's worked very hard; no one could have done more. He's almost died twice. Once when his air-line split and the other time when he almost fell on the broken mast yesterday . . .'

Nathan's jaw suddenly dropped open, and he stood up, setting down his half-empty cup as he recalled Hans Schlee's words: '*I almost fell against the broken stump of the mast at the top of the hatch.*'

L'Emir's *fore*mast was stepped adjacent to a passenger hatchway. There was none within yards of the *rear* hatchway which led to the cabin Marie-Louise Duvernet had occupied. Hans Schlee had been searching for the jewellery in the wrong place!

Nathan sprang to his feet. 'We've been searching in the wrong place! The jewellery *is* there, I *know* it. Dammit, we'll save Polrudden yet!'

At that moment, Beville was brought into the room by Rose. Nathan scooped the small boy up in his arms. 'I'm so certain it's there. You can come with me. You ought to be present when Hans Schlee makes the find that will secure your heritage for all time.'

Including Amy in his excitement, Nathan kissed her before hurrying from the room with Beville in his arms. Behind him Amy sat staring down at her plate, all the blood drained from her face. In the course of only a few minutes her hopes had been raised high – and as suddenly dashed again. More than that, by his actions Nathan had demonstrated to her that Polrudden and the son he had by his first wife were more important to him than the problems she was having to face.

Amy, too, left the table and made her way upstairs to her room. On the stairs she passed a servant and did not return the girl's greeting. Returning to the kitchen, the servant informed the staff that the mistress of Polrudden was 'having one of her turns again'.

Nathan gathered his crew on the way through Pentuan When they reached the cottage at Portgiskey a despondent Hans Schlee had already loaded his diving equipment on board *Successful,* in readiness for his return to Plymouth.

When Nathan excitedly asked the Prussian diver about the hatchway, he readily confirmed that there *was* a mast immediately adjacent to the hatchway. Questioned further, Schlee was unable to say whether the hatch was the forward or aft hatch.

'It was the only one I saw,' he explained. 'There is much marine growth at the other end of the ship. I did not even consider I might be in the wrong place.'

'Then, there's still a great chance of recovering the jewellery-box,' declared Nathan. He looked anxiously at the sky. Unlike the previous two days, it was dark and overcast, with heavy black clouds closing in from the west. 'I'm not sure we'll be able to do anything today, though.'

'Nonsense!' exclaimed Hans Schlee. 'Is the sea too

rough to take out your boat?'

'Not with this westerly wind. We'll be well sheltered in the lee of the cliffs.'

'Then, what concerns you? Rain, perhaps? You think I might get wet beneath the sea? Or are your fishermen afraid of a little rain? No, of course not. We go. If the box is there, we find it today.'

An hour later *Successful* was anchored above the wreck of *L'Emir* and Hans Schlee was dressing for his dive.

Glancing up towards Polrudden, Nathan saw lights showing from some of the rooms. The maids were lighting lamps and candles to lighten the gloom of the stormy sky outside. There was a face at Amy's window, and Nathan told Beville to wave. The small boy did so, becoming indignant when he received no acknowledgement, but he was soon engrossed in watching Hans Schlee in his strange attire, disappearing down the ladder to the depths of a rather choppy sea.

Schlee was underwater for no more than ten minutes when Nathan received a signal to pull the diver to the surface. From the foot of the ladder the diver signalled that there was a small leak somewhere in his air-tube, causing water to trickle inside his suit.

It took two frustrating and impatient hours to find the leak, and another half-hour to seal it effectively. By this time, despite Nathan's optimistic forecast, the sea was rougher, fringes of white foam topping the low waves.

Hans Schlee was determined to dive again. Replacing the helmet, he made his way awkwardly to the ladder. Once more he sank beneath the waves that slapped noisily against the side of Nathan's fishing-boat.

Half an hour passed by. Nathan had just changed the shift on the air-pump and was becoming anxious about the diver, when the safety line began to slacken in his hands. He hastily tautened it, afraid for a moment that the rope might have parted. He was relieved when he felt the resistance of the diver at the other end. As more and more rope lay coiled on the deck at his feet, he knew that Hans Schlee was returning to *Successful*. This was to be the moment of truth.

It was raining quite hard now, but every man on the fishing-boat, with the exception of the two men manning the air-pump, crowded about the top of the ladder.

When Hans Schlee's helmet broke the surface, not a man drew breath as the excitement of the moment gripped each of them.

Then, as the diver cleared the water and mounted the ladder, a groan went up. Hans Schlee had returned empty-handed.

Not until he reached the deck of the fishing-boat did Hans Schlee untie a rope which had been attached to his belt. The other end stretched down into the sea. When one of the fishermen tried to take the rope from him, Hans Schlee pulled it back out of reach, signalling that he wanted Nathan to take it.

Nathan began to pull in the rope. It became heavier as it neared the surface until, quite suddenly, an iron-bound leather chest broke the surface. Moments later it swung in the air, water pouring from it as it was pulled inboard, to the accompaniment of the cheers of the fishermen.

The chest was larger than Nathan had expected, being about two feet in length and half this in both width and height. It was locked, the lock incorporated in a stout metal band encircling the chest.

Nathan found a marlin-spike, and as the crewmen crowded about him he forced it behind the lock and began working the iron spike back and forth. It was about three minutes before the lock snapped open. Kneeling beside the chest, his heart feeling as though it were beating at twice its normal speed, Nathan raised the lid of the chest – and a gasp of wonder went up from the fishermen.

Inside the chest was a priceless tangle of gold and jewelled brooches, rings, pendants, necklaces and bracelets. Every precious stone known to man must have been represented here. It was a treasure such as no man in *Successful* had ever seen before – and none would see the like again. The fortune of the Duvernets had been recovered from the deep.

The men in the fishing-boat went wild with delight. They danced about the deck, shouting and hugging each other and slapping the back of Hans Schlee. The elated but slightly bemused diver beamed happily about him, his happiness stemming from the success of his dive rather than from the fortune he had recovered from the sea.

Only Beville seemed unmoved by the excitement about him. When Nathan showed him the contents of the treasure-chest, his only comment was 'Um. Pretty.'

It was almost an hour before *Successful* got under way, to return to Portgiskey. Hans Schlee's diving equipment had suddenly taken on a new value and needed to be stowed away with care.

A couple of miles out at sea, the man-of-war *Northumberland,* commanded by Admiral Sir George Cockburn, was butting her way south-eastwards, outward bound on her long journey to the South Atlantic. On board, transferred from *Bellerophon,* were Napoleon Bonaparte, Charles Duvernet, Jean-Paul and the other members of Bonaparte's entourage, setting off on their way to St Helena and exile.

Charles Duvernet was on deck with his son. Together they could just make out the distant outline of Deadman Point to the south of Mevagissey and only heavy cloud prevented them from seeing just a mile or two farther, to where Nathan was holding the chest that would ensure Jean-Paul would one day also enjoy his inheritance.

Successful had hardly cast off from its profitable anchorage when one of the fishermen suddenly cried: 'Look at Polrudden – it's afire!'

Nathan swung round to look at the great house and saw flames leaping from the windows of a couple of rooms on the first and attic floors. One of the rooms was Amy's.

Even as he watched in horror, the window of Amy's

room collapsed inwards and flames escaped to reach high up the outside wall.

Spinning the spoked wheel, Nathan brought *Successful* about. Catching the wind in the fishing-boat's sails, he headed towards the gap in the cliffs at the entrance to the Polrudden quarry.

'Hans, bring the chest to the house. Ahab, look after Beville. Take him to the village . . . to his grandfather's house and be sure he stays there. The rest of you come to the house with me.'

Skilfully, Nathan steered the fishing-vessel along the narrow, rock-fringed channel. By the time the wind was taken away entirely by the cliffs, *Successful* had enough way on her to run in and bump gently against the old stone-loading quay.

Nathan ran up the cliff-path to Polrudden, his crew strung out behind him. Many of the villagers from Pentuan were already at the house, using every possible utensil to carry water from the well to the flames.

Servants formed part of the water-carrying chain, and Will Hodge was organising the firefighters and trying to comfort terrified housemaids who were close to panic.

Grabbing one of the maids as she ran past, Nathan shouted: 'Where's Amy? Where's your mistress?'

The maid looked at him wildly. Breaking free, she ran off to lose herself in the crowd.

Nathan repeated the question to Will Hodge when he pushed his way through to him. The heavily perspiring groom looked grim. 'No one's seen her. The fire seems to have started in her room. By the time it was discovered the flames had spread to the room above. No one's been able to get anywhere near either room. I've sent to St Austell and to Tregony for their fire brigades, but it will be a while before either gets here . . .'

Nathan did not hear the remainder of the groom's words. He was running towards the house, brushing aside the men and women who stood in his way. He reached the top of the stairs and saw that the groom had been right. No one could get anywhere near Amy's room, although men stood nearby, dashing water against the smouldering floor in front of the blazing room, trying unsuccessfully to deny the flames access to the corridor outside.

The fire burned until nightfall. By this time two fire brigades were in action, but the fire was only finally doused by a prolonged downpour which reached the heart of the fire through the hole that had been burned in the roof.

The damage had been restricted to no more than half a dozen rooms, but these were totally gutted.

One of the rooms had been Amy's, and her charred body was recovered by the firemen and carried to the small Methodist chapel on the edge of Pentuan village.

In the last, dark hour of that grim night, Nathan sat alone in the study, a part of Polrudden untouched by the fire. Before him on the desk was the leather chest containing the Duvernet fortune. His share would be enough to make good the fire damage and ensure that Polrudden would one day belong to Sir Beville Hearle Jago, 4th Baronet of Polrudden.

Nathan had won the fight for his son's inheritance, but the cost had been high. Far too high.

The servants told him Amy had wanted a fire lit in her room. She was unwell, and the day was cold and gloomy. They would tell the same story to the coroner. It would be assumed there had been a tragic accident; that a log, carelessly placed by a maid – or even by Amy herself – had fallen from the fire. The verdict on Amy would be 'accidental death', and the coroner would extend his condolences to Nathan.

Nathan himself would never know what had really happened – and Polrudden would never reveal the truth. Nathan had now lost two wives here. The elegant, tragic Elinor and the sad and unhappy Amy. Polrudden had claimed them both. It was a house that demanded sacrifices. Nathan wondered what it would demand from him in the future . . . and from Beville.

Standing up abruptly, Nathan rubbed his face. It felt stiff and drawn. Slowly he made his way downstairs. The servants were already stirring. He suspected that many of them, like himself, had not been to bed at all.

Some of the servants passed Nathan in the corridors, averting their eyes as they went by, not knowing what to say to him.

It did not matter. Words would have been lost in the vast emptiness inside him. The servants moved on, to carry out work that was familiar to them. Life would go on. It *had* to go on, for them . . . and for Nathan.

There were many people reliant upon Nathan now. The servants, the fishermen, the women in the fish-cellar at Portgiskey – Beville.

Nathan walked wearily from the house and turned to face the sunrise. The sun had captured no more than a fiery red fraction of the sky, but caught in its glow was a solid shape that stood between darkness and a new dawn.

Its scars hidden by shadow, the house symbolised both the past and the future.

The house called Polrudden.

E. V. Thompson
Ben Retallick £2.50

In the Cornwall tin mines of the early nineteenth century, death was the working man's constant companion. Ben Retallick grew to sturdy manhood among the miners and fisherfolk through hard and hungry years. Cruel fate stole away Jesse, his dark-eyed love, and Ben searched through hiring fairs to find her again . . .

Chase the Wind £2.50

The prizewinning story of love and bitter destiny in Cornwall more than a century ago . . .

For the man who dug the Cornish earth of Bodmin Moor, the flourishing copper trade brought little but poverty and exploitation. Josh Retallick, son of a respected local family, and the wild Miriam, daughter of a drink-sodden miner, explored together the moorland until fate swept them apart . . .

'A keen eye for detail . . . astonishing energy' SUNDAY TIMES

Singing Spears £2.95

Daniel Retallick grew to manhood in the years that were a flood tide in the chronicles of Africa. The son of Josh and Miriam Retallick, he settled in a homestead in a valley of Matabeleland, with his wife and his children. But these were the 1880s. The Matabele *impis* were advancing with their singing spears towards the death-dealing Maxim guns of the white man and Daniel Retallick's loyalties, plans and dreams were swept away by destiny into the savage whirlpool of history . . . *Singing Spears* continues the saga of the Retallicks into the third generation.

E. V. Thompson
The Restless Sea £2.95

The Cornish coast of 1810 was alive with fishing boats, warships and smugglers. For Nathan Jago, a fish-cellar and boat seemed the ideal way of investing his prize-fighting winnings. But it wasn't all plain sailing to a wealthy future. For a start there was wilful young squire's daughter Elinor Hearle. And then there was Amy, with her passion for the sea and her fierce Cornish pride.

'A mightily readable adventure' OXFORD TIMES